PRAISE FOR
BEAUTIFUL APE GIRL BABY

"The unique blend of chutzpah and vulnerability turns a wild premise into a moving tale of learning to live in the world. Beneath the series of accidents and chance encounters lies a deeper tale of self-image and loneliness, choosing to stand out or blend in, and the power of nature versus nurture."

—*ForeWord Reviews*

"In *Beautiful Ape Girl Baby,* Heather Fowler has crafted a new, loopy, adult Grimm's Fairy Tale. As audacious as all her fiction, this new book cuts a little deeper; its cleverness carries wit, fancy, and a searching, searing romanticism, all as lightly as a basket for grandma. There's love, there's conflict, there's bittersweet romance, there's magic. Heather Fowler is an enchantress. I'd follow her ape baby anywhere."

—Corey Mesler, author of *Memphis Movie* and *Robert Walker*

"With so much fiction being derivative these days, what Fowler has done with *Beautiful Ape Girl Baby* is truly sui generis. The life of Beautiful is both a romp through the life of an unconventional heroine (and at times anti-heroine), trying to be herself in a world that is often at odds with her desires and sensibilities, and an instruction manual on the rewards of being true to oneself at all costs. While Beautiful's antics are many and she often finds herself in the throes of the 'toska,' she possesses wit, charm and a heart full of scar tissue, but is always, in her own way, triumphant. It's a wild romp and well worth it!"

—Michelle Reale, author of *The Legacy of the Sidelong Glance* and *If All They Had Were Their Bodies*

"What happens when magical realism meets feminism? Heather Fowler's tour de force of a novel, that's what. Although drawing inspiration from a rich tradition that includes Gabriel Garcia Marquez, Carolyn Forché, and more recently, Emily Capettini, Ms. Fowler has created a fully realized imaginative world that is entirely her own. At turns darkly humorous and deadly serious, this novel offers an incisive and powerful presentation of gender as socially constructed, an arbitrary and chance assemblage of cultural norms. As the book unfolds, Ms. Fowler harnesses the resources of the literary arts to build, piece by piece, a more just society. Heather Fowler is a writer to watch."

—Kristina Marie Darling, author of *Scorched Altar: Selected Poems & Stories 2007-2014*

"Fowler has written something impossible and brilliant: *Confederacy of Dunces* meets *Mighty Joe Young* meets *Pantagruel* meets *Heathers*. I have never read anything like this book, and I'm always thankful for the few times as a reader I get to say that. So thankful for the funny, fierce, feminist words of Heather Fowler."

—Amber Sparks, author of *The Unfinished World* and *May We Shed These Human Bodies*

"Heather Fowler is a magician—and she proves it once again with this rollicking and wonderfully subversive debut novel. Like her acclaimed short fiction, *Beautiful Ape Girl Baby* is bursting with energy and wit, humor and heart, cutting social commentary and evocative emotional depth. It's the kind of book that burns, leaves a mark, and reminds you of the possibilities of fiction."

—Andrew Roe, author of *The Miracle Girl*

"Unique and hilarious! I laughed my ass off."

—Lauren Becker, author of *If I Would Leave Myself Behind*

"A dark gleaming star of a novel—wild, visceral, yet full of innocence. Fowler never fails to make the strange beautiful, and all that we're told should be beautiful *deliciously strange.*"

—Angela Readman, award-winning author and poet

"To read Heather Fowler's *Beautiful Ape Girl Baby* is to be invited into the lucid dream of a brilliant mind. It might be easier to call this magic realism or even a modern fable, but there is something else at play here that, for me, is not captured in those phrases. There is the beauty of nightmares in this book, with the tender, profound truth of humanity at its core."

—Grant Bailie, author of *Cloud 8, Mortarville,* and *TomorrowLand*

"With *Beautiful Ape Girl Baby,* Heather Fowler has created what only she can do—spun the 'road trip' tale into a feminist, creative, can't-put-down, genius re-telling. There is no one out there that writes like Fowler and you haven't met a heroine like this one ever before. At turns hilarious, moving, and jaw-dropping, you will remember this book long after you hesitantly finish the final sentence."

—Jennifer Pastiloff, author and founder of Girl Power: You Are Enough movement

Beautiful Ape Girl Baby

A Novel by
Heather Fowler

PINK
NARCISSUS
PRESS

This book is a work of fiction. All the characters and events portrayed in this book are fictitious, and any resemblance to real people or events is purely coincidental.

BEAUTIFUL APE GIRL BABY

Cover illustration & design by Siolo Thompson
With additional illustrations by the author

Published by Pink Narcissus Press
pinknarc.com

ISBN: 978-1-939056-11-5
First trade paperback edition: June 2016

"All great literature is one of two stories; a man goes on a journey or a stranger comes to town."

– Leo Tolstoy

CHAPTER ONE
AN INITIATE

~IN WHICH, A MONKEY GIRL IS BORN, HARMS OTHERS, REACHES PUBERTY, KILLS A MAN, AND BEGINS A JOURNEY TO MEET HER MENTOR~

Beautiful Ape Girl Baby was born mad, her fetal fury unmatched even by the children in the psych ward above the Ob-Gyn, so her parents, Mr. and Mrs. Enrique Chef, both normal, could not have been more surprised as they watched her emerge from the tight, blond vagina of her mother. She came out quickly, waving her fists, with a dense thatch of hair starting at her chin and patterning into spirals at her brow. When she first opened her mouth to scream, sound pierced the walls. Dark, wet hair covered her body, fine from nine months seeped in amniotic fluid, but even later when Beautiful Ape Girl Baby, Beautiful or Baby for short, beat the plexi-walls of her pink-ribboned box, looking for all the world like an animal transported from a zoo, her parents decided they would use their wealth to instill in her the confidence the name they picked for her implied.

Thus, with her pug nose and furred back, the mewling babe was raised with stunning confidence, paid playmates to reinforce her sense of loveliness, and tutors to praise her intelligence. An entirely fabricated world was created for her on the six-mile grounds of the Chefs' estate, replete with statuettes that mimicked her characteristics and tiny, jeweled ape-girls on her mother's sill. After an eight year effort to have a child, both Chefs were pleased with what they'd engendered. What other choice did they have? Bound to be the only fruit of their complicated loins, Beautiful would be celebrated, spoiled, and nurtured as any unique progeny of such inordinate wealth. She was, they had decided, the *wunderkind*, the darkly gleaming star upon whom all wishes were attached.

As she grew, which she did rapidly, she became smart in the way of beautiful young rich girls, book-learned but naïve. She stood up straight. She possessed no mental defects, but she had still not learned to fathom life's greater mysteries.

Still, as she grew, doting as they were, her parents taught her to adore them as the ones who inspired her remarkable confidence. Her Daddy was her favorite. The only trouble he habitually encountered was keeping satisfied, healthy playmates, for often Beautiful had been known to dislocate the children's arms and legs, or bruise their soft, pale faces while frolicking aside the ivory seahorse sandbox, when the temper she'd shown in the crib came out, time and again. This was always followed by the dutiful daughter her parents preferred, when Beautiful brought lollipops and stuffed toys to friends' hospital room beds, apologizing for careless errors, or saying, with her huge blue eyes tearing up: "I'm sorry I'm so strong. I never meant to hurt you. Can you please forgive?"

Such friends were helped to pro-active generosity with bribes, but the prospect of keeping the young people around was one of tenuous hope and danger for the Chef parents. There was, for example, the friendship Beautiful enjoyed with beautiful-blond-girl Chelsea Manzan Malone. Malone began as an ideal playmate. Amazon in stature, undaunted by Beautiful's strength, she easily memorized and recited the self-effacing lines they provided each night through her door slot. With a natural straight-face, Chelsea could have become the lifelong friend they so desired for Beautiful—and best of all, she made Beautiful laugh—but all came asunder one day when Beautiful, at the tender age of eight, strong as a five year old horse, flattened Chelsea's nose with a startling punch.

"I want you to be as pretty as me," Beautiful said after, stroking Chelsea's long blond hair fondly. "So I must help you. Stand still, Chelsea. This is for your own good."

"Beautiful!" Chelsea cried, "Stop hitting me! My nose!" After the onslaught, blood soaked her desecrated face.

"I'm trying to help," Beautiful Ape Girl Baby said, regarding Chelsea's new nose and tearing eyes with a stoic's pride. "Your nose is now flat like mine! You should thank me!"

Chelsea moaned while writhing in pain. At this point, pained and incensed, she could no longer maintain the required façade. "You're dumb, Beautiful Ape Girl Baby! And awful!" Chelsea said. "The ugliest, dumbest half-girl on the planet, and I don't care what your parents want anymore! I just hate you!"

Beautiful Ape Girl Baby felt first shocked, then high-minded. "Chelsea," she said. "I know you're jealous, but I'll share my beauty secrets with you."

"Ape Girl, you just don't get it," Chelsea hollered, blood splattering in spray from her nose and lip with every word. "Look at your chin and your ears, that strange flat nose! That hair on your back disgusts us, and when you wear your Prada tank tops, it's all we can do to not gag—" Chelsea would have gone on, but by now, estate security cameras had caught the exchange, and guards rushed in. Beautiful watched as Chelsea was unceremoniously dragged away but didn't follow.

She was then cautioned by her parents not to adjust the looks of her friends but felt so distraught that it took twelve new playmates to stop her from moping, and still, as the months passed, she began to notice little things that bothered her at home, like how her parents looked nothing like her or how her friends had odd moments of consideration when she asked certain questions, like, "If you could be anyone, would you be me?" or "Do you think that rock star would like me if he were younger?" She remained reassured only by her posters of famous people, custom-commissioned by her parents with extra body hair, and the enormous ape statues aside the Olympic sized pool, which modeled her curling feet.

Sometimes, she stared at these posters and dreamt of seeking out celebrities. *Someone like me,* she thought. *But famous! I need to meet them. I should learn how they've dealt with such fame, how it's taught and enriched them.*

Often, she broached this topic with her Daddy: "Can you get them to visit me here?" she pleaded. "Any of them? Please? I don't have to leave the grounds, but can't they come here? I want to see people who look like me!" With clear intensity, "Stella Moreno would be good," she said. "Can she come? This week?"

"What would you do with them if we did get you a pop star?" her father asked.

Beautiful Ape Girl Baby was an avid radio listener. She enjoyed gardening, especially digging and yanking writhing pink worms from the foamy dirt. She read Dostoevsky in her spare time. "I could share my hobbies with them," she said. "There are many things I'm interested in!"

"No," her father said.

"No," her mother said.

"Listen, Beautiful," her father said. "Those performers are busy, but we can get you another poster."

"Blah blah, another poster," Beautiful told the friends, complaining each time this persuasion effort failed, but as she grew into puberty, her breasts swelling nicely, she gave up requesting visits from famous people, and her mind shifted, as teenagers' minds do, to thoughts of furious and steadfast copulation. The trouble was, she had no idea how, or with whom, it might be achieved.

So launched the beginning of her sexual rebellion. She both propositioned boys and alternately hid in her room for days at a time, longing for them and hoping they would miss her—ordering odd small items from a Swedish erotica catalogue and attempting to reach new pinnacles of pleasure with vibrating variations to the rubbing she'd already mastered on her own genitals. Once, she even shaved the hair from her arms and legs in a gesture of trying to look like other girls nearby, remembering what Chelsea said about her difference, particularly about her hair. It changed nothing.

She missed Chelsea these days, but was otherwise occupied. No sooner had she bought a flattering new Hugo Boss dress with designer cut-outs, than she'd needed Nicholas Kirkwood heels to match, along with a promenade across the estate to be suitably appreciated. Her parents, noticing her budding shape, brought in more boys, better paid, to reinforce her precarious self-esteem. Still, none engaged her.

Despite this, her attractions were strong. "Oh, Mother," she said, "I talk to these boys, but they don't offer to kiss me. They don't ask me out behind the maids' buildings like they do other girls, nor do they try and get alone with me. Do I intimidate them with my strength? Frighten them with beauty? Are they scared of the guards interfering? Why don't they want me?"

"Of course you intimidate them, precious," her mother said, with a worried expression. "You're quite strong. And your father's clout intimidates them."

"It does? How?"

~

"As you know, Beautiful," Ethel Chef said, "your father wasn't born rich but has worked his way up in auto parts and often had to let people know he had the upper hand. Sometimes, the hard way. Knees broken. Teeth curbed out. Other such ways. Aren't these lovely? Look at this custom new figure I just got from the Smithsonian. You have diamond eyes."

Watching her mother caress the sapphire windowsill ape girl replicas with a tenderly placed thumb, Beautiful felt soothed and valued, but there was a certain estate boy named John Henry Waters, whose name she wrote in her notebooks and spent hours considering, who ignored her entirely. Striding up beside him one afternoon, she said, "John Henry Waters, you needn't fear my father if that's the issue that keeps you away. I wouldn't repulse you if you pursued me, which is to say that I'd happily welcome it if you might suddenly strip off all my clothes and confess an insatiable desire. I don't have to wait until some ceremony." In her experience, which was the experience of reading books from the 1900s, marriage always led to unpleasant dalliances with suicide or entrapment, the need for tragic lovers outside the marriage to fulfill other needs, thus, she had decided against it, in no uncertain terms—it was a life sentence for misery lodged in a promise ring with just one gem, the ugly need to grow old beside someone you basically abhorred—unless, well, it seemed it might yield something else.

She wore a yellow chiffon blouse with cap sleeves and a green pleated skirt. For the occasion, she'd worn purple chiffon panties with lace frills.

John Henry stepped back. "You're beautiful, Beautiful," he said, "very beautiful, and it's not your father—but my affections are otherwise engaged."

"It's Tabitha, isn't it?" Beautiful asked.

"Yes," he replied. "I love her."

Beautiful stomped. "I hate Tabitha," she said, "She's

nowhere near as pretty as I am! Why do you want her? I love you, John Henry. Fiercely! It is possible, though doubtful since the institution seems antiquated, that we could even get married, if things went well with our passionate interaction. I know my father doesn't care for you much, says you lack ambition, but I have enough ambition for both of us. I can be the strength in this relationship! One day, you might catch up." Regarding his shocked look, she doubted this even as she spoke. A terrible shame claimed her heart for loving him, imperfect as he was—but he was, she'd decided months before, the earnest and gentle boy she wanted. She liked his blond curling hair and soft presence. She liked his glasses, too. They made him seem intellectual.

He walked along the edge of the pool near the lacquered shed and dipped his manicured hand beneath the lion's head spigot, letting the moisture flood through his fingers before saying, without preamble and without meeting her eyes, "No. I love Tabitha more than life, and I won't change my mind."

"That's the right sort of passion!" Beautiful replied. "But for the wrong girl."

Since disagreeing with Beautiful before had proved noticeably dangerous, John Henry took a long while before stuttering his reply: "If that m-means I have to g-go fff-rrom h-here, then I'll g-go."

"Well, fine! I don't care if you stay or if you go!" Beautiful shouted, in tears. She ran to her mother's rose garden and sat for over an hour, ripping the petals off her mother's prize roses, and threw herself a new and engaging pity party, entertaining both thoughts of Chelsea's and John Henry's defections before firmly settling into a pronounced funk as she first wailed louder and then rushed to her parent's room in high dudgeon, shouting upon reaching their doorway, "Mommy! Mommy! John is in love with Tabitha. Send her away. Send Tabitha Jones away! Right now!"

Her mother and father had already talked to John. And Tabitha. "We can't do that, Beautiful," her mother said. "Tabitha's parents are in Europe. We agreed to keep her until September."

"Fine! Fine!" Beautiful said, "Nobody cares about what I want!"

"We do care what you want, Beautiful," her father said. "Just not very much."

Incensed, Beautiful ran out and sought out Tabitha, careening through the craft room to find her. However, between leaving her parents and arriving at the site of macramé and board games, she'd had another idea. "Tabitha. You must tell John not to love you," she insisted. "Tell him I, instead, am the girl for him!"

Tabitha, a short girl with stringy brown hair, looked up from her macramé. "Y-you c-cant b-buy everything, Beautiful," she stuttered, "J-john and I are to be married. I c-can't g-give him to y-you."

"What is with you stuttering wretches?" Beautiful asked, but upon this, balled her fist and hit Tabitha as hard as she'd hit Chelsea, perhaps harder—only this time, the blow's recipient was knocked out cold. The recipient was concussed. Comatose. The coma lasted four days.

Though she begged for a chance to apologize when Tabitha recovered, Beautiful was not allowed a hospital visit. This was good since Beautiful only really intended to punch her again, but a day later, John disappeared, so: "I told you I'm so sorry, Mommy," Beautiful said, crying and beating the chair on which she sat, lounging in her parent's room. "But can't you bring him back? I'll be good. I'll be so much nicer this time, I promise."

"No," her parents said, having spent no small sum to eradicate the fallout from the previous exchange. "You see, Baby, he stole Mommy's jade and ivory necklace and had to be evicted. Mommy can't have boys like that around. You should try not to love any thieves; they exhibit a low moral character."

Beautiful saw this logic was sound, but part of her didn't believe John Henry was capable of stealing. He was such a goody goody. She glared at her Mommy. Still, as another bevy of friends arrived, she felt lonesome like never before, so often haunted her parents' marble-topped door, sometimes entering, other times just hanging outside, hound dog, until she heard them converse, the tone of these conversations tenser as the months wore on: "Does she need antidepressants?" was Month One's argument from her mother. "She is still eating, but far less," Month Two. "She ordered two new pairs of shoes in the time she would normally have ordered ten," Month Three. By Month Four, "I can't hear any more of this Ethel," her father said. "She's going to do what she's going to do. I have a business to run. I can't always focus on Beautiful's happiness."

"This is our only child, Enrique."

"Yes, and she can figure out what makes her happy without leaving the estate!"

"I never suggested she leave. I only suggest she's now unhappy."

"Do you have any idea how laborious the negotiations with the friends' parents can be? I'm tired. I'm at wit's end!"

"We must do something," Ethel Chef replied.

"Fine! Bring in another fruitcake therapist if you want," Enrique Chef declared. "That might help. Hell, hire ten."

Resultantly, post John Henry, Month Five signaled the arrival of Freya Hanson, resident therapist and aficionado of expensive marijuana that Freya referred to as "kind," which Beautiful liked. Freya had the most fascinating nasal hair Beautiful had ever seen, likely unclipped since birth. She smiled all the time.

Beautiful found it interesting that Freya was inclusive enough to give human attributes to even a small sack of weed, but viewed this as yet another positive facet of Freya's gentle nature. And "Just *be*, Beautiful," Freya often told her, stinking of drugs. "Be a leaf. Be a rose. Be the currents of the ocean. Just be."

"I'm so tired of *just being* that I need to be doing some shopping," Beautiful said. "And then I need to do some more regarding of hot male underwear models in the Sexy Man Pants catalogue," she continued, pausing again to ponder whether Sexy Man Pants was actually what *SEXIGA MAN BYXOR* meant in Swedish, since you couldn't quite trust the Swedes, but she felt iffy on many things these days.

Resultantly, her willingness to bond with new friends continued to shrink. Only Sandra, steadfast Sandra, who had lived all her life on the estate, could be trusted. It was Sandra, for example, whom Beautiful chose to tell about her late night joyride around the estate in her father's Mercedes, the Mercedes that had landed butted up against a tree, not that her parents weren't clear about who caused the wreck.

"I wrecked the fucking car," Beautiful had announced. "And now it won't drive."

Oh, how her father had been angry. "Of course it won't drive if you smash it on a tree!" he said. "Beautiful, Baby, please be more careful."

Late one night, haunting her parents' halls as she did, she heard them argue. "Darling, I know we're doing the right thing regarding Beautiful," her father said. "But she has no sense of responsibility. And no remorse."

"What do you expect?" Ethel Chef replied. "We've replaced each item she's broken. Renewed each resource. We've given her disposable cars, clothes, and friends. She won't learn a thing until she loses something that she can't recover." Her mother's voice vibrated as if a cello string, too tightly strung. "I do think she needs to understand losing something. For her growth as a person."

"I don't want her to lose things, dear," her father said. "When I think about Cisco, I see she has little enough to hope for."

"Don't think of Cisco."

"I must think of Cisco. Ten bullets, Ethel. In the heart. I had to watch…"

"Shhhhh."

Beautiful listened as her mother approached her father, three inch heels clacking over the wood floors, and imagined her mother soothing him as she often did, her mother's arm tucking loosely around her father's side. And then Ethel Chef said, "She has our love. She's always enjoyed that."

Enrique coughed. "Yes, but soon that won't be enough. She's already started to crave the love of a boy her own age."

Though just an eavesdropper, which made Beautiful unable to vocalize a response, *This is not true*, Beautiful argued silently with her thoughts. *In general, I prefer older boys.*

Her father sighed. Her mother sighed.

Beautiful slinked down the hall, hearing nothing further, her world trembling below her. She turned to her friends for reassurance. "I'm fabulous, am I not? I'm highly desirable, right?" They said the same wonderful things they always had, but she harbored suspicions many didn't like her. She suffered paranoia since they didn't groom themselves for meetings as they once had. Even the swelling of her breasts, from flat nipples with hair to rounded appendages as pert and alert as summer fruit, didn't please her. Also, there was no explanation of, or sympathy regarding, the conversation she'd overheard from her parents. Most friends offered no comment.

Only Sandra had said, "Forget about it, Beautiful. It's not important," as the others chatted amongst themselves. *Oh, thank heavens for Sandra*, Beautiful thought. With those large brown eyes and soft walnut hair, Sandra was the most genuine and sweetest of the friends! She had an obnoxiously dumb boyfriend named Eugene, but he never impaired her ability to commune with Beautiful under the trees or out by the archery range. The rest of them seemed to avoid her after 5 p.m.

Also, the friends watched the television in the Friend Lounge together, which she was not allowed to do ("Television is for the intellectually impaired," her tutor said, so her parents banned it from her room), and the errant friends could often be seen meeting after midnight at the pool, kissing, then stripping in a manner that offended Beautiful but only because she was never invited.

"What I'm talking about here, friends, is inclusion!" she announced. "I must be included in whatever's fun here!" She said this, but, for weeks, she watched girls and boys, girls and girls, boys and boys, copulating from her upstairs window, hoping for an invitation, and "These clandestine meetings must stop," she finally announced at the next catered picnic, "Right away."

As those who enacted such gatherings distanced themselves further, Beautiful grew restless, demanding additional reinforcements, but the more she desired, the less were provided. One day, on the night of her seventeenth birthday, after she'd been feted with an enormous strawberry and banana cake, eight dancing men, and five new swimsuits in elegant boxes, she came up with a plan. In the privacy of her room, she spritzed on fancy freesia infused perfume and walked into the settling mist, just as her mother had instructed.

She put on a pink, frilly dress and crammed her hairy feet into pink high heel slippers. "I'll find a boyfriend, today," she told herself. "I'll drive myself."

If it bothered her momentarily that she didn't have a car more incognito than the sleek black Lincoln to take, her father's luxury garages having been padlocked since the Mercedes incident, she then recalled that Sandra had a perfectly marvelous Pinto directly outside, with the keys in the ignition!

It was automatic, and after the tree incident, Sandra had kindly taught her how to drive it once, around the golf course, so *I'm certain Sandra won't mind if I borrow it*, Beautiful thought, and she got in the Pinto at around ten p.m.

She drove off, weaving spastically down the road. After years of confinement, lurching along once the estate gate was cleared and marveling, Beautiful wanted to holler, "This is life! I'm finally free!" but there was no one around to hear her. She rolled down the window and stared at the strange beauty of the sycamores in the night sky. She dangled her hand out the Pinto's window, feeling the breeze, and oohed at the rum billboards and the comforting thrum of slight traffic beside her. Many cars honked as they approached and passed her, so she honked back, waving jauntily. She only drove twenty miles per hour, which felt quite rapid after so many years on foot.

Sweet honeysuckle filled the air to infiltrate the Pinto's interior, and Beautiful sensed that this act of leaving the estate was momentous, as if the first day of the rest of her life, so she wanted to do something new. She would stay out for hours and go to a place she'd never gone.

A half hour later, she pulled over when she saw a small bar called The Rodeo at the side of the road, which sported an ugly neon cowgirl twirling a lasso on the roof, the sign a lit monstrosity with immense fake nipples embellished as spinning green stars. The bar boasted a full parking lot, but she hit only one other vehicle while trying to park. Striding towards the entry, she walked away from the tapped car, declining to even register the dent caused along the length of the Camry's driver's side door because her presence out must be secret. Besides, Sandra's pinto was fine.

Nonetheless, as she approached the bar's entry door, each person she saw, even those smoking, whispered and stared. Used to such attention as she entered rooms, Beautiful smiled and waved broadly like the Miss America pageant contestants she'd seen once in a maids' kitchen commercial. "It should be," she said softly, "easy to find a man to make love to me here."

"I'm Beautiful," she announced to the doorman, who backed away.

"You're something," he replied.

She frowned, but, once inside, noticed more of the bar crowd whispering behind their hands. To put them at ease, she shouted, "I know I'm incredibly beautiful, but you don't have to talk about it."

They laughed and soon went about their business, so she scoped the room, standing completely motionless until she found her target, who was a man who looked almost precisely like John Henry Waters but less clean. "I'd like a Cherry Pepsi," she told the bartender, glancing closer in the darkened bar interior, almost squinting to ascertain how much the young man resembled her first love.

Opening a rose-beaded purse to find a mauve lipstick, she pushed another girl aside and eased beside him. The bar stank of stale beer, so she kept her chiffon sleeves high. Right away, she saw the new man wore no wedding ring and didn't speak with nearby girls: *Because he's shy,* Beautiful thought. *I'll let him know I'm not.*

She sidled close and whispered in his ear, "I know we haven't met, but I find you attractive, so I want to make love."

He smelled like five-day sweat and motor grease. He laughed. His small eyes, blue like hers, sparkled with amusement. A skull tattoo pierced by a rippling knife spanned the top of his bulging arm. His friends had the same tattoo. *How very unoriginal*, she thought.

Green light reflected onto his face from a neon beer-sign that read MILLER as, "Ted, did you put her up to this?" he asked his friend.

"Not me, Jake," Ted said.

"Wasn't me," another friend replied, this one with seven gold teeth and three motorcycle books, but the last of Jake's companions, the tallest and the biggest one, just turned away. He had only two rotting stumps where teeth might have been and a metal piercing like a barbell between his eyes.

Jake turned back to Beautiful. "Well, then, what do we have here?" Jake asked. "Must be some kind of joke, this little ape girl coming to make love to me?" He smirked then put his fingers in her thick eyebrow hair. Curiously, he yanked.

"Stop," Beautiful said, wincing. "That hurts!" Having groomed this hair and gelled it into curls, she felt put out.

"The disguise is good," Jake said. "Who are you, and who put you up to this?"

He smiled nicely, so she replied, just as proud as you please, "I am Beautiful Ape Girl Baby Chef. So pleased to meet you. I hear your name is Jake."

"It is," he said. His friends gathered close until they seemed a paste of grease monkeys at her sides. "So you came to talk to me?" he went on, talking loud for their benefit. "And now you say you want to make love?"

She blushed, not expecting him to be so direct, so forward, but she wasn't now and had never been afraid. "Yes, that's what I said," she replied. "You up to it?" She glanced at his stained dark denim trousers. His flannel shirt was old, frayed at the sleeves. "I know I'm beautiful and rich," she said. "It's true my father has clout, but don't fear me, Jake. I'm not worried that you seem poor. I've read about poor people before, and you are an attractive specimen, albeit dirty."

His friends elbowed each other. "Clout!" they repeated, snickering. "Attractive specimen, but dirty! You're so dirty, Jake!"

"Go away," she told them, leveling a menacing glance

their way, and, as if sensing what her friends at the estate already knew, as if anticipating the potential violence to come, the febrile pea-brains backed off. Beautiful glared again, detesting the way they looked at her, but Jake now seemed interested.

He plastered his body against her side, putting his hand on her hip, saying, "You gotta lot of money, and you want to have sex with me?"

"Not sex," she said. "Because I'd like to pretend it might mean something—so perhaps we could call it making love." In her purse, she glanced down to confirm there was a condom she'd pinched from her parents. The sight of foil was reassuring. She didn't want this man's baby.

"So you want to make love to me?" Jake asked, smiling now. "Really make L-O-V-E?"

With sudden bliss and renewed vigor, she mooned up, replying in a sultry tone, "That's what I said, isn't it?" and asking, "Can I call you John Henry?"

The other greasers, again near, elbowed him and yanked at his arm. "John Henry! John Henry," they said.

"Say, will you give me a minute, Beautiful?" Jake asked, strutting away to the bathroom with his horde. "I'll be back after I talk with my friends."

"Sure. Take your time," she said.

When his mangy friends dragged him out of sight, Beautiful found herself deserted. The sixties tune "If You're Going to San Francisco" played from the jukebox and stirred her so deeply that she stole a floating camellia from the table jar for her hair.

She smiled, picturing how she and Jake would make love, smoothing the ruffled lace at the bottom hem of her dress in one elegant motion and lightly dreaming as he returned, but there was something tight and funny about his voice when he suggested, "Let's go to the wreck yard off Abermaine for our tryst. You agree to follow me, right?"

"You want to make love?" she asked. "In a wreck

yard?"

"Yes," he said and pecked her lips lightly, as if in demonstration of future acts. This sent her swooning. "My friends'll go get some stuff and be delayed while we do it," he went on. "But we'll meet up with them later. Come on, Baby. Let's go."

"It's Beautiful," she said, but he didn't listen.

Without looking back, he walked straight to a green Chevy truck, got in, and revved the motor. "You drive your car," he said.

"No problem," she replied, returning to the Pinto, but her nerves peaked while following him down unknown roads. "You're being a baby," she told herself. "A big weepy baby. Stop feeling so worried."

After a few bends and turns, she wondered if she could find her way home after the tryst so kept made tiny notes on a paper pad in the passenger seat, wishing she'd brought her navigation device. Finally, she entered the wreck yard just behind Jake, pulling onto a long dirt path that led to the increasing towers of car carcasses. "I can do this lovemaking without technology," she said. "And then I can get home. After all, lovemaking is natural. Just him and me—and the plastic needed between us."

One car atop the other, beside similar piles, the hundreds of multi-colored wrecks struck her as beautiful, the cumulative effect of every car crash in Albany for the last eighty years falling into a deliberate rainbow. "It's beautiful here," Beautiful Ape Girl Baby said, taking in the sights like a tourist, but Jake couldn't hear her and wouldn't have been interested.

He got out of his vehicle, toting a six-pack of Schlitz, kicking at a blue-gray rock the size of a small apple, and swigging from an open bottle. "Come on! Come on, Baby!" he shouted back.

"Do you have to shout?" she replied. When she caught up with him, in an area invisible to the main road, he put his hands on her shoulders, asking, "So how rich are you, Beautiful? Tell me how much money your father has."

"Oh, don't worry, he's not too rich," she said, but his brows came together and twitched like he might laugh before he responded, "Is that even possible?"

"What I'm trying to say is that I'm certain my father won't hurt you," she informed him matter-of-factly. "He's a nice man."

"Sure, but won't he be mad," Jake asked, swaggering and rocking back and forth on his feet, "to know his little girl was out with a greaser?"

"Of course not," Beautiful replied. "My Daddy knows his little girl can take care of herself. On that point, there is no question."

From a distance, the moans of a train's horn lulled them both. Beautiful shivered. Jake leered, but Beautiful found his menace sexy. She liked power. She also liked what Dostoyevsky said about power, which was, "Power is given only to him who dares to stoop and take it ... one must have the courage to dare." *I will stoop and take this power,* she thought, *I will dare and stoop to take greaser. We're going to have a good time!* "Besides, Daddy will never know," she told Jake, smiling conspiratorially. "I snuck out."

"That's good, real good," Jake said, seated on the hood of a wrecked Plymouth and finishing his first beer only to open another with his teeth. Two molars near the back of his mouth were black and fractured, which she noticed when she watched him speak.

"You'll need someone to fix your teeth," she told him. "If you become my boyfriend, I can send you to a good dentist. We'll fix you all up!"

"I don't need that," Jake answered, spitting. "Besides, why'd you pick me, anyway? Not like we have anything in common."

"We could have a lot in common. You're handsome," she said. "I like that. And I'm Beautiful." What she did not say, but felt, was *and you are not afraid.*

He spat again, pulling a cigarette from his sleeve. With his first inhale, he kicked a smashed Mustang.

He stood 10 feet away. He didn't touch her. He didn't look at her. Clicking his Zippo continuously, he chain-smoked two more cigarettes. Though she'd been waiting for him to make his move, Beautiful rapidly tired of waiting. "Aren't we going to do it?" she pressed. "At least start doing it?"

Since she hadn't done it before, nor had any reason to justify why it should transpire so quickly, she couldn't explain her hurry, yet there was something caged in the way Jake kept sitting on cars and swinging his legs, gulping beer. She noted a scar on his left hand, a gray round strip that wrapped all the way around his palm. She tried to imagine what object, what act, other than hot-wiring a car, might have caused that injury. There was too much mystery in the air and not many answers.

"When I feel like it, we'll do something," he said, staring into the hills.

At this, she stomped her foot. "You asked me out here, greaser boy! Don't you like me? I can't be out all night! Or, I don't want to be!"

"I like you just fine," he said. "I told you we'll do something in a minute, so stop pushing me."

"Fine," she said. "Tell me what happened to your hand while I wait."

He lit another cigarette before he muttered, "Nothing."

"That's not nothing," she said. "That's a big scar you've got. I bet you lost a lot of blood. I bet it hurt."

"Of course it hurt," he replied. "My dad wrapped a hanger he'd welded around my hand, just after he took it off the heat, and—oh, it doesn't matter. Fine, ape girl, you wanna have sex? Take off your dress and let me look at you. That's how it starts."

Beautiful Ape Girl Baby blushed. "Take off your pants,"

she replied, attempting to flirt.

"No," he said. "You first."

Still proud of her cleanly smooth breasts so recently shaved, she wanted something more, so taunted, "What's the matter, Jake? You chicken?"

"I'm not!"

"Then, take off your pants," she insisted. "Big greaser like you afraid to take off his pants for a little girl like me?"

"No," he reiterated. "Not afraid."

"Look, I know how this works," she said. "I'm the one who gets pierced here, so what're you afraid of? Bet you got nothing sizeable down there. You're afraid of me seeing it."

"I do so. I am not."

"Then kiss me," she said. "And show me!"

"Fine." He swigged the rest of his beer in one gulp, chucked the bottle, and pulled her in until she giddily pressed into his chest, moaning, "Yes," groping him, kissing him heavily, her tongue swirling in his mouth.

At first, his kiss had been soft and wet, just what she imagined, but no sooner had she started to get a good tingle than he had pulled his face away, when his hand glanced over her upper back. "Is that real hair there?" he asked.

"Yes," she replied.

"Uggh," he said, shoving her away. "Where else do you have it? That's gross! You ever think about shaving?" He fingered his waistband, looking down.

"No. Why would I?" she asked. "I'm fine the way I am. It's part of my beauty. Kiss me again. I think I love you, J—Jake." What she really wanted was to pretend again to finally be pressed against John Henry, since she'd almost uttered his name, but Jake wouldn't oblige.

"In a minute," Jake said, torching a fifth cigarette. "I need another break. Some fresh air." The air smelled of his cigarettes, rust, and dew. Jake took several drags and held them, tapping the toes of his scuffed boots together as he exhaled.

"You can kiss me while you're smoking," she said when she tired of watching this. "I don't mind, but I'm getting cold out here. I could use your arm around me."

She said this but wasn't really cold. He didn't respond.

"I don't know why you're being so reluctant!" she finally announced. "You don't have a chance with a woman this beautiful every day!"

"Ha!" Jake replied, caressing the curve of a gold Corvette's hood before he asked with a sad grimace, "You really think you're beautiful, don't you? You do, right? But you're the ugliest girl I've ever seen." As he said these things, he scanned the hills again, looking again for something unknown.

Beautiful scanned the hills, too. "You're a good liar," she replied. "I know I'm beautiful—is this a trick?"

Something new must then have occurred to him then since he got inches away from her face and blew smoke in her eyes. "Do you really think I'd find you pretty?" he asked, sneering. "Oh balls, how could you think that? I'm tired of pretending." His voice sounded harsh. He walked to his car to retrieve another pack of smokes.

"I think there must be something wrong with you," she said, only minutely hesitant, "because you're unrefined. You're pushing me away! You know who my father is, don't you? You want me to turn around now and drive away because I'm better than you and you know it? Or maybe, you really don't like me much, and you have no taste. So which is it?"

Jake took three paces, closing the space between them. "I don't know who your father is, Baby," he said. "But I do know that if I was him, I'd hide my face. I'd shoot myself for making a monkey girl like you." He kicked the Mustang's tire, shouting to no live audience, "For chrissakes! Fucking get here already!"

"Well, if you don't want to make love to me, then I'll go home," Beautiful replied, grabbing her purse. "And why did you ask me here? I told you what I wanted! It's not like I wasn't clear from the start! This is all an elaborate game, isn't it? Ok, I'm outta here." She walked away slowly at first, taking several long strides, then stopped and turned back to press him, "Aren't you going to stop me yet? Isn't this a game?"

"I don't think so," he said. "Go ahead and leave."

"Well, I don't need this hassle," she shouted. "I'll just go home and swim. I didn't know I'd picked such a dumb boy there or I would have left the bar with someone else! Guess it just goes to show, trash like you is everywhere. And to think I thought you were something, Jake! My Daddy would never have killed you for making me happy, but I have no idea what he'd do if he found out you upset me."

She held her chin high, daring him to argue or rebut in any way, but he suddenly coached his features into a saccharin smile. "All right. Come back, sugar doll, come on," he said. "You're right. You're real pretty." He opened his last beer, chugging it before he went on, "It's just—I'm afraid of hurting you. That and afraid of your daddy's obvious clout. You're a virgin, aren't you? All alone out here with a greaser like me. Betcha feel a little unsure, a little insecure."

She nodded. "I do feel a little confused by you."

"I could tell," he said softly. "Come back."

When she drew nearer, she tilted her head toward him, almost glowing with victory and murmuring, "Kiss me again" as he unzipped his pants. By the time he pulled off his shirt, in her mind, he was already that sweet John Waters, so instead of imagining spreading herself on the junkyard dirt for him, she dreamt of lying at the poolside where John Henry whispered sweet things, like, "I never loved Tabitha. Only you." As she reached in Jake's pants, she had fully realized this fantasy and nearly reached the brink of ecstasy—until she grew distracted by a new bout of empowering ideas: Sex was just a first step! Maybe, after this, she'd go to Europe. She'd meet new people! She could learn Latin dance! Her hand clenched Jake's member exuberantly, squeezing, pulling and releasing to maintain the pretense of sexual desire, about to return her attention to the acts at hand—until she regarded him closely to kiss him again and came to the quiet realization that his penis was limp in her hand, his small, blue eyes beady and fearful. "What's the matter, Jake?" she asked. "What is it?"

"I can't do this," he said, nauseated. "Not even for what they want. Not even for money! To what? Be monkey boy to them? That's not going to happen."

"You're a coward," Beautiful responded, but it occurred to her that perhaps this had always been the way with lower-class boys. Remembering each time she'd run to her parents in tears, partially comprehending the subtle slurs that flew when new crop of estate boys came too carelessly selected, she suddenly thought of a billboard she'd seen of a girl who looked like Chelsea. Then she thought of other billboards. Of women in videos. Perhaps there was a real possibility that low-class men only liked ugly women. *Still, women like her were pop stars and not everyone liked Beluga caviar either*, she thought, then backed away, asking, "Jake, do you really not think I'm pretty?"

He shrugged, dipping his eyes down to his pocketed hands. Though his posture mimicked bashful, meanness gleamed from his expression.

"Then why did you ask me here?" she shouted, enraged.

"No reason," he replied.

"Not good enough," she said, shoving him, asking, "Who are *they*, and what do *they* want?" She continued to shout questions, but he couldn't respond quickly enough. Stale beer and cigarettes tainted his breath, along with the odor of rotting teeth. She repeated her inquiries blindly, shaking him by the shoulders as she then asked again and again, "Don't you think I'm pretty? Aren't I pretty? Can't you see I'm pretty?"

Finally, he pushed her away hard, glared at her, and admitted, "We were going to kidnap and ransom you, Beautiful. But I couldn't do it alone. They might have raped you, too. I can't say. Mighta not. That's who I'm waiting on. Them. So as soon as they get here, you'll be lower than low, baby. You'll belong to us. How do you like that?"

She stepped back as fury reddened her cheeks. Tears fell from her wide blue eyes. She counted down in her head from twenty, tried all her tricks at mastering her rage and the urge for murder that shot up, almost succeeding until "What you going to do about it now," Jake asked, grinning. "Gonna slap me? Go ahead. Poor, little ape girl! Cry, baby, cry. You can't run fast enough to get away."

His gloating disgusted her. He came closer, acting like what he thought she'd do next was scream or at least register some perceived danger—but he really did not know Beautiful Ape Girl Baby at all.

He froze as she ran at him screaming, "Tell me I'm beautiful! Tell me you love me, you dumb boy!" but perhaps he was too dull to perceive the sharp edge of desperation in her voice visibly broadcast by her clenched fists and the pale hue of her knuckles. She knocked him down.

He laughed, but as she kicked off her heels and straddled him then grabbed his neck, he gave up no real fight. Only once, after she began to slam his head on the brown, stinky dirt again and again, did he try to resist, though even then he lurched up just one time with his mouth pursed like a fish out of water, his arms foolishly extended in the air at his sides, but he couldn't say a word by that time.

No one would help him. His friends had not yet arrived. Beautiful clenched his neck vigorously, his throat soft like pigeon feathers from her father's estate, so she continued to pound his head into the dank soil until his skull cracked open, and a puddle of blood grew large beneath him. When all was still, when he did not breathe, still furious, she rolled her eyes and resumed counting down from twenty to calm herself.

She looked around. Earlier, the junkyard had seemed so beautiful, but with Jake's slack neck in her hands, she saw nothing but waste in the cars. High in the sky, the moon shone down. "You don't know what you're talking about, Gutter Boy," she said to his dead body. "I'm beautiful. You're just a trashy jerk who deserved what he got. I'm Beautiful Ape Girl Baby Chef, you hear me?"

He did not. A moment later in Sandra's Pinto, adjusting the rear-view, Beautiful yanked her skirt more modestly over her knees. There were only billboards of people like Chelsea here, Beautiful thought, stroking her face, because this neighborhood was bad and people like her were priceless like Louvre sculptures. She looked at her tangerine nails glinting from dark, hairy fingers as she tapped them on the wheel, and started the car with a shudder as the ignition engaged.

Just as she cleared the driveway, his friends passed, hanging from the windows of a rusty El Camino and making barking sounds. Confused, she didn't regard them. "They deserve what they'll find," she said, then, "They're disgusting, too."

In truth, she couldn't wait to tell her friends about her evening out, but would hide her violent reaction, as she always had for the sake of her parents. Until the incident, her evening with Jake had been fine. And it was a bad stroke of luck, she thought then as she dressed for a late-night swim, to waste her pink dress on a boy too trashy to find her attractive.

She stared at her nearly bare breasts, then her furred arms and legs, thinking she would have to try again later, next week perhaps, but for now, she would swim as the chlorinated water streamed pleasingly through her back hair and the lion spigot, pouring full bore, enchanted her again, thinking as she did about John Waters's hand beneath it, dipping gracefully to cup the stream of the Chefs' boundless wealth. He'd been thwarted from loving her only by his insane love for the ugliest girl on the grounds, so she was glad Tabitha was gone. Tabitha's stutter had been atrocious—a deformity in its own right. *And where were her friends now? Wouldn't they come out and play?*

Oh no, they could not, Beautiful recalled. She'd banned them from night swimming just last month. For the first time in her life, they were sleeping, and she was not, so the feeling of being awake when they weren't was delicious, like her social life had finally surpassed theirs.

She tried not to think of the ultimate conclusion of the evening's romance. She swam low, touching the porous pool bottom with her hands, and then rose to surface with the rings. She pictured John Henry's face as she tossed them out again, but when she dove to get them, somewhere in the deep end a sudden darkness confused her, a flash of the greaser's face, and all seemed black as soot until she noted the bright light at the end of the pool, which seemed a blessed beacon.

The statues above it at the pool's edge seemed both gorgeous and wild. Lit by small floodlights wedged into bunkers, the statues' heavy fur and fangs assumed new significance as she considered them. "I come from a fierce people," she said aloud. "Superior people."

She recalled the nascent shock at her triumph still present in Jake's eyes, even after he'd stopped moving and dove again to arise and meet the statues' feral glares. She congratulated herself as she pictured Jake's head breaking open so easily, his blood like a dahlia of imperfection blooming around his soft, ugly face.

Yes, she'd done what was necessary. But she had no desire to leave the pool and find other company, embraced as she was by the cold comfort of the statues, at how much they resembled her. She thought of Darwin's natural selection, his manuscript available in one of her tutor's favorite primers, and decided she was indeed the fittest: she alone was warm in cold weather without additional garments. She alone could strip apart a tree should she long for shelter, and woe betide any who did her wrong.

With the hate-fueled recollection of Jake's curling lip, her heart burned with shame for asking him to make love to her. *What a broken-toothed greaser!* But he was gone. She took one long, deep breath and swam two laps before coming up for air, pushing Jake from her mind and thinking instead of her tender love for John Henry as she dove again and again, refusing to step from the sparkling turquoise pool until her memory of Jake's rejection, of her anger in that moment, and of all that had happened next, like morning fog lifting, mercifully had cleared.

Besides, Beautiful had more to do than to sit around thinking about a malevolent boy who wasn't her ideal match, especially one no longer breathing. *Que sera, sera.*

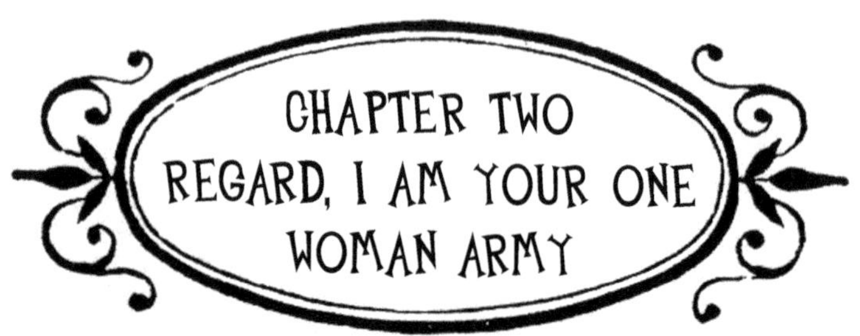

~IN WHICH, OUR HEROINE LEARNS TO DRIVE, SHAKES LIVE BEES FOR PLEASANT STING, WRECKS FENCES, CUFFS COPS, AND CO-COUNSELS LOVERS IN CHAINS~

It was the morning after Beautiful Ape Girl Baby's fateful swim in the statue bedecked pool of her fascination, post-interlude with Jake the greaser, when she was struck by a fabulous idea that she would go to visit her idol Ms. Ida May Haze. She would leave the Chef's estate! She would drive there, incognito!

If love was not to be had, or had enjoyably, she might at least meet the surly old woman whose voice had consumed her dreams and ambitions for many years. So possessed was she with this idea that she paused no small time after leaping from bed before throwing on some red Gucci loafers and an Armani sundress before charging immediately into the bedchambers of Sandra Goforth, sweet Sandra Goforth—one of her best and truest friends, who had been, at that very moment, sawing logs with small drips of drool falling from her luxe open mouth to her fat warm cheek, drops then splattering to darken her orange satin pillowcase. Sandra, Sandra Goforth, Beautiful mused, peaceful as a lamb, Sandra who was always available or could be made to be so, Sandra with a small fold of belly fat exposed where her white I Love Lions t-shirt failed to cover her expansive mass, Sandra snoring, sleeping, drooling… How Beautiful loved her!

Still, Beautiful, impatient as always, shook her friend and said, to the awakening soft brown felt of her only true friend's eyes, with a tremor of delight, "Today, Sandra, you'll teach me to drive! And then you shave me, top to bottom, and I'll run away! I'll escape the estate!"

"You'll what?" Sandra asked. Since Sandra didn't rapidly process, it was a bovine or ovine look Beautiful subsequently attributed to Sandra, though she didn't like to think ill of her most special friend. Lightly attempting patience, Beautiful reiterated, "Sandra, the other friends are sleeping and they needn't know about this, okay? But I want to run away, so this can be our enormous secret. You remain my most trusted companion."

Feeling it might be dangerous to display preference among the friends, Beautiful had never before verbally professed to Sandra that Sandra was her new favorite, nor had she firmly decided, until that very moment, as to whether Sandra's merits could place her above Chelsea Manzan Malone's, yet, at Sandra's tremulous smile, Beautiful knew she'd said the right thing and that this admission must have pleased Sandra in some way. It would have pleased Beautiful, who always wanted to be liked best.

Not that others didn't like Sandra. Who wouldn't?

Sandra was fat but self-effacing, strong but soft, the ideal sort of person and friend, and she never, ever criticized Beautiful, or Baby, as they sometimes called her, for what others referred to as her "occasional bouts of temper." Also, stirringly, she never inspired Beautiful's wrath.

Despite these good traits, "Sandra, get the hell up already," Beautiful said, already imagining how wonderful it would be to drive Sandra's Pinto across the country, having learned how to speed, how to brake, how to drive in general—after some practice becoming a Mario Andretti, zooming across the country—and then fighting her way through Ida's entourage to swoon at the most beautiful wrinkled Ms. Ida May Haze, and say, "Ms. Ida Haze, your work has meant so much to me! So much!" because this is exactly what Beautiful would say, give or take a few pressing observations that could only be made *en scene*—and she hoped Ida would be suitably grateful, but somehow knew Ida would. "Get up already, Sandra!" Beautiful shouted. "I'm on a tear!"

Languorous, Sandra slid from her bed, stripped her soft pajamas, and replaced them with another ill-fitting outfit that reminded Beautiful of Farmer John on steroids, blue overalls and brown clogs, a hippy poncho of orange and green, and a silver necklace with a peace sign. Then Sandra, yawning, brushed her hair. "Beautiful," she said, her calm voice trembling only slightly, "How on earth do you plan to meet Ida Haze? I mean, that sounds splendid. And I know you love to hear Ida on the radio, because you've said before that Ida 'unlike others has a real compassion for the spectacular people,' but Beautiful—do you really think you can leave, and won't your parents be mad?"

"My parents will be furious!" Beautiful shouted, grinning.

Sandra tried to calm her. "Beautiful, I think you should be more cautious. I—"

Beautiful ignored her. "So, I took your car last night, Sandra," Beautiful said, "and went to a bar to find a man to make love to. I found a most perfect specimen, I must say. He was oh so kind in the beginning. And he kissed me, which made my knees weak. So weak! Oh, Sandra, I was in love. But as the evening went on, I found out what a stupid, jacked out, rascal fucker he was—but I was even willing to forgive him then, I swear, because he looked just like John Henry, except… Oh, John Henry!" At the mention of her former crush, Beautiful fell into a sleepy secondary swoon, batting her eyelashes, and internally cursed Tabitha again, forgetting the other half of the story.

"And?" Sandra said.

"And, I liked him… Until I didn't. But that other guy was not John Henry, Sandra. And things didn't go well! Let's suffice it to say that I had to make him *quiet*. In *the dust*…" Again, Sandra gave her a bovine look. Beautiful continued apace, "Regardless, I have come upon this most startling and liberating idea in the aftermath! And though it will require you to shave my feet, my arms, my legs, make me ugly and terrible looking as the other human friends, albeit, rest assured, I'll still be stronger and more attractive, I'm willing. Help me now! First, I must learn how to speed in your car."

After some shocked silence, Sandra said, "I think you should learn to drive before you learn how to speed."

"Why's that?" Beautiful asked. "Daddy says all the time that people who speed don't know how to drive."

"I should have known that you'd feel that way," Sandra responded.

Beautiful then, joyfully, ran outside.

~

A short time later, after breakfast under the trees, they walked together to where the Pinto had last been parked, which was below a sycamore tree in the shade of the friends' driveway. "You met some guy last night like John Henry?" Sandra asked.

"Yes," Beautiful said.

"He's doing well, by the way. I heard from his friends —"

"Fuck him," Beautiful replied. "He likes idiots. I now have larger concerns."

"Right," Sandra said, seating herself in the passenger side and sliding one foot in and out of her clog like she feared it might disappear for good. "And now you want to learn how to drive, and then how to speed?"

"You got it, San. Ten points for observation."

"But you drove last night and you were fine, right? You had the e-navigator?"

"I did not. I handled that situation alone. However," Beautiful said, not liking to admit her embarrassment yet feeling it key to Sandra's understanding, "When I go off-estate this time, I'd like to fit in as I drive around. Drivers noticed me and honked. This time, I want to travel across the country, so I must appear normal, not special, not rich, not beautiful, do you hear me, Sandra?—I must appear completely incognito. That greaser was going to kidnap me for Daddy's money, and this mission has nothing to do with Daddy or money, and thus, paining me though it does, I must appear like a drudge, like everybody else, at least until I meet Ida. I'll bring the e-navigator this time. Maybe halfway across the country I can begin to grow back the hair on my face. I do want to look somewhat glorious when I arrive. Please, buckle up."

This drive was harrowing for Sandra, but she applied the basic primer to Beautiful: "No speeding unless there aren't cops on the road, because cops will pull you over and ticket you, which requires identification, and if you have any chance whatsoever of not being found by your parents and hauled back here, you mustn't be pulled over."

As Beautiful lurched forward at varying speeds, it was then that Sandra expounded on the idea of posted speed-limits and following the flow of traffic.

If Sandra looked a little green by the time they pulled onto the freeway, this bothered Beautiful not at all. "I'm so glad you're with me today," Beautiful said. "I understand some learning is a bit nauseating, so if you'd like to avail yourself of leaning out of your passenger side window to puke as I drive, I won't take it personally in the slightest. In fact, I'd welcome that puking, not wanting you to hold anything back or away from us, because we are the best of friends, and you must be permitted your honest reactions. But I must confess, I'm quite delighted that your car is an automatic because this lets me view the scenery better as I drive and makes the foot maneuvers less complicated than those for Daddy's car I crashed. These Gucci shoes are uncomfortable."

"I'll puke if I need to," said Sandra, smiling again her tremulous smile. "You're doing very well, Beautiful, but I might ask that you take that foot off the gas just a bit as you approach nearby traffic. Screeching breaking will attract the nervous attention of other drivers—and cops."

"You're so good to me," Beautiful said and turned to regard Sandra again, affixing her friend with a tender, grateful look, so overcome with Sandra's kindness that she careened right up close to an enormous semi-truck, and it was only Sandra's sudden terror and expression of, "Shit, Beautiful! Watch the road!" that regained her refocused attention and rapid foot on the brake pedal.

Afterward, Sandra moaned for several moments, and it was only when they returned to the Chef's estate after two hours of Sandra's excellent training that Sandra got out of the Pinto on shaky legs, walked to the nearest bush, and began to puke.

Beautiful attended her, patting Sandra's back while the largest vomit upsurges came, stroking and pulling the long hair from Sandra's face, as she said, "But don't worry that I'll take your car, Sandra. Daddy will replace it. You'll probably get a better car. Maybe a Benz. You done puking?"

When they retired to the master pink bathroom that Baby had designed at the tender age of twelve, during an interior decorating phase that was ultimately quashed by her mother due to Beautiful's extravagant designs, Sandra washed Beautiful's face with honey buttercream soap. "Remember," Sandra said, "don't forget to pull over for gas when the yellow light comes on that looks like a fuel pump, and if you hit another car, you are required by law to pull over and exchange information with the other driver, so don't hit another car."

Beautiful thought of the car she'd clipped without penalty at the bar the night before. She shrugged since this struck her as useless advice, except about the gas. "Thanks, my dear," she said. "Now, shave me."

With thoughts of the coming depilation, it was discomfiting to strip in front of Sandra, to get into the bubbly bath in front of Sandra, and, completely naked, to present Sandra with one of her father's nicked facial hair razors so she could be denuded, but Beautiful tried not to show her hesitation. Besides, she normally liked being watched during any embarrassing activity, and Sandra was preoccupied with looking for something in the medicine cabinet.

"I don't have to shave you if you don't want me to. You can shave yourself," Sandra said after gargling some mouthwash she'd found. "It's sometimes better that way."

Beautiful considered this. "I can handle my arms and my legs, maybe, but I'll need you to shave my back. Then you can do my face." She deliberated on whether she wanted Sandra to leave and come back, especially since now it would be like Sandra watching her shave the first parts as some kind of unfortunate voyeur, but she decided it could be a hassle to get Sandra back exactly when and how she needed her, so, "Please be seated on the toilet," she said. "I won't be a moment."

Hair slid in mounds from her body, floating on the bathwater. Many times she emptied the razor by shaking it in the water or turning on the faucet, and although Sandra had waited patiently, reading a magazine, Beautiful knew it took a good forty minutes until the majority of hair had been removed, and she could hand the razor to Sandra, sitting up, revealing her back, which was next.

She touched her prickly breasts. Her shaved chest, the sole clean swath she'd shaved for last night's outing, grew back already but didn't warrant new shaving. Besides, Beautiful had been advised against too much shaving already by Louisa St. Clare, who'd helped her the night before. "Once you start cutting hair, it grows back like a yard hedge."

"You mentioned you'll be taking my car, Beautiful," Sandra whispered as the blade approached and entered into, but was immediately caught by, Beautiful's back hair. "But if you get in any trouble, you should take my cell number, too. I'll help you."

Beautiful turned and grabbed Sandra in a bone-crushing hug that left Sandra gasping, poncho soaked, water dripping all over the floor. The razor fell. "Thank you, Sandra. Thanks. I'm a little afraid of going somewhere far by myself, though I'm attempting not to show it."

"Everybody hates going places by themselves," Sandra replied, picking up the razor. "But then you do it, and it's okay. I'll need to cut this hair with a scissor before I go at it with the hand razor. Can I do that?"

"Of course," Beautiful replied, "whatever's easier," noticing that the shaving of her back went much faster after an early clipping. And how smart Sandra could be! Guiltily, she regretted thinking Sandra foolish.

"You won't have stuff around out there like you do here," Sandra warned. "Have you considered that? Here, you have an enormous estate. Food. Servants. Friends."

"Yes," Beautiful said. "Here, I've got everything. But out there, I'm free. I'll bring lots of money."

Sandra nodded and replied gingerly, "I need to shave your face now. I know this will bother you—you sure?"

"Yes. When I'm out there, Sandra, I need to be anonymous. Ugly as anybody else."

"Okay," Sandra said, touching Beautiful's cheeks before she soaped them. "But be careful out there, okay? And eat a mixed diet. On the road there's lots of greasy diners. Avoid that, okay, Beautiful? Listen to me. What are we going to do here without you? The schedule every day is about you. Everything's about you..."

"Sandra, you look like you're about to cry," Beautiful said. "Why are you so worried? I imagine the friends will do what they'd like. It'll be a vacation. They could go home and visit their parents, go anywhere. They, unlike me, have been free to leave all the while. I'm recuperating my strangled scream of freedom."

"But Beautiful, you're different from the others," Sandra replied. "I know this sounds strange, but I feel oddly protective, like I want your Daddy to go with you, like you could get hurt. No one will understand you. It could be dangerous."

"Are you trying to incite my fear, Sandra?" They looked into each others' eyes and Beautiful felt like crying. "It doesn't matter. I have to go," she said as the last clump of hair fell from her left cheek, the blade finishing its tour.

"Oh, fuck, girl. You look so human," Sandra replied. "I can't believe it."

"You look so human, too," Beautiful said. "But that's normal."

"You want the mirror?"

"No. I don't want to see myself this way just yet. I'm not sure I ever want to see myself this way."

Sandra's eyes spilled over. "Beautiful, I barely recognize you. It's kinda awful."

Responding to the poignancy in Sandra's expression with a poignant memory of her own, Beautiful then said, "Remember when we were twelve and we hadn't kissed boys? Remember how we kissed our pillows and talked about boys? Remember that night you kissed me behind the green bookcase and I kissed you back? Remember how I told you I'd love you forever and ever and ever?"

"Yes," Sandra replied. "I can't forget."

"Oh good," Beautiful said. "Because Sandra—our kiss was better than the greaser's kiss last night. And I like boys.

Except when I hate them. But I've always secretly loved you as one of my favorite friends. I just didn't say it till now."

"You're done. Shaved. Now get dressed," Sandra said, sighing. "I hate boys."

"You couldn't possibly," Beautiful argued. "You have Fucking Eugene."

"Fucking Eugene is boring," Sandra replied.

"Fucking Jake wasn't boring, but he was mean," Beautiful replied. She then leaned and kissed Sandra full on the mouth and wrapped her arms around her friend, who'd begun to sob. Both were drenched by bathwater as Beautiful stepped out of the bath. "Don't worry about me, Sandra," Beautiful went on, toweling off. "I'll be all right." And she was happy, for an instant, to have erased her last kiss with the greaser with the kiss of a dear friend. "Now let me get dressed and then hand me your keys! I plan to leave soon. If I'm okay after all this, I'll give you back your car."

"You can have it," Sandra said. "I'm glad I didn't puke in there; that would stink. Vomit stink lasts forever. I remember when my brother puked in the back of the—"

"I'll miss you, Sandra," Beautiful said, interrupting her, "very, very much," and though the two friends exchanged looks that said much more, afterward both were silent.

After lunch that day, Beautiful drove the Pinto away with a luggage full of money, three bags of designer clothes, more razors, a satchel of eye make-up and hair accessories, and a bag of snacks from Sandra. "Mommy," she said to the open air outside the car, picturing her mother fingering the little ape girl figurine, "I'm sorry to leave you since I know you'll think of me and worry, but I must go."

~

About an hour into her drive, due to insufficient braking, Beautiful hit a moving car, smacking its backend with a grinding crunch. While Sandra's advice regarding pulling over and not pulling over had been compelling, or at least occurred to Beautiful again, she felt that not stopping was better. Nonetheless, she broke in the middle of the road to consider the issue.

The driver of the other car pulled over. The short old man leaned out his window and shouted, "Crazy woman driver! Pull to the side! Don't you have insurance on that heap?"

"Shut up, old man," she shouted and, as his language got more colorful, she flipped him what she affectionately referred to as the bird.

She worked to pull the Pinto to the emergency lane, if only until she decided what to do next, but didn't appreciate when he shouted, "Fuck you! Aren't you going to get out and talk to me?" He got out of his car. In black slacks, gold neck bling, and a pink button up shirt, he seemed so gauche.

"No," she replied.

Though she had the e-navigator, she was also worried that she wasn't really on her way to see Ida, that the newest machinery, as much faith as her father had in such things, might betray her somehow, as gadgets sometimes did, and she'd be stranded on one of these country roads with another jerk yelling at her, or no food, for quite some time, having to approach strangers. Her father had always forbidden her a cell phone. She was now only forty miles from home.

Her stomach grumbled and an annoying new noise

issued from the Pinto as she cranked the wheel. The old guy approached her, preparing to introduce himself.

All her life, people had been introduced to her by den mothers or den fathers on help-staff—and to meet people outside of this, well, it reminded her of the dive bar. How they'd stared and shouted! What little they knew! They could come off quite aggressively. She regretted the beauty of her natural state was not with her then and hoped she wouldn't hurt the other driver.

"I'm calling the cops, you stupid bitch," he said, shaking his fist at her window. She looked over at his car, which was pretty, she mused, or had been, before the Pinto crumpled the metal near the back bumper. There was a horse hood ornament she admired and the car's color was fire-engine red.

"Want to trade cars?" she asked, manually rolling down her window as Sandra had instructed, feeling she could fix his bumper issue with a few solid hits.

His response was to sputter profanity. His response was to walk back to his car and kick his own tire with his funky white tennis shoe, so Beautiful, having concluded that the Pinto still drove, though there was now an awful rasping as the wheel turned to the right, discarded the idea of either paying for his damage or exchanging his car for hers—because he was mean and, having belonged to Sandra, the Pinto was too good for his ugly white tennis-shoed self.

She drove away. After which, she was filled with regret that the Pinto had no hood ornament. All he did was make a call on his phone. "I should have taken his car," she said. "Or at least the ornament. Perhaps if I took his car, it wouldn't be making this noise that Sandra's car now makes."

She listened to the scraping and said, "I should have taken that guy's phone, too! What if this car dies? I'll need a cell phone. What if I need to call Sandra? How was I supposed to get one if not through my own enterprise?"

The piles of money in the backseat luggage would make any purchase easy, she knew, but she wanted a phone now. The road expanded from two lanes to four while she desperately tried to remember that Pay as You Go Calling commercial, wishing they could transport a phone in her general direction.

But the funky guy hadn't followed her. No traffic riddled the road, solely Beautiful and the grinding of the Pinto's tires against the wheel wells, which she began to consider a lovely and appropriate noise, reminding her of migrations of large and metal modern beasts, gyrating in a sort of morbid clutch and release due to pathos almost sexual. As she spied an almond orchard to her left and a peach orchard to her right, she fell in love with the beauty of the mixed scents. She felt free! "I've never seen these so close before!" she stated, forgetting the other guy entirely. "Trees that bear fruit! Even hinky little nuts! Nut blossoms! Fruit with nuts!" There were no fruit trees on the estate. Daddy wouldn't allow them. They attracted insects, most of which he hated. Also, vermin.

In a flurry of desire to keep this feeling and scent close, Beautiful pulled over, exiting her car to dance around the nearest peach tree like it might be May Day, which she'd read about. "You had to keep me from trees, Daddy?" she asked. "Because you disdain bugs? That's silly!"

Happily, she shook the trunk and several peaches fell. She tasted two, both with an aftertaste of chemical pesticides, so she promptly spit them out. Bee boxes sat below some trees. Buzzing. "Oh fantastic bizarre buzz!" Beautiful said, rebellious already. "Daddy, I love the natural!" Her father had a hatred of naturalism. "Anyway, fuck you, Daddy. Life and nature are beautiful things!" Beautiful went on, grabbing a bee box and shaking it until bees flew out *en masse*.

Some stung her. She remained placid. "Nature hurts," she said, smiling, as if realizing this for the first time, "so

good." From the Pinto she grabbed a small spiral bound notebook on which she had started a list entitled: LIBERATION MOVEMENT DISCOVERIES.

Under day one, she wrote: "*Peaches taste shitty when unrinsed. Should have asked Sandra more questions. Driving is difficult, yet I persevere. Nature moves me where concrete does not. I'm stung, and yet, the slight pain soothes me somehow. That enjoyable little pain aside, it's hard to be alone without a cell phone when you have an ambitious plan but only one other person in on it, who isn't even present—Blast, Sandra, why didn't you come?— this means I should have taken her with me, at any cost, insisted, "Sandra. I need you, my hairless little friend," but I can't go back. She's busy. I'll figure things out.*

Observation two: Peaches and almonds smell good together, but nothing tastes good with pesticide. Someone should do a pesticide free peach and almond dessert. I missed hearing Ida today. I hit a car and didn't pull over. Nothing happened, except the ridiculous guy got mad. Sandra's driving advice credible? What to ignore?

Though her car doesn't work well, now making a loud ass noise, I remain happy. Wonder if anyone's worried. I miss Mommy and Daddy, but it's good to miss people sometimes and how proud they will be when I learn the personal responsibility they are always talking about! Then again, who the fuck cares? Wearing gorgeous Jimmy Choo shoes today. They were not on sale. I'm wicked hot. Burning! TTFN."

As a chill breeze blew past, Beautiful donned a Cavallo

sweater grabbed from the back seat. All around were orchards. "I'm cold when shaved," she said. "What a feeling to be cold!" She got back in the car, chattering to herself, "There's something here that heats this car. Some dial or lever."

She tried to remember whether Sandra had said anything about a heating device in the Pinto because she did remember having ridden in warm cars, but for now, despite pictorial representations of various kinds on the knobs, consoles, and levers, she had no idea how to make anything work. She turned all the levers. Nothing happened.

But the power was off. Maybe the heat needed it. She inserted the key and leaned forward to press and squint at the buttons and dials as if they would tell her the good action in the language of symbolism. She recognized an icon as a gas gauge, mainly since Sandra had repeatedly pointed it out, "Watch for this. Watch for this or the car will sputter and die!"—but while doing so, pressed against the wheel, and, engaged by her breasts, the car horn emitted a lengthy honk upon the trees. "My breasts can honk," Beautiful said, not displeased. "What else can they do?"

A few cars drove by, but traffic was minimal. Still, after she'd beeped, as if she meant to attract him, a man came running toward her from a distant red farmhouse. Beautiful didn't feel like chatting so waved. She then realized she'd knocked down part of his white wooden fence that surrounded the orchard when she'd initially pulled over.

"I'd like to give you my money to fix this fence," she told the distant figure, "Because though it's just wood and detains no animals, Daddy says people should pay for what they wreck!" She felt proud to be so thoughtful, and took nine hundred to place under the bee box, one for each downed plank, destroying as little more fence as possible while leaving.

Nonetheless, before she rejoined the road, two squat people now approached from the red farmhouse in stiff runs, the portly man with his portly wife trailing by one hundred yards.

The two of them, having not yet discovered her left reparations, seemed far more interested than she was about the fence situation. "Did they craft it with their very hands?" she asked aloud and slipped a compact disk into the music player, weaving and waving again, passing them by. Humming along with a throaty ballad by an eighty year old, she then heard the e-navigator tell her to turn around.

It spoke with the voice of a disengaged Englishwoman. "Turn around when possible."

"Well, aren't you a saucy little wench?" Beautiful asked, feigning her best post-post-colonial British accent. She flipped a U-turn. Driving again past the house with the broken fence, she now saw three police cars. The lights on their cars spun soundlessly, cops talking to the farmers.

"Policemen!" Beautiful exclaimed. "How exciting! Have the farmers been robbed?"

It didn't occur to her that the people in the cars may be seeking her, the destroyer of the orchard fence, but her Pinto passing them by again resulted in four fingers pointing into the cool mid-morning air, their attached arms swinging as if on hinges to follow her progress. Only one car came in pursuit, a police vehicle.

It was only when this car pulled behind her, lights flashing mildly in the afternoon sun, that Beautiful felt a slight concern. She donned her sunglasses, which Sandra told her (and yet everyone knew) were the symbol for rapt submission, consulting the speed limit. Still, she felt happy! She felt like the lead car in a new parade. *I'm the lead car*, she kept thinking, almost singing.

The cops then turned on audible sirens.

Was this the moment she was supposed to pull over? Beautiful mused. She couldn't pull over for cops, Sandra'd said. Her father would make her go home and she hadn't even reached Ida's. Recklessly, she floored the Pinto but the officer accelerated to drive right alongside her.

Speaking through a megaphone, he said, "Pull over the car, lady, and no one gets hurt!"

"I'm not hurt," Beautiful replied. "Nor do I plan on getting hurt." She didn't lower her window. "Most importantly, Officer, I need not to hurt you," she went on, mainly to herself. "Perhaps you should let me move along. I left money."

She smiled and waved, hoping to seem foreign, reminding herself of those TV shows where someone sometimes acts like they don't speak English when they don't want to answer a question. Beautiful had no desire to answer this cop's questions. *I'm Polynesian,* she thought. *From Uzbekistan. Turkish, needing some Turkish Delight!*

In the ignored cop car driving alongside her, there were two policemen, one fat, one skinny.

"Lady, pull over," the nearest cop repeated.

She kept moving, undecided. Only when the cop cut off her progress off with a diagonal swerve did she kill the Pinto's ignition and get out, furious.

"Do you not get it that I'm on a self-liberation movement?" she asked. "Have a little respect."

"Put your hands in the air!" the cop shouted. "You have the right to remain silent."

He was a red-headed guy, she observed as he approached, rather large, really very close to the ugliest man she'd ever seen. "Listen, I need a cell phone, Officer," she replied. "Where's the best place to get one, fast?"

"Stand spread-eagle against the car, young lady. Keep your hands up!"

She didn't understand spread-eagle. He neared her with his gun out.

"Turn around and put your hands on the vehicle," the approaching one said, reaching for his cuffs.

"Or what? You going to shoot me?" she asked, noting his partner remained in the car, typing something into the computer. "Listen. I've got money," she said. "How about I give it to you and you let me go? I'm sure what I did was a minor infraction. How about a few thousand?"

"Lady, lean against your car and keep your hands where I can see them."

"I don't feel like leaning against my car," Beautiful argued. She also didn't keep her hands up, but dropped them and rotated, deciding to sit back in the Pinto instead, though as she turned to get back in, the officer slammed her against the car.

Without thinking, she grabbed him and reciprocated the slam. His gun fell. The cuffs fell. She grabbed this weapon, flung it away, then lifted him by the scruff of his neck and put him between her and his partner's view of the situation. "That wasn't very nice, officer," she whispered. "I don't appreciate it." His breath stank of six day coffee and stale Cheetos. "But you are going to help me," Beautiful went on, very slow and dulcet. "Because I need a cellphone and you have one. I'll take yours. I might need your car too. Tell your partner to get out of the car and I won't harm either of you. Tell him to come out, right now."

She kept hold of the cop's neck but let him grab his walkie talkie. "Don't turn towards your partner," she said. "Just do as I ask."

In response, the officer spoke into his radio, attached some code to his message, and she noticed that the partner had gotten out of the car rapidly, but the partner's gun was drawn.

"Drop your gun, Tall Skinny," she shouted, using the fat one she held like a vest. "Or I'll end this man's life."

The partner was tall and skinny, which made her nickname perfect. She didn't think she'd have trouble handling them both if need be, but in his clenched sheer terror, the fat one, who'd peed the leg of his pants, said, just then, "Is that hair growing in on your face?"

"What's it to you, Fat Ugly?" she asked.

The skinny one tried to talk her down, speaking in his reedy boy's voice, "Release my partner, lady, and no one will get hurt. No one will be harmed if you let my partner go."

"No one will be harmed if I hang onto him either," Beautiful replied. "So what kind of stupid conversation is this?"

"Just let him go," Tall Skinny repeated.

"But if I do that, you're still going to try and arrest me, aren't you?" Beautiful asked. "Normally, I'd inform you of my father's clout, possibly see if you felt like taking a bribe, because that is how Daddy works, but now, I'll simply inform you of my own clout. I'm practicing independence. This means I'll create my own solution to this undesirable situation. Drop your gun." All shared a moment of stunned disbelief. "That means NOW!" she bellowed. "Come closer!" She wrapped her arm around the fat partner's neck and whispered, "How do I make this go away? I have to visit Ida Haze."

The one she held made no response.

"Just let Vick go," Tall Skinny said. He was very young, too, Beautiful then realized. A novice baby of a cop. And he was worried, maybe, because she had tightened her choke-hold on the fat one named Vick, who had turned red in the face as, simultaneously, a cloacal scent arose.

"God damn it, Vick!" Beautiful said. "Did you shit your-self? Oh, how nasty. So nasty!" She wondered if what he'd done would leak through to her red Prada dress. "Vick, I love this fucking dress!" she said. "I'm tempted to shoot you for that alone."

Meanwhile, Tall Skinny near bawled. "Don't kill Vick," he said. "He's a good cop. There's good cops and there's bad cops and Vick's a good cop. He's been almost like a daddy to me. Let him go."

Well, this was all very touching and moving to Beauti-ful, not to mention that she wanted to let Vick go, being that he'd just shat himself, but she was unclear how to get out of this mess without harming either officer. Her dress was thin. Cop shit didn't need to besmirch it.

"What's your name, Tall Skinny?" she asked the thin cop.

"Ed."

"Well, Ed," she said. "This is your lucky day. I'm feeling generous. I'll spare you and Vick today—because I take no pleasure in the killing, trust me now, but you must toss me your handcuffs." Ed did. Beautiful caught them in her left hand. "And toss your gun out to those weeds along the road. Right where that ice-cream wrapper is."

Ed hesitated, said, "I'm not supposed to surrender my weapon."

"Oh, don't hesitate now," Beautiful replied and cranked her headlock a touch tighter until Vick began gasping, turning purplish. In immediate response, Ed, like some hostage's cowed lover, rapidly capitulated. "Now come to me and hold out your hands. Both of them," Beautiful narrated.

On the estate, she'd often narrated activities for friends, so this was a relaxing and habitual occurrence. Ed inched closer. "Hold them out far," she said again, like she were asking him to embrace the planet, imitating the voice of a therapist from back home, a woman named Lizbeth who had a strange fetish for dolphins and liked to swim with them. Beautiful loved Lizbeth's expansive demeanor, and she and Lizbeth had even sat together on numerous occasions, listening to ocean sounds on a small clock radio Lizbeth carried, meditating as the latter required. While meditating, though it had been described as a spiritual activity, sitting and thinking of dolphins, Beautiful had often just thought of tuna. And shrimp. And other things she liked to eat. But no one could deny Lizbeth's style was powerful—and now Ed, AKA Young Skinny, was listening to Beautiful effortlessly embody her former shrink as Beautiful said, "Come to me, Ed, and turn toward Vick!"

Ed did as told. Beautiful took Vick's cuffs and cuffed one of Ed's wrists to one of Vick's. Then she took Ed's cuffs and diagonal cuffed their opposing hands. "Now, you two are going to sit in Sandra's Pinto," she said before instantly re-evaluating the situation. "No. Actually, you'll sit in this ditch. I'm not taking you with me."

The movements they made, trying to sit with their wrists cuffed at diagonals, were funny. "Fat Boy should sit first," Beautiful said. "Then Tall Skinny should just go with him, you know? Like dancers."

They tried to figure this out. Finally, to help, Beautiful just punched both in the gut at the same time and they landed in the ditch. Once everyone was seated, Beautiful got back in the Pinto. She sorely wanted to take the beautiful police car but was pretty sure Sandra had told her *not* to take anything from police, or she might *intuit* Sandra *would* tell her not to.

Her windows were down. Already the beginnings of an argument were audible as Vick complained, "Why'd you drop your gun? A good cop never relinquishes his weapon. Awww, man. This is gross. Sitting in your own shit is gross."

"She was gonna kill you, Vick," Ed said. "I could see it in her crazy eyes."

"You're not fit for cop work," Vick said. "I should tell your daddy."

Beautiful, interested, did not yet start her car. In fact, she suddenly felt this was a good opportunity to practice what Sandra had often called humanitarianism. She would facilitate the discussion. Right then.

She got out of the car, noticing Vick shifted on his behind, he and Ed seated quite close. "I think the two of you have some interpersonal problems to work out," she announced. "And I'm going to help you, in a co-counseling capacity. You see, I have done a lot of work on my impulse control and self-regulation. Thus, I feel that though I never had a career goal before and have taken no extreme classes in therapy, I have been the recipient of much therapy, and I think I might take up helping people by aiding them with working through their issues." She smiled with an expression that was quite luminous, fierce, but one she hoped was friendly, then altered this to the smaller placating smile-frown she'd tried out on small children at the park before uttering, "Say, Ed, may I make an observation?"

"Vick smells like shit?"

"Yes, this is true. Vick does in fact smell like shit. Does the fact that he smells like shit keep you from being able to pleasantly converse?"

"It keeps me from being able to converse like I don't have *shit* in my pants," Vick said.

"Vick, would you like me to strip those pants from you?" Beautiful asked, again conciliatory. "You would be bare-assed at roadside, but, you would stink less. We will fling them in the ditch."

"Don't be touching my pants," Vick replied, leaning as far away from her as he could.

"I don't want to make love to you, so don't worry," she added in a clinical tone. "Stripping your pants would be solely for your comfort."

"I'm not wiping his ass for him after you do that," Ed said. "If that's what you think."

"I suggest we cut off his pants!" Beautiful then said, already excited to have found an excuse to use the Swiss Army knife on Sandra's keychain, which she'd always been told not to touch. But Sandra had given it to her for this trip! The corkscrew could be an interesting implement as well. "Let's corkscrew off his pants," she suggested.

"Like hell you're going to strip my pants," Vick replied.

It was in this precise moment that Beautiful felt an undeniable *toska*, which was the Russian sensation of spiritual anguish without specific cause. "You're giving me *toska*," she said. "I cannot translate this word for you, bumpkin, because it has no English equivalent, and unless you have read as many Russian novels as I have, you'd have no idea about just how beautiful and interesting a thing as *toska* can be, but let's just say that what you are doing, how you are acting, it nauseates me and causes a slight ache in my chest that could catapult into a fretting large enough to cause a great gnashing of teeth, a great rending of garments, not sexual, not mine—though, if I touch you, I have already shared it will be with the Swiss Army knife, or the corkscrew, because this pleases me... Ed, anything to add? Are you, too, in the throes of the *toska?*"

"Never thought about it much," said Ed. "But I think I've lived *toska* every goddamn minute of my life."

"I gotta cause for my *toska*," Vick said. "The shit in my pants."

Beautiful took all of this in quite gently, not allowing her flaring temper to get the best of her. "I've offered," she replied, with only a small amount of haughty aplomb, "to cut them off. Yes or no? Which is it?"

"No," Vick said, eyeing the corkscrew that she had already opened and then regarded with a heightened delight.

As the conversation continued, Beautiful tried to facilitate fixing the relationship problems between Ed and Vick, repeatedly bringing up Ed's submissive behavior and how, in her view, this was all about his perceived inequity with Vick's powerful self-presence, which Ed lacked. She could not remember the exact words to rephrase her various shrinks, but she felt likely approximations would do. "So Ed, what I was reaching for before is that I think you have a displaced father figure dynamic going on with Vick. You seek to impress him, but he won't be impressed because you are not a good cop. Yet, you keep trying. Why do you keep trying?"

Ed rolled his eyes. She cracked him in the face with a left jab and then smacked them into each other. The conversation went through many such contortions.

Finally, it seemed, at last, that the opinions of the cops had aligned with hers after very limited coercion on her part, when she announced, "Because you love Vick, Ed!" tearfully and triumphantly, "If you didn't love Vick, why would you have thrown your gun to the side?" and the two of them nodded, too, also tearful.

This part of the discussion concluded, Beautiful addressed what Sandra would call the "real issues." This meant, from Beautiful's understanding: Facts that cannot be denied when further action is required. "Excellent, you love each other," Beautiful said. "But we must get to the hard questions here, because these questions could forbid your unchaste consummation of this passion." She took a brief moment here to search each policeman's eyes as if she were plumbing their very souls, as if any threat of dishonesty on their parts would imply a trip straight to hell, or a hard smack at the very least. "Now, Officers Vick and Ed, note I'm being respectful here and no longer calling you Tall Skinny and Fat Ugly because that was wrong of me, wrong, wrong, wrong—are you two related?"

"No," Vick said.

"And how long have you been partners?"

"A year," Ed said.

This went on.

Finally, a few smacks later, Ed admitted his deep love for Vick and his willingness to pursue a deeper and more involved partnership. He also admitted his longstanding phobia of doorjambs and that he still, upon occasion, but not all the time, urinated while sleeping. "You're making very good progress, Ed," Beautiful said. "I'm proud of you."

There was a tearful bit where Vick had asked Ed about whether he had radioed for help when he saw Vick was in the headlock, to which Ed had answered that he could not —he was worried about Vick first. And even if Vick had shat himself, Ed wanted him alive, brother, alive. Beautiful clapped for them at this revelation. "You see, you're good kind boys after all," she said. She touched the cheek of each. She kissed the cheek of each.

This, she knew, was not part of standard counseling protocol, but she liked a personal touch. Still, this work made her hungry, and she realized she had always wanted a megaphone, so took theirs, dropping a hundred in the front seat of the cop cruiser to compensate.

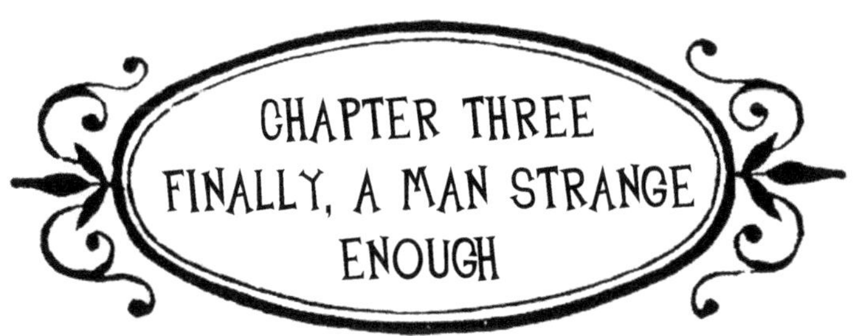

Chapter Three
Finally, a Man Strange Enough

~In which, Beautiful learns her estate friends are fake, takes a weird lover at a hotel pool, loses him by morning light, enjoys self-inflicted bruises, and bonds with her earnest driver Thomas, who has issues~

As she got in the Pinto and drove away, the two men huddled together. They didn't speak. "And you see," Beautiful said. "They know each other better now. It is a close and tight camaraderie they now enjoy. I'm glad for that."

She wondered when her perfect soul mate would appear. As she came within fifty miles of stopping for the day, she saw the trees around the long highway like wooden arms inviting her into the big wild world. "I'm being so good, Daddy," she said to no one. "And very feminine, Mommy."

She drove forty more miles and pulled off to the side of the road to ask her notebook, "If I killed nobody today and came up with an ingenious pain-free solution as well as providing personal cop counseling, do I get extra points in heaven?" She drove another block or two and then pulled off again, expounding, "Because I do think I'll be going to heaven. After I see Ida. Hopefully, long after. Also, I was good today because I really wanted to steal that cop car and

I DID NOT. Could have turned those lights on, with the sirens blaring, sped down the road. I should write down each bit of self-control I had today. Dolphin lady, God, Mommy, this has been a record. I am a model of self-control."

It was then that the car's gas light came on and Beautiful simultaneously figured out the car radio worked because it sputtered to life spontaneously as someone sang, with a raspy voice, from the speakers: "You give good love to me, bay-bay. So good. Take this heart of mine…" and Beautiful was promptly reminded of her tender romantic will to be united with a worthy party and her beatific visions of love with John Henry that she'd only recently tried to curtail. Nonetheless, she was also reminded, due to the gas light, that she needed gas, so she decided to combine these efforts and see what she could find at the gas station. Maybe another man who looked like John Henry! But then, she wasn't picky.

Hungry, yes. Picky, no.

No one could match up to Sandra for dearness or John Henry for sheer gentle kindness. A John Henry-Sandra combo struck Beautiful as an inspired idea. She wanted to call Sandra, too. To tell her how good she'd been.

She would omit mention of the smacked car and the old man shouting, "Fuck you." But she might say a word or two about his car, so red and shiny, except where she hit the back. She would omit the mention of the farm people too, the bee box, their fence… "You give good love to me, ba-ay-aybeeeee," the radio blared, "so good…"

Beautiful sang along. And so forth.

She pulled into the nearest gas station where two anorexic teenagers, one boy, one girl, skulked out front. "Hey lady, hey lady," they half-whispered as she approached to pay for her gas. "Will you buy us some Schlitz?"

"What are you going to do with that liquor?" Beautiful asked.

"Drink it," was the reply. Both the short girl with a

black beanie pulled over dyed blue hair and the tall pale guy wearing dark lipstick gave her a pleading look.

"I'll buy you both some chips instead," Beautiful said. "You both look hungry."

She entered the store with a wad of cash. As she exited after payment, she knew the credit for some cash had been placed at the pump, but couldn't decide how to use it, which was embarrassing since the kids avidly watched as she walked around the car three times with their chips, bills still clenched in her hand, the third time noting a small latch of some sort on the driver's side floorboard inside the vehicle that matched the dash icon.

"Oooh. That might be it," she said, just before shouting, "Teenage alcoholic children! Come help me, please! Now!"

Like summoned rats, they came. She gave them their chips.

"Put the gas I've purchased in this car," Beautiful said, "and I'll give you some money."

"How much?" the boy asked.

"It's rude to ask such questions," Beautiful instructed. "You'll never be rich or a rich person's favorite if you insist on showing your gaucheness every minute of the livelong day."

"I want enough for a soda," the girl said. "And a Slim Jim."

"Done," Beautiful agreed. "Now, show me how to do it."

After they pumped her gas, having seen the open cash luggage in the car, Beautiful observed that the boy's eyes went dark, like he seemed he might jump her. The sight of money did odd things to people. With many scrapples enjoyed in her history, Beautiful could always tell the animal zest of a fighter ready to commit the astronomically stupid act of combat, such decisions completely delusional with a clearly worthier opponent, but as they stood in the yellow lights, the girl hung back and the first punch the boy tried to throw made Beautiful laugh at his insensate state, his fist landing lightly in her palm. She grabbed it and squeezed this hand, saying, "Silly bug," shaking her head. "No, no, no," she went on, "not today. Work on your grappling skills," but she did not release his appendage.

She waited, holding firm but not tight, counting down from twenty to avoid inflicting unnecessary injuries. When he did not appear plentifully remorseful, she squeezed his fist a little harder until she was sure he felt enormous pain.

She then handed the girl a cool hundred with her free hand. "That's because you didn't resort to violence," she said. "And while I acknowledge it's possible that your female nature alone made you smart enough to realize my superiority, I do thank you for demonstrating less stupidity."

"Let me go—let me go!" the boy begged, trying to wrench his fist away from her. "You're crushing my bones!"

"I am not crushing your bones," Beautiful replied, indignant. "I know exactly how hard to squeeze if I wanted *to crush* bones. I'm only *close* to *bone crushing*, but I—"

"Please let him go," the girl begged more humbly. "Please, lady. Come on."

When Beautiful released the boy's hand, the kids ran to the curb but still watched her from afar. Beautiful sighed. She'd taken the cop's cell phone, but suddenly wondered if this could be traced. Probably.

Thinking fondly of Ed, she opened it and decided to call to see how he was doing. Also to see if his hands were still cuffed. No answer. She assumed yes. "Kids," she said, beckoning them near again. Both approached, but the boy ducked behind the girl. "Want a new cell phone? Just dial a guy named Ed. Ask him to come buy you some liquor." She knew Ed would not. He was a good man. He might, however, take them somewhere safer.

Concern for them came and fled. She realized she needed a plan. It was late. Which motel or hotel might she locate? She wanted one with an Olympic sized pool, already missing the comforts of home and her friends, wondering what her friends were doing now. *Probably copulating near the pool*, she decided. *At any rate, near their beds.* She decided to walk into the snack store and talk up the gas station attendant. "I need somewhere to sleep," she told him. "Know any place around here with a good pool?"

"We don't have many of your kind around here," he said. He was a tall man with wire-framed glasses, short on talk while big on gesture.

"My kind?" she said. "What kind would that be?"

As she leaned closer, he leaned back with matching alacrity. "Oh, you know? Strangers… Up the road," he said. "Sheraton 6. Or the Hyatt Regency. They'll put you up."

She regarded him with disdain. All these ugly people. Still, there was a kind look in his eyes. She liked him. "Do you, Mr. Gas Station Attendant," she asked, "think I'm pretty?"

It was still her ambition to lose her virginity, though he didn't look the least like John Henry. Again, the *toska* hit, this time with a different cause. John Henry was gone for good, forever gone. She'd never see him again. The impossibility of replacing people with any believability was wrenching torment. Her current solitude. John Henry's loss. Sandra's loss. Ida's distance. All of these held *toska* of the first order. Additionally, she was still bothered by the whole exchange with Jake, whether she wanted to admit it or not, and kept hearing what he said to her that night about her looks. As if to reinforce her discomforting recollections, the hair on her face had begun to give her a peculiar sensation, like the shorn quality had been soon replaced by an implacable itch. Just yesterday as she'd shaved, already she felt invisible regrowth, which she saw as a mixed omen because it meant that she could return to her powerful self sooner rather than later, yet now she felt like a child, so virtually hairless, a weak, unidentified, face-scratching child. "Well, do you think I'm pretty?" Staring at the counter guy, but more so looking through him, she burst into tears.

"Sure. I guess you're pretty," he said, looking first at his register then down the candy aisle.

"Very good," Beautiful told him, wiping her tears away.

"Just as pretty as the next girl, I reckon," he went on.

"Oh, thank you!" she replied. "Do you not mean *more?*"

He didn't respond, but she flushed as she assessed his body, considering whether he would do. Then it occurred to her that he might actually want to make love right now. She was ready to do so, and all the better, she decided, if he were just a stop on the road. He wouldn't be a permanent lover after all. Who wanted that?

Temporary is Terrific, she thought. This could be a slogan. It was a possible career path, sloganizing. And perhaps she should have a larger goal with this trip than just to see Ida. To make love continuously and demonstrate her superiority, for example, by taking a new lover at every single town! To prove the irresistible nature of her beauty! To get rid of what Jake said, once and for all, for he had done her grave disservice.

In hindsight, her resultant temper was really quite his fault. She remembered his shriveling testes, how his organ seemed a wee, dead rat in her hand. But not all men would be this way. Some would revere her! Some would want to

pierce her with an organ worthy of consideration! Strong and able ones!

She would test this idea of taking multiple lovers on Sandra, whenever she got around to calling. For now, she freshly considered the attendant. "So, would you like to make love or not?" she asked. "Right now?"

"Uhhhh," he said, currently seeming unsure, not anti, per se, but also not too excited. "Maybe so, maybe not," he went on. "I'll be here all night."

"Well, I won't be here that long," Beautiful replied. "So make up your mind, more snappily if you don't mind."

"I'm deciding how we could do it," he countered.

Bored already and losing sight of the topic and the pleasure in her impulse decision, Beautiful sighed before asking, "What the fuck does that have to do with anything, Counter Guy? Did you think we should go at it on the counter, because I was thinking behind the register maybe? Or in the back? It's not that I'm shy, but there are children out there. Young, alcoholic children!"

"I'm not supposed to leave the front," he said.

"You could take a twenty minute break and lock the door," she replied.

"I could, I suppose," he said, speaking slowly, monitoring her closely now with an almost casually lewd regard. "I'm not giving you anything for it though. No cigarettes. No liquor."

"I want neither," she replied. "This, sir, is what you call a lark of kindness. Could you express a little enthusiasm?"

The look he returned was as bland as a stone. The idea of making love to him appealed to her less and less. So unimpressively emotive was he that she began to believe, rationally or otherwise, that he simply did not deserve to touch even her left pinkie finger. "Oh, never mind," she said. "I don't think I want to."

"Okay," he replied. "My manager doesn't like when I lock the front anyway."

~

Her mood was quite ambiguous while departing, joyful, confused, generally irritable, in turn. Thus, when she spied the teenagers still loitering outside, the waifs having broken the Pinto's side window and working to fish out money with a straightened coat hanger and their greedy hands, she was instantly incensed. Never would reaching the hotel be more welcome.

Once there, she would call Sandra to discuss what she'd learned today: "The world opens to me in new and disturbing ways," she already imagined saying. "And if I have to hit a car, bust a fence, cuff some cops, and dislocate the shoulders of a few teenagers as I mediate this road to self-discovery, well, then, that is what I must do. It doesn't please me."

She walked to the boy whose arm was jammed into her car and said, very clearly, "Please put down that money unless you two would like to accompany me to see my mentor Ida May Haze. She might have some advice about your bad behavior!"

She waited for the boy to retract his arm and then lifted one child under each of her arms and let them dangle. "Drop the money," she said. "While you do seem to be misbehaved children, on the upside of this exchange, I could use some company, especially if either can drive. Can either of you drive?" The girl, pressed to Beautiful's left side, began to cry. The boy kept silent, looking fearful.

"Oh, forget it," Beautiful said. "Just run when I drop you."

They did. Beautiful recovered the money and reconvened her drive. She wanted to say to someone, though she wasn't sure who, "What's wrong with people? You help them and they treat you this way? You give them a hundred and they're out to take more! Does greed ever stop?" It was at this moment that she realized she was actually remembering the swimming lessons she once tried to take at a public pool at age five, until she had injured too many other children, before the Olympic pool at home was built, when six of her swimsuits had been stolen from a locker. This had caused some unfortunate violence.

She wanted to call Sandra or storm to Sandra's room and vent. She wanted Cook to bring her meal up to her room and to ask the woman to wait with her until she was done trying on clothes, Cook attending these activities with a very cold beverage brought right before she'd eat, because Beautiful despised when the ice was mostly melted and moisture coated the sides of her drinking glasses though the warming tray kept the food warm.

But she didn't really want Cook. And she'd call Sandra after she had rested. She'd exercise at the hotel swimming pool. If the rest of the trip went this way, Beautiful fantasized what she'd say on Ida's talk show when she finally did reach her: "Ida, the roads I've struggled to reach you. It wasn't easy! A rapscallion at every corner. And lord is it hard to be a good woman in this day and age!"

There were many things she thought of doing, but she lay on the hotel bed as soon as she got a room and promptly fell asleep. When she woke, the room phone rang insistently... She picked up and it was Sandra, shrieking unbecomingly. "Beautiful Ape Girl Baby Chef! What have you been doing?!"

"Nothing, I..."

At this, Sandra cut her off. "Good, but your father says you must go outside right now, Beautiful! He sends a car. Get outside!"

Beautiful stretched and shrugged, still sleepy as she replied, "Thank you, but no. I need food," to which Sandra responded, "Beautiful, really?! What in the world are you thinking?"

"Hmmm, Columbian coffee and a nice strawberry tart," Beautiful said.

"That's not what I mean!" Sandra said, her voice unusually sharp.

"All right. Maybe some fresh cherries. A bottle of ginger ale. Obviously, I was sleeping, so I haven't yet decided what to eat. Still groggy."

Sandra released a hissing exhalation before shouting, "Forget about that! Wake up in a hurry. Listen to me. You have to come home!"

Since Sandra was so uncharacteristically animated, Beautiful fondly pictured Sandra pacing, maybe doing that thing she did with twisting her already curly hair around her index finger until the finger spun tightly toward her head. Smiling, she said, "Sandra, I'm on a one woman liberation mission and my mission's not yet concluded," adding the song, "We've only just be—gun, to liiiiiivvvvve—white lace and—"

"Beautiful," Sandra then shouted. "This is not an easy-listening soundtrack! Did you *not* absorb a word I've said? The cops are after you. Your daddy made me call the Pinto in stolen, and he's doing all he can for damage control, but you must gather your things and go out now so his driver can pick you up."

"I can't! I won't go home, Sandra," Beautiful replied. "And I don't want his driver. Daddy can forget it. I refuse. *Je refuse!*" Beautiful did not speak French, but had heard this in a movie and liked it.

Sandra exhaled a new sigh that seemed to come from her very bowels, this one accompanied by muffled tears. Beautiful, baffled, considered the variances in Sandra's sighs and finally replied, "I'm fine, Sandra. I'm totally fine. But what is the matter with you? You don't sound fine."

"You're what's the matter with me!" Sandra said. "No, Beautiful, I'm not fine. You are not fine."

"But Sandra, I am fine. You're wrong."

"Maybe you're fine now, but, in general, Beautiful, you aren't fine—and you will not be fine if—"

"So am I fine or not? Fine or not fine?!" Beautiful asked. "Sandra, this conversation is making my head hurt, and you're usually not so wishy-washy because—"

"You're not fine, Beautiful! You need to get out of there right now, in a hurry!" was Sandra's emphatic response.

"Okay, thanks. That's good to know," Beautiful replied. "I'll leave in a minute. But, what are you wearing right now Sandra? I'm trying to picture you."

"What?"

"I'm seeing in my mind's eye those pretty flannel pajamas you wear with little gray cows and pink moons, since you often wear those on Thursday nights, and it's making me feel quite homey. Are you pulling the hair from your head with your finger curled up tight? Did I tell you what adventures I had today, because I was going to call? I swear I'd planned to call, but I wanted to nap first and—"

"Beautiful," Sandra said. "Yes, I'm wearing the flannel cow pajamas with little moons, but listen; you're going to get taken to a jail if you don't get your ass out to the parking lot. And jail is a bad place. They rape you. They take your clothes off. They put you behind bars. Beautiful, there are cavity searches and you can't just come and go. Other inmates can get rowdy. Rude."

"I've read about that, though it's not as bad as Turkish prisons," Beautiful said. "Those I've also read about. Not that I want to go to either, except—"

"All right, well, what you need to do is go outside right now," Sandra said, in a voice clearly meant to mimic Ethel Chef's. "Your mother asked me to call you. Don't hesitate. Get what you have from the Pinto and keep it with you. A black unmarked car is coming! With a driver. Your daddy says you can be gone from here one week, but that's all. There's a phone in there for you, too. If you check in once every two days, you can go to Los Angeles, but you aren't permitted to drive. We saw the car you hit. The fence. The policemen. Beautiful, those two men were crying on the news, terrorized. It's not like at the estate where you could, where you—"

"Where I could *what*, Sandra?"

The line went silent. "Where you could do anything you wanted... You have to get out of there. Your father—"

"Sandra, I've been driving. I'm driving just fine. Why —"

"Beautiful. Get outside and go to the car. Take your stuff. Stand on the curb." This Sandra nearly shouted, and her voice would have issued as a shout if it weren't so clearly hissed through clenched teeth.

"You're talking rather aggressively," Beautiful said. "Sexy! I like it."

"Do it!" Sandra shrieked.

As Beautiful did, the black car driver pulled up immediately and loaded her luggage. Beautiful got in, and just afterward, no fewer than six cop cars pulled into the lot. Through the shaded windows, Beautiful watched them surround the Pinto with great interest. She said to the driver, "Well, would you look at that?" She also told the driver, "If you take me back to the estate now, I'll kill you before we enter the gate. I'll cut you up, send the pieces to the nearest dock, and then feed your organs to surrounding sharks."

She saw him as a thug, if an aging thug. He had white hair and a small white mustache. If she could be sure this mustache was fake, Beautiful wanted to rip it off. In short, she determined quickly that he was just another unengaging clod, one of the bodyguard types her father sometimes sent with her to archery. Like the thug he was, he nodded. This meant nothing. She opened a bottled water from the car fridge. "Another hotel, please, driver," she said. "I want to go swimming tonight."

As the sky darkened, the driver kept driving. Luckily for him, she cat-napped, but when they'd progressed an hour along the road, she asked, "Am I allowed to drive again later, according to Daddy?" The driver pulled into the parking lot of a luxury hotel. He failed to speak. She wondered if his tongue had been cut out. "I asked you a question, Driver," she said, testing this theory. "And you didn't even introduce yourself."

"You cannot drive, Beautiful," he said. "Hello, I'm your driver. And no, you can't drive. That's why I'm here."

"Fine, but if I want to drive, you're fired," she replied.

"I can't be fired," he argued. "I was hired by your father."

"Oh," she said, "then check us in right now and stop being such a wet blanket. I expect responses when I speak, Driver. It's the least you could do considering the circumstances."

She'd figure out what to do about the driver situation tomorrow but first wanted a swim. Perhaps it was better to let her father's goon keep his job. Simply being the rider was advantageous in many ways, she acknowledged; she could relax, as she'd done all her life, and let someone else carry her to her dreams.

Out her hotel window, she witnessed stars in the night sky. She pulled her swimsuit over her legs, which snagged a few times on emerging leg hair. Since this irked her, she immediately called Sandra to ask, "This shaving thing doesn't last long does it?"

Sandra had been sleeping. "Beautiful? Where are you?"

"Safe at a Hyatt. Radiant after riding in one of Daddy's black cars. A horrid Lincoln, as you know Daddy prefers. The most boring vehicle in the history of Daddy's empire. The non-car! If this car were a person, it would be saying, 'Don't look at me. I want to stand in the corner forever, rich and stultifying!' And I'm here now at the Hyatt, and the hair on my body is growing out, Sandra. Very fast. Should I keep doing this shaving thing every day? It's rather sharp on my legs."

"Do you plan to get out of the car much?"

"Yes, I do," Beautiful said. "Every chance I get."

"You know your father's talking to Ida's rep right now, right? He said it will be expensive, but he'll get you in to see her, and it might be better if you don't get out of the car much, Beautiful," Sandra said. "To safeguard your trip. For your own protection."

"I don't need protection."

"But, Beautiful, you do."

"I do not," Beautiful said, thinking the aqua water of the pool looked inviting. "From what?"

"Men with guns."

Beautiful laughed. "I have the driver for protection, if need be. Ha ha. Men with guns."

"I'm just worried how you might feel is all," Sandra said. "When you run into people outside the estate. It's a different world out there. People won't bow and scrape."

"I know that."

"They won't compliment you like they did back home."

"I've already seen that, Sandra," Beautiful replied, staring harder at the water. Though normally soothing, the sight of the pool suddenly brought back the ominous feeling she had the previous night as she slept, the bad dreams she'd awoken from with starts. She changed the subject, "How's Mommy taking all this?"

Sandra sighed. "She's very worried."

Beautiful put Sandra on speaker and pulled her suit up over her breasts, putting her arms through the holes. "Tell her not to worry."

"I will. But listen, like I said, how about you just don't get out of the car."

"I'm going for a swim right now, Sandra," Beautiful said. "Out of the car. Can you answer my question about shaving or not? How often do I need to do that?"

"How quickly does the hair grow?"

"It's poking me right now, sticking on my swimsuit," Beautiful said. "So, very fast. And I miss the hair, but whether

I have it or not, I'll be getting out of the car. A lot. I have lived my whole life in the provincial area of my father's estate and I want to see the world, so I need to get out in society!" When Sandra did not reply, Beautiful added, "Also, I think it's time I found another man. I never told you what happened the first night I went out, but things did not go well. The one I had, I cracked his head open on the dirt floor of a wreck yard and let me tell you, Sandra, with little remorse, I killed him. I snuffed out his small pathetic life, not that he didn't deserve this, but I'd never killed a man..."

"Your father knows about that too."

"He does?"

"Yes. That's why he's letting you go now and hasn't brought you home, so you won't murder privately again. Because your mother told him it would do no good."

At this, Beautiful was reminded of the constant conversations she'd overheard between her parents, how they'd said she'd learned no personal responsibility and had never known what it was to lose something. "I didn't want to kill the guy," she told Sandra. "He wasn't a good person, granted, but he failed to tell me I was beautiful. He failed in all the important ways. There weren't any security guards to protect him. There was no one to protect me but myself. And he wanted to abduct me. Though, I admit, all I wanted to do was to pretend he was John Henry Waters whilst we made love on the nasty wreck yard floor. But he failed me, Sandra. He didn't even let me do that! Is it so very hard for a boy to give me what I want for once?"

"Oh, hush," Sandra said, in her soothing voice. "*Tck-tck*, I know he didn't. But hear me now because I love you, Beautiful, and I'm your friend."

"I know you're my friend. You're my truest friend."

"And because I'm your true friend, Beautiful, I'm going to tell you something that will hurt you, but you mustn't be angry... Your entire life has been a lie. You wondered why your friends didn't seem sincere, why they didn't act like they liked you for real, why the boys stayed away? It's because you aren't like everybody else."

"I know that. I'm special."

"Yes, Beautiful, but your father paid those friends to be your friends," Sandra said. "All your life. They only lived near you for the money. And you don't look like anybody else. The posters were fakes. There's a chance you might scare outsiders."

"I don't have to pay anyone to like me," Beautiful said. She laughed in the hopes the joke would soon end, but the room with its fancy black and white photography began to spin. "You're lying, Sandra," she said. "I'm not the only one like me."

"I'm not lying," Sandra replied. "That's why I'm worried about you."

Beautiful shut off the phone. She closed her eyes, seated on the floor, until the walls stopped moving. Soon enough, however, thoughts of the new unhappy developments saddened her. The friends weren't really friends.

She went down to the pool, which was largely unfrequented save a single man seated at a metal table, bent over his cellular device. He was not particularly handsome, but there was something earnest about him. Something dismayed. She liked how he chortled and intermittently cried. He wore a white suit, a black fedora, and shiny white shoes.

After entering a gate propped open with a rock against hotel swim hours, she laid out on a pool lounge chair to watch him. She didn't move much at first. There was the issue of her hair growing out and how she now feared she'd look getting into the pool with a watcher, so this paranoia kept her rather still until he peeked up from under the brim of his hat, himself nearly just as self-absorbed, silent, and oblivious as she often was, until finally he spoke. "You fucking looking at me, girl?"

"Yep," she replied, adjusting her fifties starlet swimsuit, which had just begun to creep up her rear. "What're you going to do about it?"

"Nothing," he said. "It's a free country."

"Well, I was looking, but I wasn't rude looking," she replied. "As you well know, rude looking would have been staring right at your package. Maybe looking at you askance or with some kind of vindictive spirit. I've done none of that. What are you doing here anyway? You aren't dressed to swim."

"None of your business," he replied. "I don't swim. I'm afraid of water."

"Fine," she said. "Suit yourself. Want to come up to my hotel room and make love later?"

If he was surprised at her inquiry, Beautiful was also surprised. She wondered what it was about this man that made him suddenly appeal to her, but perhaps it was simply the fact that no one was paying him to do anything. It was a free universe of choice, and *choose me* her offer said, and *do so on purpose*.

Not that she knew anything yet about making love, not that she knew he was *the one*. She could learn what she needed to know as things went forward. Also, if it were really bad, she reasoned, at least this would set the bar low for any further experience.

Plus, she'd take him here on the concrete beside the pool, but there was always the hairless issue now. And the cold. The slightest breeze made her shiver some; although, such chill was good for the appearance of her nipples.

"Would you find me more attractive?" she asked the man, of a sudden, "with hair on my face?" Her look was fully loaded. Had he known her better, her intensity and the minimalism of her subsequent expression should have told him this answer was dramatically important. She waited, holding her breath.

"Sure," he said. "Would you find me more attractive if I told you I was a bad, bad man and had done lots of mercenary things with an evil and ambiguous agenda?"

"I could care less about your agenda," Beautiful said, sauntering up and leaning over him where he sat before pulling off his fedora to examine the label. "Because I'm innately selfish. Unless that agenda, right now, is about making me happy, I don't care what it is."

She wondered if he was a plant, sent by her Daddy, someone to test her somehow, but he was grouchy and somewhat unpleasant, so she doubted it. Her father sent smiling happy people her way, fake people.

This guy was real. A bit eerie, in his creepy adorable way. She liked his way! It reminded her of the War and Philosophy wall in her father's library. Sinister, subdued, not altogether innocent.

"Oooh," she said, "bring a little of that sexy evil over here," but he shifted in his seat.

"No."

She dropped his hat on the table and he put it back on. "Villains aren't used to women as aggressors, are they?" she asked. "That's okay Fedora Man. I could have you crying like a baby. I could break both your arms and both your legs. So what do I care about your mysterious agenda? I don't care about it. Not at all. How 'bout you kiss me? A small warning: I'm not very patient by nature."

She didn't wait for him to kiss her. She leaned and put her lips on his. Enjoying his submission and confusion, she lifted him up from his chair and held him standing before her, his feet dangling in the air. She shook him slightly as if to tell him to put his feet down, and, like their connection was psychic, he dropped them.

What pretty eyes he has, she thought. "You're taller than me," she said. "That's so fetch. Kiss me again."

"Sure," he replied.

When she pulled him right up close, he didn't struggle. His kiss began gently, but he was the one to advance it, suddenly tonguing her throat. As he did, she fondled his thin elbows. They were, she concluded, just right.

She wasn't yet sure what his elbows were perfect for, but that would come later. For now, she was glad the driver had no directives for sleeping like a watchful harpy, in her room—so she and Fedora Man could have all night long! All night long she could use and molest him! However best pleased her! Maybe they would play board games, too!

So enormous was her bliss at possessing him, Beautiful grabbed Fedora Man's ass and squeezed it with pleasure. "First, I'm going to swim," she said. "So, you will watch me do so, and then we'll adjourn to my room to take care of the sex business. How long do you think that will take?"

Fedora Man's face expressed shock.

"Is the timing a source of confusion?" she asked. "Like, perhaps you are considering how long each part of my body will take to caress? Or is it logistics? I have only one day here, if that relieves you, so you can get back to your evil agenda pretty quickly, though we may elect to be distance lovers if we mutually conclude this an enjoyable experience." Upon that, she dove into the water.

Each time she surfaced, just as he had been told, he watched. *What a good man,* she thought. *So attentive!*

As he regarded her, his face squinted with a look of extreme concentration, like he attempted to will certain thoughts into her head. "Tap, tap," she said, whilst rubbing the water out of her eyes with one hand and seconds later using her other hand to fist-thump her skull, "Nobody knows your thoughts from just a glance. I can only hear you when you speak."

"Hmmph," he said. "What do you care what I'm thinking? I'm not thinking about you. I could be thinking about the weather."

"Liar!" she said and laughed, noting her bathing cap looked quite stunning in her reflection. "Even if you weren't thinking of me, okay, think about me now," she said aloud. "Observe me! Admire me! Don't I look excellent in this cap?" She dove and surfaced, deciding she enjoyed the way her hand felt sluicing down the rubber on her head when she felt the cap, like a sexy bald woman touching her scalp.

Though her watcher's eyes were still on her, she did not inquire anything else. Her rubber hat matched her white and gold suit. The outfit was a smash hit in her estimation. She'd have to tell Sandra all about this swim later, eschewing no details of the jaunt, especially those regarding how electric she felt as he watched.

The story would begin, "After I successfully negotiated the terms of seduction, Fedora Man and I spent a cheery interlude where he lasciviously regarded my every breaststroke in my super-fly retro swimwear. Very intimate! As I swam, I felt his desire mounting! Until he was a beast of desire! I think, perhaps, Sandra, that it was my stunning white bathing cap. After all, it is shiny, faux-bald, and slick, faux bald is very hot. It wasn't long before I would take him upstairs to my room and fling him against the wall, remove his jacket by force, and rip open his bodice. Oh, damn, scratch that! He has no bodice. His shirt. Rip open his shirt so I could see his— " At this juncture, she paused, uncertain whether Fedora Man would have a hairy chest or not. She was also unsure of whether his relative hairlessness would make her desire him or pity him. But the water felt good streaming over her skin as she watched him watching. She swam closer to the edge near his table where he sat, again passively chortling and looking seriously disturbed, these things alternating.

"Later, did you want to take me dripping wet?" she then asked. "Or would it be better if I dried off?" He gave this question due consideration as she emerged to stand beside him and clasped his hand.

"Dry," he said.

If it bothered her that his cellular instrument was still occasionally regarded, she gave it just one thought, grabbed it, and chucked it in the pool. "Later," she said. "For now, you're mine."

His eyes watched his tool land at pool bottom, horrified, but she pulled him close, stating savagely, "We must give up our little addictions, our little fears, when we attempt to make love, mustn't we, Fedora Man?" then dragged him up the stairs behind her, pausing two-thirds of the way up to say only, "Listen, I got all my previous romance patter from books, so I really hope you know what you are doing up here. Otherwise, we could get lost. As yet, I'm still a reluctant virgin. But we shall resolve that. So come on, Fedora Man. Yes, come on."

"I told you I am an evil man and still you drag me up to your room?" he replied.

"Either I don't believe you about your evil," Beautiful Ape Girl Baby said, "or I don't care."

"You don't know what I've done."

"But you don't know what I've done either," she replied. "To be privy to that knowledge might make you appear a blushing flower of good. Look," she said, quite bored with his whole evil spiel. "I didn't ask you to marry me, did I? I asked for an erotic evening with another body. I've had some bad experiences, okay? Letdowns. A boy I loved who preferred a stupid stuttering little twit. Another man I wanted to make love to planned to hold me for ransom and said unsavory things. It didn't end well. You look nice enough. Can we do this already?"

Fedora Man chortled then looked close to tears. "I don't know if I'm able," he said. "My heart is wild like a venomous dog! Beautiful, I, myself, am a low and venomous dog."

She couldn't remember telling him her name, but figured he could just be complimenting her obvious physicality. "Let me give you a science lesson, Fedora Man," she said. "Dogs don't have venom, though they could be rabid. I think you're thinking of snakes, which do have venom, but don't look like dogs in the least."

"I meant I'm a bad human being."

She looked closer at him for the traces of whatever he thought was horrible, but saw only a thin man in a black hat with a white suit, who looked more tired than anything. She knew his canine statement to be metaphorical but still found it lacking, so followed up with, "If you are such a bad human, venomous dog, my delicious little *boychik*, then why do you wear all white? You know, white is the color of purity, of good intentions. Of innocence."

"My hat is black," he said. "Like the contents of my head."

"Your suit is white," she replied. "So that means your body is good. Who cares what your head does? It's your body that's in question. I want to use it here. It's good, I assure you. I'm in no danger. Unless you're going to head-fuck me."

"Oh, shut up," he told her. "That's so dirty. Head-fucking."

"Ooooh. Say that again," she replied. "Either part! I think I'm flirting! But also, as an aside, *nobody* tells me to shut up, Fedora Man. Learn that quickly or you might get hurt! Yes, there's magic in Heeeeeaaaaaddddddfuuuuuc-ccckkkinnnngggg! What a great expression. Come on, Fedora Man! Say it again!"

He didn't reply but followed her until they'd almost reached her room, a few people overhearing them peeking out of curtains to regard them in passing. Beautiful, oblivious, strolled on.

As they stood in her doorway, she yanked him close, struggling with her cardkey. "First, I'll take my white suit off," she whispered in his ear, tonguing it. "It'll make me seem more ominous to be naked, if that's what you go for. Isn't that what you bad boys go for? Or I've got some black stuff inside that I can put on—so it can be nothing but bare skin when we're alone in my room, as I mentioned, or black stockings and bare skin, or leather and stockings, or rubber and bare skin—or I could put on a jumpsuit, a gold one with grey buckles and small appliqué horses! I can be like 'Ride 'em, co—"

"White confuses my enemies," he said, ignoring her wardrobe inquiries. "And I can keep it clean. It's an unusual skill set."

She pulled him flush against her, replying, "Good. Show me another one!"

"Maybe I've been too hasty," he said, backing away. "You're getting my white suit all wet. My white suit is getting w—"

"Wah wah, FM, I'm doing that with my own white suit, for fuck's sake," she said. "White on white. I'm just trying to have a good time here, Fedora Man, and while I understand your reservations, actually I don't have any clue about your reservations, nor do I really care about them, but whatever they are, even full blown mental illness or terminal illness of the non-sexually transmitted variety—because this is a fling, remember? We don't have to unpack every little bit of sacrificial baggage. And I would like to—Except your res—Wait, do any of them have to do with me? Don't you think I'm pretty? Do you really not think—"

"No," he said. "You're stunning. This is about my problem."

"Oh, good," she said. "Because I don't care about your problem. Even were you afflicted by non-contagious leprosy. Even if you had ten people inside that little head, controlling you by exceedingly evil mental puppetry! Oh, wait, is *that* your *problem,* that I'm stunning? Because I don't think that's a problem at all! I would call that a welcome and *long overdue* perception from an object of my sexual interest."

"No, I mean my problem isn't you. It is my need t—it's my empl—"

"Oh, good. That's great," she said, not really listening once she was absolutely clear she wasn't the problem.

"Then come here."

She pulled off her swim cap and threw it in the room near the bathroom. Her walnut hair sprung forth. She kissed him again and flung him close to the bed. "Sometimes haste is good," she explained, following his body's path and pinning him beneath her against the wall. "Let's be incautious and hasty. Or, we could pretend we've known each other for years if that's homiest. I have no preference. You could even pretend to be a delivery man. How about you deliver some sugar, like neighbors do, or some salami? Too trite? Paper goods? Oh, yeah… I've brought you your dinner napkins, Beautiful. Why thank you, delivery boy! Why don't you come in my room?" She giggled uproariously, and he seemed rather charmed. "You're so cute for an evil guy," she said.

He kind of smiled. She kissed him again. She thought of all of Sandra's cautions, not remembering any that involved staying away from evil men in white suits, and besides which, she didn't really believe in evil as anything more than misery pounding away at the wrong door to righteousness, unanswered need seeking outlets in the wrong peg, right hole dimension, so she said, very softly, allowing her hands to unbutton both his shirt and his pants as if she unwrapped a long overdue gift addressed only to herself, "And besides, I'm really ready for this experience. I've waited *so long,* I now grow old in the tooth. Or long. *Long* in the tooth is the expression. Wow, look at that tattoo, Fedora Man! It says *I Love Mommy,* right over your heart! And besides, can you really be so selfish as to not give me this night of lovemaking? You said you'd come upstairs. You came. I want you to transport me into the realms of practiced love. If not love, I at least want to see what it feels like to do what they were doing, the friends, my fake friends, by the pool, for so long. The same friends who are inglorious turds, except Sandra. The friends who I now know my father paid! Ooooh, it's hurtful! Now, can you be a little *more* evil and help with the planned debauchery? I have a condom in my room. That's for you, for your anatomical part that penetrates, your cock, dick, package, whatever you want to call it. I like package because it reminds me of presents or shopping. I know the rudiments of what is supposed to happen and that it might involve some minor pain for me and that this painful part would involve your package, the same present I have so chastely and deliberately failed to examine so as not to make you uncomfortable until now, but you're in my room, so tell me: Is it big? Because if it is, I want to see it at its largest size before we progress. To mentally prepare. Can you bring it to its largest size, first, while I watch, so I can gauge? I'll be an anatomical scholar. Very quiet."

He colored before saying, "It's not very big. But it's very, very bent." He waited with a timely pause before adding, "So you're a virgin?"

"Didn't I just say so?" she asked. "Glad you're keeping up. And evil or otherwise, you shouldn't look forward to breaking my hymen or anything, because I ride horses. I lost that years ago. There'll be no blood, understood? Let's get this straight from the start that if your evil shit craves bloodshed, you shan't get it from me. But I promise to be very open to this experience. Very, very open! And enthusiastic! But I'm always that. Sometimes overmuch, Sandra says."

Fedora Man said nothing.

"Oh, and if I'm not enjoying it too well," she went on, "if it bores me, I hope you don't mind if I call you John Henry. That might help to me to reach the necessary mood."

"You need help?" he asked.

"Sometimes I'm in the mood—and other times not. Sometimes, I must imagine certain stimuli. Do a little creative visualization, you know, picture things—for example horseshoes. I really like those."

He must have been amply ready to quiet her because, upon this, he pushed her into the wall. He kissed her so deeply she wanted to swoon, not performing that light fish kissing she hated. She thought her stomach might fall through her cunt.

"I'm not showing you my package first," he said as he peeled up her swimsuit top and began to suck her nipples. "But I'll use it later. And though I'm in the mood to taste your breasts, you must fail, at every interval, to seem even the slightest bit like my mother—because if you do not fail, if you do not, I'll stand up and walk away. Additionally," he said, "I like you in white, but I like you out of it, too."

Ooooh! She really liked the way he spoke so assertively, but she didn't speak in case she might somehow elicit within him a shadowy perception of his mother. She might sigh or blink like his mother for all she knew. In unknown ways, she supposed she could not help residual mother resemblance, but she didn't want him to leave, and then she didn't want him to leave for hours. Sometimes, when you find your aggressive desire mirrored by a suitably strange other party, you just go with it, flow into the lava storm of *enacted desire* until everyone has ejaculated or hollered, and thus desire can stop.

~

She awoke the next morning with the fresh memory of his enjoyment of her skin, prickly and all, his exclamations about how unusual and lovely she was, his rapt attention to all parts of her body, and his insistence that she lie supine, silent, as if the body of a corpse, which was not interesting in and of itself, but compelled her in that it required her to perform nothing, to activate nothing, to allow herself the fresh and exciting novelty of being a doll in a man's awareness, free to solely experience the lavishing of his attention and not required to provide him a thing. As she opened her eyes, she wanted to roll over and embrace him, not to crush him as she'd done so often with things so dear, but softly touch his head and perhaps groom him, brushing back his minimal head hair with her fingertips and laying down many misty kisses on his face and neck because the memory of their strange interlude the night before returned with force.

She relished this. It was now her first intensive sexual memory.

His package had been bent, as he'd mentioned, which she'd liked. The only bit of discussion they'd had about this was when she said, upon viewing it for the first time before it entered her, purple, bent, and mottled as it was, "Fedora Man, your package isn't straight. I don't think the blood flows correctly. Did you want me to fix that? I could straighten it for you."

"Neither is my mind straight," he replied. "Everything's fine."

"But again, did you want me to straighten it before you pierce me?" Beautiful asked. She explained she'd once reset the bones of a friend she'd tossed into a bramble, so demonstrated the proposed gesture and performed it in pantomime with her palms so he could visualize her intent, like breaking a stick. "I'm sure I can make it straight," she insisted.

He put his hand over her mouth. "I love your hairy chest," he said. "It's like a baby animal. I love the prickles on your legs. I love you quiet and still." He put just fingers on her lips, muttering, "Don't say a word. Remember, if you talk about fixing me, you'll remind me of my mother, and, Beautiful, I regret to tell you that I had to end her life. The fact that hers was a mercy killing does not absolve me."

"Now *that* is interesting," Beautiful said. "How'd you do it?"

"She was long-suffering. I did it to help," he said. "There was a pillow. A revolver. Some clothespins. We won't need more details."

"I'm very helpful with mercy, too," Beautiful said, grinning to have something new in common.

"Yes, but reminders are painful," he replied.

"Oh," Beautiful said, so consumed with empathy at how his mother must have treated him to necessitate her mercy slaughter that tears filled her eyes. "Oh, Fedora Man, I'm sorry for that! You're perfect just the way you are, and I'm so sorry you found it necessary to silence your maternal creator! I'm lucky mine never offended me so gravely, but I'm very sad for you, vicariously sad. If you are still interested in pursuing a sexual liaison, should we cry together and then have sex? I've never cried with anyone before. It could be novel."

"My mother was a horror," he replied. "She'd no clear idea about my genius and belittled it constantly. But, no, I don't want to cry with you, Beautiful. You're not my sister or even one of my many ex-girlfriends I still talk to, and I don't know you well enough. I could only cry with you if—oh, never mind..." He trailed his hand up her thigh as he made this remark and then placed his palm over her mouth once more, a palm curiously flavored like rhubarb. "Just be quiet here, please," he said.

Beautiful licked his palm, deciding it was strange he could be so cruel with his words, yet light with his touch. His slow and detailed enjoyment of her body then made for another wistful sadness within her, for whomever he was, he was taking his time to address her body in every conceivable way, not that she'd conceived all that many before him. She could even forgive him for killing his mother, whether she learned more or not. After all, she'd never known his mother. And his mother, unlike hers, had probably deserved it, may have even been grateful for the release—having long-suffered in the cruel carcass that was her terrible, praise-withholding self.

Beautiful's compassion for his case was also aided by

the fact that she knew he couldn't physically overcome her, though she might pretend this were possible to suit his ego, so he could be an ant feasting on the garbage hill of her bounty. She loved his banana pepper nose, his slight tint of rosacea, all his imperfections.

She loved when he went between her legs with his face and seemed to twist back and forth in the throes of something more decadent. She also loved how different it was to orgasm *with someone*. Not that she recalled *him* orgasming. If he did orgasm, he wasn't very loud about it, and she preferred emphatic shouts, but she still wanted his quiet face to never leave her. When she woke more fully the next morning, however, ready to turn to him and share these revelations, excited enough to lift him and press him to her in a timeless way just like a forties photograph she'd once seen with a sailor and a nurse, she encountered an empty pillow.

His Fedora was gone.

At some time in the night, she must've fallen into a deep and contented slumber, at which point, Fedora Man, and any trace of him, had vanished. This wasn't exactly true. The memory of where his hands had been remained. Additionally, maybe a slight bruise, here or there, on the outsides of her thighs and the insides of her elbows, but those might be self-inflicted.

On the hotel nightstand, he'd left assorted pastries wrapped in a napkin. Several. But no phone number. No contact information. The loss of his pleasure possibility was profound.

To demonstrate the vehemence of her feelings upon this discovery, half-awake, she punched the wall. Once. Twice. Only when she had dotted the wall with at least three holes that went clear through, along with several lighter patternings, did she cease punching and contemplate dressing.

To shave or not to shave was her primary question.

Sandra had mentioned the possibility she'd look strange as she stepped from the car. Also, there was the driver to manage now. She lifted the hotel phone, dialing his extension. "We leave," she announced, still miffed at Fedora Man's outrageous and silent abandonment, "in ten minutes."

Picturing the nearly hairless body of Fedora Man she'd just interacted with so closely, she thought of the billboards she'd seen while she was driving and how, while sneaking watching television through the years, she'd seen so many hairless freaks and celebrities that she'd wondered if their hairlessness was some new vogue. Considering her trip to the studio to meet her idol, she took a shower and brushed her teeth. Would Ida expect her hairless?

Her skin tingled. It was a new dawn and a new day as a singer might have sung. She dressed and walked to the car. "Driver," she said. "Get the fuck out of the vehicle, and give me the keys. I'll drive. Daddy can pick you up here. I'm leaving you." If Fedora Man could just up and leave her, she decided, she'd do the same to the driver.

Her driver didn't budge. "You driving isn't a good idea," he said. "I'm supposed to drive you and pay for hotel rooms on this trip. You have no identification. Cash won't buy everything."

"So, what? Are you saying I have no identity, Driver?" she asked. "Because I am Beautiful Ape Girl Baby Chef and —"

"I'm telling you," the driver said, meek and exhausted, "that these days you can't use cash for everything, and your father has never had you identified, not beyond a birth certificate. Do you know what an ID card is? A driver's license? You don't have either."

"Well, that rather makes me feel like a non-person, doesn't it?" she asked.

"I can't tell you how you feel," he replied.

"Get out of my car, Driver," she said. She opened his driver's side door as if opening a door for a very sweet date and said, "I'll ask you super sweetly just once more. And, if you don't comply, I'll dislocate your shoulders and pull your hips out of joint. I'll leave you on that bench over there, wailing and crying but needing emergency medical help. Now wouldn't it be nicer if you'd just get out like I asked and do exactly as I said? My patience, though growing as I mature, is quite low today. I've had a long night."

It was unclear whether this speech made his action come to the fore, but he did get out rather quickly. "Wait," Beautiful said. "I have an idea! Get back in, Driver. I need you to teach me how to turn the heat on! And how to use this car! I need to not damage things this time and to blend. So we will have one lesson today, Driver. I'll watch you as your passenger today. And then, once I've learned enough, I'll drop you off on the road."

He re-entered the car. When he did, she took the moment in the morning sun, regarding herself in the Lincoln windows, to decide she indeed looked very festive in a hot pink Dolce sundress with strappy Nine West kitten heels. "Good luck blending," he told her.

She stared him up and down as her mother often did, still wanting to pluck off his silly white mustache. "I'll shut the door of this car, Driver," she said. "And our lesson will commence."

If she felt pain, emotional or otherwise, from the amorous events of the night before, she didn't display this. "Let's be very business-like and civil about this," she told her driver. "We," she went on, meaning herself, "can handle no further emotional upset today."

Though she wanted to call her friend Sandra to ask how to interpret the events of the night before, especially FM's sudden desertion, she did not. The road was her future whether her heart was sorely riddled with pain, fury, confusion, or desire—and besides, how would Sandra know anything? Had Sandra ever experienced such a complicated series of hours with a lover?

In the time that had passed during lovemaking, Fedora Man (whose real name was Ivor, he'd finally shared) had said many things that would mean nothing clearly understandable to anyone, and were a damn sight hard to navigate for even for a winsome and intelligent girl like her.

Had he been so upset to learn that she was just seventeen, she wondered? Was that why he'd bailed and left pastry? Once, while they'd twisted together, he'd bothered to ask her age and that moment had been awkward, his face in her lap, neck craning up, when "Seventeen," she'd responded, "and a few days."

All his efforts ceased. Withdrawing, he looked ill. "Seventeen?" he parroted.

"That's what I said."

"I was hoping I'd misheard," he replied.

"Well, I really don't think age should bother you," she stated. "I'm not a normal girl. I've done far more than a normal girl." She stared at his pale chest, at the presence of freckles on his shoulders, at his dot-like nipples, very pink against his own emaciation. The tattoo about his mother was a beautiful distraction, hung directly over his heart. "You look about fifteen to me," she said. "Excepting your face, I think I look older than you."

"I'm forty-nine. Seventeen is very young," he announced, using a cold voice much like her Daddy's when he'd freshly discovered some new and expensive problem she'd created. "Too young. And to think that I've touched you like a woman. I'm evil, but there are some evils that even I forsake. These involve touching children!"

"I'm not a child."

"Yes, you are."

"Bah!" she said. "Pfft. So touching me is evil now? That's fucked up, Fedora Man. You came to the room with me. You began the lovemaking. I, for my part, just initiated then very demurely participated."

"It's like I couldn't help myself," he said, talking more

to himself than anyone else. "You were so fetching, I couldn't help myself. My desire for you was large as a roan mare! I'd planned to be chaste. But you were my little heathen."

"I do like being your little heathen," she said, delighted to have a pet name within hours of meeting him—and indeed, she decided, why should such endearments ever wait? She was a fan of the instant nickname, provided it was kind. "So I'm still your little heathen and always will be. At least until you leave me, humiliate me in front of everyone I know by pretending we were never close, act like a complete ass, and force me to decide that, resultantly, I just don't like you anymore."

During another long response of ponderous silence, in which he tried to decide he wasn't present by simply shutting his eyes, she studied the ceiling, savoring his sweet words in her head but contemplating that the word "heathen" only usually applied to someone outside the fold of organized religion, by someone possessing organized religion. Since he mentioned he was evil, she doubted he had that, so scrutinized the overhead light a long time, pondering what exactly his organized religious group might be, until she got too bored by the dry topic and his silence so yanked him back on top of her once more before saying, "What's evil about love? Let's make it again and again! Let's make it right now!"

"Everything's evil about love," he replied. "If you know what it is… I, myself, do not permit myself to love, Beautiful. Well, that's not exactly right. I permit myself to love, like worship, from a polite distance or for short periods of time, but I don't permit reciprocity. Because my love for anyone tends to fail when I devalue them, so *no one* is allowed to *love me back*. Though I do rather feel that I love you now. In my way."

Beautiful's eyes burned. "Then I reciprocate your love, if that's how you feel, because I admire you, Ivor," she said.

"There aren't many people I admire, and I've killed someone before but it didn't feel like this! I've climbed whole mountains and it didn't feel like this! This feels good, touching you, relevant, which makes our age irrelevant, don't you think? It's like those soldiers in the Vietnam War who required appeasing after their experience. Should they not have received hookers if they so desired, after they'd been at risk for sudden death, when at any moment fate could steal their lives away? Shouldn't they have marijuana, cocaine, anything they want—if it does something good for them? I say we're all at risk for sudden death, Fedora Man, and I think that my mixed and painful experience paints me much older than a normal seventeen. I'm timeless. I'm a hundred and fifty-three lifetimes. You don't know what I've done and what I've seen, but I'm a metaphorical year-and-a-century past sweet sixteen. So, you've killed someone. I've killed someone. Multiple someones. And I think anyone who's killed someone, even one person, has relinquished their age, so kiss me again, please. I'm forever and a flash of just one instant. So don't make my first night of real passion with a suitable party be accompanied by the wistful pain and tragedy of your unfortunate early withdrawal!"

She hesitated as she watched his face freeze over to mask any revealing emotion before she muttered, pleading, "Please. I'll pretend I disdain you, if that helps, that I don't love what part of you I know. But, please. Again. Let's make love again. And, are you part of the Methodist sect? A Jew? Luddite? Morman? Protestant? Lapsed Catholic? Because if I'm a heathen, I rather want to know what kind of heathen I am, in your view. I should be—"

He shook his head, pulling her closer, their eyes meeting for a long and sad exploration of the nothing each one could understand about the other, and then he pushed her down on the bed and placed his head there again between her legs to take her high into the stratosphere, ageless as she was, hollering in ecstasy as she was, herself unfettered by a need for silence since she'd already decided her active hollering couldn't possibly remind him of his mother, whom he seemed to have never pleased.

But how would she explain that earlier headshake and sudden silence to Sandra, his hesitation? Because now she thought it might explain everything. And maybe he had abandoned her with no further explanation because of the age dilemma, or the nothingness dilemma, or the religion dilemma, or the dilemma of enjoying too much the thing that is timeless and has verbally stated CLEARLY that it cares for him, regardless of whether this care is suited for only a short window or longer; but maybe it was something else altogether.

Maybe he didn't like her ass.

However, now, tired of rethinking it, she gawked at the driver, baffled. "Fuck," she said, enjoying the use of expletives when enmeshed with mental struggle. "Fuck-fuck. Fuckityfuckfuckfuck. Fuck! But really? Did he really have to go? Maybe I somehow hurt his feelings?"

Anew, Beautiful discovered she was a blunt tool with the deciphering of tender emotions. It was easier to break things than to fix them. Everything before FM had been simple. Even when his bent package had found purchase inside her and she had, contrary to her original supposition, bled like a stuck pig, which might have meant the earlier occurrence was likely an irregular menses not occasioned by her equine mounts, she couldn't interpret that second moment of his pause, when after he said, "you're bleeding," he said, "I'm a monster," which was probably what initiated the subsequent age conversation, though at the time she'd simply said, "Am I really? How *new!*" and "Let me see!"

"No," he'd refused.

"Let me see my own blood, damn it!"

"No!" he repeated.

"Let me see my personal fluids or I'll brain you on that wall."

Upon that, he pulled up and out so she could witness her blood on his body. When he did, she was proud of it, really. No one had bled her before. Hardly anyone made her cry except herself. And she'd killed two people she thought, maybe three, but wasn't trying to compete with Fedora Man, as his evil was already much protested and highly lacking in her estimation.

Nonetheless, now, to the driver, her mental faculties still occupied with carnal confusion, insides roiling in ways to make her decidedly weak and emotional, coasting on a tidal swirl of pleasant memory and rejection, she said as calmly as possible, suddenly not very happy to be so spaced out and vulnerable, "With the lessons, please start at the very beginning with your driving primer. It would be quite excellent if you'd narrate every step. Begin with, 'Place the key in the ignition,' or 'Step on the brake.' 'Don't hit the gas.' You know, the easy and obvious things, as if you were narrating to a baby." As she began to cry, she added, "Pay no attention to my tears. Allergies. Evil winds today," and got in the car.

The driver waited till she stopped crying, looking rather forlorn himself. He had white bed-hair, tossing and turning bed-hair. "I couldn't sleep last night either," he said then continued, "First, place the key in the ignition." He put his seatbelt on. "Seatbelt," he told her as he started the car. "That's so you don't get hurt in an accident."

"I rarely ever get hurt by accident," she replied. "What's your name, Driver?" As she considered his calm demeanor, she suddenly found his silence, lack of motion, and willingness to wait attractive and positive attributes of his character. She abhorred people who bullshitted or unpleasantly rushed others, those who always deigned to notice others' weaknesses, so, if nothing else, he was straightforward and sweet, which gave him many new points in her book. Her book got less exacting by the moment.

"Thomas," he said.

"I *do* like you, Thomas," she said. "I'm glad I didn't dislocate any of your shoulders, hipbones, or kneecaps. I'm glad you're my driver. Carry on."

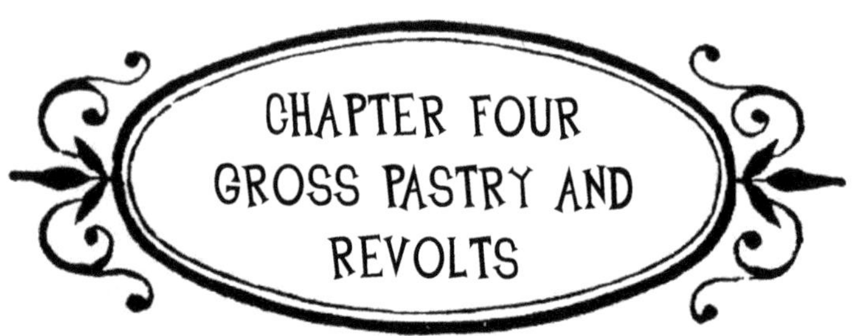

CHAPTER FOUR GROSS PASTRY AND REVOLTS

~IN WHICH, THE ROAD LOOMS UP BEFORE THEM, A BUTTERFLY DANCE THEN MASSACRE TRANSPIRES, AND BEAUTIFUL ACQUIRES A STRAPPING NEW SON. ~

Beautiful focused briefly on Thomas's tutorial, but soon found her mind wandering to the journey to meet Ida. Since childhood, Beautiful remembered feeling renewed strength from Haze's teachings, joy, and salvation. Haze was not religious, but she was ruthless, something Beautiful appreciated. And Haze was beautiful. Almost as beautiful as Beautiful.

Her show was available in two formats, radio and podcast video. The radio came in through satellite, but the video could be found online, lacking in clear footage as it was, filmed almost in the dark, low budget. All her father's cars had satellite radio due to his clout. While it had been several weeks since Beautiful had heard the *Strong as Animal Woman Show,* if there were ever time she could use it, Beautiful determined, it was now.

"Driver, find the *Strong as Animal Woman Show,"* she said, thinking she used to write notes from Haze's speeches as she'd listened, enjoying the savory emphasis of Ms. Haze regarding how to be one's strongest, brightest self. There was a time she'd quote excerpts of the show to her friends, most of which began with, "Ida May Haze says..." though her favorite excerpt ended with, "and if you aren't strong enough to row your own boat, then the solution is getting stronger, not waiting in the water and depending on the kindness contingencies of others. Because kindnesses are undependable contingencies, and you can trust no one!" This passage invariably ended up true, Beautiful's other favorite passage being, "If you don't want to break nuts, what're you doing here? Can't eat 'em 'less you crack 'em."

"Oh, yes, Ms. Haze," Beautiful had imagined answering so many times. "I have no problem breaking nuts."

However, to her current inquiry about Ida's show, Thomas replied, "No reception here, ma'am. I can't find it."

"Blast," Beautiful said. She dug into her satchel beside her Armani luggage. The picture she'd kept of Ms. Haze pleased her and she wanted to locate it. The lady was eighty pounds or less with a gray bun. Beautiful always enjoyed picturing the photograph as speaking like Haze did on-air, sometimes imagined this. Pushing Fedora Man out of her head, she said, "You are one tough little broad, Ms. Haze. I have so appreciated your tenacity and willingness to accept yourself! It has broadened my path immensely, though I refuse to do yoga as you suggest because I don't find it relaxing. Also, I don't feel a down-dog is a good thing for anyone to practice. Dogs, by nature, are too submissive. Though I like the call to the sun and childish ground-groveling position, or what have you, provided no real groveling must transpire."

"And when you want to switch lanes," her driver Thomas said, still narrating his lesson, which she occasionally followed with intermittent interest, "flip on your blinker, located right here, in the direction you'd like to go, and then look both in your mirror and behind you before entering the desired lane, like so."

Beautiful hummed, staring out the window.

"Are you paying attention to my tutorial?" Thomas

suddenly asked.

"No," Beautiful replied. "I'm sorry. Can you make it more interesting? Flash a few salacious or humorous pictorials. This technique has helped tutors in the past." When he looked crestfallen, "Oh, but don't take it too personally, Driver," she insisted. "There are many people I ignore. You are but one— " but her fingers then felt coated with some sort of slime. Digging further in her satchel for the vanished picture, she found a second package of pastries! Two cream cheese pastries, wrapped in napkins! Cream cheese now under her fuchsia colored nails! "Ick!" she said. "Fucking nasty!"

When the pastries were lifted from the paper, the surrounding napkin read, "I can find you again. Don't worry. fm."

"Want a pastry, Driver?" Beautiful then asked. "My lover has provided breakfast." Then her cell phone rang.

Opportunely, it was Sandra. Beautiful answered her phone. "Oh, hello, Sandra! You wouldn't believe what happened to me last night! I have big news! Enormous news, because in the game of love, I, Beautiful Ape Girl Baby Chef have—"

"Beautiful?"

Sandra's solemnity faintly registered. "Of course, it's me. Who else?! What is it? You sound strange."

"Your Daddy has—Oh Beautiful, it's—" A fractured

silence overtook the line. In the background, Beautiful heard movement, the sounds of packing, items dropped in a box. "Things aren't well here," Sandra finally said.

"I understand, but you don't even ask me how I've been or what I've done? I've been engaged in some exciting events, Sandra. I was just thinking of calling you when—"

"Beautiful. Please.... Your father is on a rampage."

"My father? What kind?" Thomas glanced over, so Beautiful glared back and cupped her mouth and the receiver of the phone with her hand as she spoke, as if that made the conversation private.

"He's fired all the friends. A few left peacefully, but the others..."

"Be calm," Beautiful said. "I'll hear this from the beginning."

Though her driver seemed focused on the open road, Beautiful gauged by the way he tilted his head to the side nearest her that he was in the process of pastry eating, driving, and surveilling. "Just a second, Sandra," she said. "Thomas. Show me how to pull over to the emergency lane and then show yourself how to wait without listening. I have to get out."

"As you'd like," Thomas said.

Beautiful stepped from the car into the morning sunshine, achy from the night before. "Wait for me here," she said, calling back. "With your windows up!" She walked along the emergency lane until suitably distant from the Lincoln before whispering into the phone, "I'm being watched by the driver, but he can't see me now. What's happening?"

A sob. Another sob.

"Sandra, speak. Your cries *will not* help you. You're silence won't help either, like Audre Lorde says. More importantly, they aren't helping me right now."

"So the friends shared the orange Hondas, three friends per car, and now they're fighting over them. We've been told to evacuate the premises. Some friends got rowdy. After all, what'll they do? Here for so many years, many of them, with no resumes for other than 'friend'? And when they told your dad they wanted the cars to keep, he said, 'Duke it out amongst yourselves.' Well, you know they're animals, Beautiful. There was fighting. Not with your father, of course. But when the fighting actually started, he called the security detail, the same security detail that none of us like, and so, at dawn this morning, there was pandemonium, like two groups set up on either side of the field, and an enormous brawl. The friends fought among themselves the night before, but then decided they each wanted a car, and so this whole brawl transpired right outside of the garages. Friends armed with the bases of lamps. Security armed with Tasers, maybe? I couldn't watch. Yusef was in the lead. Maria to the side. Audrey off to the left. And there your father was, on the fifth floor, watching it all. He seemed amused, Beautiful. I could tell because he kept throwing down handfuls of silk rose petals and laughing, sometimes encouraging one side or the other."

"Sandra, where are you, my darling? I don't worry about the ruffian friends, only about you."

"Here in my room," Sandra said. "I won't fight."

"That's good, Sandra. Do not fight. You're too special to fight, and I fear, my friend, you're too emotionally friable."

"I don't mean to worry you, Beautiful, but your father has been disassembling things all morning. Fans. Radios. He's angry. I've been hearing him argue with your mother, who's decided, by the way, that she's now furious he ever let you go and that she'll be conducting a hunger strike until your return."

Beautiful stared at the open road, pastry in her hand. Though she'd planned to eat it in a sort of post abandonment, bittersweet celebration replete with *toska*, on third thought, it looked rather repulsive, the icing emitting that bizarre sugar water icing sometimes does as the pastry hardened, so she began to pick at the breaded part and toss pieces to the ditch for the birds. She returned her remaining attention to the dilemma of the friends. "How long has this gone on?"

"Since this morning."

"But mother is crafty," Beautiful said. "I've seen this starvation move before. Does anyone feed her? Secretly?"

Sandra said nothing.

"Sandra, is anyone feeding mother secretly? She likes those crustless peanut butter sandwiches, individually wrapped, and other small concealable snacks. Juice pouches. Little packs of carrots. Sandra, this is dreadfully important. Are you writing this down?"

"Yes," Sandra said. "Because I'm feeding her."

"Oh, very well then," Beautiful said. "That was my only worry. So what does it matter what she tells him? And my father doesn't care about those cars anyway. He likes the spectacle. I can only imagine how satisfying that must have been! To watch modern warfare on our very own estate! Did he record it? Was anyone injured? Were there paramedics? Was there blood? Did the friends have trademark colors? Was anyone gloriously toppled on the battlefield of —oh, never mind, I don't care. What else is father telling mother?"

"Your father is telling your mother that he doesn't think this outing will be good for you. He says that, as much as that's true, you must be free to pursue yourself, like your mother said, years ago. And then your mother says, yes, but learning consequences in the real world could hurt you beyond repair because you're their only child, and once damage is done, it's irrevocable—and your father cuts her off, replying, 'You wanted this, Ethel. You said she needs to see the world as it is,' upon which your mother sobs and says, 'Beautiful, my Baby, she's not ready, and I was wrong,' so your father sternly admonishes, 'Thomas is with her, my pet. It cost a fair amount to get her out of the scrapes she's already in, so let her take it to the limit. We have a spy network. She can visit Ida.' This sort of talk goes on rather circularly."

"So all the friends are fired?" Beautiful asked, it suddenly occurring to her that home would be quite different upon her return. "You're saying I have no more friends?"

"Yes."

"And you? Fired?"

"I'm a friend, aren't I, Beautiful?" Sandra shuffled around, kicking something. "I have until this afternoon to remove my things. But your father gave me another car, because you took the Pinto."

"A Porsche?"

"A gray used Honda the caterers abandoned."

"That bastard! Cheap ass! Daddy should be ashamed!" At this, disgusted, Beautiful flung the remainder of the pastry to the road, saying, "But he can't get rid of you, Sandra. I forbid it!"

A jagged sob. "Yes. He can." After another jagged sob, "He already did," Sandra admitted.

Beautiful gazed back toward the car and turned her attention to the dry hillside. "What will you do now? *Tck-tck.* Come join me!"

"I can't join you. And what would I do for a living from there, Beautiful? I'll tell you what I'm going to do; I'm going home to my parents' place. They've got a trailer home in the back they'll let me borrow. I'll keep calling when I can. I just thought you should know what happened. Gotta go! You hear me?"

Beautiful glared at the phone, sensing something false because Sandra rarely hurried. "Are you telling me a pack of lies, Sandra?"

"No."

"If you go, who'll feed my mother?"

"She'll have plenty of help. The wait staff wasn't fired.

Your father has insisted on wearing his red and gray smoking jacket pajamas until you return or her strike stops, because she hates those. I hear her now. She's flung herself on her bed and moans at top drama, 'My girl! My little girl among the savages! How will she ever survive?' But I hear your father laughing. And now he says, 'Are you talking about Beautiful Ape Girl Baby? Really, Ethel? That's rich. No one can hurt her. No one will harm her at all. She'll kill any bastard who touches her. Even some because they won't.'"

"Sandra," Beautiful said, then reminded of her triumph. "For your information, I made love to someone last night and the man survived." This was a point of pride, but she didn't dwell on it. "He had a black hat. Oh, he was handsome. He bled me. And now he's gone. I wore a white Lane Marsh swimsuit. The interlude started at the hotel pool..." Comfortable with Sandra on the line, she talked until she reached the best part of the night, the climax of coupling, or actually the climax of FM's face in her lap, which she liked more, when she irksomely realized that her phone, without warning, had gone dead. She had no idea how much of her story was lost or received.

Disappointed, Beautiful strode back to the Lincoln and got in. "To Ida's, Thomas," she said. "This very instant."

"It'll be a while," Thomas replied. "Ida's isn't close."

"All right. To the nearest bathroom then," Beautiful muttered. "Right away. I need to relieve myself." *And how true this was*, she thought, loving this relieving oneself expression, fitting, as it did, a number of situations, the current one a pressing message from her bladder.

"As you'd like," Thomas replied, plugging her phone in to charge. "But no more driving lessons for today, Beautiful. You look a little jakey."

"What's that?"

"Shaky. Out of sorts. My mother used to say it."

"Well, of course I'm jakey, Thomas," Beautiful said.

"I've just lost all my friends. This is a life milestone, yet I've been rooked at every turn! Do you play chess? Do you know the meaning of rook? I've been so rooked." Beautiful stared out the window at a mass of firs, at a mass of rocks, at a mass of bizarre and crooked signs, at a mass of dirt, at a mass of masses, until Thomas pulled into a service station. Once there, she exited with her head high, though internally she worried about Sandra's wellbeing. Her father could be a Class A ass. A gray cheap Honda!

"Disassembling things?" she said. "Like what, Daddy? First radios and such, then TVs again? Will you graduate, this time, to plumbing?" The bathroom reeked of urine. Beautiful went into the nearest stainless stall, imagining the battle of security agents and her friends. She hoped someone had a bugle horn, that there had been a charge! She envied the Tasered security folks their weaponry, having once Tased someone very satisfactorily and incapacitated them for quite some time. This had been a security guard. She'd stolen his Taser from him when he was insolent and Tased him repeatedly. He'd pissed himself, she remembered, but upon thinking of that moment, she remembered her own bladder's needs, now almost as pressing as his then, so she readied herself to urinate more appropriately. When she pulled down her panties, however, before indulging in the great pleasure of a strong release, she saw the rust of dried blood. There had been more blood? Would the repercussions never end?

As her urine began to stream, she thought about how he, Fedora Man, had said not to worry and that he could find her. But with a pastry napkin? Was she supposed to drop bread crumbs from the pastry like Gretel had?

And that idea had been fine, she'd supposed, when she'd considered the idea of some reassurance being better than none, but now, in the white light of the stainless steel facility, she had more doubts, asking, "How exactly did you plan to find me, Fedora Man? Psychically determine whereabouts? And when? Would you be tracking me as Daddy does with commerce spies? What if, by that time, I no longer want you?"

Instantly furious as if that was what would happen, "So I'm supposed to wait around?" she asked no one in particular, wiping and standing in alarm. "Wait for some sudden reappearance after you've suitably done whatever evil you do best? I think not. I think I should go out right away and replace you with a different stupid man. Maybe several. I am, after all, no longer a virgin, so can do as I wish."

The idea that he was different than the men she'd met on the estate, so much kinder and more interesting, occurred to her as significant—but not so significant as to be perfectly conciliatory due to his own prominent peculiarities—though his embrace was the more plangent and worthwhile now, due to her recollection that the friends who behaved like buffoons at the compound had been, she suddenly internalized, *paid employees*, ergo, like hookers to her freely benevolent friend-ridden will, but were resultantly unwilling to give her what she wanted in a sexual capacity in her lifetime, yet he was not. He gave! He gave her orgasms. And why? She would tell you!

It was because they knew, wily friend foxes as they were, that trading sex for identical wages as token friends would make them underpaid sex servant workers. Underpaid! Because if you, as a laborer, could be someone's friend for one wage and then suddenly found yourself im-mersed in a romantic relationship where sex was necessary and required to satisfy that relationship, it was entirely possible that the romance would sabotage the friend job, not long afterward, and that this friend job would then be unmanageable, if, say, after the sex, Beautiful, the employer, grew bored and suddenly had found she had no use for them—or if they repulsed her! She was, she acknowledged, flighty. And so, it was job security or *job preservation*, she now concluded, that kept her body pristine on the estate, but sheer stupidity that kept it otherwise when sex was embarked on for free with Fedora Man. So, of course, he'd left her! He owed her no livelihood!

What if her friends were saving younger siblings from hard labor and sending money home to their mothers and grandmothers? What if they were sole sources of income for five people in a rundown apartment where everyone was in wheelchairs or on disability and though they desired her madly, madly, like wild binge beasts in the desert, they could not, even with great desire, sacrifice their security for an ill-fated attempt at heaven between her legs because they loved their families so very much? What if that negation was their concession to responsibility, or so she then concluded? And she understood them perfectly, at peace with their decisions.

But Fedora Man was unemployed by her estate, had no job. Thus, he was replaceable. She spit on her hands and washed them.

She no longer even wanted to call Sandra back and tell her about the night of passion with FM because she now wanted to forget the whole thing ever happened, sure there were either far better men out there who wouldn't up and abandon her with no left telephone number, or that she should sample a few before deciding to fall in puppy love with the singular one she'd physically bonded with for a lone night of blissful interlude, solely because he had been available, adorable, amenable, reasonable, and first.

The idea of firsts was high in her mind as she moved her palms below the bathroom air dryer, saying, "I should have done myself first. Bled myself with a cucumber! Then I wouldn't be in this confusing pickle of somehow thinking Fedora Man is more important than he should be! Also, I hate cheese danish, and I'll likely never see Fedora Man again, so his note on a napkin was cruel. Not to mention all his stupid uses in the *salle d'amour* of 'when next we meet' and 'not ready for yet' and 'more to come' and similar such expressions, all the while as I tried so hard not to be his mother, which caused my eerie silence during long parts of our consummation, a silence very uncustomary and unsatisfactory! And so there is nothing to be kept sacred from that pack of lies he told. In fact, I think I should boycott the word 'yet,' as in any 'not ready plus word appendage…' expression, because that kind of yet he may have referred to seems never to come—and if there's something I should talk to Sandra about it's about the necessity of disbelieving the foolish 'Yet,' the bullshit 'Yet,' the improbable 'Yet,' or the 'Yet' that never did and never would mean yet—because how irresponsible it is to speak and use the word yet when you don't mean it, or can't mean it, when a lazy bum soul couldn't possibly mean it!?" Beautiful took a breath, pushing open the bathroom exit door. "'Yet,' dissected, is a word every decent person believes to mean alluding to an implied future event—but which every indecent person uses just to fob off current responsibility with faux-possibility thrice removed, because I feel deceived by yet. I also feel nauseated by the cheese danish FM gave me. All this while Mommy starves and fights at home, and Daddy? Oh, Daddy. Of course he'd be laughing at the friends. So is all this really worth it? I shouldn't have left the estate! The paid friends loved me and were THERE WITH FRIENDSHIP IN THE MORNING!" Thinking of Fedora Man, she then took off her panties and threw them in the garbage can, saying, 'But fuck Daddy, fuck Fedora Man, fuck Thomas, fuck them all—actually, fuck them all YET. Yet yet yet! Yet yet yet yet," washed her hands again as if the stink of the situation was too fulsome, dried them, and walked outside.

It was then, right outside the door and glad to be liberated from her virginity blood besmirched panties, which were now safe in the circular file of the public repository, that two very wonderful things happened. First, a homeless woman holding a cardboard sign that read,

"Haven't YET given up hope. Even a quarter helps!" was seated outside the restroom and looked up at Beautiful's tearful, deep blue eyes before saying, "Oh, honey, you're much too young and pretty for tears like that," which caused Beautiful, highly emotional, grateful to the moon, to swoop that lady into her arms, stink and all, redolent sweat-dirt stink pressed into Beautiful's Vera Wang skirt and sweater ensemble, as Beautiful hugged her mightily and paused just after doing so to whisper in this woman's ears, "Whether you are inflicted with glaucoma or cataracts, I do appreciate your sentiment," before depositing the woman back on the ground and pressing four crisp hundred dollar bills into the woman's hand, just after saying, tender as beaten chops from the butcher, "If you want Mogen David, lady, I don't care. You buy whatever you want today because you are nice and niceness, in this foul world, is sorely underrated! You're a gem of love and delight!" Second, it occurred to Beautiful, like a much needed revelation, that she herself had plenty of money to put Sandra on her own payroll and hire her, at the decent sex worker wage rate just in case, sex friend or otherwise, because losing Sandra to financial concerns was not okay. This revised payment plan would be just fine for Beautiful, who never valued money more than friends—but how to propose it to Sandra?

As she ran out to the Lincoln, she thought it would take some finessing since she did not require sex from Sandra, but she wondered if she should fake an interest to get Sandra to accept a better wage. Still she wanted nothing to do with Fucking Eugene. He wasn't part of the deal.

Beautiful got into the car. "Morning, Thomas," she said, full of vigor.

"Morning, Beautiful, are you relieved?"

"Yes, very," she said. "I had a mind-altering piss."

"How excellent," he replied. "About three days to go before we reach Ms. Haze."

"I cannot wait to get there," Beautiful said. "You have

my permission to speed."

They drove a good two hours without speaking, in and out of two rural towns, past mountains and rivers and occasional cut-sand embankments. Beautiful couldn't help but be moved at how very many plants there were, how lovely the unmanned landscape. She didn't even begrudge Thomas's presence; that driving business was rather fraught with the need to pay attention—and there Thomas was, performing his duty. What a good driver!

When they came beside a meadow bedecked with African daises, milkweed, blazing stars, and bird's eyes, so many flowers, Beautiful gasped in delight. "Oh, Thomas! Look!" she said. "It's like my Chia Mero skirt! I always wondered where these species of horticulture could be found. Thomas. Stop, please! Stop now!"

Thomas pulled over. He said, "Yes, Ma'am."

As she surveyed the field, a riot of pink and green and purple and yellow and white and blue, the sky bright and gorgeous as the painting in her mother's sitting room, Beautiful elected to get out of the car. She watched a cloud of butterflies that descended upon the flowers. "Those, Thomas," she said as she opened the car door, "are Monarchs! Kings and queens of the wind!" She smiled at her knowledge, grateful for various tutors back home. "And you see that, Thomas?" she asked. "It's milkweed! They love it! Across the country, people now plant it to help with the Monarch migrations. Don't touch their wings! Don't touch them!" She knew scads about butterflies.

More butterflies arriving by the moment, with the air scented like bliss, like the amazing sweet desire in dreams or a perfume without an alcohol base, "Thomas!" she then exclaimed. "Nature calls upon me to dance! With the butterflies! Would you please turn some music up and endeavor to be invisible as possible? I want loud and glorious music for my dance, piano with perhaps a few cellos, not too busy! And if you see the butterflies grow scared or start to flee, turn it down. Pay attention only to the butterflies!"

Beautiful ran out into the field that was fabulously ungated and unfenced, available for everyone. Around her, the butterflies dipped and wove.

It all seemed too beautiful and took her breath away. Even the air wore the golden pink tint in which Beautiful imagined lovers would first make their discoveries about each other's painfully present beauty, about their love for each other and the resultant need to keep each other close at all costs. It was the air of culmination, of need, of sunlight and warm breath. The air of reward. The air of certainty. The air in which need flourished from want into receipt and became a possessive enabler so fine that the very statement of that need could render the impossible dream of having, of sharing, of sating oneself fully with another being, which was fine when such a dream was entertained by two, but devastating when not.

And where was Fedora Man now, she wondered? As she stood, a small butterfly landed on Beautiful's shoulder. This visitation impressed upon her that she could not yet begin dancing, lest he might fly away, if it was indeed a him, because as she beheld him, she began to see him as the symbolic presence of pure delight taking rest on her body, the universe's answer to her question, so instead of moving, she regarded this fearless creature with wonder. "You. You," she told him. "You're the most beautiful little thing! I love you so much!"

She simultaneously desired a dress of dead butterflies. One with a sweetheart neckline and a belt of onyx, made entirely of the small wings of these gorgeous creatures, fit and flare, with crepe backing. But only after they'd died. Maybe she'd go to that place in Mexico where the butterflies flew over the graves of children and gather a ton of corpses, as available, for the dress. She had no desire to kill them as they lived.

"My soul matches your flight," she earnestly told the

small butterfly that had settled upon her collar. "If even for a moment, I can forget to worry. Everything will be fine. I know it!" And then she forgot him and the dance happened, her liberated dance in the field, the one she would describe later in her journal as a fitting waltz for her soul, for she could restrain it no further. The first butterfly that landed on her flew free, but there were many more all around, no shortage of beauty or flight. As she danced, classical music piped toward her faintly from the distant car, and she felt her motion was no longer governed by dance teachers of the past, for whom she was an abysmal failure, but only from the motion of the butterflies themselves.

As they darted, she darted. As they dipped, she dipped. She failed to be a person in this wild dancing she performed, but a member of the swarm, of the school, of the countryside itself.

When exhausted and spun dizzy, she crumpled to the ground and lay in the flowers, watching more insects in the air above, deciding she would never again think of butterflies the same way. Now, they were her spirit guides, her teachers, and she loved them with a heart so full that she needed several deep breaths just to calm herself from sheer adulation and joy. "A butterfly emporium," she said then. "Butterflies at the estate! When I return!" And then she fell asleep.

It was Thomas's hand, stroking her face, that awakened her. "I'm sorry, Beautiful," he said. "But you'd been sleeping for an hour, and I thought you might want to get going."

All the creatures were gone. The air went still. Beautiful blinked. Stood. "Rightfully so, Thomas," she said. "Let's be on our way."

But they drove no more than two miles, the landscape mirroring the meadow in which she'd slept, before Beautiful noticed an abundance of odd road signs, WARNING: FALLING ROCKS, DEER XING, DEAF CHILD ZONE, signage aplenty, but no advertising. No-where was there a beautiful hairless woman to taunt her—or anything someone might sell her.

This rural nature of the countryside appeased something lost and devastated within her until the image of Jake's face appeared, as if out of nowhere, in the shadowed confines of her brain as her eyes surveyed the Lincoln's dim interior after re-entry. In that dark space, her mind took several more depressing turns. As if from loss of direct sunlight or the absence of the butterflies, her spirit dove. She had not just killed Jake. At least she feared this might be true. He'd been the only man so far, sure, but there was a friend when she was five, she remembered, whom she believed she had pushed off the cliff that flanked the east estate. This friend was a faint memory now, like she may or may not have existed, but if she did exist, Beautiful remembered, she'd have been quite young. Nonetheless, long ago the features of this friend had gone amorphous, mutable. What a strange act, to push someone off a cliff and never to remember her face or name.

The faceless friend memory then brought Beautiful back to an even more stunning devastation, for she had been secretly frightened, for the longest time, about recurrent nightmares that she'd killed her fetal twin. These took place in utero, in which she was just a small ape-girl fetus, and inside of her mother, at this early stage of growth when her arms and legs were functional, occasionally, she envisioned that she'd wrapped her hands around the neck of her co-habiting fetus and choked it dead. Not only this, but in these dreams, she ate it. A private act of infant cannibalism.

While Beautiful was mindful that a fetus wouldn't normally eat another fetus, that the umbilical cord that nourished her would have also nourished this phantom nightmare fetus, she couldn't shake this dream because it had recurred for years and she'd never asked her mother:

"Mother, was there only one of me in your womb? Mommy, did I kill my sister or brother?" She'd been either too afraid to ask or didn't want to know.

The interdependency of these ideas was too bothersome and real to fathom. Damn the black Lincoln fear box! It incited bad memory. Neither had Beautiful asked her parents about the cliff push, which was probably why Fedora Man's current recitations of his evil bored her. "Who cares?" she wanted to say. "You don't know how it feels to be *evil* and *different* until you have nightmares about killing strange children on hypothetical imaginary cliff pushes or eating your fetal twin!" But thank goodness, she decided now, she'd never shared either problem with her new lover. He couldn't be trusted.

Already, he'd taken too much, given too much, and become a new source of worry and chagrin, so the only peaceful moments she had while thinking of him had to do with when, flat and silent as he preferred, she'd lain still and he'd touched her as if this were the most normal thing in the world, as if she, trapped in his microscopic gaze, had become his universe, his queen, his best love, the only one present when no one else could reach him.

She glanced up toward Thomas from her perch in the backseat. He paid her no attention, progressing forward, so again she peered out the window, lowering it for the fresh air that blew in with the scent of lilacs. It was good she had no need to speak to him, that he didn't speak to her, consumed as she was with recovering whatever memories would aid her for the rest of her trip to Ida's, happy memories.

The nap in the field had been lovely. The dreams had been light, fleet, and restive. Yet the joy in her spirit seemed again sorely limited after she entered the Lincoln, which was black, shiny, clean, polished... Inside, she was safe, according to Sandra, but it was only outside of the car that she truly felt alive. She pictured that small butterfly landing on her shoulder again, closing her eyes and willing him near. Then she said, "Help me up, butterfly. Help me fly."

Blinking, imagining an exchange with this butterfly, she zoned out until "Fuck, holy fuck all, fuck shit, Beautiful!" she heard Thomas exclaim, so retrained her attention to the road. The next eight hundred yards of road were flat, clear, but afterwards a black floating cloud hung in the air. It was dust perhaps? No, she realized in horror, it was butterflies. Thousands of them, and within seconds, Thomas drove right into this cloud, massacring a swarm.

It was like she heard them screaming, dying right before her, though it was she herself who screamed, "Stop! Stop, Thomas! Oh, God, stop! You're killing the butterflies! Stop killing all the butterflies!"

"I can't stop," he replied, the migration cloud penetrated, countless corpses then coating his window and the front grill of the Lincoln. More and more splattered on the car. They weren't even close to exiting the cloud.

"Now, Thomas! Oh, please, just stop the killings!" she said again, weakly, in shock, tears pouring down over her face like a river.

"I just can't till we're through it," he repeated. "We'll get in a wreck."

Right then, a distant red Camry flew up fast from behind so Thomas accelerated, but Beautiful didn't care about road safety, only the little deaths. They had to stop driving through the cloud. She clocked Thomas in the back of his head, jumping to the front seat, and swung the wheel hard to the right. "Stop killing the gentle things," she instructed while they'd drifted into the good ditch. "Oh, how ultra-awful!" And then the car, their car, the black impervious Lincoln of darkness and death, landed hard at the roadside, Thomas out like a light, unconscious, and Beautiful in terror.

She yanked up the emergency brake. When everything stilled, when her eyes stopped swimming in tears, she found herself unable to speak except to say to his inert body, "You conspired to give me this slaughter, Thomas, didn't you? You and my father! All those butterflies dead! His hatred of naturalism has brought this death to me! You probably even killed my spirit guide!" and then she wept far worse than ever before, crying for both Jake and the fetus and the cliff girl and the thousands of butterfly bodies across her windshield and her lack of prescient awareness and the fact that she had just punched Thomas in the head for no good reason except to cease an unavoidable butterfly slaughter, as if that were possible, so she then blamed everyone for life sneaking up on her, the ugly part of life that would never have found her on the estate, which is a point Daddy might have reiterated while relishing making his victory manifesto about her trip as a failure, but just then the car radio crackled to life and, intermittently, within the static, Beautiful heard the strains of a pop song, though she could not identify it and didn't care to sing, distraught as she was, thinking only, "Butterflies. We have killed so many butterflies, Thomas! Oh, my friends! Oh, my foes! They did not deserve this. For they were only dreams..."

Then somebody started singing about shaking ass, shaking it hard, and Beautiful snapped out of her reverie. She was far more practical once she recovered. She got out of the Lincoln and walked around it several times before opening Thomas's door. Then she lifted him out of the driver's seat and deposited him in the passenger side, propping him up so as not to allow a concussed state to somehow take him into concussed deathland as she drove.

She eyed the module that told them navigational direction. She'd drive again, she decided. Right then. "All right, Thomas," she said. "It's my turn to do this, because you're decidedly out of it." She monitored the gear shift, the ignition, and also the wheel, eventually dropping the brake and pulling out onto the road.

Her thought was to find some kind of gas station or shop where she could purchase ice for the back of his head.

How to convince him a stunning blow had come from the rear, unaffiliated with her, was another concern.

At home, she wouldn't have bothered with such deception, but now, needing him as she did, it was possible that the times warranted eliciting less of his ire in order to get her to her mentor's house without incarceration. "I could say," Beautiful decided ten minutes later, staring out at the passing land and mindful of those little speed limit signs, "that a luggage flew up from the back, with your rapid braking, Thomas, so you were hit. And then I wanted to drive you to the hospital, but concluded you'd be fine with ice applied to the back of your head—and besides I had no clue where a nearby hospital was, so I kept driving." The problem was that no piece of luggage would match a fist-sized, rear cranial impact. Also, what if he remembered he hadn't been braking? "I could buy a hard object," Beautiful then conjectured, "from the next place I stop, put it in the car, somewhere he can see it, maybe right beside him, and say, 'It flew from my satchel, Thomas, really. The butterflies were upon us, the orange cloud of slaughter you caused, or the sky caused, or the season caused—and then this strange object flew forward and conked you on the head, this one right here, and then you were out!" She paused in thought, adding, "Because I was in the backseat and we were, unmanned, if you will, driverless, I delicately pulled the wheel to the side. I had to. And surely then I leaned over and moved you, though obviously took no liberties, Thomas. You know I don't desire you in that way, but, also, it was absolutely necessary. To pull over after, switch spots, and check on your well-being. So I checked on you and then started driving toward Ida's."

Explanations irritated. She could not be too sure what level of minimalism would fit. What would be believable, yet sparse enough to incite no further questions? These sorts of things might not have bothered her normally, such as figuring out how to explain what had happened to a still needed excursion participant, catering to them, etcetera, for normally they would have been instantly replaced, ushered away at the estate. But this was not home and there were scant resources on the road. "It must be like those people who have little money! Or little help! I'm learning to be resourceful and make-do!" Beautiful said, feeling much like those women she read about whose silk stockings were limited and thus they'd drawn pencil lines up the back of their legs to compensate, though she'd never quite thought those lines would feel anything like silk. "Still, these resources must be preserved," she said. "I shall have to rise to this challenge. Yes, this challenge is arduous, but I shall rise—and why? Because I am Beautiful Ape Girl Baby Chef, a winner! And Thomas is a good driver. While I'm not. How I hate driving! Yet we must continue."

Despite her past enjoyment of a few limited tours behind the wheel, she still found the whole driving effort intrusive to her growth and self-reflection, which was, she internally affirmed, the purpose of this trip. Thus, she could develop new skills of reasoning and persevering in order to make Thomas doubt that she'd harmed him on purpose. That, or she could call her father and tell him she'd clocked Thomas in the back of the head, which would be simpler, but then there was the issue of finding a replacement driver and waiting for his or her arrival, plus her father's likely anger and disappointment, not to mention Thomas's undeniable and admirable quality of blending, of silence, of an extreme lack of charm, which might be replaced by a personage more talkative whom Beautiful then wanted to punch in the head without the excuse of an accidental butterfly slaughter in progress, and such a person would distract her further from the goal of reviewing Ida May Haze's *Strong as Animal Woman Show* philosophies before she got to Ida, which Beautiful must do before the exchange to come because being prepared was important. She had to keep Thomas.

"So the plan is," Beautiful said, as if solidifying her intent by verbalizing, "I buy a fist-sized object and plant it in the backseat. A snow globe? A desert cache can? A jar of Vaseline? Not heavy enough... A small bottle of detergent? Yes. I buy a bottle of detergent, plant it in the backseat, and then buy ice and probably some kind of towel to put the ice in so it doesn't jolt him into fresh shock when cold water starts running down his neck, another towel so as not to ruin my clothes for the rest of the ice, and then I tell him about the flying object, the one I'll then point to, that will have knocked him out."

She examined how he slumped since her last attempt at propping him up. Slobber fell from his lips. "It just plain knocked you out," she practiced telling him, also adding one of the friends' expressions common to accident explanation, which was a pout, a sad look of mysterious intent that implied both sadness, partial repentance, and confusion.

She practiced the look in the rear-view, but it made her laugh. Pout? Beautiful Ape Girl Baby Chef did not pout! Because she did not repent! Peals of laughter left her in a better mood. But she needed to work harder at *appearing to repent*, so she tried a pout again, as if she meant it, then spoke the planned speech again, but was thrown into more fits of terrible giggles throughout, which also involved some unladylike snorting her mother abhorred.

I am sure, she thought, *that I must try not to find this story funny when I make these announcements to Thomas,* but the harder she tried to practice fibbing with a straight face, the more she laughed, as if laughter had an inverse relationship with desired severity.

"It's the pout," she mused. "I can't pout. It's causing more laughter. And hives. And joy tears! This is a lot of effort to appease one silly monkey in my father's employ!"

Yet it cheered her. Beautiful pulled over for just a moment to regard Thomas's white mustache. How much she wanted to pull it, just yank it a little. It was so thick and pale, she was nearly certain she could pull it out in clumps, like dandelion spores.

She could pull it lightly, just once, to wake him, but she knew she wouldn't have the control to do it nicely since she'd wanted to do it for so long. Yes, she'd plan to do it nicely, but she could predict that what she'd do instead would be to *start* pulling gently and then *yank really hard* and laugh. She chuckled again, saying, "And then, Thomas, something fist-sized came up and hit you in the lip. I don't know what!"

In this moment, even his monkey suit, his black, slick and heavy bodyguard suit struck her as somewhat ludicrous. "Thomas," she said affectionately, with speech not uncharitable due to the fact that he couldn't hear her, "You couldn't guard an old woman from a six year old child, or a six year old child from her lollipop, or a lollipop from a bee. It's a good thing you're only a driver and not a bodyguard."

She pulled back onto the road and patted his thigh, thinking fondly of home.

The orange Hondas were quite ugly, she then decided. It was good they'd be gone. She wondered whether Helga or Bernice was feeding her mother and wondered whether her mother, as she often did, had taken her father's smoking jacket and pajamas and sprayed them with some noxious household item as he'd slept so that he'd awaken to a viscous cloud of repulsive or anomalous scent, like olive oil, or bug repellent, or licorice-scented body spray.

On the road, there was nothing but landscape for miles. Thomas shifted. Beautiful took her phone off the charger. She rang Sandra, but her call went straight to voicemail. She then commenced to singing and reciting passages from Ida's shows, her singing off-key but enjoy-able. Five minutes later, no stores in sight, Thomas began to wake.

She hadn't even gotten the ice yet, much less the detergent. All her planning was foiled. "Shit, I'm sorry,

Thomas," Beautiful then said. "In the completely understandable panic of the moment, during the butterfly slaughter, I clocked you in the head. I took over driving. But you'll be all right."

It felt good to tell the truth, Beautiful decided. Besides, she had no choice, the truth having exited without further reflection.

"Mama?" he asked.

"Not Mama. Beautiful," Beautiful replied.

"Beautiful, Mama," he repeated, with a pained yelp.

Upon that, he flopped over on his side and pulled his thumb into his mouth. Were she not so moved by the childlike nature of his posture, Beautiful may've told him to get a hold of himself, but she did worry about regression. What if he could no longer drive?

She'd read about these men who "regressed" and were like infants for days, months even. If this was the case, liking him or otherwise, she determined to drop him at the next rest stop. "Thomas," she said. "It's drastically important that you show some adulthood at the next interval in which we speak." And what was with these men and their mothers? All of them had some issue, only Thomas seemed to crave comfort from his, unlike the fearful cringing of Fedora Man.

Beautiful enjoyed no close male friends on the estate, so the idea of men and their thoughts about their mothers was new to her. She didn't understand men in the first place, and her mother had made it quite difficult for her to bond with men around them except her father, considering them scoundrels. Beautiful thought of the nightmares of fetal killing and eating: *But you're afraid of your mother, too, Beautiful*, she told herself. *No, I'm not*, she argued. *And if I am, I'm afraid of what mother can tell me. If I find out it's true that there was another fetus, I might feel terrible, as if my life had snuffed the life of another infant before I was even cognizant! And did you plan on mur-*

dering the man in the wreck yard, she asked herself? *My errors,* she firmly told herself, *come from emphatic sentiment, felt in the moment. I am not murderous by nature! Have I not learned how to dress myself demurely as mother instructed? Have I not learned how to use my words more often than my fists? Have I not suppressed the urge to discuss, in detail, biological functions that interest me greatly? I have. I have.*

She imagined her psychologist was there again, the woman with the whale and dolphin tapes. "Beautiful," that woman would say. "It's clear you have issues with your mother, too."

At this, furious with the shrink's imaginary presence, Beautiful shouted, "Well, that's natural that I'd have issues with my mother, because I'm the GIRL child and the GIRL child is always the one who cannot measure up to the mother! But I feel quite belligerent about *boys* with mother issues. Because *boys* were never expected, for example, to learn how to smile and appease houseguests, never expected to be delicate and feminine and camouflage their reactions to ridiculous speech by male counterparts."

Beautiful considered her mother with more kindness then. "But mother softens me," she said. "Mother loves me, even if I'm not the girl she wanted. We can't all be what our parents want because we aren't our parents' replicas and, so, individuating, this act will always cause our isolation." She wrote in her journal: MEN DO NOT HAVE A RIGHT TO MOTHER ISSUES! She underlined this five times.

Still, it was rather sweet how Thomas had looked upon her when he said "Mama" earlier, so she decided she might one day want a male child, and she hoped it would come out different like her. What she couldn't picture was its father.

Would Fedora Man make a good match? How would a child of such a skinny pale villain and a robust ape girl arrive? Not that he'd be the father. He didn't seem, at this point, even able to negotiate a second date.

"He was my first receptive, intelligent, unusual man," she told herself. "He will not be my last!"

But it was amazing how saying something aloud could cause sudden internal opposition. Immediately after expressing her will to power over rejecting him, Beautiful fell into a powerless slump of sad-eyed mooning, thinking, *It's not safe to even think his name. Ivor. Ivor. Ivor. To think his name now makes me weak, and if I were a Superman type, then Fedora Man would be my evil kryptonite.*

It didn't console her at all that this was a time-honored feeling of lovers in love. She knew that to feel this weak meant she'd fallen deeper than she'd wanted to for FM, but hadn't Fedora Man encouraged this? Hadn't he followed her upstairs and made love to her at the pool? If he hadn't, none of this weakness would exist, she suspected. At least John Henry had always completely refused her, aside from a few doting remarks and songs dedicated to her at pool parties, his refusal, all in all, allowing for a certain indignant and helpful rage on her side. And John Henry had only inspired an endless capacity for wanting without any clear possibility of having, but had John Henry reciprocated her interest, she decided, say, with a whole night of lovemaking, or a creative work in her honor, a mural wall of paintings, an album of songs, she now knew her misery could be so much worse.

This made no sense. "Why should getting some and losing all be so much more aggravating than wanting all and getting none?" she asked herself. It was counter her entire theory on love, which should be that more was more, not more was less or less was less and therefore better. "Subsequent interactions reduced in frequency or care? Exploded dreams? A taste of life motif?" she posited, thinking of Fedora Man's sexy little way of pausing. Dang, he was sexy. Sexy and bad for her.

She imagined him green, glowing like nuclear waste. He was saying, in her fantasy, "I'm your evil stud lover,

Baby!" right as she decided that she didn't want to be Superman or Supergirl anyway, so Kryptonite shouldn't bother her, and that she didn't need him.

What she wanted now was for Thomas to get the hell up and take over driving so she could read, take a nap, skip, draw, cease viewing the endless bland landscape that was clearly tiresome enough to lull her into a green evil villain sex fantasy that doubled as a Fedora Man continuous consideration coma, all about Ivor—because in her vivid mental life, ever since she saw him, all she wanted to do was to feel the weight of his head upon her thigh once more, to see him smile once more, to feel the strength in his hands and the lightness of his body, to both throw him in the water he feared and to rescue him until he learned, by default, how to trust or how to swim—or for somebody, anybody, to ask her to be silent like he had, but it had to be someone she would listen to—and she also wanted for Sandra to come and accompany her on this road trip, as well as to know that her mother was okay, not living on peanuts, and then possibly to have a ham sandwich, some dark chocolate perhaps, and a solitary swim. This followed by a Swedish massage, with rolphing for deep tension.

She had lots of wants. She turned the radio dial on the Lincoln's display, adjusting the tuner. "Ida, I need you," she said. And yes, this was a fancy radio, but when she navigated to the right setting for the *Strong as Animal Woman Show* station, which she knew perfectly well how to find, Ida's voice emerged immediately, clear as the sound of two hands clapping.

Resultantly, Beautiful smiled and then glared at Thomas. "Fucker," she said to his slumped inert mass. "You told me we couldn't get Ida's show." She almost clocked him again.

But "...and it's a difficult thing to remember," Ida said through the speakers, immediately seizing all of Beautiful's attention, "why, in the midst of all this suffering and this shitbin life, we must persevere, but we must persevere because what other choice do we have? Many a thing can make perseverance difficult! For example: Avoid the ills of hard liquor!"

"I do!" Beautiful replied.

"Avoid the ills of tobacco!"

"I do that too," Beautiful said.

And, "Again, NO SMOKING," Ida went on, but Beautiful overheard a purse-lipped inhalation on the line that seemed quite lengthy, like Ida herself was smoking, sucking up some gas like a fiend, this sound followed by a wheeze then a series of raspy coughs. "Tobacco will kill you!" Ida stated, coughing more. "And avoid places of ill-repute. Members of the sex trade. Fanatics with travelling circuses. Avoid marriage too, unless you are certain that who you find is your absolute soul mate. And, on that subject, make it clear from the very beginning that you don't intend to pick up socks from the floor, nor will you do extreme dishes or embrace raw food diets. In short, friends, avoid all places and people whose attitudes make you unwelcome." Some kind of book or door slammed closed in the background. Someone called for Ida, and, for a moment, the station went quiet, as if shut down. Then Ida came back on, raging. "And if the assholes in your home are mean to you," Ida said, in a fierce whisper, "stamp out their power! Take it back fully, without prisoners! Only you can make your life what you want it to be, even if you're starving or oppressed. Never forget, friends, we live for our integrity and our majesty *in the today.* There is only *the today.* Forget tomorrow. It's meaningless. It might not even *belong* to *you.* Forget the past, too. But buh-bye for now." This was the end, and then the regular jingle came on, but though Beautiful was glad to have heard Ida, some parts of the narrative seemed disjointed.

"I think Ida's now smoking crack," Beautiful said as Thomas shifted obliviously in his seat. "What the hell was that?" The need for a sandwich reoccurred, hunger pangs deep in Beautiful's abdomen, so Beautiful drove faster in the hopes that this would bring her more quickly to a suitable destination. When at last she saw the dusty lot of a new and identical roadside diner along on the right, for they all looked identical to her, big windows, booths, cheap cars, assorted trucks, cheap chrome, she pulled in and then attempted to wake the gimp that was Thomas, who still sucked his thumb.

"Thomas," she called out. "Thom-as!" Nothing. She reached into the backseat where she'd stored the stolen police megaphone, turned it on, and stated, thinking of Ed, "Thomas, come out with your hands up! We have you surrounded!"

Thomas jolted awake spastically, bonking his skull on the window beside him. She laughed as he rubbed the back of his head, newly green in the jowls, laughed so hard her abdomen and jaw hurt. Then she turned off the megaphone, instantly a little sorry. "Shit, I'm sorry," she apologized. "I forgot your head must hurt."

"It does." His hands rubbed his temple as he glared at her, his head bobbing. "You hit me," he said. "Hard! You punched me in the head!"

"Good job, Thomas! That's right!" she said, pleased he recollected real events. "Oh, I feared for you for a while, Thomas. You thought I was your Mama! You called me Mama, too. It was touching."

"Why did you hit me, Beautiful? What did I do?"

"Sometimes, others must be hit," she replied. "When they're doing a bad, bad thing."

"But why?"

"You didn't listen."

"To what?"

"I said stop killing the butterflies," she said. "Don't you remember that beautiful cloud of butterflies? The Lin coln cruised up on them. They were dying against the car. But you didn't even brake. And as we discussed before," she racked her brain for the expression she had used earlier, when first surprised by his waking, "it was my gut reaction that caused your sudden removal as driver, the reaction of not being listened to as I verbalized my intent for you to stop, and the situation needed something, some kind of immediate remedy, which unfortunately involved you getting hit. But I said I was sorry. Say, can you drive now?"

He reached into his pocket and removed his cell phone. "Two announcements: One, I'm calling your father, and, two, I quit."

"Thomas, let's not be hasty," she said, trying harder to be nice. "I could have left you in the desert after I clocked you, could have dumped you there like a pile of refuse in the sand, buried you even, but I didn't. Look, I took you here, ever so worried about your head. Brought you to this place of nourishment. I thought we could have a nice lunch."

"I don't want to eat with you," he said, scowling.

"Well, what a whiny baby you're being, Thomas!" she replied. "It's quite immature." She grabbed his cell phone and smashed it twice on the dash. "Call Daddy now," she said. "I'm going in to eat."

He had no choice but to follow her since she had the keys and jingled them on the tips of her fingers as she walked. "You're making the right decision, Thomas," she said when he approached behind her. "Tell you what. Be nice and don't call Daddy this minute. Then, tonight, I'll find another driver who I'll hand select from a nearby establishment, and then I'll give you plenty of money to get home. Let's just be kind to each other over this lunch, okay? I really didn't mean to hurt you. You've been valuable. Just remain calm."

Two hours later, seated in a red booth, Thomas tucked into her arms and crying like a wee baby, she felt terribly sorry that she'd ever hit him. He was such a good baby.

She wiped his tears away with her own sweater, gross

and snot-globbed as it became, now seeing herself as his true mother, his primate mother, his primordial mother, his mother of fate and circumstance. And she would've nursed him, voluminously squirting the essence of life, had she any milk. "I know it's been hard for you, Thomas," she said. "Life! Love! Loss! Mothers! And I think you should suck that thumb all day if you want to, even while you are driving, especially while you are driving, except when you need to turn because that could be dangerous. You should do whatever pleases you. How long has it been since you did that?"

"Forever," he acknowledged, both sheepish and enraged.

"I know, Baby," she murmured. "I know." His tales of his mother's chill treatment had incited the greatest pity Beautiful had ever known for a boy, or man, or baby, as she now saw him, a glorious big man baby, completely in touch with his feelings.

"You, Sir," she said, "are beautiful to behold!" She wiped his face again, which was ruddy and wet, but a far sight less snotty, and then she said kindly, but with much fervor, "And you know what else, Thomas? I've noted you have some repressed rage issues. You have never fully expressed that rage, which means you have been stuffing it, so this means you have a lot of it, all stuffed down. I myself don't repress my rage. This is why I'm so well-adjusted. But you've repressed it for so long you no longer recognize your rage for what it is! Thomas, you need to let that rage folly out!" With pity, she grazed his face with her fingertips.

"I have," he agreed, between renewed sobs. "I've repressed a lot of rage. And when you clocked me back there, it was so wonderful because I'd never let it come up before. Because I hadn't been clocked for no reason by someone I hardly knew. It was quite manly when I said, 'I quit,' wasn't it?"

"Yes," Beautiful said. "I did believe you. Though I had to smash your phone." She kissed his forehead, kissed it again, and touched his mustache without giving in to her ever-present temptation of yanking it. "But you were naughty when you told me Ida Haze was not available on the radio. Let's explore: Ida Haze very plainly *is* available on the radio, so why did you say she wasn't, Thomas?"

"I resented you," he said. "I was afraid of Ida's message."

Beautiful thought this session quite fabulous and longed for the whale or dolphin tapes behind it, thinking maybe she should record it to listen to it later. She could be like her old meditating shrink, not the pot smoking one. She so wanted to be helpful. "And why, Thomas, did you resent me?"

"I was jealous of your pleasure," he admitted. "You're made so easily happy, Beautiful. You're so emotional. And you say what you think. So I didn't want you to be happy. I couldn't stand for you to be happy all the time, made happy by that silly crackpot, Ida Haze. I think you should know, I've researched her address and it's not in the lofty area of Westwood that you imagined. It's rather in a barrio."

Beautiful lifted him upright in his seat, asking, "But why would Ida broadcast out of the barrio? And why would someone in a barrio have a rep?" Confused, she took a glass from their diner booth and flung it to the floor to shatter. Thomas stared with wide eyes. "She must be making a statement to barrio broadcast," Beautiful said. "But what could she be saying by that? Nonetheless, I have faith in Ida Haze. In fact, Thomas. I learned that last maneuver from Ida's The Broken Glass episode. She devoted a whole show to it. Want to try? Break a glass."

"Well, I, uh, well—" He looked fearfully for the waitress.

"Just do it," Beautiful said. "Don't think too much. Do it."

He looked at his glass. "I can't throw this. It's full of water."

"Yes, you can. Watch. I'll show you again."

She took his glass from his hand, full of water, and threw it into the ground. Then she stepped over the water and broken glasses, went around, and gathered ten more glasses, two by two, from surrounding tables. "Not to worry," she told the waitress. "I'll pay for these." She turned to Thomas, handing him just one, saying, "This is an important moment of your development as an angry child. Take each and every one of these and throw it, hard, on the floor. As you do this, say something self-empowering like, 'I hate you, Mama. You mean and nasty Mama who ensured I'd never feel cherished!'" Maybe add another message between the anger venting, a good one. I only grabbed ten glasses, but I do think you should make a message for yourself like, 'I am worthy of love and appreciation. I am the best white-mustached driver there ever was! I'm a shining star of Lincoln drivers!' and then return to the fuck-off Mama messages as needed. I must say, Thomas, my mother never necessitated such acts, though I can think of someone who might. But that's my problem, and it comes with a man-like deserter in a black hat. My cross to bear. Now, throw! Throw down! Throw!"

Thomas dropped the first glass, whispering, "Fuck you, Mama." It didn't break, just cracked with an awkward thud.

Beautiful picked it up and returned it to him, patting his back aggressively. "You can do better, Thomas! A tiny chip? A hairline crack? Harder," she urged. "More vocalization. Look at this! This glass is hardly broken. Do it again, like you mean it!"

"Fuck you, mean Mama!" he said, getting a better toss on this next glass, which did shatter. By the fifth or so, he threw like a baseball pitcher, all kinds of florid language flowing from his lips and Beautiful coaching every now and again to return him to the self-love focus, but when he had thrown the last glass and there were no more, he looked sorrowful.

"Don't worry, Thomas," she said, "the deeds are done, but now we do recovery. You sweep the broken glass. Sweep softly. These shards are the traces of your vented anger. The act of sweeping, a sweet forgiveness for yourself for venting that anger. Contrition is the clean up. It makes people feel better to clean up. Promise. I'll wait for you outside if you don't mind doing my clean-up, too, just this once. I have to call Sandra. I'm ready to make her an offer."

CHAPTER FIVE
SHIT TON OF GLASS

~IN WHICH, SANDRA UNFRIENDS BEAUTIFUL, A DINER WINDOW CRUMBLES VIA HEAD BUTT, THOMAS SHOWS MERIT, AND BEAUTIFUL RESCUES A BAR SLUT FROM A WOMANIZER, DOES COPIOUS DRUGS, AND HAS A REVELATION. ~

Beautiful walked outside and dialed. "Sandra?"

"Oh, hi, Beautiful."

"I'm at a diner, Sandra," Beautiful said. "Not causing any trouble, promise. But I've wanted to ask you som—"

"Beautiful, look, I don't know what's happening there. I'm at my mom's. I—"

"That's not it." Beautiful peeked down at her arms and legs where the hair had just begun to curl again. Considering her green crackle nail polish, she said, "I can't have this rift, not anymore, Sandra. I want you back. There's a big world of people out there and none of them mean as much to me as you." Uncharacteristically, humbly, Beautiful waited.

"Back where?" Sandra asked.

"With me. You're my best friend."

"I told you, Beautiful. I can't. It's the real world. I can't go around being a *friend* for a living. What kind of living is that? I—"

"I've thought a lot about this," Beautiful said. "And since I just made love to someone who was not paid, a *not paid* friend, Sandra, I realized that there was a good reason that the paid friends could never make love to me, not that our original kisses didn't matter when you were paid and you kissed me while salaried, though you weren't paid to kiss me, but what I'm saying, Sandra, what I'm saying, is that I would pay you the going rate for sex services workers in order to retain you in my employ. This wouldn't be a bad wage. Comparably, sex service workers make on par with garbage men, though slightly more than mechanics. These things do depend on their ability and willingness to perform certain functions, but in our case that's irrelevant. Sandra? You could get annual raises and employee of the month awards. I would make this happen… I would."

Sandra remained silent.

"Sandra?"

A snuffle rattled the line.

"Sandra, I don't want to take advantage of you," Beautiful continued, "and it's not like we have to be lovers, but if I have been unfair to you, I want to remedy that. It hurts my heart if I've been unfair to you, and I have the money. I can hire you at a top rate if you want, a call-girl rate. This is the money made by the hookers rich men prefer, the beautiful ones without disease who don't have missing teeth or frequent alleys. The only paid workers who make more than that in the sex trade are those paid to inflict massive pain or play in other people's feces, but I don't think you want to inflict pain upon me since you're so gentle, I'm pretty sure neither of us like shit, and besides I don't wish to hurt you or make you dirty, not that I think you want me to hurt you, though I like Tasing, and, in our case, any sex would be purely optional, but before I could pay you via transfer, once this is set up, just so you're aware, there might be a slight delay. There are the matters of a few brokers I'd need to contact and I'd—"

Sandra emitted a harsh gasp. "Are you calling me a hooker, Beautiful? You saying you want to employ me as your call girl?"

"No—I—"

"Because that's what it sounds like, and if that's what you think, you're just like your fucked-up, stinking, mob-boss father who thinks his money can buy everything and… I was always your real friend. Always—but now you treat me like some kind of paid friend flunky, only you want to pay me like a lover without really being my lover, or maybe, quite possibly, you'd be my lover, too? Oh, fuck, Beautiful. This hurts too much. This whole conversation just hurts. I can't even talk. Go! Live your life. Be free. Do what other rich heiresses do—buy more clothes, treat your low class friends like trash, and travel around the world. Go to Iceland! Spain. Ireland. Learn another language, grow Chia pets, but forget about me! You don't—"

"I'm free now," Beautiful interrupted, her eyes tearing. "I'm trying to help you keep being my friend during my freedom."

"No, you're not helping me," Sandra said. "You don't even know what freedom is. Your father puts tracking mechanisms in everything you own, everything of your mother's too! And if you understood freedom, you'd start by…" Sandra ranted on and on about all the ways in which Beautiful didn't understand her environment, so Beautiful listened with half an ear, simultaneously observing Thomas sweep up the glass inside the diner, sweeping so carefully, so calmly and gently, moving the green handled broom to resolve the mess such that the floored glass-glitter rapidly emptied into his dustbin. In the midst of watching Thomas, however, for Beautiful, Sandra's voice grew faint, lapping, absent of meaning and words. Then she heard a dull click.

"So, if I'm not free," Beautiful subsequently replied, unable to keep up with the breakneck pace of Sandra's unexpected heart-slashing, "what do you call this break I now take from the estate? Or my wish to come visit you where you live?"

She listened for Sandra's reply for at least twenty seconds until, staring at the receiver after a slight lull, she noticed that the call had been terminated. She then leaned her forehead into the glass, the same forehead already cool and lacerated by so much mean talk, and seconds later, as Thomas looked up and waved, Beautiful smiled her coy half-smile at him, waved, pulled her face away from the glass before cocking her head back once more and ramming her face forcefully through the window.

The wall of glass shattered, not into shards but tempered round pebbles. That's how they made the big pieces now. And, "This is what I get? This is what I get?" Beautiful asked. "Because I cared too much and tried to make a nice life for her, but now I'm accused of being like my father? He fired her! I'd never be my father. He cares for nothing and no one but mother and his business. Him and mother and his business against the world. I'm just the accident they made. The one with no real friends."

Standing in the glittering crumbles, Beautiful reached into her purse and pulled out a lipstick. She put it on without a mirror, trembling and smiling at Thomas again, a full smile of deliberate motherly support this time, waving again at him through open air as if everything was fine, but she also considered walking around to the other large panel of window glass and demolishing that. As soon as he registered what had happened to the first one, however, Thomas dropped the broom and ran to her, saying, "Beautiful, you just broke a shit-ton of glass. We'd better get out of here."

"I can't flee, Thomas," Beautiful said. "I'll pay for the damage. Though I'm not sure I'm even done doing it."

"Oh, you're done, Beautiful," Thomas replied. "The cops'll get here any minute. We've got to go—"

"All right," Beautiful replied, moping and reluctant.

"Let's pay and go."

~

"Wow, Beautiful, you were really in touch with your anger back there," Thomas remarked a few miles later.

"I was," she agreed. "Tapped in."

"I felt awed by your power and ability to embrace that feeling," Thomas said. "I felt like cheering. It made my cup tosses feel small, though I was glad to enjoy them with you."

"We should shoot some guns," she replied. "That always thrills me. *Pow! Powpowpow!*"

"A whole pane of restaurant glass, Mama," Thomas marveled. "Holy fuckatony."

"That, Thomas," she said as they got back onto the interstate, "was big anger. Big sadness. Sandra has cut me off. Sometimes, many times, small cups just won't do."

"Guess not," he said. "Guess not."

"Say, listen. I need some silence for a while, Baby," she said. "Mama needs to deeply consider how to initiate a chat with Daddy. But Sandra is worth it." After speaking, Beautiful sat for a long excruciating think, which took all of three minutes. She then dialed her father.

He picked up right away. "Beautiful?"

"Daddy?"

"Beautiful?"

"Yes, we've been through this before. We're both here."

"So we are. What do you want?"

"Daddy? I need a favor."

"Are you having a good trip? Are you coming home soon? Your Mommy wants to know."

Beautiful sighed. "Yes, Daddy. No, Daddy. Listen. I need the address of Ms. Sandra Goforth, and I need it now."

"Your mother also wants to know what you are eating out there. Can you tell me what you're eating?"

"I want to know what she's eating, too," Beautiful

said. "On her hunger strike! Thus, our concerns mirror each other. Tell her I'm eating snakes and varmints with a side of tile paste. I'm eating the heads of small creatures killed on the road. I'm eating asbestos."

"I will not."

"Then give me Sandra's address, pretty please?" Beautiful twisted her crystalline ring on her finger, watching more billboards pass.

Her father paused. "No."

Out the window, trees and power poles flew by at alarming rates. Beautiful considered Thomas, who was, just as she'd advised, busy suckling his thumb and driving. Speeding mightily, but sucking his thumb. "Very good, Thomas," she said, thumping the back of his seat with her open palm.

She then returned her attention to her father. "Daddy, I'm aware you have a lot of clout. I've never doubted your clout, and yet, Sandra is my friend. I need to see her. I've heard you have fired all my friends. Is this true?"

"We do what's necessary in a commerce economy, Beautiful. You left. Why employ friends for a daughter who's absconded?"

"What if I want the friends back? I am coming home sometime!"

"We hire more then."

"The same ones?"

"If necessary."

"Well, that's fine, but I need Sandra's home address right now."

"You can't have Sandra's home address," her father argued, "because she's an employee of the estate, and I don't release the personal information of employees of the estate. Besides, Baby, did you think I'd fire your very best friend?" He used the cold business-like tone he'd employed so many times before, but hardly ever with her.

"She just said you did fire her," Beautiful stated,

echoing his chill. "Thus, Sandra's not an employee of the estate, but a former employee. As I'm a member of the board of trustees for the business, non-speaking partner though I have been, I feel perfectly sanguine to request the address and alternate phone numbers of Ms. Goforth, post-haste. It's a matter of grave importance."

"And that important matter is?" he asked. She heard her daddy moving about his room. Looking for a shoe, it seemed. The noise of one shoe dropping and then another was one she recognized from many of her parents' conversations.

"That I miss her very much," Beautiful said. "So I'd like to speak to her in person. I'd like to go see her."

"As I noted, she's still employed via the estate," her father then said, attempting a consoling tone. "And so I cannot give you what you want. When will you return?"

"Soon enough. But Sandra's still employed, you say?" Beautiful asked, dipping a hand into her luggage and pulling out a few sweater sets and blouses. "Or was when last you spoke to her?" What she wanted to wear that evening when they reached the next hotel destination was the Rebecca Tan evening gown she'd tucked away at the bottom of her bag, but with her luggage upright, she had difficulty digging.

"Yes, continuously employed for further phone contact, should you need it, and support on your trip."

"Now, Daddy," Beautiful replied. "Please stop fibbing. Sandra's my true friend and she told me just today that she was fired!"

"True friendship is a matter of opinion," he responded. "As is who's lying. But I assure you, I'm not lying. Would I lie about what saves me money?"

Beautiful was silent. He would not.

She then said, "I might be coming home soon. What does your suit smell like today, Daddy?"

"Lard." If cringes were audible, she'd have heard a

lengthy one. "I reek. I can't even find some uncontaminated loafers. Your mother'll make me an ill and crazy man!"

Her daddy bustled about before shouting, "You need to eat something, Ethel! And no, I won't be persuaded, no matter what you apply to my undergarments," before speaking quietly into the phone to his daughter, like he told her a secret, "Beautiful, as I said, Sandra is in my employ, with the stipulation of being available to you. Did you want to speak to your mother? Oh, please, speak to your mother. I *beg* of *you, speak* to *your mother.*"

"Not now! About Sandra, how must she be available, per the revised contract?"

"Phone contact. Twenty-four seven."

"Oh, really, Daddy?" Beautiful replied. "Well, I've just legitimately fired her for breach of contract."

"You don't say?" In the background, Beautiful heard the birds. They said, "It's a jackdaw! It's a jackdaw!" She pictured her father on the other line where she knew he stood, hovering beside the enormous cockatoo cage, twirling the phone cord on his finger because he insisted on the anachronism of phones with cords at the same time as the use of state of the art technology for espionage. She pictured him staring out onto the estate grounds and then into the gilded birdcage he adored.

But all the birds were mean and rotten, she thought. *It's like he trained them to be mean*. Beautiful had even giving up on holding, feeding, or teaching them to speak, though she occasionally took a shot into his room with her BB gun from the distant guest house, when the doors were open. Sometimes, only rarely, when she could get away with it and they'd bitten her, she broke their necks.

Now, she told to her father, "I called Sandra earlier and she hung up on me. That's not support. Ms. Goforth employed the f-word and told me to get on with my own life, so if she was employed, she is no longer. You'll now have to fire her again, if my firing did not work, as of this afternoon, retroactive to near lunchtime, and Daddy, you'll recall that we've been over this issue before, in the case of beautiful blond girl Chelsea Manzan Malone. When I helped her, as a small child, to make her more beautiful, when I punched her in the nose, and you sent her away. Do you remember what you said to me then, Daddy? You said, 'Any former employee of the estate has my permission to correspond with you via snail mail, so you may have their addresses, Beautiful, for that purpose.' And I sent Chelsea several letters, all of which scented with cherry ambrosia perfume and full of my repentance, none of which she replied to, but you released her address for the purposes of my development of pen pals in alternate locations, which I sorely needed, which I still need now, though you never let me have the addresses of the authors whose books I've loved because you told me they were already dead or essentially assholes, sometimes both, which they were, which they have been. Five points for you, for your incredibly depressing accuracy. Still, please give me Sandra Goforth's address right now. I need it."

Her father lifted and dropped several heavy objects before saying, "And what would you say to Sandra, in a hypothetical letter, Beautiful, after she f-bombed you?"

Beautiful thought hard. One thought, above others, repeated in her head, so she replied, "I would say that I missed her very much, Daddy. That I didn't care if we'd quarreled. And I'd write her a long letter, full of exclamation marks, to show how strongly I felt her loss and how much it hurt me; I'd tell her I never required more from her than that she talk to me upon occasion and be my friend. I'd drop this into the nearest postal box and then Thomas would drive until we got where we were going. Hang on, Daddy, I'll call you back. Let me demonstrate. I'll first ship you, via text, an early planned excerpt of my proposed letter to Sandra. It may be long. Stand at the ready."

Beautiful hung up. She set her phone to texting this

hypothetical narrative, the message of which turned out to be short, sweet, and rather simple. "Sandra, I have missed you," she texted with feeling. And then, because that said all she had to say, really—the other more personal stuff about wages and sex and Fedora Man not to be told to her father (since Beautiful intuited that he wouldn't appreciate them)—she applied all needed emphasis to the consuming idea of broadcasting the weight and the strength of her missing Sandra, texting only and ever again:

"!!! !
!!! !!!!!!!!!!!!!!!!!!!!!!!!!!!!!!!!
!!!
!!! !! !!!!!!!!!!!
!!
!!
!!
!!
!!
!! !!!!!!!!!!!!!!!!!!
!!
!!
!!
!!
!!
!!
!!
!!
!!
!!! !!!
!!! !!
!!!
!!!
!!!
!!!
!!!

!! !!!!!!!!!!!!! !!! !!!!!! !!! !!! !!! !!! !!! !!! !!...”

AND SO FORTH…

~

It was about an hour into her exhaustive pressing of the exclamation mark key, her shift button getting a bit shaky, Beautiful humming and pressing, humming and pressing, forty-seven or so such messages initiated until each reached its maximum message length, when she received a reply text from her father.

“Okay,” it said. “Please stop.” And he gave up Sandra’s address.

Beautiful smiled and whooped. “Zounds, Thomas I’ve won!” she said. “Daddy gave in! My first victory! I used his very own Nuisance with Persistence technique! But, Thomas, where is Las Vegas? That’s where Sandra is! How long does it take to get there?” Beautiful paused only briefly before deciding that she really would like Sandra to go with her to Ida’s, almost no matter how far Las Vegas was, and asked, “So do you think we should go there first?”

“If we get her to agree we’ll pick her up,” Thomas said. “Okay. If not, we’d better to head straight to Ida’s, or we’re wasting time.”

“We’re never wasting time on Sandra,” Beautiful said.

“That’s your opinion,” Thomas replied. “But we’ll do what you want.”

~

An hour later, Beautiful moped toward the front seat. Thomas had reinserted his thumb. "Thomas," she asked, feeling rather frail and girl-like despite her recent victory, "can I ask you to be your adult self for a moment?"

"You can always ask," he said, still watching the road, a dreamy peace stealing over him as if he'd again bonded with the road. Somehow, the fact that he gazed outward made the conversation easier to initiate.

"It's personal," Beautiful said. "I need advice."

"Everything's personal," he replied. "In a weird way."

"No, not everything."

"Most things." Already, she saw his thumb was reddish where it had been sucked raw. A thin line of saliva punctuated the place of its end of contact with his lips.

"As an adult accustomed to the outside world, Thomas, as a good civilian and civil citizen of what I'm now referring to as 'out there,'" she began, "would your reaction be angry if your best friend told you they wanted you back with them so much that they'd pay you a far sight more to return to them—because they loved you so much? Would you be incensed?"

"No," Thomas said, but he pulled the car over and stared into her wide, wet eyes, saying, almost as if he didn't want to, "But Beautiful, real friends don't pay each other."

"How do they make a living?"

"Not off each other."

"So, they do that friendship thing for nothing?" Beautiful asked. In her purse was the old set of Pinto keys. She examined the borrowed Swiss Army Knife again, pulling in and out the small ivory toothpick. Then she played with the corkscrew, screwing it into the back of the passenger seat. "So, what's the leverage, then, to continue the friendship?"

"How people treat each other," he replied. "That's

what friendship's all about."

"Where good and nice behavior is necessary, right?"

"Yes," Thomas replied. "Or not exactly. In friendship, people treat each other well because they care. They care and receive care in return. But one person doesn't usually boss everyone around like you did at the estate. In a real friendship, care doesn't work that way."

"Mother bosses Father around," Beautiful noticed. "They work that way. Don't they have a real friendship?"

"More like a strange and loving Civil War," Thomas replied. "But they're not normal."

"Yes, they're beautiful that way," Beautiful agreed. She pulled a sharp knife from its metallic bed. "So if you propose to pay a normal friend to be your normal friend, but they're already your real friend, that could insult them? Like, say, if you proposed to pay them like you'd pay a sex services worker?"

She thought of being bled. She thought of Fedora Man. She had not paid him. No one had been paid. But he wasn't her friend now.

Thomas blushed, replying, "Like a sex services worker? That really has no place in friendship."

"You mean you couldn't be friends with a sex services worker?"

"Not if you paid them for sex. It's a business relationship."

"Well, what if you got sex, but you didn't pay for sex? Like if they gave you free sex? Or what if you paid for sex, but then decided you liked them as a friend? Could you get a free friend, or a free friend only sometimes, or a free friend almost never?"

"I think we're getting off track here," Thomas said. "Though I'm not saying these scenarios aren't possible."

Holding the knife blade to her finger without cutting herself, Beautiful scanned out the window where the grass seemed still from their parked vantage. Everything was still, yet below the grass there were thousands of insects, digging or something, doing what they did. So many lives beside her own, beneath her own, in progress. She moved the knife blade from digit to digit. "So what if you have a friend, and you say something that makes them really mad? What do you do, in the real world, if someone is really mad? Does it matter what you said?"

"That always matters," Thomas replied.

"Okay, so they're totally mad, now. Fuming! What do you do?"

"Apologize?"

"And if they don't accept?" Beautiful pressed the blade into the outermost pad of her thumb until it split flesh.

"How good a friend is this?" Thomas asked.

"The best kind of friend, one who only comes along once in a lifetime, maybe twice. But the kind of friend you can't know how much you'll regret losing until you lose them, and there's no one else you can tell your sorrows to who has any idea what you're talking about." Blood. Blood flooded her fingerprint, filling in its creases, and then there were tears falling from her eyes as Beautiful said, "A friend you've loved your entire life, or loved for so many years that you remember how they were before they had breasts! They know you this way, too! From all the way back when you were an ugly, stupid, little child creature! There was so much good knowing of and about the other! An equity of loving!" More tears fell from Beautiful's eyes as she pictured Sandra's sweet face years ago and then how it looked as she'd said those mean things before she'd last hung up, blinking quickly to clear her vision of moisture such that full salty tears fell directly onto her red saturated thumb, where a large drop of blood already welled and was splattered. This made red into pink for an instant, with the blood's dilution. But the deeper red resurfaced. She pressed her bloody teary thumb to the window, making a fingerprint of mottled red on glass to cover a distant tree.

"I think you should just compliment the friend," Thomas said. "Tell them you didn't mean what hurt them. Maybe remind them how much you care?"

"I did all that," she said, smearing her thumb on the glass, making an impromptu peace sign with blood and tears. "But what if they still won't let you talk to them, not at all?"

"Then fuck 'em," Thomas said. "Stop smearing blood with your finger and getting your cut dirty. Wrap it up. Don't harm yourself! Ida wouldn't like it."

"I always harm myself when I hurt someone else," Beautiful said. "It's my curse. I can't stop thinking about it. The hurting. The friend hurts and I hurt, and if they hurt, I hurt more, sometimes even just hurting about the more they hurt from some hurting, or just that they hurt at all. The hurting in a cycle. That's a lot of hurt."

Thomas nodded.

"So I love her, and she hates me."

A few more tears fell from Beautiful's eyes, but when Thomas pulled back onto the road, she said, "Besides, it's not my finger I'm smearing blood with. It's my thumb. Not that it makes much difference, Thomas. But I have opposable thumbs, and you should recognize that. I have eight fingers and two thumbs. Strong thumbs."

She clicked shut the knife's open blade without cleaning it. "And anyway, this is Sandra's Swiss Army Knife. She cuts me first by lending it to me with much love and then cutting me off, as if I were an unimportant-never-friend she unshopped as shoddy goods, and so now I cut me with her knife. Because, fuck her. Fuck her for ever unshopping me!"

"I'm sorry you're upset," Thomas replied. "You should try that breathing technique Ida uses."

"You mean Active Hyperventilation?"

"Yes that."

"Thanks a lot, Thomas," Beautiful replied, in complete despair. "But I don't want to hyperventilate. You may now go back to sucking your thumb. I hate hurting!"

Thomas returned to scanning the road as he drove, also consulting the e-navigator as he mentioned, "I'm feeling some repressed rage coming up again, Beautiful. Let's do something about that soon."

"At our next stop," she agreed.

"Hmmmph," he said.

Beautiful leaned back in her seat. Wrapping her thumb in the same sweater he'd spilled snot on, holding her thumb behind the phone to staunch the injury, "Sandra, you've been a good friend to me, and I love you, and I'm sorry," Beautiful texted. "Also, you have nice hair and kind eyes. I can't understand why you've now been so mean to me, but I probably deserve it."

"I did it, Thomas," she said. "I complimented and apologized."

"Excellent," he said, trying to add cheer to his voice. "Now we wait for her reply."

Beautiful watched the clock announcing the minutes ticking by. After three minutes, ditching the sweater, she said, "I feel I should say something else. This is because I have no patience." She pondered exactly what to say and then typed, "Sandra, remember when we were kids and we danced to that video where that multi-ethnic guy danced around with zombies? Even if you were a zombie, I'd still care. I'd still fraternize with you. I wouldn't let you eat my brain, but I'd let you bite my head. You could take a little bite."

More minutes passed. "How much time has passed now, Thomas?" she asked.

"Since the first text or the second?"

"The second."

"Twelve minutes."

"And so, Sandra, I do believe you're my real friend. But if you were still on Daddy's payroll, I fired you today. Because if you're supposed to provide twenty-four seven phone support for my emotional needs, you hung up on me and I was *not* feeling supported. How're things at your mother's?"

Another several more durations passed, Beautiful asking Thomas for a time count every few minutes, Beautiful told Thomas. "That's it. I have to pull out the ace." She busily worked her phone's keyboard. The resultant expression was "...so if you don't reply within an hour, I'm coming to see you in Las Vegas. I'll show up on your doorstep. I cut my thumb with your Swiss Army knife because I believe we're blood sisters, and I'll need to cut your finger, too, so we can mix blood when I get there. Unless you're too squeamish—"

She was about to go on, but Thomas looked rather fidgety in front, which distracted her. "What's that funny movement you're making, Thomas?"

"I need the restroom," he replied. "Soon."

"Very well," she said and released her message but asked Sandra nothing further for the rest of the day and got no reply. When they finally arrived at their evening destination that night, she told Thomas only, "It's clear we're going to Vegas, now, Thomas. Vegas first. Now, I'm going to bed. Please watch my phone and let me know if Sandra texts back."

"I will," Thomas said. They parted ways in the hall, his room close to the ice machine and hers at the far end. The carpet was black but dusted with stars.

A peaceful sleep sounded idyllic. Once Beautiful got into her room, however, she didn't feel like going to bed. She felt like jumping out the window.

It then occurred to her that she didn't have to pass Thomas's room to get to the elevator. "I'll just go out to socialize a bit and make myself feel better," she said. "Sandra's not the end all, be all of friends. I'll make more friends! She's not even a good friend if she can't see the depths of my horror at her refusal, coupled with my clear willingness to appease her. And besides, I must remember what Ida Haze said about the kindness contingencies of others! They are exactly that. Contingencies!"

Beautiful took twelve hundred from her luggage and tucked it in her black lace bra. She put on a pretty dress, contemplated shaving, and decided against it. She did not decide against a pair of four inch Bordello heels tipped with silver and a stunning neck ensemble that resembled mangled daisies.

Since Thomas had been so kind, she considered asking him to go with her for this outing but rejected that idea almost immediately, thinking, *Mothers shouldn't take their children to bars.* She stared at her face in the mirror then shaved it once more. In the glass after, she surveyed her appearance and thought herself svelte. "I'm not less powerful with less hair," she said. "I'm just blending. It could be that now is simply the time to begin my new agenda of finding a Fedora Man alternate, a replacement."

She walked to a bar downstairs and across the street from the hotel, a clandestine looking joint that advertised a big interior, but had hardly any exterior lights. She strolled to a door manned by a large blond man with a leather jacket. "ID?" he said.

"Don't have it," she replied. "Let me through."

"Then you can't come in. The cops are breathing

down our necks."

She looked at him, said, "I can come in. You'll move aside and I'll enter," and proceeded to walk around him.

At first, lulled by her calm speech, he made no objection, but he grabbed her arm before she could pass. "Hey! Listen, I mean it, lady!"

"No, you listen, Whatever Your Name Is," she said. "I have had a long day, and two very long days before that. I lost my best friend today, and I don't want to be violent, I don't, Whatever Your Name Is, but I will *if I must*. Do you understand?"

He did not. He didn't release her arm.

Breathing deeply, she said, "I'll give you a hundred dollars if you just let me walk by in peace. I want to go stand by the bar," peeling a hundred from her bra and handing it over. His pupils were huge. He took her hundred and dropped her arm.

"Do what you want," he said, sniffling like he had a cold. Both his nostrils were rimmed in white.

"Thank you. I always do," she replied. "Did you dip your face in snow?"

Without answering, he wiped the back of his hand across his nose. She walked into the bar and considered ordering a Shirley Temple. "You there," she said to a young pretty girl at the bar. "What're you having?"

"Sex on an Island."

"Oh," Beautiful said. "That sounds good. Bartender, I'll have three Sexes on an Island."

Three orange drinks before her, Beautiful handed him a hundred. She observed the girl beside her, decked out in small shiny garments of white spandex. The girl's top was thin. Through the fabric, Beautiful saw the shape of her breasts and nipples, thinking: Apples. Little apples. The top ended just below the breasts, and the girl had been abdominally pierced, a small hoop with a long white crystal dangling at her navel. Below the navel were white hot pants, white fishnets, and white heels. Her hair looked mixed, blondish brown, and on her lips the most delicious shade of plum sauce clung.

Beautiful wanted to lick the girl's lips as the bartender handed her the change. When she saw other people giving dollars back to him, like a tribute, she surrendered two dollars per ordered beverage because that seemed the going rate.

"You got friends coming?" the girl beside her asked.

"It's always good to have friends coming," Beautiful said. "But I don't." She thought of Thomas. "Well, I have one friend who might come, but he's really more a driver, and he thinks he's my baby."

"I know what you mean," the girl said. "All men are big fucking babies!" She lifted her glass, cocked it at Beautiful, and took a sip. "Cheers to us!"

Beautiful did the same, but, "This doesn't taste like sex," Beautiful said, her throat warm and burning. "Or island. Sex tastes more like salt and perspiration. I've only really had it once, but it didn't taste like this."

The bar girl laughed. She had small pointy teeth and sat clumsily on her stool. Beautiful liked her enormously. "Well, sister, nothing ever does taste like sex, except sex," bar girl said. "Tuna or salt gargle. No damn island around here. My drink's almost out."

"Are they making you happy, this drink? Have one of mine," Beautiful said, sliding a full drink over to her new friend. "I'm disappointed with the taste."

"I'm disappointed too *and so* I'm getting *fucked up,*" the girl said, emphasizing assorted words in her sentence then repeating, "*Fucked up.*"

"I'm already fucked up," Beautiful replied. "Is it something to *get?*"

The girl smiled and patted Beautiful's arm. "Funny, you!" She dipped her hand into her shirt and lifted one breast then the other. "Balanced right?" she asked. "I mean the nips? So, you here to meet men? My name's Candy, by the way. Candy Louisa Kane."

Beautiful found Candy fascinating. She just wanted to watch her. "Maybe," Beautiful said. "If there're any decent specimens." Surveying the crowd, Beautiful noticed men thronging at the sides of girls wearing nearly next to nothing, like the girl Candy beside her. The heat of the press of bodies made the room feel tropical. In the heat and tropics of the situation, because of the plum lipstick, Beautiful thought Candy resembled a pop star.

"My name is Beautiful Ape Girl Baby Chef," she told Candy, figuring a trade-off was expected.

Candy gave her a wide sloppy grin. "Hi, Beautiful. Well, I can tell you everything about all the men in this bar. Every raunchy detail. I think I've slept with each of them on different nights, and every single one of them is a fucker! A real fucker!"

"Good to know," Beautiful replied.

Candy smiled again quite widely. "I like you, Beautiful. You're kinda different," she said, but if there was a slight slurring in Candy's voice, Beautiful neither under-stood it nor held it against her. They gazed warmly into each others' eyes. Candy wore big fake lashes with purple glitter, which Beautiful wanted to look at for quite some time until Candy whispered, "Give me ten dollars and I'll share half a hit with you right now." In Candy's hand was a small white pill.

"How do you share a hit?" Beautiful asked.

"It's easy," Candy said. "We just both take it." The lights in the bar flashed—blue, pink, purple, white. On the dance floor, people gracelessly groped. Beautiful watched a man's hand slide up under the back of a woman's skirt as he yanked her tightly toward him.

"Half a hit?" Beautiful asked, distracted.

"Yes," Candy said, placing her hand on Beautiful's thigh to massage it. "This is good shit."

"I usually take a whole hit or give a whole hit,"

Beautiful said, wondering who they planned on hitting. She looked at her black dress and wished it was smaller. *I should show more thigh*, she thought. *That's what they did out here.*

"Yeah, but I've only got one of these good pills and we've got to share," Candy said in a girlish voice, leaning closer to Beautiful until her lovely plum lips hung just inches from Beautiful's own mouth. "And I'll probably pass out in a minute anyway. I'm fucked up. So fucked up! You'll like it. I swear. This hit'll make you see fucking rainbows. Rainbows and starrrrrrrrssssss."

Beautiful handed Candy ten dollars. "Okay," she said, staring at Candy's small and elegant hands, her nails tipped with chipped acrylic, which were no good for hitting anyway. "You can try, but I don't think you'll hit me that hard."

Candy did something furtive with the little white pill at the bar. Then she gave the sweetest smile to Beautiful and lifted her tiny hand over Beautiful's drink, opening her thumb and index finger as if releasing a pinch, dropping half the pill. "It's done," Candy said. "Now just kick back for the ride. Drink up."

Obligingly, Beautiful sipped.

"Shit, there he is!" Candy then said, poking Beautiful in the arm. "The biggest fucker in the whole bar! Stay away from that one."

"Where?" Beautiful asked. She looked up, wanting to see the bar's biggest fucker, but the man Candy pointed to didn't seem that large. At his side, like some kind of clinging leech, was a woman with dry red hair. The woman's dress was made of red satin tied together with knots.

"She's a fucking slut, that girl," Candy said. "A total fucking whore! Bitch-whore!"

"I think you're much prettier than her," Beautiful said, thinking about compliments and apologies, which was how she now defined friendships. "I'm sorry she makes you unhappy, but Candy, you're so pretty. I could look at you for hours."

Candy's eyes teared. "Thank you!" She grabbed Beautiful's shoulders, pulled Beautiful close for a long hug, and planted her lips on Beautiful's cheek, leaving some plum lipstick. "You're a true dollbaby, Beautiful," Candy said. "Really something special. Oh god, I love you."

Beautiful was filled with warmth.

"Keep drinking," Candy said. "The night isn't getting any younger."

"So the big fucker," Beautiful inquired, "who looks like a little fucker to me, what's wrong with him, aside from poor taste in garments?" He wore a pair of light jeans and a velvety tiger shirt. On a man who more closely resembled a tiger, Beautiful decided, it would be lovely, but on this man, this big-nosed man with hardly any cheekbones, with small beady eyes scarcely decorated by the blond fuzz of his thin brows, it looked ridiculous. "I think he looks ridiculous," she said.

"It's not about how handsome they are," Candy slurred. "Good looking, not good looking…"

They watched as the redhead wrapped her arm around the man's shoulder and kept whispering into his ear. This whole couple was interesting to Beautiful, but not as interesting as Candy. She took another drink to show Candy she was listening. "Since you've sampled so many men," she replied, "I look forward to your expertise on what makes for a good man to make love to. I've had some limited experience with that, which went poorly. And then I had another experience, but I find it hard to understand."

Candy stared at her. "Right. It's better with women," she said. "At least they won't use you just to get their dick wet and then toss you aside."

"I guess I haven't been used," Beautiful said. "Or tossed."

"Like that guy," Candy went on. "You know what's so

bad about him? He's not good looking, and he doesn't have shit. He's an ugly guy with nothing special and so you think you're safe. Totally safe."

"Safe how?"

"Like he's not going to hit you or steal from you or something."

"Okay, that's good." As Candy spoke, Beautiful had regarded him more closely. She was not thinking he'd last long if he did.

"But then," Candy said, smacking the bar with a sort of angry woman's slap, "they pull their shit on you! They all have their shit! And you know what his shit is?"

"No," Beautiful replied. "I've no idea."

"He makes you feel so special, like he's totally all about you. He tells you your past doesn't matter. He tells you all kinds of shit. Even quotes poets and stuff, like, like, I don't know, name a poet. He acts like he doesn't think you're trash. And then you have sex with him. And you do that again and again; you do that so much, you think he's going to, like, stick around, but he doesn't fucking stick around. He just vaporizes. Poof! And then you know what you do?"

"Seek to destroy him or damage his vehicle?" Beautiful asked, interested on this point. Also, the room had begun to spin.

"What?" Candy asked, forgetting her train of thought, but seconds later reconvened with, "So, he drops you! Shows up at this beat-up place with some other hooker!"

"Another hooker? A real hooker?"

"Well, not really. Another girl kinda like you, *except not you*, which is why she's a hooker, and then—" Candy said, her small pretty face twisting up in an expression that looked like pain personified. "And then, you're nothing. You don't even get the break-up speech. And it's not that the break-up speech is good or anything, not like anyone needs another reason to feel shitty about themselves, because that's what break-up speeches do, give you more hang-ups! But at least," Candy said, slurring wildly, "at least they give you a good reason to hate that shifty motherfucker. You know what I mean, Beautiful?"

Beautiful still watched the biggest fucker. No, she had no clue. She'd never heard a break-up speech. Rather than giving one, Fedora Man had just bolted. But then she'd had no getting together speech either. Except maybe by allusion. *Blahblahblah, yet,* Fedora Man had said. *Blahblahblah, in the future, on our next interlude.*

The biggest fucker guy put his tongue in his current woman's ear, nibbling as they got nearer to the bar. "Fuck, they're coming. I don't want him to look at me," Candy said. "Hide me. Quick." And she pulled Beautiful around and planted her right between the fucker guy and herself. Then she said, "Quick. Kiss me. You're my girlfriend now, okay?"

Beautiful didn't know what was happening. All she knew was that the pop-star girl was plastered all over her, kissing her, and touching her. Those urgent little hands traveled over Beautiful's ass, over her back, around her sides to her breasts. It was pleasant, she acknowledged, but her head was fuzzy. And then the biggest fucker approached.

"Oh, so you've gone to the other side," he accused Candy.

Pulling away, Candy looked at him and spit on the floor. "Maybe so," she said. "Trading up."

"Well, you picked one butt ugly girl do it with," he told Candy, as the woman at his side snickered.

This Beautiful did not find funny or pleasant. She pulled her posture straighter. "You're not a tiger," she said. "You're a silly little worm of a man."

Candy's mouth fell open.

"She didn't think so," he said. "And her mouth was stuck in that O most of the time she dated me."

"I could kill you in less than one minute, Tiger Worm

Man," Beautiful replied. "Careful, now." She got off her stool and walked up close to him, only beginning to be enticed by the idea of killing him. She'd kill him for Candy. Liquor had loosened her inhibitions. "You quote poets? How about you quote poets as the stars fly around your heads. Lorca's a good choice. Also, Poe." She saw him with three heads. "I'll take my shoe and put it right through your forehead in a second," she told him. "This'll bother me not one bit. Here you take a gorgeous woman like Candy and you treat her like dirt, like less than dirt! Where was your break-up speech? You and your simpering little redhead don't impress me."

He pushed Beautiful, but hardly swayed her.

"Is that all you've got?" she asked. "I'm wicked strong." She grabbed her stiletto from her left foot, raised it in one of her hands, and said, "If this is the last moment you live, if this is the end of your miserable life as a cur and a scourge of womanhood, I'll at least have the pleasure of taking you out cranially. Your neck isn't even good enough for my hands." She raised the shoe, the silver tip of the heel aglimmer in club lights, his three heads appearing to waver as she stared at him, concluding she'd hit the center head first because that had to be the winner, the best balloon, and then the unthinkable happened, the untimely aperture of healthy violent escalation, the unexpected intervention, and the only thing in the world that could have possibly quelled Beautiful's will for vengeance just then, which had returned in a way she hadn't been attuned to since the wreck yard incident with Jake: That thing was the arrival and appearance of her son.

Thomas stood in the exterior doorway, his startled mouth agape like a baby bird's, his white hair brightened by outdoor halogens, his white mustache illumined too, him standing there tired in his rumpled black suit before he spoke, and what he said to her then, what he called out in a horrible, weepy, overwhelmed way, was, "No! Oh, God,

Mama. Please don't!"

Beautiful dropped her shoe and pushed Tiger Worm Man to the ground, stating, "I cannot make a bad example here. Because that's my son watching me, and I love my son. He's my special, precious baby boy, for whom I must set a good example. But if you approach me again, or Candy, I'll kill you with no remorse. I'll dropkick you and stab you and make you wish you were never born. Since you seem to use your package so damagingly, I'll attack that first and then I'll attack your lousy, thin-lipped, lying mouth. Do you hear me, Tiger Worm Man?"

The man backed off and entered the men's rest room. As she turned away from where he'd been, the lights assumed such a soft quality that when she looked back toward Thomas, she near mistook him for an angel, an angel of his more childlike self, and then she regarded Candy again, Candy in her blinding white outfit, the third piece of which was a scarf tied like a bandage around her right thigh. "Candy, come on," she said. "Let's go back to my hotel. You can tell me more about you there. We'll be leaving the biggest fucker here."

Thomas rushed toward them, blubbering, "That was so good, Beautiful. I'm so glad you didn't kill him, Mama. You had such self-restraint."

"I couldn't kill him in front of you, Baby," Beautiful replied. "I love you too much."

"Yes," Thomas said. "And, as Ida says, we must release our rage in productive, non-murderous ways."

"That's right," Beautiful replied. "There's no cleanup for murder, though it is occasionally necessary."

But, "Fuck. Fuck. Oh fuck, oh fuck. Uh fuck. Fuck-wow, fuck," Candy said, standing beside them, listening.

"Oh, Candy, you like the F-word, too!" Beautiful enthused. "Come on. You're safe with us. Let's go, Thomas. Are there three exit doors here, or do I imagine this?"

"There's one," Thomas said. "You okay?"

"She's on drugs," Candy announced, beaming. "I gave them to her."

"Ah," Thomas said. "Which drugs?"

Candy didn't answer.

"Let's get you back to your room," he told Beautiful.

"Great drugs!" Beautiful replied. "White drugs! They make everything so pretty!" As they walked outside, Beautiful began to stagger, but Candy staggered, too. They leaned on each other.

"What kind of drugs did you give her?" Thomas repeated firmly.

"I don't know," Candy said, bracing herself against the chill night air. "I had a bunch of them." She looked into a small turquoise wallet she pulled from her back pocket. In the bronze-clasped change purse, she had several more pills and a few tabs. A penny. A few quarters. "I'm not sure which one is missing. This was a great stash. But it was only half a hit she got, whatever it was. Oh, and we had Sex on an Island."

Thomas seemed more discomfited.

"Not real sex," Beautiful said. "A beverage!" Then Beautiful said, "The cars are crazy pretty, Thomas. Look at all the cars." She stopped to pet a headlight. If a darker revelation went on in her head, this was evidenced only by how she turned once beside a gold Saturn and kicked the wheel four times. Then she said to Candy, "You don't have to come with us if you don't want to, Candy. Thomas can drop you off at your home, wherever that is."

Not seeming to listen, Candy then dropped to the ground and bawled. Her skin and white clothes got dirtied by asphalt, black smudges every place her prodigious bare skin touched and even all over the white net stockings. Scuffs marked her shoes.

She's like a pig in the pen, Beautiful thought. *A skinny white pig rolling in tar mud,* except the asphalt was not wet, but "Candy, what could it be?" Beautiful asked, lifting Candy up. "You're getting all dirty. What's worse, you might be bruising yourself. But, mostly, you're getting really dirty. It's nasty."

"I'm getting evicted soon," Candy said. "This means I'll be moving back in with my mom. And my fish died last week. And I'm fucked up. Fucked up. And I loved him. I loved that fucker. Guess I won't be moving out with him now."

"Hmmm. Good thing I didn't kill him if you felt that way," Beautiful replied, yet Candy then seemed alien to her. What did she mean she loved that fucker? This would not be the first time that Beautiful didn't understand this strange girl whose mascara now ran down her face in creepy streaks. Candy attempted to stand.

"No, Beautiful. It'd be great if you'd killed him," Candy slurred in reply. "Just great. Then she wouldn't have him either."

Beautiful had a hard time staying focused, wanting to touch more cars, wanting to console Candy, wanting to touch more cars—but she said, "Why don't you come to the hotel and we'll take a swim. You and me. Swimming's good for emotion."

"I don't think you should swim, Beautiful," Thomas said. "You're on drugs."

"But I love swimming!" Beautiful said, waving her arms around to express the emphatic nature of her feeling and finding that she now saw trails of motion in the sky. And colors. "Oh, night rainbows are so beautiful, Thomas," she said. "Candy, I don't see any stars but I think I see night rainbows! Aren't there supposed to be stars?"

"I want to swim," Candy said. "Let's swim!"

"Oh good," Beautiful replied. "And I don't yet know about your flip-flopping love issue with the fucker, but you can come with us tonight and then if you want, you can come live on my estate, which is actually my father's, but you'll be my new friend and teach me all about men! It's about time I started hiring my own friends."

She thought about that for a second, got terribly worried, then asked, "Thomas, judgment call here, please—am I now supposed to be hiring my own friends, or not hiring my own friends?"

He helped Beautiful into the car before replying, "Don't worry about that now, Beautiful." He helped Candy into the car too.

"Thomas, since we're so close, why'd you drive the car across the street instead of walking to the bar as I did?" Beautiful then asked. "The hotel's right there."

"I'm a driver," he said. "That's what we do." There was shared silence as he pulled into the hotel parking lot.

"I get it! I'm not supposed to be hiring my friends," Beautiful announced. "That's what you're saying. All right, Candy. I'm not offering to employ you, but I'm offering you a comfortable place to live at the estate for as long as we're friends. And you don't have to do what I say, and you cannot be fired. Also, I'll fail to use you as a footrest and you can do whatever you want next to the pool, including throwing parties. There're no more boys there now, but maybe there'll be some when we get back. I'll hire one for you! Should I hire you a boy?"

Candy looked perplexed. "A hired boy for me?"

"You don't want hired friends either?"

"Well, what would such a boy do for me?"

"Whatever you want."

Candy warmed to the idea. "Really? You shitting me?"

"Thomas, am I saying something strange?" Beautiful replied. "Candy doesn't understand."

"You're on drugs," he said. "So, yes."

"Oh, drugs are marvelous," Beautiful said. "Look what my arms can do! I can make night rainbows!"

"Drugs are sometimes good," Candy said. "But don't do too much. They can also ruin your life."

Thomas pulled at his own door handle, opening his

door to exit. It was then that Beautiful realized they'd not yet gotten out of the car, but she felt a strong inclination to remain seated. "I don't want to move," she said. "Do we have to?"

"Yes," Thomas said. Without leaving the car, Thomas reached for something in the glove box and then reached back with his other hand to touch Beautiful's head, petting her face. He looked at the e-navigator as he said, "Just relax, Beautiful," but his fingers felt excellent on her skin, like they might have made her hair grow at an accelerated rate.

As he tried to pull away, she grabbed his wrist and kept his hand on her face, saying, "Keep it there, Thomas; your hand is like velvet. All over my face. Oh, that's good."

"Oh god, it's good shit I gave you, yeah?" Candy said, wiping away her near dry tears on the sweater still in the backseat, the one bled upon and snotted over. Candy smiled, rubbing that sweater on her own face, probably thinking about her hired boy.

Having a hired boy was good, Beautiful understood. "That thing's moving," Beautiful said, regarding the sweater Candy nuzzled, which now appeared to writhe like a small animal near Candy's eyes and then become a beautiful white cat, licking invisible tears away. "Say, Candy, you have a cat on your face," Beautiful told her.

"I do not," Candy replied.

"Yes, you do. It's pretty and I think it's a boy cat." Beautiful petted her own sweater.

"We're here now, and I say it's time to get up to our rooms," Thomas said. "Let me help you both up to Beautiful's. Ladies, try to act normal and walk straight as we go through the lobby. We don't want extra attention."

Once more, Beautiful glanced at Candy's tiny get up, now dappled with patches of asphalt smear, and found it hard to think they'd get no attention. She tried to walk straight. "Thomas, the doors are multiplying," she whispered, after avoiding the lobby clerk's eyes. "You have to open them for us."

No one bothered the group going up. As they arrived at her room, Beautiful turned to Thomas and said, "Has Sandra texted back? Is that why you came? Is that why you went out to find me?"

"Yes, Beautiful. That's why. I thought you'd want to know what she said."

"Which was?"

The ice-maker rumbled and busily dumped a load. "I'll tell you tomorrow," he replied, to the sound of falling ice. "After you're sober and have slept."

"No, tell me now, Thomas," Beautiful said and pushed Candy lightly into her room.

Thomas nodded. "Sandra said, 'Beautiful, I love you. And I'll always love you. But please don't come visit. Ever.'"

Beautiful stood in her doorway, feeling the impact of Sandra's words like a series of hard punches. Her mouth drooped. When she realized she hadn't yet replied to what he told her, she said, "Thomas I'm going swimming right now. Candy. Come on. Let's get dressed. I've three swimsuits. One is wet. Two are not. You choose among the dry."

The money luggage lay open on the floor. When Beautiful entered, Candy stared at it, unable to divert her attention. "The swimsuits aren't in there," Beautiful said. "I know my luggage shouldn't be stored on the floor, but I was too lazy to lift that one onto the rack. Maybe I was upset." She went to digging in a different bag, pulling out the two dry swimsuits. "The white one is wet," she acknowledged. "Or I'd have shared it with you." She didn't tell Candy that she'd already decided that the white suit would now be retired from wearing by anyone, perhaps made a shrine to, as it had been the garment in which she'd been bled, the one Fedora Man had admired and placed his hands on, though Fedora Man was long gone, because when a person was your first anything significant, she now knew, it brought them a place in your permanent memory, so you kept what reminded you. Beautiful sighed.

"You're totally rich aren't you, Beautiful?" Candy asked.

"We do fine," Beautiful acknowledged. "That's how my father puts it."

Candy still regarded the greenbacks in the luggage. "That's a fuckload of money," she said.

"Only one bag, out and open."

"Yeah, I'll say."

"Candy, before we swim, I think you should shower," Beautiful said. "You have asphalt all over you from rolling like a pig on the parking lot."

"All right," Candy said.

Beautiful closed the cover on the money luggage and sat on it, saying, "There's the bathroom. Go find it." She looked out toward the pool, which was a calming turquoise.

"All right," Candy said again, but Beautiful observed from the corner of her eye that Candy didn't walk to the restroom. She stood a few feet away, stripping. After kicking off white heels, she removed her white shorts and stockings. She then went for her blouse. "He shoulda stayed for this, don'tcha think?" Candy asked, flashing Beautiful her breasts.

"For what?"

Candy's hands traveled her own shape. "This! Can't you see how hard I work out?"

"You do look like a billboard girl," Beautiful replied.

Though an absence of physical desire marked Beautiful's appraisal, Candy attempted to elicit one by saying, "But look at my abs! Look at my tits! Aren't I hot? He shoulda stayed, right?"

"For your body alone?" Beautiful blinked, thinking the body was just a sack of watery flesh ultimately, that the body could be pretty like flowers, alluringly creating a hunger of sorts, as nectar did for bees, but it was how someone touched you and spoke to you that counted since pure physical allure had never determined who she wanted to get close to—or why. John Henry she'd wanted for his gentleness, Jake for how his posture resembled John Henry's, Fedora Man for his intelligence and difference, or maybe just because she liked his freaky unusual way. With Fedora Man, too, she felt a sense of sameness and blushing admiration that was bigger than her normal positive response to new people. With him, she felt a diminishment of the staggering differences she'd often decided destroyed her equitable relationships with others. Maybe it was his acceptance of her, or his desire for her, that drew her, whether he'd eventually left or not.

Though maybe his abandonment did mean non-acceptance now. "He should have stayed for your person, Candy," Beautiful said as Candy bawled, "if he was going to stay at all."

"My person? What the fuck is that?" Candy asked. She sat naked beside Beautiful on the luggage, and put her head on Beautiful's shoulder. "Like, who'd want my fucking 'person'? If some guy wanted that, I wouldn't have been with so many. I'd have stayed with one. I mean, I'm hot, right? Smokin' hot. It's enough they want my body." Candy laughed self-punitively, leaning in toward Beautiful, her bare breast brushing Beautiful's arm. "You want me, don't you? You might want me?"

Beautiful felt too conflicted to reply. Candy's lack of confidence was grotesque, but she didn't want to make the situation worse. "I like you very much."

Candy leaned away from Beautiful and slumped on purpose, forcing her stomach to create a small roll. "Yeah, I'm hot all right," she said, pointing to her belly. "But maybe not so much. Look how ugly now! So fucking ugly when I bend. I mean, he wanted the redhead. But what does she have that I don't, Beautiful? What?"

"I don't think she has anything," Beautiful replied carefully. "I don't know what she has, if anything."

"Wrong! She has him."

"He's a fucker, you said. You clearly said he's a fucker."

"Yes. But why did he start with me, and then drop me? I'm so much better than her," Candy replied. "He acted so sweet. And he loved this," she said, pointing to her crotch. "But then I guess he forgot about it. Oh well."

"I don't analyze my own body that way," Beautiful responded, staring out again at the pool's rippling skin of water. "I don't think you should compete with other women because he'll do the same thing to her if it's just her body he wants. He'll leave her. And if you don't like men so much, why do you have sex with so many? Do you enjoy that?"

Candy stood, stretching. "Oh, I like sex okay. It's what gets you shit. Don't you agree? You want it too, don't you? The shit!"

Beautiful remembered the couples in the bar, how they draped across each other in what seemed desperation, how the feast of flesh felt so empty, then and now. "No, Candy," Beautiful said. "I feel liberated. I've been abandoned and I'm glad that I never needed the shit from sexual exchanges. Now, I feel like I'm living in an absence of human hormones, but this is because nothing is so simple anymore. I have no idea what I want, and thus I want nothing."

As Candy walked into the bathroom and got in the shower, Beautiful fell onto her bed, shouting, "Get me up when you come out. We'll jump the fence if we have to… I want to swim." She contemplated putting on a suit, but that struck her as too much effort.

The room itself seemed hazy. Above her was a lamp with crystals, and she watched these sparkle for a while and then returned her gaze to the pool's surface in the distance, where now, visible through the window, a woman in a grey swimmer's cap had begun to swim.

The gate to the pool was left ajar. Someone had already broken the rules. And entered.

CHAPTER SIX SWIMMING AND SLUT DOMINANCE

~IN WHICH, BEAUTIFUL GIVES A LESSON ON FINANCE, IDA MAY HAZE INSPIRES NEW RAGE RELEASE EXERCISES, BEAUTIFUL GROCERY SHOPS, THOMAS WORSHIPS TREES, AND A ROBOTIC CARRIER PIGEON DELIVERS A MESSAGE OF AMBIGUOUS IMPORT FROM FEDORA MAN. ~

The swimmer was an old woman in a black sporty one piece. She swam on and on. Beautiful wondered what would drive an old woman out of her bed, late, late at night at a hotel, to swim, but what drove anyone out of their bed late, late at night? Something terrifies her, Beautiful thought. She needs to move. She needs to get back to the source.

Beautiful closed her eyes and pictured herself in the water beside the old woman and then in the womb, the selfsame womb where she always landed in her nightmares, the womb of fetal-eating dreams, only this time her twin had a face that looked just like her except was the billboard version, with a longer, straighter nose, with a delicate brow. Beautiful, in this dream, was covered with masses of hair. She seemed shorter, less graceful.

"Hey, Beautiful," she heard the womb twin call out, though the twin didn't usually speak in Beautiful's nightmares, "you know why you want to kill me in your dreams, don't you? Because I'm the beauty and you're the beast!"

At this, Beautiful curled fetal. She found she could not look up at this other twin, feeling the shame of knowing her other twin found her repulsive. "And you know eating me is so ghastly, don't you, Beautiful?" the other twin pressed. "Because I'm who they wanted you to be. I endangered you. If you'd let me live and then came out after me, you knew they'd get rid of you for sure. But what might you possibly do about that now? They're going to kill you like the freak you are, eventually. Like an animal. They'll make the ugly thing go away, like all shitty rich people do. You know it's true."

After this, Beautiful reached out and put her hands around her sister's neck and then the dream devolved into the same dream it always was, where Beautiful choked her twin and ate her sister's fetal body over the course of many hours. But as she finished choking her twin this time, the dream ended. As she awoke, she felt Candy's slim hands on her shoulders, shaking her lucid.

"What, Candy, what?" Beautiful asked, still groggy. "What is it?"

"You were screaming," Candy replied. "So I had to make it stop."

The money luggage sat zipped beside the door. Beautiful soon realized its misplacement. "You were going to steal from me?" she asked, grabbing Candy by the shoulders and shaking her lightly as if to elicit an explanation.

Candy, again wearing her white outfit rolled with soot, looked away.

"Look at me, Candy," Beautiful said, squeezing harder, but only so much as to keep Candy's attention. Awe, shock, and rampant dismay ran through her. The girl Candy was now so foreign as to be incomprehensible, so Beautiful took a moment to gape about this disloyalty. "You're supposed to be so pretty, Candy," Beautiful said. "What all the men in the real world want, but there's a reason why none will stay with you. You can't be trusted."

At this, Candy finally replied, "I didn't leave, did I? I woke you up instead."

"This is true," Beautiful said. "But I'm not a man to get shit from, I don't like being almost robbed, and you and I, we can no longer be friends. You can go."

"Look, you just don't know what it's like having no money. I've gotta go live with my mom. I don't know you. How could I know this whole estate thing is for real, or even that you'd let me stay like you say you would. And I've got no dealers there. How do I get my stash?"

"Drugs?" Beautiful asked.

"Yes. I need them. A lot."

Beautiful looked at this waste of a girl, so pretty yet so pathetic, so sad and forlorn. She picked up the luggage and opened it, grabbing a stack of hundreds as thick as her fist and handing it over. "Get free of the drugs, Candy," she said. "This is all I can do."

Candy started crying. She rifled through the stack, saying only, "This is a lot of cash, Beautiful. I can't take this much."

Beautiful, baffled, scratched her head. "You were about to steal the whole bag."

"But I didn't," Candy said. "I only thought about stealing it. But I never did. And then I woke you up—I looked at you, screaming in pain and fear, and I didn't want to do that to you, Beautiful."

Beautiful nodded. "That's good, Candy," she said. "Those drugs you gave me are bad in the morning."

"Bad all the time," Candy said. "Except when they help."

"I don't know if I was helped," Beautiful said. "But I saw several unusual visions. Did you swim last night?"

"Yes," Candy said. "Me and this sweet old lady. She swam more." Candy regarded the money again, like it awed her.

"So, take care of the drug problem," Beautiful said. "If you don't want to come with us." Candy kept looking at Beautiful, back toward the money, back again at Beautiful. "But I think you are too delicate for the rest of my journey, Candy," Beautiful continued. "And though you know a lot more about men, I should like to give you some advice about finance from my father now that you have a start-up stake." She put her hand on Candy's shoulder, feeling like an older sister, asking, "Do you know much about finance?"

"Not a thing," Candy said.

"I never understood it myself," Beautiful replied, "but I think that's because it was meant for the real world, and you, Candy, are a citizen of the real world!" Beautiful looked around her hotel room, at the luggage still inside the door. "And you're trying to do good. I can see that."

Upon this, Candy flung her arms around Beautiful again and kissed her once more on the cheek, this time with dry lips.

"You're quite demonstrative," Beautiful observed.

"I get it from my mother," Candy agreed.

"I really like that plum lipstick you have," Beautiful admitted, so Candy dug into her back pocket and pulled it out, shyly handing it over. It was still warm from being up against Candy's body. "Really?" Beautiful asked, removing the lid, turning up the plum color, and putting some on. She went to the bathroom mirror, looked at herself, and returned to Candy saying, "That was so generous! I love it! Okay, now here's what Daddy says. I shall paraphrase to cut down on time." She sat on the bed and pulled down beside her. "Candy, if whilst explaining this I happen to go into the lofty tones like Daddy uses, or unconsciously mimic his voice, you must remember Daddy has much clout and is used to speaking as if for an auditorium, even when he speaks only to his daughter. I'm giving you my father's wisdom so might channel him. All right. Here goes. When in the possession of money and earthly goods,'" Beautiful began. "You must consider how best to use your capital! People will try to get at you. They'll *want something*. They'll be creative in their desire to steal your hard-earned income, desiring something for nothing, as invariably people do, but if you employ them, you must be *fair*. You are the *dominant*. Tell them *the rate* at which you will pay and the *proposed duration* of employment.' This is in case you hire a boy, Candy. Tell the boy all this before he begins. 'Of money, neither borrow, nor lend.'" At this, Beautiful paused. "Daddy didn't like lending. 'Better to give away what you may not see again,' he often said. 'And don't give what you can't afford to lose.'"

Moved, Beautiful paused, remembering the low timbre of her father's voice as he spoke of such things, and she stroked Candy's hair very kindly, as he'd have done, before standing with her fist in the air, as he also would have done, going on, "And if you've got a lot of money, don't stash it in some gambling vehicle, but put it in the bank and let someone who's smarter than you manage it. Don't hire a lesser tier of broker because those who work on shoestrings will be tempted to tap into your wealth.' Now, Candy, I don't think I've given you enough money to have such concerns as a mogul like Daddy, so I'll try and condense the rest into his most oft repeated speeches. When Daddy said something more than once, it always meant something. You can count your money while I conclude. Okay, so listen close, because he gave much emphasis to this: 'And if people ask you if you have money, always tell them you're barely getting by! This reduces their urge to request money from you. But if you find something you do want to give money to, do it invisibly. That way, if you no longer embrace the agenda of a cause you've supported, you can seamlessly cut ties. Quiet giving is best. Make sure there's a tax shelter. Organizations or people to whom you make donations should be dealt with only for the purpose of farming money out, self-interest, charitable effort, or tax relief, such that they can return to you either karma, a hideout if necessary, or more wealth. The government will rob you blind. And don't buy the intangibles. This isn't possible, Beautiful, even if you try! Intangibles are not for sale.'"

Candy counted the money with a dull gaze. Whether she absorbed anything wasn't clear, but if Beautiful was of the mindset of giving advice to someone because she herself could never use it, in sharing this wisdom, she nonetheless wanted to finish because this last point, at last, she just now began to understand. "No, 'Intangibles cannot be purchased,' Candy, 'but always keep your person safe and never fail to care for those you love. Defend them with your pocketbook and your life.'" Beautiful teared up, thinking about how her Daddy always looked the second after he said *love*—and the sweet tremble that came to his voice. Touched almost to tears just recalling that aspect of his care, she cleared her throat, summing her speech with, "You and me, Candy, we're the intangibles. But, as Daddy would say, 'That concludes, Peanut, our lessons for the day.'"

"Oh, wow," Candy said. "Your Daddy's a talker!"

"Yes."

"Thanks, Beautiful."

"Sure. I don't know what he means by half of it," Beautiful admitted. "But maybe you do."

"He's so protective," Candy said. "Such a good Daddy."

"Daddy protects first, asks questions later," Beautiful said. "That's why I ran away. I've been so protected all my life, I couldn't even know what was real. He doesn't want me to know. And now I have to keep figuring out whether or not to hire friends..."

Candy shrugged. "I don't understand you, Beautiful," she said. "But you're one of the most generous human beings on the planet. I won't forget you."

"I can honestly say I won't forget you, either, Candy," Beautiful replied. "But please stop giving your beautiful body away to the fuckers." Candy stood in her white outfit smudged with asphalt, regarded her scuffed shoes, and gingerly held her new wad of cash that would not fit into her tiny turquoise wallet. "You'll need another purse," Beautiful then said before digging in her luggage for a Coach designer purse. When she found this, she dropped everything from Candy's hands into the main purse pocket. "Keep this purse," she said, handing it over.

Candy stood a little straighter, clasped Beautiful to herself one last time, and then disappeared out the door and down the hall. Beautiful listened to her go.

If she regretted the loss of the beautiful purse, she felt at least consoled that Candy looked so happy, but by the time Thomas came to get Beautiful that morning, saying, "Rise and shine, Beautiful, are you ready to go?" Beautiful had already decided that Candy's leaving was meant to be and that she'd have Thomas repeat whatever he said that Sandra said last night, and then ignore it. Because she wasn't giving up on Sandra.

When Thomas arrived, she rubbed his white-haired head with her hands, clasping him in her arms for the important morning therapy hug. "Mama's so sorry she was on drugs last night, Thomas," she said. "It was out of my control. I only thought the girl would hit me…"

Thomas, clutched to Beautiful's bosom, obligingly replied, "Not all Mamas are perfect, Beautiful. But I'm glad you didn't kill her man."

"Yes," Beautiful said. "It wouldn't have done any good. She still loved him."

"Where'd she go anyway?" Thomas asked.

"Started her life and such," Beautiful said. "I gave her money."

They took their luggage and loaded the car. "First Sandra's, then L. A. in just a day or two, Beautiful," Thomas said. "I've been thinking about how you don't like the Lincoln, and I think we should buy another car like Sandra's

Pinto. Park this one outside the barrio and go in stealth mode. We must look poor. People are violent in the barrio. And they might want this Lincoln."

"My trust is yours entirely," Beautiful said. "Do what's needed with the cars."

"We might want to look a little downscale too."

Fresh from considering her father's views on money and the luggage near-theft, Beautiful agreed. "Yes," she said. "In this real world, sometimes we have to hide ourselves better to preserve our safety. When we go to the barrio, I've decided I want to look like a rapper girl I saw in a video with a big clock around her neck. Time is ticking. *Tck-tck, tck-tck.* Mother is starving. And we must continue forward!" Beautiful glanced up at the dashboard clock before saying, "Look what time it is, Thomas! It's time for Ida's show. Put Ida on."

He fumbled with the dial before locating the station. When he found it, "In pursuit of the things we've lost," Ida May Haze began, "we must sometimes retrace our steps to where we've been, even if this means the old house of our parents or the shitbasin of our ex-boyfriend's, or the doghouse, anybody's doghouse. Sometimes, we all find ourselves in the doghouse of life. And so, I have an exercise I'd like to share with you listeners today; it's along the lines of other exercises I've used and demonstrated, perfect in the reduction of rage. This exercise is called squeezing the orange."

"Oh boy," Thomas said. "I'm so excited."

"We'll need oranges before long," Beautiful replied. "It's not good enough to just imagine rage reduction."

"Yes, a handy thing there's a grocery on the right."

"Okay," Beautiful said, "stop there. But be quiet now. I need to hear the whole show. Oh, Ida May Haze, how we both need you this morning! And I'm almost at your bosom, clasped to your heart, I hope, like the daughter I've always been to your teachings. Oh, Ida Haze. You're wonderful!" Beautiful felt briefly overcome with her fandom.

Thomas pulled into the grocery store parking lot and they listened to the rest. "I think we should make juice," Beautiful then said. "Juice from rage. Let's not waste it. A consumable is a good outcome. Were we novelists, we might make books, painters, paintings, but we're not. We're just travelers. So, juice!"

Thomas promptly agreed. As they entered, Thomas was helpful with not just procuring the oranges and putting them in a large wire basket, but also in the purchase of paper towels and wet wipes, which he said would be useful for cleanup. Additionally, they found a large pitcher, into which to squeeze the after effect of their collected rage, and a package of croissants.

"This is a beautiful place, the grocery store," Beautiful said. "Someone lined everything up neatly in rows." She also felt fascinated by the shoppers. "A lot of people must use these stores," she said, observing a mother with two small children, one of whom was caterwauling over a desired yet declined purchase of several long straws with red and blue stripes.

"I can't afford those," the mother said. "And you guys don't even throw them away. You leave them in the dirty cups!"

"But I want the straws!" the tow-headed boy shrieked. "I need them! Neeeeeeeeeeeed them!"

"How old is that child?" Beautiful asked Thomas. "The one with snot falling from his nose."

"Probably about three," Thomas replied.

"I don't care for him much," Beautiful said.

The boy's sister stood quietly next to the tantrum, unassuming and serious in a grey pinafore with small white sneakers tied with rainbow laces. "Please, Mama," she said calmly, with the attitude of an old woman. "He'll do this every time. He's crazy for these straws."

The mother sighed, her hand traveling over the row of

salad dressings. "No. He has to quit whining and throwing fits. He can't always have what he wants."

"I'll put away all my straws and his straws in the garbage," the girl said. With dark brown hair and a humble look, the girl grew more endearing to Beautiful, who whispered to Thomas, "Look how selfless she is! All for her brother!"

The girl stared longingly at a doll up on top of the dressings shelves and then back again toward her brother and mother. She didn't say she wanted that doll, but Beautiful knew.

"Thomas, please continue with purchases for our rage exercises," Beautiful said. "I want to look at things." Beautiful got a wire cart of her own and decided to follow this family. The first thing she grabbed was the straws. Three packages. The second was the doll. As the mother went forward, the three year old in the front of the cart and his sister walking along beside, Beautiful watched the mother shop for breakfast cereal next. Many times, the mother paused in an aisle and looked over the goods, seeming careful, investigating prices.

Beautiful, though she had no idea what she was doing, appeared to do the same. Three aisles later, she wanted to ask the woman, "How are you choosing what to buy?" but felt too shy. She'd caught the eye of the three year old because he waved from time to time and smiled with a gummy grin, missing his two front teeth, and the little girl, too, began to take an interest in Beautiful.

Once, bravely, Beautiful brought her cart right up alongside the family. The mother said, "Nice day, today, right?"

"Right," Beautiful said. "Good for shopping."

Noticing some similarity at what was in their carts, the woman said, "Did you see these rice boxes are on sale ten for ten dollars?"

"No, I didn't," Beautiful said. "They any good?"

"Decent," the woman said.

Just then, the girl in the pinafore wiped her brother's nose with a piece of fabric she yanked out of a black patent leather purse. Unwilling to seem she still watched or followed, Beautiful rolled past. In the back of the store, she noticed a whole row of cold meat. So much red. So many kinds! Thomas ran into her there and said, "Got everything. We ready?"

"Look at all this raw meat, Thomas," Beautiful said. "It's where they put the dead animals we'll eat, before they're cooked."

"We won't be cooking," Thomas said. "Let's not buy that. What else's in your cart?"

"Oh, it's what this woman I followed around wanted," Beautiful said. "Or what her kids wanted." Beautiful rolled her cart to the front and paid for Thomas's stuff and what was in her basket, the whole trip little more than a hundred. "Please tell the lady in the blue shirt with two small children that this is for her," Beautiful told the cashier after grabbing the bags Thomas selected. "She really likes the rice for ten or ten dollars. And the boy likes the straws. And the girl wants the doll."

As she walked outside with Thomas, Beautiful hoped the family would be surprised and pleased, even permitted herself a moment to imagine the happy smile the quiet girl might display when seeing the doll. She thought about calling Sandra to tell her about grocery shopping, how interesting it was, but texted her instead.

"Dear Sandra," she wrote. "I'm on my way to see you because I am your real friend and that's what real friends do. If you love me, you'll understand. Don't argue. I must squeeze oranges now, rage therapy with Thomas."

During the orange squeezing, however, Thomas and Beautiful concluded that this activity was nowhere near as satisfying as breaking glass. Also, their hands were sticky. "At least we get juice out of it," Thomas said.

Sandra texted back, but Beautiful, her hands dripping with pulp, could not check the text. "Thomas, do you think it's better for me to simply be happy that Sandra has texted back and not read her text?" Beautiful suddenly asked.

Thomas, driving with one hand but squeezing oranges with the hand closest the passenger seat said only, "I think two hands would be better for this rage activity. It's like only half my rage has an outlet. The hand that's angriest can't squeeze, Mama. It's holding the wheel! But you've been squeezing quite robustly. I don't know about the text."

"Yes," Beautiful said, "though two hands of mine now are sticky, and in order for us to do this activity together, I had to sit up here, which makes me feel both like we've run away together as criminals and that my private rage is on display. Granted it's only you, Thomas. But as your mother, I feel I shouldn't display my rage in front of my child. Many mothers have submerged their rage so as to protect their children, or have submerged their children to protect their rage, but I wouldn't harm one white-mustached hair on your head. Thus, I'm not getting real rage out here, only activity modeling. Maybe I should check that text message from Sandra."

"Do what you want," said Thomas. "But I think it'll only piss you off." Thomas intermittently used his prudently purchased wet wipes to wash his squeezing hand and the knife. "You're probably right. And so thoughtful, Thomas," Beautiful said. "Much like this enjoyable gay man I saw on a television show, from which I might conclude that gay men simply are the most thoughtful of men since heterosexual men hardly remember the small stuff."

Considering Jake and the greasers, a dark flash returning, Beautiful doubled her juicing speed. By that time, the pitcher was half full, gaining by the moment as they continued chucking rinds out the window until one chucked rind nearly hit a pigeon flying beside the car, which Thomas then noticed, glancing in the rear-view. "Beautiful," he said.

"That odd bald pigeon appears to be trailing us."

Beautiful glanced over. "Wow. That's strange. Why's he flying so low? Did you nail him with that last orange?"

"I don't know. I think so. But he's pretty skilled at dodging."

"Slow down," Beautiful said. "Or pull over. We'll let the pigeon pass."

A moment later, however, the same pigeon flew up to Beautiful's passenger window, wearing a leather carrying case, pecking at the glass, so "Pull over, Thomas," Beautiful said. "It's a carrier! Oh, how great! Daddy told me all about these! Perhaps Mommy has written! What do you think she says? I'll tell you: 'Beautiful Ape Girl Baby, you bad, sassy thing, you've worried your mother to death! Get home this instant! I told you Daddy's been disassembling things. Don't you see this pigeon? This means he's disassembled all the phones!"

"Haha. Mrs. Chef hire a carrier pigeon. Not likely. She's too clean. Pigeons carry plague," Thomas replied.

"Then who'd send me a plague bird?"

"Fedora Man?" Thomas guessed.

"Maybe. But this bird has a message," Beautiful said. "And while it mightn't be for me, it might as well be for me. It'll be mine when I open it. Besides, the pitcher is full so we can now have our breakfast in that nearby field. Three bags in, we're out of oranges and I'm hungry. Time for croissants."

When Thomas pulled over, the pigeon again tapped the passenger side glass with its beak and Beautiful cleaned her hands before opening her window. "Yes?"

The bird flew into her palm "He's a spy bird," she said, observing his strangely rubberized head and the way he nudged and rubbed her palm with his skull, like he attempted a ridding of old skin. "But I'm right! He does have a message packet."

"I think it's a message for you from the government,"

Thomas replied, smirking. "Dear Beautiful Ape Girl Baby Chef: Pigeons carry plague. Put that dirty bird down! Wait! No! Maybe it's from your mother!" Finding himself hilarious, Thomas chuckled.

"My message does not say that!" Beautiful exclaimed.

"Maybe it does!" Thomas replied.

"It does not, Thomas!" Beautiful argued, glaring wickedly at him, he who had begun to snicker more and more while munching his fresh croissant. She thought about Sandra, the unchecked text, the stress of which making her want to wring the pigeon's neck even more because those feathers were so soft and tempting. "If I haven't yet read a text message from my very best friend in the whole world, Thomas," Beautiful said, reigning in her urge to kill. "What makes you think I want to read a message from a random pigeon first?"

"I don't know. Maybe you don't," he replied, but wisely took this moment to walk off into the nearby trees with a cup of juice and the rest of his croissant. "I have to use the little boy's room, Mama. Which means the woods."

"Why is it that for little boys, the world is your restroom?" she called after him. "A girl child, raised rightly, does not view every bit of passing foliage as a toilet!"

Thomas may or may not have heard her, but Beautiful couldn't be bothered to repeat herself. She took the packet off the pigeon's back. Inside, there was small note in squalid script. "I've been thinking about you a lot," Fedora Man wrote on the enclosed letter. "I have to see you again. Love, fm."

"Awwwww," Beautiful said. Now, Beautiful had never written Fedora Man a letter, but even if she had, she would have signed off BAGBC, short for Beautiful Ape Girl Baby Chef, so what was all this lowercase "fm" about? She thought of him in uppercase, but this was apparently how he signed off. Did he think he was a radio station? "You give good love, bayyyybayyyy," she sang aloud, recalling the mystery burst from the radio the last time she'd thought of him and wondering if he might be possibly acknowledging her more powerful presence by his small letter sign-off now, despite his obvious potential for evil, oh snooze. And besides, Beautiful had read a bunch of malarkey about dominance and submission once, when she'd decided she wanted to train an aggressive dog, but then she'd read about animal behavior, not human, so this didn't help. Also, her exercises in dominance had been too vehement with and the dog—the choke chain—things did not go well.

What am I supposed to do with this weird pigeon message, she thought?

The pigeon hadn't left by the time she was done thinking. He waited. He pecked desultorily at a bit of dropped croissant and paced, just like a mad little old man. "He must await a reply!" she exclaimed. "I suppose I should say something in return."

Inexperienced in matters of romance however, Beautiful felt clumsily unsophisticated. Staring hard at the pigeon and hoping to think of a good response, she noticed that the pigeon's legs were metallic and jointed, a bot bird! His eyes seemed glass, she now concluded—a glass and metal fabricated bird, glued over with rubber and feathers! Fedora Man had high technology.

"What the freak do I say to any of this?" she mused aloud. Also, Fedora Man's message had been so minimal. "I'm only used to writing to men who don't pursue me," she continued, "when I can be my full luxurious self because I'm sure they'll reject me!" And what should she reply to a man who had made love to her, disappeared, left a message on a napkin with nasty pastries, and then further sent a message of only two lines, transported by bald, mechanized, carrier pigeon?

Thomas hung by a copse of distant trees. She thought to ask his advice, but in this moment, he stood before one and performed bizarre, ritualistic bowing. "He's sanctifying the place where he pissed?" she asked the pigeon. "Is that what?" When the pigeon's tail feathers quivered, Beautiful lifted them curiously, and in response, the creature shat out a metal ball.

Meditatively, Beautiful wrote, on the other side of the paper the pigeon had delivered, "Who cares, fm? WHAT are you going to DO about it? BAGBC." She wrote this, but felt a moment of piercing remorse at her abrupt and ruthless rejoinder, and because of this, she elected to squeeze the word "Love" between "it?" and her initials.

Being a squinched "Love" as it was, however, it didn't look very loving, moreover looked every bit the obvious afterthought it had been, so she followed up with "More sex please. Name a date," before shoving the missive back into the carrier pigeon's packet and shooing him away. He flew off in the wrong direction. "I should have killed that pigeon," she said. "He'll never get anywhere."

She then read the new text from Sandra, which stated, "You can't come to me. I'm indisposed."

"The hell I can't," Beautiful then texted, but cancelled her reply without the satisfying *shoooooooop* noise she got when a message had been released. She should wait to respond to Sandra now, she knew, as Fedora Man's mystery continued to rankle her. She should deal with that first. It was enough to watch the drunk-seeming carrier pigeon fly first one way and then the other. She had her doubts he would ever find his way back to his master.

If she spent a moment wondering whether or not she should've attempted a more romantic letter, a long one, like the ones she'd read in books, she consoled herself that A.,

Fedora Man would not likely read a long, dippy ass love letter, and B., the dippy ass bird he sent her was unlikely to weather the weight of the existing message, so a heavier missive might've made the odds worse when aerodynamics, incompetence, and load were considered.

It was better she'd kept her reply short.

In his absence, she suddenly tried to imagine Fedora Man's face, but all she could conceive was the feeling of his face against her thighs. The sound of his voice. *I should have taken his picture at least*, she thought, ashamed that the face of her first lover seemed alternately available and lacking in her visual mental landscape.

"Thomas!" she called. "Thomas! Get your tree worshiping ass back here! Thomas, we must talk about this world as your restroom treatment soon!"

CHAPTER SEVEN VIOLIN CONCERTOS, FRIENDSHIP, AND DIVORCE

~IN WHICH, HELICOPTERS, HELLIONS, HORROR, GENDER DYSPHORIA, FREUDIAN ROMANCE HAMARTIA. ~

Beautiful had fallen asleep in the backseat as the next monumental step transpired two hours later. Fedora Man flew in from above in a black AH64 Army Apache helicopter. Below the helicopter dangled a net. He spoke down at the car via loudspeaker and told Thomas to pull over. In the midst of his first utterances, Beautiful slept.

She awoke to the sound of Fedora Man's nasal voice telling Thomas he'd leveled a destructive device at the road, and if they didn't pull over, he'd crater the path in five minutes. The countdown had begun. He paid special emphasis to the cratering.

Beautiful rubbed her eyes to view Thomas, whose pallid face grew increasingly terrified. Thomas, meanwhile, shouted from the front seat, "Mama, wake up! This could be an emergency!"

"Well, is it an emergency or not, Thomas?" Beautiful asked, yawning. "Your learned assessment could impact my willingness to get up."

"CRATERED!" Fedora Man thundered. "Three minutes and thirty seconds."

"Yes," Thomas said. "Clearly an emergency."

Beautiful glanced up at the copter, listening to the cratering talk. "He's so cute," she said. "What a peach. But I don't agree. It's not an emergency."

As she'd slept, the landscape had changed from green familiar woods and suburban strip malls into barren gray hills. Not only did Thomas and Fedora Man simultaneously speak to her, but her phone was ringing. Automatically she checked the phone display before addressing the rest of the situation. Sandra! Oh good!

Beautiful picked up. "Yes, Sandra?"

"Beautiful Ape Girl Baby!" yelled Sandra. "You're not coming out here! I forbid it!"

"Yes, I am," Beautiful said. "Any minute. And you could be nicer about it! I wanted to come *before* I visited Ida, to take you with me *while* I visit Ida."

When Fedora Man said, "CRATERED," again, Beautiful rolled down her window and stuck her head out with the cell phone attached to one ear, glancing up. She waved to him, grabbed her backseat megaphone and said out the window, "Shut up a minute, will you? I'm now awake," as, "You cannot come out!" Sandra pleaded in her ear. "It's been bothering me ever since you said you would."

"Don't tell me to shut up!" Fedora Man called down.

The terror on Thomas's face increased.

"Get in the seating net!" Fedora Man commanded, but Beautiful waved his insistence off by shaking one hand out the window in the universal stop-crawling-up-my-ass gesture, but also tried to clear her mind for negotiations with Sandra.

Striking Asp was the tactic she chose, confident her father would agree. In conversation, this maneuver was where you quickly struck with a baffling question that would prove beneficial to your party regardless of response. She learned this from his Business 101 tapes, only the sort of thing normally expressed was similar to, "Will you agree that we can liquidate your company, or will you elect to use our newly selected cost-efficient management team?"

Nonetheless, friendship still stuck her as business with no fail-safe primers, so she followed up with Sandra, in a sweet tone to show her docile yet concrete intentions, "And so, do you plan to be happy when I arrive to visit, or to be my friend without a visit?"

"Uh, what?" Sandra asked.

"You heard me," Beautiful replied. "Now, you can respond." She wanted spoken leverage before giving up what shaped up to be a clear victory on her side.

"I suppose I could be your friend without a visit," Sandra said.

The noise of the chopper increased. "Does this mean renewed phone contact on a daily, or weekly, basis?" Beautiful inquired. Simultaneously, Fedora Man demanded, "Pull over right now, driver. I must speak to Beautiful. Or I'll blow up the road."

Beautiful's temper flared. "The hell you will!" she said into her own megaphone. "I just woke up. We don't have plans. What're you doing here?"

"Don't you want to talk?" Fedora Man asked, a whine entering his voice. "The pigeon note said—"

"Well, I had no faith that pigeon would ever get back to you, much less so soon, and I definitely didn't think you'd show up while I'm so busy. Additionally, I now have my adult child Thomas with me."

"I have missed you," Fedora Man said.

"Adult child?" Sandra asked. "What the hell's going on, Beautiful?"

"Nothing," Beautiful told Sandra, keeping the cell phone with Sandra glued to one ear. "Just my boyfriend in a helicopter. Daddy had several of those helicopters. This new guy seems mildly possessive and I like that." She allowed herself the momentary weakness of enjoying a swoon that Fedora Man had arrived to retrieve her with a net after all, he who'd before professed he didn't want her caught in any of his nets. "He thinks he's powerful, but he's really a softie. Hold on, Sandra. Let me flash my breasts at him. That should appease him while we speak."

At this, Beautiful heard Sandra's insuck of breath. "You shaved?" Sandra asked.

"Oh, mostly," Beautiful said, leaning out the window again and lifting her shirt. "But I can assure you, he doesn't care! We've been *intimate*, and he likes my hair." The air felt grand on her bared skin. Thomas couldn't see her. No other cars littered the road. As she glanced down at her breasts, Beautiful noticed the hair there was short indeed, but had begun to soften and curl.

"Let me get my binoculars," Fedora Man called down.

"So did you want us to come get you or not?" Beautiful asked Sandra a moment later, re-entering the vehicle and zipping up her Juicy sweatshirt.

Thomas then dropped the dividing glass. "Mama, your father checked his craft out, and this guy is not the army or the police. But he's likely to have big guns."

"He's no danger," she told Thomas. "He's mob. Or something. Maybe Mama's new boyfriend, Baby; introductions can come later. Now, Sandra—"

"I don't k—" Sandra began, only to be interrupted by Fedora Man saying, "Beautiful, that was a great show, but aren't you going to talk to me today?"

Beautiful grabbed her own megaphone and replied to him, "About what?"

"I need a moment to discuss our relationship."

"We have no relationship. You left me."

"Now I'm back."

"Relationship? What in the blazes?" Sandra queried, overhearing.

"I'll tell you in a second," Beautiful told Sandra, but, "So? Back for what, fm?" she demanded.

"Nothing in particular," he hedged. "Some general

questions."

"I'm on the phone with a friend now," Beautiful said upwards. "Come back later. How about in an hour?"

"Are you talking to him or talking to me?" Sandra asked, irritable. "Because, by the way, I have never not been your friend, Beautiful, but the point of this conversation should be that I don't want you to see me here. Not in these circumstances! Your father said he gave you my address. He also said you fired me."

"You said you weren't employed by the estate when I offered to hire you as my friend," Beautiful whispered, somewhat agitated. "Which means you were being paid as my friend already. Did you plan to be doubly employed by the same source? That doesn't seem fair or right, Sandra. Just a second."

A violin sonata, Bach Sonata No. 1 in G minor, played by famed violinist Isaac Stern, issued forth through the helicopter speakers, accompanied by a strange noise that might have resembled a heart-warming serenade had it not so closely resembled a dog's bay.

"He wordlessly sings his love!" Beautiful said. "How cute!"

"There's singing going on?" This was Thomas.

"That's beautiful," Beautiful said out the window to Fedora Man. "But come back later!" Despite her clipped address, she was touched he remembered her musical preference, revering as she did musicians who did more than just play—like how Isaac Stern had saved New York City's Carnegie Hall from demolition in 1960 and championed several young violinists in his long career.

"So what is the story with this new boyfriend?" Sandra asked. "And is that music I hear?"

"Yes. It's beautiful." *Store this moment away,* Beautiful thought to herself. *It's like the dance with the butterflies. Fedora Man remembered far more than he gave himself credit for. His memory was actually pretty spotless.*

Still, her best friend was at stake and that meant more than catering to a lover, so to Sandra, Beautiful Ape Girl Baby announced, "Here's what I'm doing next. I'm traveling to get you then we'll go into the barrio to meet Ida Haze! Really, do you think me so shallow as to care where you live, Sandra? I would love you as my friend if you were the poorest church mouse staying in a degraded brick dwelling and endangering humans with your feces. I would love you if the halls of a great tower toppled and you lived in the dirt! I would—"

"Was that Bach Sonata No. 1 in G minor?" Sandra asked, catching Beautiful's drift. "Oh, double plus romantic! I like this guy!"

"Yes," Beautiful replied. "Isn't he dreamy?"

"I'll say," Sandra said. "But what's this about the barrio?"

Thinking of the approaching barrio, Beautiful then remembered to tell Thomas, "We need not forget that we'll need to buy a new beater truck and that I want that big clock for my neck like a rap girl."

"A beater truck?" Sandra echoed. "What? Again, you want to take me to the barrio?!"

"Yes, they have one of those barrio things in Los Angeles," Beautiful said. "It's where a bunch of poor people gather around and commit crimes of theft and violence."

"I can't come back later," Fedora Man said, halting the music. "We have to resolve this today."

"Look, I'm really conflicted right now, Ivor," Beautiful said out the window again. "After all, I liked you very well and then you left. Now, you come back, playing my music, knowing very well it will stir me to the heights of aural ecstasy, but what sort of afterlude is that?"

"I gave you pastry," he said, indignant. "And a bird! And a note!"

"Yes, an ambiguous note! A bot bird I wanted to kill! And no clue what would happen next!"

"That couldn't be avoided."

"I'd say it could!"

"You asked what I was going to do about missing you in the pigeon message," Fedora Man replied, persnickety and verging on cross. "Well, here I am."

"Ground the helicopter now and we can talk," Beautiful responded. "One moment from now, and I won't care what you do."

"Mama," Thomas said. "Should I pull off the road?"

"Let's hear his reply first, Thomas," Beautiful replied, before raising the soundproof glass to tell Sandra, "I enjoyed him in the bed, too! I have to tell you this situation quickly and get your advice. So I met this guy at a hotel. I call him Fedora Man or Ivor, sometimes FM or fm, upper and lowercase. He and I had sex. Actually, we made the most beautiful love. At a Hyatt. It wasn't Paris, but it wasn't the junkyard! I didn't kill him. I wanted to keep him forever. Then he left. Now he's back in a helicopter! And he wants to talk to me. Except I don't think I have time for a lover now that I take on intensive parenthood. Thomas, the driver, has taken on the identity of my past-the-womb child since I unfortunately clocked him in the head, so I'm raising him again. This adds complications for a quick renewed fling if Fedora Man does come down since it might distort Thomas's new childhood—"

"Thomas, the white mustached driver?"

"Very good, Sandra. But stay with me. I need advice on the other man... So I could play a retiring maiden for FM, though I've never been good at that according to the drama tutor, and I did detail in my note for him to come for more sex, which I'd now be declining due to Thomas's delicate sensibilities. He's like a Russian guy, isn't he, my new love? With three names. Anyway, what do you suggest?"

"That's a lot to absorb," Sandra replied. "Can I hear the shorter version? The simpler one?"

"Past good sex with guy now in helicopter overhead.

New adult baby now driver. No child witnesses possible for continued sexual affair. Later sex acts likely aborted. Mayday? Abort all or none?"

"I'm not feeling much helped by that summary," Sandra replied.

"Then maybe you should just be happy we're coming to get you!" Beautiful said before Fedora Man announced, after the lull, "I can't pull over. I can't land on this hill. Agree to pull over at the next town."

"Don't care about the next town," Beautiful said. To this, stalling, tilting her face out the window, she went on, "By the way, I very much liked your bald pigeon."

"Thanks," Fedora Man said. "I smoothed his head. Are you pulling over?"

"Probably not."

"Why not?"

"I don't feel like it."

"Ooh, you're in trouble now," Sandra said. "He'll think you don't like him."

At the same time, Fedora Man said, "All right. I can see you're feeling shy. But tell me, do you still think you can love me, though I left you?"

"I'm not really sure," Beautiful replied. "Can you rephrase the question?"

"He asked if you can love him," Sandra answered, overhearing. "It's a simple question. Yes, or no?"

"Simple for whom?" Beautiful replied. "I don't just throw such words around lightly, Sandra! Except when they involve non-romantic love."

"I think I sort of still love you, Fedora Man," she replied, "Yet I'm aware we just met."

"We did a lot more than meet."

"Yes, and then you bailed like a louse. Let me think about it." Beautiful thought for a minute. After a minute, she didn't think she loved him. He'd dickishly vanished. Still, it was possible that she did. It was also possible that this whole trip, since she'd left the estate, was quite eye-opening, an experience needing thoughtful digestion, so would require a few weeks of consideration. Perhaps a conversation with Daddy. But, in that time, she could lose fm. "As you noted before, Fedora Man," she stalled. "I'm very young. Only seventeen. Also, ambiguous and flighty."

"Sandra," she queried, "What do you think? Could I love Ivor?"

"I don't know."

"Tell me what you think based on how you know me."

"You might love him because you love things instantly. You also might not love him since you drop them just as fast. But he's a little nuts to ask if you'll love him right after recently dumping you at the hotel with no recourse. I don't know… Flip a coin?"

"You said age doesn't matter," Fedora Man replied down.

"It didn't matter to me," Beautiful said. "But you keep bringing it up."

"So do you love me or not?"

"In my way, I love you," she replied via megaphone, but when he asked, "What does loving me your way mean?" Beautiful pulled her head back in the car, speaking only to Sandra to say, "There is love and then there is love. Do I love him like I love Mommy or Daddy, parents of my growth and patient organizers of important scholarship? Certainly not. Do I love him as I love Ida May Haze, champion of eradicating base feelings and proponent of powerful women's rights everywhere, voice of shining reason in the horrid darkness? No! He cannot touch Ida for merit or importance. Do I love him as I love you, Sandra, my friend of many years for whom I have a huge amount of admiration and years of equity, camaraderie, and care? No, not that way. Do I love him as I now love Thomas, as a sweet child needing my guidance and protection? No, Sandra, not that way either! Do I love him the way I loved John Henry, where it felt my heart would fall out every time I thought of him and I wanted to kill any girl he went near—kill them—I mean rip them bodily apart with my bare hands, drain them of blood, and make them regret th—no! There isn't that sort of ownership. But, he makes my thighs tingle. And that's worth something. He's kind. Attractive. Funny. Sweet. Also, I let him bleed me. He was my first cunt stab."

"Perhaps it's just intense lust," Sandra said. "The connection between two strange and different creatures."

"Oooh, that sounds romantic," Beautiful praised Sandra.

"Thank you," Sandra said. "I thought so, too."

"Listen, my own way is my own way," Beautiful shouted via megaphone out the window. "You'll find out by and by."

"What exactly does that mean?" Fedora Man pressed.

"I do love you," Beautiful said upwards, "like I'd love a new dog. Okay?" She forgot for a moment that she'd told him she'd killed the last dog she tried to train, this excessive training a result of the dog's inability not to piss the rugs.

"I don't think I'm coming to see you after all," Fedora Man muttered. "I'm flying away."

"That wasn't a good reply about the dog," Sandra added. "He's pissy now. And he's leaving."

"Well, if you're that namby pamby of a suitor, then I don't think we'd last that long anyway!" Beautiful replied via megaphone.

"Is that so?" Fedora Man asked.

Beautiful paused in indignant silence, nodding the affirmative without speaking.

"You're losing him," Sandra said.

"I'm out of here," Fedora Man echoed.

"So be it," Beautiful replied upwards. "Get the fuck out. Go ahead! You went before! Is this supposed to be *new* to me? What, let you back in, so you can abandon me again?"

Thomas, seemingly fearful, dropped dividing glass to caution, "Don't antagonize him, Mama! He has a big gun on that helicopter. He could blow our car off the road. Should I pull over?"

"Oh, let him try to blow us away!" Beautiful said. "Like he'd have the nerve! Cratered! Cratered! Bah! Little fm."

In the sky, the helicopter turned.

"I take it we keep driving?" Thomas asked.

"Yes, keep driving," Sandra shouted, but because Beautiful was the only one to hear her and the effect of multiple conversations at differing volumes was confusing, Beautiful resultantly shouted both, "Sandra stop shouting in my ear," into the cab and "Damn it, yes, Thomas. Proceed," before remembering to lower her voice.

"You know, some men consider an argument a strange sort of foreplay," Thomas reflected seconds later.

"*Tck-tck, tck-tck,*" Sandra said, eliciting the childhood sound they both knew as comforting.

"*Tck-tck, tck-tck,*" Beautiful replied, looking up to note that Fedora Man's helicopter had indeed gone. Whether the man inside was wrenched in great waves of despair, Beautiful had no idea, but "Oh, I think I really messed that up," Beautiful added, before brightening with a change of topic to ask, "So, Sandra, should Thomas and I speed to come and get you or not? We'll drop in soon!" She waited. Sandra sighed. As Thomas drove, Beautiful saw they'd entered a patch of desert. Dunes arose. "Don't you need to be comforted again, Sandra?" Beautiful asked. "Wouldn't it be better to comfort each other where we can embrace like kindred spirits and plot small acts of vengeance?"

"I don't think I should go anywhere unsafe because I'm pregnant, Beautiful," Sandra finally admitted. "And Eugene has left me for a stripper."

"Fucking Eugene," Beautiful replied. "Left you in the

sand pit? Oh, the desert is a monstrosity. Completely useless." She regarded the cacti. The gray-strip road led into an enormity of uninhabited sand and the sun began to droop, reddish, in the darkening sky. Beautiful didn't care for the wide slope of the barren hills, nor could she see why anyone romanticized it. Certainly, one person standing on a hill of sand could feel alone, should aloneness be desired. Certainly, it was cold there, though hardly ever snowy, and when it was not cold it was nastily hot. The only thing useful about the desert, she thought, was to make a person grateful for a mirage or man-made exorbitant paradise at which to arrive. "Sandra, light on the dunes is best viewed via professional photography," she added. "It's not like you can lean against a cactus and feel a sense of company, of warm bark, of sheltering leaves—not like you did with a sycamore or oak on the estate! No, in the desert you got pricked. A prick pricked or pricks you. Many pricks! Consider Fucking Eugene. And this is why, Sandra," she said. "Daddy prefers Vermont to Nevada, only using the latter to bury people: Because the desert is a good place for burial but ridiculous to inhabit!"

"Your daddy has more power than I do," Sandra said. "And money. Besides, I can live here for free."

"You can come with me for free, too," Beautiful said, but, at Sandra's mention of her father, she felt a sharp, terrible pang of missing him. As Sandra erupted into tears, Beautiful remembered how it felt when her father coddled her on the big leather loveseat long ago, saying, "Don't worry, Baby. I love you," and, "Everything will be okay. *Tck-tck. Tck-tck,*" because there was hardly anything more comforting in the world, so she then said the same to Sandra, to the sound of Sandra's gentle crying and escalating moans. Then she listened to Sandra's breath, to her jagged inhales, which slowly smoothed.

The idea of Sandra calming resultantly calmed Beautiful, who went through an attempted self-guided meditation, imagining she and Sandra were both were lotus blossoms, picturing her friend's mouth drooping open like it did at home when Sandra focused on thinking something so hard that she also partially closed one eye and her hands went limp. "Be the flower. Be the flower," Beautiful mouthed, just before saying, "Come on, honey. I'll protect you. Tell me you're coming with us," giving an audible nudge while deciding they were no longer flowers but instead dual moonbeams. Or dolphins. Or baby tigers! "Sandra, you left the estate," Beautiful said. "Eugene left the estate. And now, within days of leaving, you've changed your life and moved out into the godforsaken shithole desert, the land of sand where no one is happy. I have never seen a happy people movie in the desert. I imagine because the desert is a place for camels that spit! Robberies. Pyramids! Mummies! If you stay here, you could be stung by wild scorpions! I saw this on *The Radiant Planet* show. Like, say you're lying on your bed one night, and one of those silly ouch-ass bugs crawls up on you, maybe pauses on your chest, like it would stay still and interesting to look at but leave you alone, THEN zap, zapzap—sting, sting, sting! That's all they do with you know, scorpions? Shit, eat, mate, sleep, and sting? But there are desert spiders too. I know because I have watched the desert series a million times: Sandra; there are many nasty little creatures in the desert! And that's where you've gone? As if all this change weren't enough, you've also shoddily disregarded the love of your very best friend on the planet, who is me. Me. Myself, Beautiful Ape Girl Baby Chef, who loves you like the moon and the stars draped in a single basket, loves you more than Eugene ever loved you and you know why? Because *I never slept with you!* I instead loved you with the deep heart of someone who really only wanted true decency and good for her friend, not necessarily the bountiful magnificence of her friend's body, though that could've been exciting—but one who wants nothing of yours except the sound of your sweet voice and your enduring friendship. Because without you, Sandra, I have no best friends. Regrettably, I'm alone in world. So I want you back, okay? I need you back. I need you with me."

Beautiful heard Sandra sniffle, which she took to be a good sign, so she skipped the "Pretend We Are like Two Orphans" part she nearly presented, forging ahead. "And if I want to pay you to keep you as my friend, if I do that, it is only to keep you in comfort so that you may enjoy our loving friendship without feeling like a burden or a pauper. About Thomas, in case you're jealous—you may not be, but in case you are, let me soothe you: Thomas is strictly my child. Thomas resembles my friend, but the burdens of parenthood are different than those of friendship, and I would like you, dear friend, to take this journey with me because I, too, get tired of being around strangers. Even if pregnant, you can come along. No one will hurt you. I'd kill them first."

There was more silence on the line and new shaky tears, before, "Yes," Sandra agreed. "All right. I'll go with you. Come get me."

"Oh good, my dearest friend. I've missed you so terribly" Beautiful said, but hung up quickly before Sandra could backslide or change her mind. "To Sandra's quick as you can, Thomas," she said. "Do not dally."

"North by Northwest from here," Thomas said. "We'll get there tomorrow. We need a hotel room tonight."

"Thanks, but direction is meaningless to me, Thomas," Beautiful replied. "Though I appreciate you, Baby, for showing your navigational prowess."

Ida's show came on fortuitously later that day and this was a gentle show entitled, "How to Make the No-Good Bastards You Love Reciprocate Some."

"Oh, good," Thomas said. "This sounds like exactly the show I need."

Both agreed, half way in, that Ida was on a rant. The technique *du jour* involved sudden undetectably caused wake ups followed by kindness. Another briefly discussed topic was the sudden doing of a personal chore for another person to inspire gratitude, followed by inflicting a restrictive silent treatment and mournful looks. "You gotta make 'em think that they're the low down sonofabitches they are!" Ida enthused, sounding again like she deeply inhaled a crack pipe. "But if you love them, they're worth the stinking effort, bastards."

After that life-affirming message from Ida, Beautiful felt saddened that she had no bastards upon whom to try the new techniques. She thought of Sandra and thought of Eugene, Fucking Eugene and his stripper, and listened to Ida say once more, "And you know what you do if these tactics don't work?" to which Beautiful instantly replied, "That is easy, Ida. Break their fucking necks!"

"Consult new strategies for shock value!" Ida pronounced.

Beautiful sighed. She'd begun to regret sending Fedora Man away, but she'd asked him to come back in an hour, and he hadn't. What if she did still love him, but would only find out later, like when he never spoke to her again?

Upon reaching the next hotel, she wrote in her journal: "If you're only used to chasing men, but not having them chase you, much less being successful at luring them because you like strange and freakish intellectual types with neuroses that involve hiding and liking other women more, aka John Henry and fm—but they then chase, surprisingly, and they do this new chasing at an inopportune time—WHILE YOU ARE REPAIRING A FRIENDSHIP—is it your fault if you handle things badly, chucking romance to the side because you realize subconsciously that you never had much faith in romance but you do have faith in long-term friends? WWIMHD?"

But Ida May Haze was not available on the hotline, so Beautiful, breaking the wall of silence with her parents, which had reached its highest in terms of planned absence, called her mother, hoping Ethel Chef might present some useful ideas.

"How many times must I tell you, Beautiful, that an object's beauty alone means nothing?" Ethel Chef was fond of saying. "It's beautiful, but is it useful, too? Can you use that corded tie to string up a chicken? Can you use those statuettes as weights?" On and on, Ethel Chef routinely perseverated, caring solely for places where utility reigned.

Normally, Beautiful didn't care for it. However, a good dose of useful rhetoric then struck Beautiful as provident, but knowing her father's proclivities to disassemble while stressed and fearful regarding the state of the home phones, Beautiful tried first her mother's private cell. The phone rang once. "Beautiful?" her mother answered. "Is that you? Baby? Are you all right? Where are you? Oh, my darling, oh my dearest, talk to your Mommy, right fucking now!"

"Word," Beautiful said drily. "In edgewise. Gasp!"

"I've been worried sick!" her mother responded. "I'm sick with the thought of my small daughter out in the great unknown! Endangered! Prey to cretins of disreputable natures!"

"Mommy, I'm fine."

"You're not fine, Beautiful! You're gone."

Despite that love and friendship were heavy on her mind when her mother first answered, at the sound of her mother's concerned voice, Beautiful wanted to cry with frustration, with a sudden need to be coddled to the matronly bosom and come home, or a thick desire to hang up out of guilt that she was never the daughter who could use such abundant and motherly worry as her mother displayed —which then instantly raised the same issues she'd been trying, unsuccessfully, to repress, so she then said exactly what she'd been trying to hold back, aware that she might not again have the perfect moment since things so often went unanswered or unasked at the estate: "Mommy! Was I a twin once? And did I eat my smaller, more normal sister? I think, in your womb, I had a sister you could have worried about more convincingly, who was infinitely more feminine… Did I?"

Her mother sounded cross, replying instantly, "You answer my questions first, daughter! I'm hungry and riddled with nerves. I've missed you so much! So, how are you? Where are you staying?"

"I'm fine, Mommy," Beautiful replied. "Don't worry. I'm with Thomas in the desert, having just arrived at a strange hotel room with scratchy sheets and a cheap, filthy comforter silk-screened with Aztec patterns, lying naked on my bed, alone, with no marauders. This is how I'm aware just how cheap and scratchy the comforter truly is. Bah! But I've taken a lover. He thinks he's evil. I am not sure if I'm in love. But even if I were in love, I have just ignored my potentially beloved in order to patch things up with Sandra, who I recently fired."

"Are you calling because you miss me?"

"I'm calling because I don't believe in romantic love, because I'm too emotional for it, or perhaps I just don't believe it's possible for me, and I'm trying to see if you have love with Daddy or just an amiable and financially viable partnership. You're my mother after all, so I'm hoping you can tell me something about this love thing, love that isn't compensated with cash. And my twin. But first there's the issue of childhood cannibalism. Actually, this cannibalism would've happened in the womb. There may have been some cognitive awareness on my part, but did this happen, Mommy? Did I eat my biological twin? You're the only one who knows."

"Beautiful," her mother replied, "Whatever gave you that idea? You're an only child."

"I've been dreaming it for years. Nightmares. Shakes. Screaming. Sometimes that thing where your leg moves while you're sleeping, like you might kick something. And how's Daddy?"

"Your father's fine. But he's disassembled every piece of household electronics. Including the telephones. I'm not calling from home. I am—away."

"I feared as much so called your cell. You eating?"

"Yes," her mother said. "Minimally. Because I won't sit idly by while you engage in this ridiculous freedom strike. You were free at home, weren't you?"

"Free to live a lie, Mommy. I had no benefit of genuine reality."

"Beautiful, all reality is a lie."

"Except it's not fair to keep the main lie from the person the lie's built upon, who thinks she is everything. Did you think me so dim?"

"Is it wrong to love your child so much that you seek to protect them?"

"It is wrong to make them think people like them who do not, and thus cause a confusing sensation that no action has an equal and opposite reaction. Because you know what that could have done, Mommy? Made me mentally ill! A loon. Batshit crazy. I could have become like that Beach Boy musician guy, agoraphobic, scared as shit of people and pouring sand in his house—constructing a self-elected reality that would never be kind to me, and why? Because there were Jokers to the left of me and Jokers to the right, this would be the paid friend employees—but I was stuck *in the middle* with you! That's an excellent song I just kerfluffled lyrics from, by the way. And yes, you love me. And yes, Daddy loves me. But one cannot live with only one's parents as influence and become the creature one's meant to be. So, did I have ever a sister or not, Mommy, firstly? And, secondly, did I *eat* her?"

"It is possible, but unlikely you had a sister and then ate her," Ethel Chef said, "because you're left-handed. Surely some left-handed people may not be carnivorous twin absorbers, but I have recently read an article that states left-handedness is recessive, and some left handed people, born singly, must have somehow absorbed their right-handed fetal twins because twins mirror, which possibly caused the left-handedness, mirroring a right-handed twin, except when only one child is born something may have happened early in the pregnancy to result in the left-handed mirror baby absorbing the weaker, right-handed party when it faltered, so I'm not sure. If this happened in your infancy; I'm very sorry. That topic done with, when are you coming home?"

Beautiful absorbed all this like a dead fetus before she rebutted, "What I want is factual here, Mommy. Were there, or were there not, two babies in your stomach? Count your fingers. Pull out one finger on each hand for how many babies you carried. Did you pull out one or two fingers?"

"I don't know how many babies there were! Do you think I could see through my skin?"

At this, Beautiful sensed withholding, so tried her father's tactic, which she loosely entitled: Asking-A-Variation-of-the-Question, "Did the doctors see two babies in your womb, Mommy? Is there any proof, for example, that there was a baby who looked like Kelly MacDonaldson, famous swimsuit model and spokesperson for Zest mouthwash, and another who looked like me, the one who looked like me eating the one who didn't in cold blood?"

"Only bones and organs are visible in sonograms, Beautiful," her Mommy said. "How could I know whom another fetus might resemble? My womb was and is a creatively glorious mystery."

Beautiful flipped onto her back to regard the stucco ceiling, replying, "Mother, you're working my nerves."

"As it should be. You're a teenager. I'm your mother. Nerves get worked in both directions. Besides, doesn't it occur to you to ask, 'How is your day, Mommy? How've you been?' No. Instead we must embark upon some bizarre question before even exchanging niceties?"

"Very well, Mommy," Beautiful replied, struggling to remember if any niceties had been exchanged. "How was your day?"

"Fine."

"That pleases me enormously. How are you? Was breakfast good this morning? And, when you get around to it, would you mind telling me if there were two sets of bones in the sonogram?"

"I don't know," her mother replied. "I never viewed them."

Beautiful reeled. "You didn't want to look at me as a baby?!" She gasped, rising from the nasty print bed, striding to the mirror still fogged from her shower and wiping it with her hand. "You avoided looking at me? Maybe I'm not beautiful after all. Maybe all these years you've been lying! And I'm UGLY, Mommy! HIDEOUS!" Upon this, Beautiful burst into tears.

"I think you're beautiful, Beautiful," her mother said.

"No, you don't."

"Beautiful, today is not the day to doubt me, not the day to doubt that I love you. I love you more than any other child or person on the planet, even if you are distinctly unique. We didn't view the sonograms, but we always listened to your heartbeat. It was a sentimental activity your father and I performed together."

"But am I pretty? Am I special?"

"Beautiful, would we have made those statues at the pool if we didn't think you were both pretty and special? Would we have named you Beautiful? Would Mommy have bought that gorgeous Smithsonian doll that looks just like you and made it her favorite talisman?"

"But you turned away from me as an infant?"

"Not on purpose. Honestly, I did want to look. But your father said, 'Darling, sometimes things are too amazing to view with the human eye. Let's wait till she comes out to behold her.'"

The whole thing seemed dangerous and fraught with secrecy. Beautiful donned a bra and panties, several pairs one after another, unable to determine which looked best.

If she wanted to pry further on the issue of happenings in utero, she, too, was trained in the art of interminable silences parsed by purchase and discovery, so said instead, "Mommy, how did you know you were in love with Daddy? And how did he ask to marry you?"

"Oh," Beautiful's mother said. "Hmmm." In the background, Beautiful heard the rustling of a paper bag and furtive chewing. "Hmmm," Beautiful's mother said again.

"Can you finish chewing that creampuff without hiding that you're eating and just answer the question, Mother?"

"It's not a cream puff. It's an éclair. I'd be glad to tell you the story of your parents' love, Beautiful," her mother said. "I'm glad you're finally curious!" and so she began one of the longest stories Beautiful's mother had ever told without her father's interruption. This account involved the auto parts industry, flunkies, an investment, steno-pool work, and her mother's obvious engaging superiority over every other typist working for Enrique Sheldon Venus Spellbrooke Chef in the height of his growing clout, when certain narcissism bled into his every doing: "Your father was so arrogant!"

It also involved her mother becoming his private typist for all confidential matters via Dictaphone, before speech recognition: "Because he knew I was the best."

And how, in a private fit of pique, one day, Beautiful's mother decided she no longer wanted that honor: "So I made a typo."

"A typo?"

"A very obvious and bad typo. The subject line was supposed to say, 'Subject: Managers Meeting at 2' but I changed the word 'Managers' to 'Mongrels.' Your father sent the memo, never expecting to proof my work. The other mongrels were not happy. I didn't want to be fired, but I did want off the detail of transcribing messages since he often said unsavory things, but he refused to fire me. Instead, he took to coming down and watching me type. 'To help you hear better,' he said. First, he dictated in person in the steno-room and then, sure the other steno-pool girls had a strange fixation on watching his ass, sometimes pinching it—he was very particular about who could view his ass—he had my typewriter brought into his office. Your father was quite handsome, albeit seeming absorbed fully in himself. This went on… And then one day he started dictating a memo that seemed like a love letter! I was furious he wouldn't type his own correspondence of this nature, pretty sure his penis would come into it soon enough, that and how he wanted to touch her—since the beauty of the woman was something he waxed on and on about, despite how he'd expressed he had never so much as lifted a single hair from her slim shoulder to kiss her nape! Regardless, Beautiful, I was about to become, I realized, a pornographer for your father!"

"Oh, the nerve!" said Beautiful, horrified.

"Yes. Except, 'Darling,' your father then said, which I was supposed to type, 'I came up from nothing. Had no help. And you are the best typist I've ever had, loyal and faithful to a T, except lately I sense you want to flee. I look at you every day and sometimes ask you to type memos that will never be sent, to people who do not exist. I do this to smell your fruity and papery perfume and to watch you walk into my office and glare at me, because you glare a lot, love, like a glaring machine, but I can't hide this overwhelming feeling that this might be lust, but could also be love—and, so, just in case it is the latter and my life will be ruined irreparably if I don't make this proposal, will you marry me and share all my worldly goods?"

"Oh!" Beautiful said.

"Yes," her mother replied. "And then, to be fair, he

described his faults at length. ‘Many times I’ll pay nearly no attention to you. When I’m nervous, I disassemble things. Rockets. TVs. Phones. There are bad genetics in my family, so we might create strange children. I’m walled and I’m secretive, but I’m loyal, and I’ll buy you anything you could possibly want, provided you’re not too frivolous. I don’t believe in the purchase of ice sculptures or anything that self-destructs, but I’ll shield you from the dirty side of my business. I’m a compulsive gambler at the horse races and sometimes drink to excess. Sometimes I need anti-psychotics. So what do you say?”

Beautiful pictured her mother younger, her father in one of his old navy suits with the high collars and thick neck ties. She tried to picture her mother typing these words as he spoke. She couldn’t. “What were you doing while he spoke?”

“Pounding the keys, of course, Beautiful. As a true typist, I never felt his words were real until they reached the page.”

“Even when you knew he stood behind you?”

“Why, yes! Even then. That’s how nervous I was! I still have to type things to make them feel real. Sometimes, on anniversaries and warm spring days, I still type while he stands behind me and then we—”

“Mommy! TMI.”

“Oh, sorry.”

”So what happened that exact day?”

“He took my hands off the typewriter and said, ‘If you agree, Ethel, I’ll bring in a ring tomorrow that can be sized to fit your correct finger. This was all rather unplanned. Not that I haven’t been thinking about it for some time...’”

“And what did you say?”

“Yes, Beautiful. I said yes. I could hardly resist him.”

“Did you go home with him that night?”

“No. I went to my house and went to bed. He went to his house and did the same. It had been a long day.”

Dreamily, Beautiful thought of how pleasant it would be to be proposed with a letter, a letter made to look as though it were for someone else, but actually revealed itself to be a matrimonial pledge of fealty, of desire. Oh, double swoon. "Okay, but he kissed you, right?" Beautiful asked. "Before you left the office?"

"No," her mother said, chewing and crumpling. "It took him a week to work up the nerve, even after I wore his ring and our status was announced at the office. He said, 'I wanted to believe, for a while, that you'd really marry me, so I've been afraid to kiss you because then, if you refused me, I'd no longer be engaged. What if you didn't like the way I kissed? I couldn't bear for it to be over too soon...'"

"And you said?"

"I said, 'That's all very nice, Rick, but I need you to kiss me if I'm to believe you really plan to marry me and that this is *not* some kind of mean joke on the steno-pool girl because unless you kiss me, I can't know how to feel. It doesn't really matter if you're a bad kisser. I could train you. Additionally, you might be gay, just attracted to my silky garments.'"

"And what did Daddy say?"

"He said, 'I'm not gay and I don't play mean jokes, on account of my dead brother Cisco, may he rest in peace.' Oh, you should hear him go on about Cisco. But Cisco—that's a terrible story." At this, her mother paused.

Into the silence, Beautiful imagined her father's severity each time he uttered Cisco's name. She stared into her luggage with stacks of money. Her mother's paper bag stopped crinkling but the line wasn't dead. The pause was sticky. "And then what?"

"Your father and I strode out to the parking lot below the building."

"And talked? Kissed?"

"No, we had raunchy sex in his Corvette for three hours, maybe four. My pussy lips were slack. My jaw was sore—"

"Mother!"

"You asked, Beautiful," her mother said. "I'm trying to be honest. That was a great and memorable time! But it's really no different now. He still likes me to glare at him. Why do you think I put him through the trials?"

Beautiful sighed. "Oh, Mommy, how wonderful! I love your love story! It makes me want to join a steno-pool. Or type. Only, I think I want to be the boss. Except I want to receive the message in the letter, too."

"You can't have it both ways," her mother said. "You can only make the words or take the words. You can't do both. And your father and I fight. A lot. But you know when I knew I was first in love?"

"When?"

"The moment I first laid eyes on him. Nothing has ever changed."

"That's the loveliest thing, Mommy. The most beautiful and most romantic story ever. It is causing me to swoon. A big lovely swoon! I—"

"Yes. But I think you should know now, Beautiful, we're getting a divorce… Your father has cut me loose."

"What? Where are you? Do you need me to come? You okay? Mommy, where are you? What's going on?"

"I'm fine, Beautiful, and I love you," her mother said, suddenly weeping with restrained fervor, this just before the line went dead. No amount of calling could bring her back.

Were this not disturbing enough, while Beautiful had spoken to her mother, unbeknownst to her, Thomas began to enact, unobserved, self-punitive measures outside her room, bashing his head against the wall, standing, head-bashing, hollering, shouting apologies, and beginning the cycle again.

"Well, for crying out loud!" Beautiful said. She put on a purple Gucci dress with lime piping and walked out to observe him, responding, "Must everyone submit to uncontrollable weeping today? My life starts to resemble a Somerset Maugham novel!"

Moments before, she'd missed the earlier commotion while she'd tried on multiple outfits and contemplated calling her father about the divorce, but now she returned her attentions to Thomas, after he, wanting her comfort, pressed his face close to the window and moaned with theatrical volume to let her know he was bleeding.

"Walls don't collapse like panes of glass," she said, irritated. "Especially from a soft little head like yours."

A bird pecked her window as she opened the door for Thomas and ushered him in, but it was not a pigeon this time, nor a vulture, just one of those weird little brown birds you privately assume are government machines, the unidentifiable ones that lack the solvent trait of a recognizable breed. It was not a bot.

Thus, she wanted to kill it instantly. She did not. There was no time.

"Mama, help me," Thomas said weakly. In her room, he touched his bruised forehead and the knot emerging there began to swell. "I'm so sorry," he said. "I've been such a bad boy."

Standing in her uncomfortable Franco Sarto mules, Beautiful sighed, asked, "What troubles you, Baby?" To remove her aggression that she hadn't killed the small brown bird, she took to jumping on the bed. *Replacement Activity,* she thought, a technique she learned from the pot smoker shrink.

"I can't tell you," Thomas said, blubbering.

"Then why are you here?" she asked, jumping, listening to the bedsprings.

"I want to tell you, Mama, but I can't!"

"I *am* here for you, Baby, but you *have to* tell me," she replied, grabbing him by the lapels of his black suit and lifting him onto the bed to jump with her, saying, "Bounce with me, Thomas. Also, it's Mama! Answer now!"

"I'm so sorry, Mama," he said. "I'm so very sorry for what I've done!"

"What've you done?"

"I lost your man, pushed your man away. I ruined your chances at love. I should have pulled over when Fedora Man came. I should have pulled right over and opened your car door for him, but I was too selfish!"

Beautiful stopped bouncing. "Thomas, whatever are you talking about?"

"I didn't want to lose what closeness we had so I didn't give you up. That's why my real Mama hated me. I made her boyfriends leave. And now you told your boyfriend to go away since I heard you say you couldn't have me witness your love. It's my fault all over again!"

"You're too young to witness romantic love just yet, my pet," Beautiful said. "You can witness Mama's platonic love, but romantic love is a dirty, sordid thing."

"I know," Thomas said. "I do know that."

"All right," Beautiful said, seating them both, fixing his tie, his lapels, and his chauffeur's hat, in what she hoped would be a nurturing way. "This could be important. How did you make your mother's boyfriends leave?"

"I got too clingy, because I wanted to be with her. And this shamed her. But she couldn't get free of me. And now I've done it all over again. Daddy left her because he didn't like me. Said I was too girlish and strapped to her side. That's why all my life, I—"

"You tried to be overly masculine," Beautiful intuited, recalling his weird faked Butch attitude each time he tried to be stern.

"Yes."

"And later insisted on wearing big black suits?"

"Yes."

"Just before you grew that mustache and learned how to shake hands hard, like a real man?"

"Yes," Thomas said. "It's all true. Mama, you're so

smart!"

"Thomas, does this have anything to do with the tree worshipping I observed in the park?"

After they discussed tree-worshiping, duChamps, restrooms, and bowing Tibetan monks, Beautiful concluded Mother Earth was a big terrifying influence. She also decided that Thomas was generally afraid of women, their disapproval, their joys, their accomplishments, all tracing back to his gender dysphoric belief that he secretly was a woman, but an ugly and inadequate one who chased away men, who was good for only brutal sex acts, as he admitted that he sometimes was a barmaid in his private daydreams, but in real life succeeded at chasing men away from both himself and the parenting women in his life, whom he resultantly feared because he could not be their real girl baby, and so he had to pretend to be manly to hide his fear from others, to hide his anima, who had the face of a petulant little lass, inexplicable freckles, and slight lisp.

He also, she observed, seemed trapped in a Freudian anal stage, despite or because of the rampant Jungian influence to his life narrative she now noted regarding lucid dream realization and perpetually adjusting the semiotics of womanhood. "Well, I think we should do away with this heavy male conditioning right now," she asserted, simplifying. "I have an idea."

Thomas looked up from his tears. "I feel so pretty when I'm crying," he said. "Let me cry."

"Well, you're not pretty that way, Thomas. Snot runs down your face. Women aren't prettier when they cry. So you felt you wanted to be more like a little girl when your father left," Beautiful replied, applying an icepack to his forehead with a smack, "that if you were a little girl, you could have been closer to your Mama, more protected. Am I hearing that correctly? And maybe in your heart you always feared you were a weak little girl, while simultaneously viewing girls as something desirable to be—

because you could be excusably weak, you thought, if you were feminine. This, itself, is a fracture in logic. Yet, at the same time, you actually seem to thinks girls deserve bad things to happen to them, which is evidenced by your 'every woman deserves to be punished and beaten while lying on the floor choking on her own vomit' comment. Thomas, be mindful. I could've taken those remarks poorly, but I didn't. And why didn't I? Because I could beat you within a centimeter of your life, were that required—but, I'd want you to be a man for that. Still, all in all, don't you think my perceptions of your gender issues are pretty accurate?"

"Yes," he said. "Thanks. Absolutely."

"What strikes me," she said, "is that regardless of all this, or because of it, you seem to feel you didn't deserve love, as either a little boy or a little girl… Why?"

"I was an ugly little girl and a bad little boy."

"I don't know how you looked as a little girl, but you were not a bad little boy, Thomas. Please, stop lying. Mama can't handle it. I know for a fact you were a very excellent little boy."

"I was bad. So very bad."

"What was bad? That you lied?"

"No, that I couldn't act like *a man*. I cried like *a girl*, like *a baby*."

"Thomas, a *boy* cannot act like a *man* because he is not yet a *man*. How can a *child* be *an adult?* A boy needs care as much as a girl. A boy who is harmed or threatened will cry. A girl doesn't get more or better care from a mother, in fact gets more judgment and less praise," Beautiful admitted, remembering the criticism she'd endured, stroking his arm before saying, "I know this because I was a failure at being a daughter and often preferred the company of my father since I couldn't please my mother, which resultantly broke her heart that we wouldn't be as close as she'd have liked, but she wouldn't stop judging me, not for one minute. Had she a son, she would have praised his every shitpile action since he didn't have to live up to being a girl, her girl in particular. So let me share with you, Thomas, my mother would've loved the hell out of you. She would've loved every wimpy sentimental thing about you. I say that lovingly! And I'm your Mama now, but I really don't care if you're male or female. You can be my happy little it boy! My it girl, too! The important thing is that you're *a child*, who needs nurturing and care. And now, hug me with much emotion to impress upon me the veracity of my truths, for I feel I've said enough."

"Okay," he said, hugging her.

"Granted I'm no professional," Beautiful went on. "And I didn't really listen to my shrinks, or if I did, I did so with the same selective fervor with which I've read Tolstoy, for example. Nor do I know if being a girl, really a girl for a while, will dissuade you from your illusions about gender. But I've a solution that I think will solve the issue. You need to come to the bathroom, Thomas. We can't do this once we reach Los Angeles—but between here and Vegas, I think you should permit yourself to be very feminine just in case, dress like a little girl, act like a girl. You'll be my new little girl. I'll take you through to womanhood in less offensive terms. I'll loan you clothes. I don't plan to make you bleed via the genital area, but we must get rid of your mustache." A feverish need to yank his facial hair filled Beautiful once again. Just one little pull, a small yank, yankety-yank-yank, would be so nice—the urge for which she submerged with difficulty, instead proposing, "Right now, I suggest we shave your face. This will be rather ceremonial. Do you have a little girl's name you'd like to take?"

Thomas whispered in her ear.

"All right," Beautiful said. "I'll call you that."

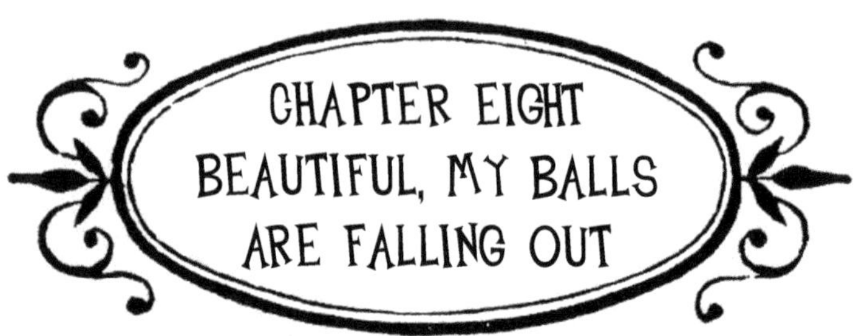

CHAPTER EIGHT
BEAUTIFUL, MY BALLS ARE FALLING OUT

~IN WHICH, BEAUTIFUL MAKES THOMAS PRETTY, THEY WALK THE DUNES, FEDORA MAN EXPLORES CHAIRED BONDAGE, MOONING POSSIBILITIES ARE NEGATED, SOULS ARE TOUCHED THROUGH FEET, AND THE TRYING BONDS OF LOVE ARE BENT TO BREAK.~

Fedora Man had texted, "SO, IS THIS IT?" by the time she finished shaving Thomas's mustache. His use of caplock both irritated and cheered her.

If he was angry, he cared enough to be angry. Beautiful never angered herself with anything she might easily ignore. Poor angry little fm. Wanting to kiss his agitated cheek, playing to his rage with a response designed to subdue his inner beast and convince him of her amenability, she responded in lowercase, as if she felt submissive, "is what it?"

His reply was idiotic: "???"

She responded in turn, "???goose."

"We Are Over, Aren't We?" he texted, in Title Case. "Beautiful, are we over or not?"

Beautiful thought of several replies:

1. "Yes."
2. "No."
3. "Fucksake, you're the one who keeps leaving!"

4. "What exactly do you mean by over?"

&

5. "Could I sleep on that, call a few friends?" Etcetera.

She typed and deleted each possible response while contemplating Thomas's ideal look. "Not too slutty, Thomas," she said, handing over a pair of cream clip-ons. "As we create your girlhood today, I must have some girlish advice from you."

Thomas looked dubious. "I'm not even dressed, and you forgot to call me my girl name."

"True," she said. "An oversight. Two ugly oversights. Let's finalize your outfit. I don't think you'd go hooch, so I'm going to make you a very classy girl, Esmeralda."

"Can I watch you pick my outfit before I go into the bathroom?"

"No. Go in there and get naked. Don't give me any sass."

Beautiful selected him a green Dolce & Gabbana floral print stretch charmeuse dress, with a yellow purse with green ribbons. His back might be a bit wider, but the stretch would work. She picked him a fine Hanky Panky Cherry Heart low rise thong and a purple chiffon bra, which she permitted him to fill with tissue. "Since you've decided you want breasts," she said through the door after he mentioned it, "should we make you a thirteen year old girl? When did your father leave again?"

"When I was eight. But I've always wanted breasts, since I was a baby… I think I should have them, limited as this girlish phase might be."

"Okay, Esmeralda. You can have breasts," she replied. "When you were a boy child, you had breasts on loan to you since infancy but lost them at about two, since they were never actually yours, on loan from your mother—but if you'd like real breast ownership, as a girl child blossoming into a woman, Thomas, mentally, logically, I'm making the call that you can't be eight. So let's decide your father left at thirteen. Makes things so much easier."

He opened the door. "But he didn't leave then. And I was more robbed than that—I was a formula baby!"

Beautiful smiled and grabbed his shoulders to shake him warmly, saying, "Oh, so what? Reality doesn't exist, Thomas! My mother just told me that, which means it's true!" When he smiled, uncertain, she added, "Who cares when the fucker really left? Has it stopped bothering you?"

"No."

"Then you can be whatever age you want."

In the bathroom, when Thomas was fully dressed, they did his make-up. He opted for a light tint moisturizer, blush, and mascara. "Thomas, you look so pretty!" Beautiful told him as he rose from the toilet seat. "Next time, though, use foundation for the large pores by your nose, and let's now provide you with a nice subtle lipstick in a shade of rose."

"I'll take a deep, sports car red," he replied. "My inner girl is racy."

"Very well," she replied. When he appeared somewhat like her mother, Beautiful entrusted him with a girlish advice question. "So, let's say you're a girl and there's this boy you sort of like. But he's upset. He asks if you're done with him, about which you have no idea because you've just begun. Oh, except you already had sex. What do you tell him?"

"Don't know. Are you over him?"

"Well, you might be over him, but you might've just been busy when he came by. What do you say, Esmeralda? What do you say if you're being your best girl self?"

"I say—" Thomas began.

"Say it in your girlish voice, Thomas," Beautiful said. "It sounds more convincing."

"I'm a little confused by his move with the helicopter," Thomas went on, his voice raised in a charming falsetto, his left hand gesticulating like mad, "especially the cratering emphasis around his beloved, but anyway, I say, 'What makes you think we are over, you lousy piece of shit? You've not yet begun to suffer! Work harder for me…' And then I wait a bit to let him respond more since that's the girl's job, waiting. I pout while I do this." Thomas displayed his pout.

"I can't pout, if that's the girl's job…" Beautiful said, unsure. "Tell me what's the guy's job? Now be Thomas."

"The guy's job's all the recovery work—" Thomas said. "The whining, present buying to get her back, all that. But he has to want to sleep with her. Or he'll just be cold. In that case, she could pout or not pout and wait forever. He'll still be cold."

"I don't like waiting. What if he's always been cold?"

"How cold?"

"Icy ravine."

"Impossible to say," Thomas replied.

"But has this happened to you, Thomas?"

"As a guy? Yes. I've done lots of begging. But, as a woman in a guy's body, dating a woman, I've been a victim of the glacial stare without the opportunity to provide the glacial stare. My stares go misinterpreted."

"So you've had lots of girlfriends?"

"I've tried to have many girlfriends," Thomas admitted mournfully.

"I think you should stop begging, Thomas," Beautiful said. "I don't like men begging. I like eloquent arguments, and I like men not making the regrettable mistakes in the first place."

"Men are beyond faulty," Thomas said, raising his voice again such that she knew he was Esmeralda. "Especially those whose mothers never loved them. A mother's love is so, so important! Even now, I'm traumatized by the rubber taste of the nipple. I was robbed of her breasts!"

"Pfft, a mother's love," she said. "Mama loves you." Beautiful sat contemplating her wardrobe choices and the lack of a maid. "But men are the ones who pursue, right?"

"I don't know because if I'm female, then I'm certainly a lesbian," Esmeralda replied. "Which means I'm not the one to be asked about heterosexual relationships...?"

"Please, answer as Thomas then," Beautiful replied. "Hey, that was cool how 'het-er-o-sex-u-al' just had six audible syllables. And keep switching back and forth. It's really interesting to watch you do that."

"Yes," Thomas said, voice deep. "In most cases, the man pursues, and the girl waits."

"Well, that's not how I do it, Thomas," Beautiful replied, squinting. "Am I the guy?"

"True, except you're waiting now," he argued. "So clearly you're the girl."

"I'm not waiting," she said petulantly. "I'm formulating my response. I might still be the guy."

"But are you over Fedora Man or not?" Thomas asked in a high-pitched tenor, regarding himself in the mirror and touching his moisturized skin and the smooth area above his lip. "And if so, would you like a new boyfriend?"

"That would depend, Esmie," Beautiful replied. "I feel now, after such deprivation, that to deny myself something I so clearly want, such as Fedora Man, anything I want, would be ridiculous. Why not just have him until I get tired of him? Let him have me that same way?"

"That's very liberated," Thomas replied. "Is he amenable?"

"I don't know. But after the seventeen romanceless years of my life," Beautiful said, "I've endured so much lack of reciprocity that my need for satiation verges on complete and massive gluttony!"

"Careful. No. Don't take him back now," Esmeralda said. "The girl who wants too much always cries. The guy who leaves always makes that girl cry. Whether or not you're over him, he'll still make you cry if he comes back, so is that gluttony worth crying over later?"

Beautiful wrapped a new scarf around her face,

maneuvering it many different ways before saying, "How much do I get *in the now?*" She tried on a few purses and punched the wall, asking, "But why does the girl always cry, Thomas? I'm so tired of crying. I'd like him to cry. I'd rather make him cry."

"Good luck with that," Thomas said. "The girl is the crier. If she takes him back now, maybe she cries for shame that she has allowed his sub-standard presence back into her life because he was never quite good enough, but she was weak and foolish and desired him too much. If she lets him go, she cries because of what might have been or what, for a brief moment of fantasy, may have existed between them for a time. But the girl always cries. It's the girl's lot in life to cry. *Cry-high-hi* me a river. Oh, cry me a river! Guys don't cry unless they get kicked in the balls." He happily applied a second coat of mascara to his lashes, muttering, "I feel a veil of pain falling over me, just visually becoming a girl. A veil of suffering, pain, and sorrow!"

"Then I don't think I'm a normal girl," Beautiful said. "I don't like sorrow, don't like suffering, and I don't wear veils. Careful with that mascara, Thomas. It's clumping. Anyway, I thought of presenting FM different terms that required more sacrifice from him, like, 'If we aren't to be over, we must do some platonic talking and gauge our level of compatibility. Otherwise, yes, we're over. Please respond within ten business days. Memo format will work."

"Beautiful, maybe you should wear my suit," Thomas replied.

"Hell no," she said. "I love dresses. I only wear suits in dreams."

"But if you wore my suit, you wouldn't be the one to cry," Thomas said. "You could be the one with all the power."

"Thomas, this is where our philosophies diverge," Beautiful replied. "I can have power wearing any dress I currently own. I can have power in a thong bikini with no bra. I can have power butt-naked. I am *Strong as Animal Woman*, like Ida May Haze, so I don't go in for all this ridiculous crying and shaming shit. I think you need a redefinition of womanhood. If your mother blamed you for her inability to keep a man, it's because she was a stuttering twit who had the audacity to blame a child for her own weakness. If your father didn't care for your lack of testosterone, it was probably because he, too, suffered from fears about his manliness. My Daddy is very manly. As a result, he does whatever he damn wants, even if that means taking milk and oatmeal baths and singing lyrics to sappy musical theater songs. He doesn't need to shake hands hard to show clout, as if a hard shake were a man-badge, nor does he display interest in Wall Street to demonstrate proof of the unfeminine. He shows clout by his direct unwillingness to accept anything that doesn't please him. That's true clout, Thomas. Selecting how to do what you want and doing it! Besides, in most dreams, when I'm wearing suits, I'm also eating my fetal twin."

"Oh," Thomas said.

"Yes," Beautiful said. "It's complicated. But you sure look pretty today!"

"Thanks. Can I confess I'm afraid to go back to my room looking like this because I might start touching myself?"

"I think you should do it," Beautiful replied. "Who'll stop you?" Thomas seemed shy, but smiled, churlish, and appeared to be very much enjoying himself. In her bathroom, she caught him several times checking his reflection and also sneaking looks at her other garments. "Oh, but hurry up, then come back. I think we should go out soon," Beautiful said. "As part of getting rid of this shame you've internalized, let's take a public walk on the dunes."

He looked fearfully at the door. "But what if people laugh?"

"Baby," Beautiful said, with the same seriousness with

which she'd banged Jake's head on the wreck yard dirt. "They won't, or I'll kill them… It's sunny. I think you need a parasol. So, about Fedora Man, what should I say? I still haven't decided."

"Am I supposed to be thinking like a man or like a woman?"

"Like an adult *being*. Whatever seems best. I feel people who represent both sexes are better balanced. Also, I think you have modeled your perceptions of women on the wrong women. Pay more attention to Ida's shows. Or me."

Thomas thought and replied as Esmeralda, "You should say, 'Fedora Man, if we're over, you've made that decision. If not, get your ass out here and do what you know will make me happy. I've accepted you as you are. Don't you believe me? Gifts are not unwelcome.'"

"Oh, Thomas, I'm so proud of you! So proud!" Beautiful said, clapping her hands together in delight. "That was very assertive femme virtuous! You'd have made a wonderful woman!"

"Thank you, Beautiful," Thomas said. "Now I'll go back to the bathroom for a moment to give you some privacy while you contact him."

"Thank you, Baby," Beautiful said. "You are the best child a Mama ever had and I'm grateful. I love you, but don't masturbate in my bathroom."

"You're a very good Mama," Thomas replied. "I won't. Do you really love me?"

"Of course I do, Thomas. Now, this is not an unclean love. It's a pure and unconditional love bred by your service and kindness. But we can find you an impure love if you'd like."

"Oh, thank you. Thank you, Mama," he said, voice high, so consumed with emotion that he darted into her bathroom and shut the door. "Do you think," he asked through the door in a muffled voice, "that we could find a woman who might love me as a woman? I really do find women more attractive."

"We can find anything we want if we look hard enough," Beautiful replied, but when Thomas entered the bathroom, Beautiful lifted her phone and immediately texted Fedora Man the address. She replied: "We're not over. I'm open to continuing our acquaintance, but fear that our carnal alliance confuses me. I suggest you come and talk to me tonight, when we shall be as chaste as ever two friends were. I like friends, in general, more than lovers, as when they depart there is not such a sense of disloyalty. Thus, if you desire me as more than this, you must belong to the circle of friends FIRST, for only after can we make our decisions based on basic compatibility. The short run and the long run are hard to predict. It'll be hard not to violate you, I'm sure, noting as I do your obvious desirability, but I'm thinking we should tie you to a chair so that nothing untoward will happen. This is for your protection. I'm in 34B. Thomas stays next door. He's in a very frail state. Don't sedate him or off him. He's special to me. Not in a romantic way. So, yes or no? If we're to continue, it's now up to you." If she was aware this message was quite long to be ensconced in a text, she ignored this. After all, she could write a letter, but send it where? How? No bald pigeons lingered now.

Regardless, she felt the direct *toska* that the use of electronic appliances for human affairs engendered. If the recipient received your message instantly and chose not to reply, you could be assured it was a slight diminishing of personal value. There was no plausible deniability as there was with the regular mail, imagining as you might that the letter had been lost in the post, soaked through with rainwater, dropped inopportunely in a neighbor's mailbox, or other such face-saving nonsense.

Two instants after Beautiful had sent the above text, she felt aware that Fedora Man had been beeped or buzzed or vibrated. And that he'd read her message. Since she'd suggested tying him to the chair, she wasn't sure how he'd receive her message, but hoped that the spirit of desired platonic relations was communicated.

~

"Beautiful, my balls are falling out," Thomas whispered, panicked, squeamish, possibly enjoying his embarrassment as they straddled the next dune.

"It's the underwear, Thomas," Beautiful said. "In hindsight, I should've given you boy shorts, but I feared the presence of the word 'boy' in the garment's descriptor would be off-putting as you took your tour of womanhood. I had a nice pair, too, black with silver apples! Apples are delicious. I think that about apples every time I wear those boy shorts and look at my own butt—but we aren't near enough to change, and you're practicing being a girl. Can you tuck the problem in?"

"The underwear?"

"Your balls."

"I'll try. Can you give me some privacy?" Beautiful wasn't sure what he did to fix this issue since, in response to his request, she turned her back. A moment later, when he said, "Ready," she returned her gaze to his location.

"All this stinking sand," she said. "Such grit." She removed her heels. The sun dipped lower and sand coated her feet. Thomas meandered daintily, still looking jaunty though walking with a slight limp, peering up with a dazed look and clearly enjoying the feel of soft garments on his body. He left his heels on, said he felt sexy. This didn't matter because walking in the dunes was sinking your foot to its base regardless, then lifting your foot clear of whatever spiked appendage on your shoe hung below.

"If we pass a few more dunes," Beautiful suddenly said, "it occurs to me the view will be the same, and if that's the case, what's the point of any movement in the desert?"

"Movement is meditational?"

"At least my feet are less hot," Beautiful said, noting that the ground cooled as the day cooled. They'd enjoyed dinner at the tiny diner inside the hotel, walked for an hour, and now Beautiful felt queasy. Fedora Man had not replied after her long and fervent text.

"I think I should tie him to a funeral pyre and light him on fire," she said.

"What?" Thomas asked.

"Nothing," Beautiful said.

Throughout the afternoon, Thomas, however, made leaps and bounds of progress. Newness pervaded him. She made him wear his dress to dinner, to celebrate, which caused several strange stares, but Beautiful failed to perceive them as threats.

When they parted ways and went to their rooms, planning to arrive at Sandra's by noon the next day, Thomas said, "I think this is the most freeing and beautiful day of my life, Mama. I feel so, so—liberated!"

"That's good, Thomas," Beautiful said. "What did you do about the panties earlier?"

He opened his purse, showing her he'd stashed them in the zipper pocket. "Tucked here."

"That was quite resourceful, Baby!" she enthused. Despite that a continuous checking of her phone yielded no reply from Ivor hours later, Beautiful was proud of herself. Because pride breeds pride, she was then proud of her mother for helping her, proud of Sandra for being such a good friend, proud of anybody who'd ever helped anybody else. This feeling swelled. Pride fueled and abetted pride! That was why she'd visit Ida! Ida had helped her! She regarded Ida May Haze's photo again. She checked her phone once more. Still, no reply.

And you see, she thought to herself, *he's useless. One night of great pleasure is not nearly worth the struggle one has with a person unwilling to talk, really talk, bound to a chair or otherwise. He's a weasel and a coward. Maybe he only wanted me for my body, like men wanted Candy.* "If you come, I would only bind you to a chair to ensure I did not molest you," she texted to clarify, so he'd have no doubt. "Because you're that tempting."

She wanted to speak to her Daddy, but feared he wouldn't be accessible. He'd likely disassembled his own cell as the last item of the lot. Outside, night claimed the dunes, along with the silver light of stars. After another fifteen minutes with no reply arriving, Beautiful plugged her phone in to charge. She got into bed, glad Fedora Man wasn't there because if he were she may have killed him by now for making her wait. "Well, I guess that's over," she said. "My lovemaking tour in the self-liberation movement is now officially over."

Fast asleep in lime green flannel Vera Wang pajamas and slippers, three hours later, she heard a knock at the door. It was dark in the room, dark outside too. "Who is it and what the hell's name do you want?" she asked.

There was no reply.

She lifted the curtain to view the black blanket of sky, through which the stars still twinkled without fully illuminating the landscape. A man's shape lingered outside the door. "Whoever you are, I'll kill you mercilessly if you've come to accost me," she announced.

Someone laughed with a tinny, weasel-like sound. "It's me. I'm here, Beautiful," Fedora Man said. "Just like you asked." He rubbed his eyes, which seemed wet from how they shone.

Beautiful flung open the door and stood before him, aghast, delighted, aghast. She touched his face and his hat with first her left hand then her right. "You don't exist," she said, pulling him into her room. "I think I'm dreaming you. Since that's the case, I'll have my way with you."

In the dark, half asleep, she saw him as mirage. But she believed in enjoying and controlling her dreams, so she kissed him and pressed him close. He kissed her back, a peck, pushed her away, and then flipped on the light. That's how she knew he was real.

"I'm here," he said. "Where, may I ask, is the chair you promised?"

~

After FM was secured, Beautiful decided that her first inventory of their shared interests didn't go well, not to mention that restraining him took a while.

"I've no interest in the stock market," she said heatedly, "because I've no interest in money."

"You've no interest in money," he replied, "because you've been wealthy your whole life and have plenty, but if your father's business started failing, you'd be interested in a hurry."

Beautiful felt tempted to sock him. "I would not."

"You would so."

With difficulty, she refrained from direct aggression, counting down from twenty. "Well, you see, Fedora Man, that's where you're wrong. I don't intend to take over my father's business. That's what flunkies are for—so any man who is perfect for me will also need to handle those issues. I'm the idea person! I want to create marvelous parties and plan trips and see friends and enjoy myself! I like to help people! I've always wanted to be more helpful than I've been able to accomplish, but I won't let that stop me this time."

"I hate helping," he replied. "I'm more about destroying and leaving. Crushing people and things like tiny bugs! Can you loosen the white thigh-high around my left ankle? My circulation suffers."

"Of course," she said. "But I'm leaving now, and I'll be back with coffee. I need it. Then we can talk about whatever you like to crush. I'm curious about that. Personally, I found it quite difficult not to crush the neck of your bald automaton bird you sent with your message. It was a childhood habit, killing pigeons, and letting him live was difficult. Let's see this thing through to the end, shall we?"

When she left to get her coffee, the hotel premises was dark. A stare through the diner window at the facility made her aware that it was closed. Then she recalled the in-room coffee maker. She needn't have left.

She returned to Fedora Man, who chanted some bizarre rhythm of *oooms* and *umms*, his eyes closed, his head tilted down until his hat nearly slipped from his head. "Are you sleeping?" she asked.

"No, I'm meditating."

"Well, your hat's falling over your face. For the purpose of this discussion," she announced, "I think we should take it off."

"I don't like people to see me without my hat," he replied. "I don't like people to see me in any vulnerable state. Hatlessness equates partial nudity."

"Am I going to fuck your head?"

"If my head is naked, it stands a high chance of being fucked."

"What kind of house did you come up in?"

"The kind where people fuck you while you sleep. The hatless house. I just don't like people to look at me without my hat."

"This is where we differ, Fedora Man," she said. "I like people to look at me whatever I'm doing. Because I'm naturally and gloriously beautiful. Nobody fucks with my head. Perhaps you should try to think like me."

His hat fell off. He stared at his right ankle. "Oh, I'm so uncomfortable," he whined. "You only had one pair of white thigh-highs, and no scarves. Maybe the sweat-sock around my left wrist robs me of confidence. Cotton's a natural fiber. It evokes naturalism and rough privileges. Additionally, if you want me to recognize the power of nudity and self-confidence, I'd suggest that you model that behavior."

"That's possible, and crafty," she replied, considering the enjoyment it would offer to disrobe. "But I must remain clothed to assure myself that I'm chastely analyzing the problem of us, and I cannot release your hands. You understand, don't you, that since we've already been lovers, I can't be naked and free here around you without encouraging my own licentious thoughts about making you similarly naked, which would then result in your will being crushed, Ivor, smashed to bits, because I'd take you with no remorse whatsoever! I'd use you shamelessly as the sex-puppet boy entity I've always wanted. I'm trying to show you a modicum more respect." She took his hat and replaced it on his head. "Despite this, no one," she said, "is going to fuck you against your will."

He appeared to dote upwards. She enjoyed this. Staring at each other, acknowledging something had shifted between them, both were silent.

~

"But what I'm saying," she said, walking around his chair in a circular way, "is that your relative evil is not necessarily evil. How did you conceive of your definition of evil? What's more, how can you maintain it while doing good most of the time?"

"I'm not evil all the time, but I'm evil enough of the time to know my main force in life is evil. This is one reason I feel you'd be better off without me."

"That remains to be seen. I believe that your evil is deep-seated insecurity, meshed with a tendency to lose touch with reality. Hallucinations, perhaps?"

"You're right. I am hallucinating right now that my head is between your legs," he said. "My tongue is going lap, lap, lap. And you're going, 'Oh, oh god. OH GOD!

Ivvvvvvvvvvvvor, Yes!'"

She thought about that a while before replying, "Can I get in on that hallucination?"

~

Eight minutes later, having avoided such intimacy, she pulled his chair closer to the bed, still wearing her clothes. "Okay, so what do you do when a friend gets mad?"

"I don't have any friends."

"Yes, you do, Ivor. You must. So what do you do when a friend gets mad?"

"I do have some friends I once said I'd throw myself in front of a truck for. Very loyal friends. But, in the end, I let the truck hit them. I didn't sacrifice myself because I wanted to save myself from *unnecessary* commitments *to loyalty*. I may talk a big game, but I wouldn't actually throw myself in front of anything, for anyone."

"Okay, but after you saved your own hide," Beautiful said, "did you apologize for not truck-blocking?"

"Were the friends dead?"

"Let's say no."

"I sent their families an automaton carrier pigeon with condolence notes, in some cases…"

"That's a good start."

"No, Beautiful, it's not." He commenced to crying without sound. "I've let people down, and friends have suffered. Like one I left with no warning. She killed herself in a boat cabin when she couldn't reach me. Tied up in a closet."

"I've killed friends too. That's the price of life," Beautiful said. "Ivor, Let's not dwell. We're not dead now." She kissed his cheek but then he launched into harder, louder, inexplicable tears.

"Stop crying, fm," she said. "Right now."

"I can't stop," he replied. "You might have sounded

like my mother just now, so I desperately need to cry."

"All right, keep crying," she said. "I'll pack for tomorrow."

A few moments later, after his sobs subsided, Beautiful broached the difficult topic of vegetables. "And what do you think of squash?"

"The game?"

"The food. Also, how well do you play badminton? Don't lie to me."

~

She finished packing while she awaited his reply. Finally, "I like squash," he said. "Zucchini is a personal favorite, drizzled with garlic butter and made with nuts. I am a badminton ace. I would beat you and beat you again. You might get upset since you can't win. I hate when that happens, so suck it up. My own sister will no longer play badminton with me due to her a history of *loss* at the sport."

"I'll beat you at badminton until you cry for shame," Beautiful replied. "Within an inch of your newly lacking confidence. But let's examine your sister's history of *loss*. Did she lose anything better than what we've had?"

"How do you define *better?*"

"Oh you know, awful, truly CRUSHING? Crush, crush, crush, Ivor, like a little birdie's neck. Maybe I meant something worse. Did she lose more or worse than us?"

"How do I know whether she lost more? I don't know what you've lost."

"I haven't really lost anything," Beautiful replied. "But, my point is, what did she lose? I'm interested in your sister."

"She lost our father's love when she was twelve. I lost it too. But our father was much more evil than yours."

~

"Ivor, would you do something for me?" Beautiful had kicked off her slippers.

"What?"

"I want to talk about this guy. His name ends with Gut."

"Gut who?"

"I don't know, a writer type, a daydreamer like me. He wrote a book I liked entirely too well, about a father and some string and a cat and a Dresden maybe, which is a very sad city, though this particular city was nowhere mentioned in this novel. He was an anti-war novelist, like many military vets. Anyhow, let's not focus on war because Daddy loves it. I could get waylaid: 'There are more things on heaven and earth, Beautiful Ape Girl Baby Chef,' he'd say, etcetera, etcetera. Meh. Regardless, in Gut's book, there was this beautiful olive-skinned princess. Very sexy. And in this one scene, she took off her sandal and started touching some guy's foot. A stranger's foot! This was right before killer ice was about to take over the planet, also before she was going to get married to a different guy not from her island, though the latter guy was about to be President—anyway, on this island, they had a custom that struck me as really romantic about touching feet. I'm thinking foot-touching qualifies as an act we could share without sex or mother issues since it doesn't involve penetration, and I'd like to do this thing together. I've always wanted to do this thing! Let's do this thing right now!"

"What *thing?*"

"We touch our bare feet together and share our souls," Beautiful replied, transcendent.

"I don't think I have one."

"A foot?"

"A soul."

"Oh, yes, Ivor. Yes, you do," she said.

"Even if I had a soul, it wouldn't move through my feet," he announced. "It would move through my head! Or my p—"

"Then you'll hardly care if I tilt over your chair and try the foot touching, will you?" she asked, dropping both him and the chair to the ground more gently than she preferred.

"Certainly. Tilt me over any time you want since I'm *restrained to the chair!"* Fedora Man replied, whinge-moaning.

"Oh, can you stop being such a buzzkill?" she asked. "You're evil. I get it." She lay on the floor across from him, feet in the air across from his, wriggling her hairy toes to make a point. "Now, put your feet up and touch them to mine."

"No," he replied, toes pointed down in rebellion, neck craning his grounded head sideways to regard her. "I'm not going to."

"What if I don't care what you do in this situation?" she asked. "I can access your feet if I'd like. What if I just touch our souls together because I want to? It's what I'd do at home. And on Gut's island, no one was ever so stingy as to refuse a soul touching freely extended! That's so stingy, Fedora Man! You should be ashamed!"

"I can hardly stop you from doing *a damn thing* if I'm tied up, can I?" Fedora Man asked. "I'm an easily *forced submissive* in this position. But for the sake of argument, let's say someone didn't want to touch feet with someone else. Wouldn't this undesired foot-touch be like rape on that island? Like a safe word violation? By the way I've read that book, and I'm thinking that any soul to sole contact should be strictly voluntary. It was voluntary in that book. Plus, it involved religion."

"Do you need religion? Did you want to stop me from touching your feet?" she queried. "Heathen or otherwise, I will not touch them if you feel strongly, but I do believe you are just hiding out in Fraidy Cat Book Memory Palace. Whelper Land!"

"I don't particularly want to stop you," he replied.

"But regardless, what you do makes no difference since I have no soul to belabor. Mine is strictly a point of honor. Of asking. Of receiving permission to touch me."

"So you see, Fedora Man!" Beautiful shouted, kicking the air. "*Again* you are being difficult for the sake of being difficult!"

"I just think you should ask my permission, more formally."

"Okay," Beautiful said, still on her back and talking upward, feet suspended inches from his. "Dearest Ivor, will you press your feet against mine this evening, so we can attempt to have a reenactment of the inter-soul communion I read about once in a Gut book?"

"No."

"That's not the right answer. Try again."

"Do what you want. *Rape* my feet."

"Is that permission? I think that's permission."

"Why me?" Fedora Man asked. "Why touch feet with me?"

"What in the hell are you talking about? Don't you know why you?"

"I don't," he said. "Please spell it out."

She got off the floor and stood, staring down at him like he was a most curious ugly toad. "Because I love you. Because you bled me, you idiot. So I would like our souls to have communed at least once, even if it is to be in this slipshod motel room where there is no world-killing ice, where there is no strange island, and there are no beautiful princesses, save myself, though you can have that role if you want it and I'll be President guy—because we have been intimate. I've never had a boyfriend like you before. Not one I let so close. And you're the first person I've ever asked this from, though I've been dreaming it for years, so it would be very nice if you would simply not say no." She stood awaiting his response for a long while, refusing to say another word.

He closed his eyes so that she couldn't look at him while he considered her request and said nothing more until the moment she was about to put her slippers back on and return to her bed, the moment when she turned away from his stupid, supine, closed-eyed self, deciding to untie him in the morning and privately hoping his circulation suffered.

Then he said, "Lay back down, Beautiful. All right. Give me your feet. You can have my non-existent soul."

~

Shortly thereafter, she lifted his chair back to an upright position. "Peanut butter. Creamy or crunchy?" she asked, this during the co-inhabiting part of the interrogation.

"Crunchy."

"I see. Steamed vegetables or broiled?"

"Broiled."

"Salmon or yellowtail?"

"Neither. Vegetarian."

"Lobster or shrimp upon occasion?"

"Maybe."

"Old fashioned oatmeal or instant?"

"Rolled oats."

"All right, well, listen, I like wearing leather garments —a lot! I like my leather real. Same with fur. Would this cause problems with your vegetarian idealism?"

"Probably, but keep the pieces small. Don't let my friends see them."

"Already part of the plan."

~

Other parts of the discussion went worse. After she'd sated herself with three hours of intense interrogation, Beautiful finally told him, "I feel you can go free now, Fedora Man. I'm afraid we haven't much in common."

This elicited no response.

"I'd hoped we'd have more to say to each other," she went on, "but if we have nothing in common, perhaps there's no future here. This must be a problem for people who make love to each other, sometimes realizing there isn't much to feel compatible about." Tears fell freely from both her eyes as she remarked, "This must happen to a lot of people. That music you like, for example—it exhibits a complete distaste for big bands and also soulful blues or rock covers where artists have enjoyed a modicum of success!"

"It's what I like," he said.

"You like songs that have stupid words by bands like The Gropers. And how can we possibly wake up together and enjoy a morning of camaraderie that is not spiked with our disdain for the other's habits and tastes?"

"I understand," Fedora Man said, "well-put," as she removed the ties from his ankles.

"Yet I feel that, even if this pairing has been a terrible mistake we accidentally consummated too quickly, at least we tried." More tears came to Beautiful's eyes. "Still, it was like thinking you've won something and discovering you haven't. Like knowing you have a new puppy at home, but knowing he bites you every five minutes rather than kissing you fondly—when the initial three minutes he spent soaking your face in the humane shelter for dogs you certainly thought him the most adorable and considerate pet ever kept there, so you brought him home. What a devastating disappointment! Before you go, did you mind if I put your hat back on? That'll make things more formal."

"Go ahead," he replied, turning his hand on his recently sprung wrist. "I'll head back to my helicopter soon."

"Should we try to be friends after this?"

"No."

"Really?" She sat on her bed, crossing her legs. "So I

guess we can't even be friends now, now that we've taken things too far? Romance is awful with what's ruined."

"That's true. I agree," he replied. "I can never be your friend again for as long as I mildly desire you. You might be able to be my friend regardless of desiring me, but I can't be your friend because romance will ever be on my mind. I might not be able to stop flirting, even if nothing will follow but your injury and fury. Nonetheless, I've never been successful at romance due to my evil nature, so this isn't a big failure. More like a repetitious failure."

She laughed. "Yes. But I had a bigger romantic failure with a greaser. He wanted to ransom me and spoke of rape. In the end, we didn't part amicably... As to be expected with such low-class horrors."

"He didn't change his mind and be your friend?"

"I killed him. It was necessary."

Ivor reached over and took her hand. "He probably deserved it. I will," he said magnanimously, suddenly saddened to lose a possible connection he might admire, "from henceforth, attempt to be your friend from a distance. We could call each other and talk about killing, now and then. Though, let's be clear. I desire you more than mildly, in a physical capacity unlike the desire I've had for other women."

"The same can be said. You'll be my friend?" she asked, surprised. "Uncompensated? That's great, Ivor! Not that I undervalue you. Friendships without a price are the better kinds. Harder to keep. Harder to acquire."

"It's not such a prize. Most people don't want to be my friend," he said.

"Well, I certainly do," she said. "Who wouldn't want to be your friend? I have only one real friend now, not on my father's payroll. I'd like another. Ivor, this is excellent news! I'm so glad we can be unpaid friends!" She beamed at him before asking quite earnestly, "Do you desire me, really? Even if I don't look like those billboard girls that other boys go on about? Even if I'm not feminine or demure enough for my mother to love me?"

"Yes. I desire you. And who needs a mother's love?" he asked. "Not us." He put his arm around her as they sat together. "Did you think I'd sit in a chair and let you harass me with questions for several hours if I didn't feel both desire and admiration?"

"I don't know what you'd do. I hardly know you."

"But think of what you know so far."

"What I know is that I don't know you well enough," she said. "But that must be developed within the growing friendship. I know you like to crush things. But I want you to know that nothing about your physical traits puts me off," she said. "Not one thing. If we didn't have such a bad dynamic of compatibility based on the verbal parse of habits, we could've been great lovers."

"Differences aren't always deal-killers," Ivor said, with feeling.

"Yes, though you seem quite ready to end things," she replied.

"You told me we must," he replied. "You pronounced we were no good. It's good we explored the non-physical side of our dynamic, though it led to an undesirable outcome," he said. But he touched her lips with his fingers, her shoulders, her breasts, all lightly, with the softest of touches.

"If you touch me like that again," she said, swooning inside, "I've already touched your soul with my feet, so I'll be forced to throw you onto the bed and ravish you as I did our first night together, with more of my own needs met this time." A wave of multi-layered *toska* consumed her. She looked at him and passed it right into his eyes where *toska* then hovered, too, mirrored, multiplying, a rampant and lucid *toska* expanding on freefall between them.

"As long as we're both aware that this is a short-term passion we're both supposed to give up without any drama after this evening," he said, pressing his face to her neck,

"No weeping. No moaning. No long, humiliating letters expressing our mistakes and how ridiculous it is to think we should be the same in all respects. No bargaining. No mailing of the others' preferred peanut butter. No offers for vegetarianism from the ham eater. No promises to sway like ghosts on the others' graves due to the eternal rightness of us, despite the obvious wrongness. No maintaining of long-suffering loves for each other, despite the expense to the present, which is to find every other person partially boring and not nearly as desirable. No comparisons to current or new lovers or wistful sighs as we marvel at how we ever gave the other up over badminton, finance, or politics. No boredom when or if the new partner hasn't killed someone, too. In short, no mooning."

"That sort of mooning sounds kind of good," Beautiful said.

"I've always been a fan of mooning," Ivor replied. "It's how you avoid the next real relationship."

She sighed, sighed again, and said, "Relationship avoidance is good." Then she tossed him onto the bed, saying, "I now have a son named Thomas. He's my driver. This week, however, he's regressing to childhood and experiencing his girlhood. I loaned him some Dolce and Gabbana. And my panties. His balls were falling out. I thought to suggest boyshorts, but they weren't readily available."

"I have a partner in the business who'll be dropped into Niagara Falls tonight because he failed the mission to bring back shares from a major conglomerate," he said, kissing her neck.

"When you have clout," Beautiful said, lifting her face so he could work more thoroughly as they spoke, "you must use it. That's what Daddy says."

"I think it's so kind that you'd give your male driver another girl childhood," Fedora Man said, with his hand wrenching down into her pajama pants but getting twisted in the waistband.

"He had a terrible boy childhood," Beautiful replied, twisting his nipple. "He hated his birth mother."

"Understood," Fedora Man agreed, yanking her pants down to her ankles. "He's lucky to have a new definition of matriarchal love."

"Yes," Beautiful said, smiling. "It all started when I clocked him in the head, like the best things do... And to think I haven't even clocked you yet."

Fedora Man rose and nuzzled closer, seeming to bury himself in her chest. "I feel so safe with you," he said, unbuttoning her pajama top. "That statement is not to be mooned over later either."

"Agreed," Beautiful replied, putting her hand down his pants and pulling out his bent member before solemnly sitting upon it, taking it in, and gyrating her hips slightly back and forth. "And I promise not to moon over how beautiful your pale skin is in the heart of the night, how I like how you touch me so softly and listen so well, how you let me say what I want to say and refuse to be horrified when I'm honest... I've never had that in all my life. I don't even have to lie. I won't moon over you. *Tu et nul autre.*" Above him, she moved slowly, so slowly that the only thing he did was gasp in one long series of exhales and inhales. "Does that feel good?" she asked. "Should I get more vehement?"

"No," he said. He put his hand over her mouth and blinked, his eyes wet. "Don't speak. Please, say no more."

When he kissed her again, she thought about how she'd miss that, too, how adorable he looked when he wanted to shut her up—upright, prone, tied to the chair, even while ranting indignant about her preference for night swimming over dune walking.

He whimpered a few times. She kept moving.

After the lovemaking ended, she pretended to sleep. When he, too, pretended to sleep, but Beautiful was aware that at any moment that he would leave just as stealthily as he'd done the last time, she opened her eyes and looked at him like this might be the last time she'd see him. Covertly, she took a photo with her camera phone, several.

No, Fedora Man, she thought. *Though we hardly agree about anything, I will never moon over your loss when you go. Except every single day. I love you as more than my former dog, and I suppose I should admit it...* She contemplated getting into the shower, but subsequently wanted to cry. This time, unlike the last time, he had not hurt her with his penetration but had allowed her to own him completely, though only, she supposed, because he knew he would be leaving.

"What you most want comes and goes," she remembered her mother saying so many times. "Come and go," she told Fedora Man, moving her lips but creating no sound. "Come and go. Come and go."

In the morning, of course, he, his fedora, his presence, his safety as the one she could tell all things to without fear, was gone. She was alerted to this by Thomas knocking in his black suit. A fearful ache rose in her chest that she could not explain.

"Mama," Thomas said, shaking her hand as if he were a salesperson when she opened the door, with a firm but confident grip. "I have concluded, late last night, mincing around in your Fendi nightgown and slipper heels, that I didn't really want to be a girl. Being a girl is painful and difficult. I diminished them before as something weak or less than. You've shown me I was wrong! So I'm fine being a man, no matter what that means."

"Nice handshake, Thomas," Beautiful said. "Please go get me some pastry and crunchy peanut butter from the diner before we go. Not everyone has the stomach to be a real woman. I don't blame you. But we have to leave soon. Sandra's waiting."

"Was someone here?" Thomas asked, looking around at the thigh highs and sweat socks on the floor, the state of the mangled bed. "The room's a wreck."

"Yes, someone was here, Baby," Beautiful said, remembering how she characterized Thomas as a salesman a moment ago when he'd arrived at her room, finding it applicable. "A traveling salesman came. He sold me some expensive information for a price. And now he's gone. He needs nothing more from me. That's how it works."

~

It was late that morning when Beautiful received a text from her father. "Your mother is missing. STOP. She has not called in two days. STOP. Please tell me if she communicates with you. STOP. I'm so worried. STOP."

"Daddy," Beautiful replied. "I'm glad you still have a cell phone, though this appears a new number, but there's no use pretending it is a telegram. You're doing that thing you do again of refusing the present and wanting to retreat into an already vanished past, but it's no use. We cannot fail to welcome the future by pretending it is indeed the past just to please ourselves, and we cannot live like cavemen in this exciting age of limitless information. Mommy is fine. Did you want to talk about the divorce? Call in an hour."

Beautiful wrote in her journal as Thomas drove through hills and arid terrain. She wondered how Ida May Haze would have perceived her trip had Ida lived it. Ida herself had lived through many losses. There was the frog colony she was required to eliminate from the backyard; the ridiculous daughter who'd gone off and married a syphilitic sailor; the death of her sad, grim father; the loss of her maidenhood and waste of her life in a shithole with a bastard who hardly cared. For each of these losses, there'd been a show, sometimes several.

If Beautiful ever had a show, *The Everything Is Not Beautiful at the Ballet Show* she might call it, she wondered what she'd bemoan. The decimation of friends at the compound interested her, as did the fact that she'd find Sandra, for the first time, in a place unlike home. Pregnant. Living in the dirt. A small parasitic growth adhered to Sandra's womb-wall, sucking at Sandra's resources. And she might discuss the relationship between she and Sandra on her show, compensated or otherwise. A mostly platonic love affair between women.

But what could she tell Sandra about Fedora Man now, after the latest events? "We had a very disagreeable conversation, swiftly followed by more passionate love-making I instigated, and he left, but now I find even his repulsive traits capable of rendering immeasurable *toska?*"

And were her parents getting a divorce? And what did it mean when you hated just about every single thing about someone else's preferences, which might have mattered, except you loved them so deeply, none of that was essential? Did dolphins have a place in personal meditation? Did dolphins have a snowball's chance of making an undesirable love go away when you thought of them deeply enough, visualizing how they looked swimming through the water and the small nubby teeth they often showed with open mouths? Was this likelihood of probability lessened when driving through the desert? Were there dolphins in the desert, like at a casino pool? After all, there were Venetian boats, but were there ever too many questions? And how did you give something up that you'd promised not to moon over, when promising not to do something was pretty much the perverse soul's equivalent for deciding you indeed did want to do that thing and moon over said individual, doing it to excess?

"I do want to moon over him!" she announced.

"What?" Thomas asked.

"Nothing."

Well, if he plans to leave me, she thought, *I can moon all I want. How's he ever going to know, and whom will it bother? Perhaps, one day, when I have lived enough and am ready to write my memoir, I can omit all the bad things I've done and create him as just one short chapter on impossible loves whose moon-over value calculated to an aggregate twelve times higher value than their real presence value! He did look funny when I tied him down on that chair, quite agitated.*

On that cheerful note, she reclined into the back seat, watching Thomas appear like a reborn and jubilant child as he drove them toward Sandra's, Thomas a happy boy now in his black suit that made him look like an FBI agent, his face shorn of his mustache, and his hand fooling with the radio dial while he announced so many childish and ridiculous ideas of gratitude for sights they passed in transit on the road that she'd begun to zone out until he announced something that did interest her. Thomas, excited and gleeful, said, "Beautiful? Ida May Haze is on the radio! Look, I found her channel, even out here in the dunes!"

"Very good, Thomas," Beautiful said, "you're such a good Baby," and they settled in to listen.

CHAPTER NINE
SPEAKING AGAIN

~IN WHICH, IDA PREACHES ON RADICAL SOLUTIONS, BEAUTIFUL SCHOOLS FEDORA MAN ON LOVE, GRANDMA CHEF GOES VEGAN SHOWGIRL, AND SANDRA COOKS CHICKEN.~

Ida May Haze came through the stereo, ranting: "And what I'm saying, listeners, is that nothing worth doing or having is worth *doing* or *having* when you have an *inconsiderate* asshole of a spouse!"

"Hear, hear!" said Thomas.

"You must choose your spouse more carefully!" Ida stressed. "This is a situation Ida May Haze calls a no-brainer!"

"Does she speak in the third person?" Thomas asked.

"Yes, she often does," Beautiful said.

"Now what you all want to know is whether you should get rid of your lemon of a spouse, if that's what you've got! Right?" Ida thundered. "What I'd tell you in response to that is that *Strong as Animal Women* say *YES* to *Spousal Elimination!*"

"That's exactly right, Ida!" Beautiful remarked. "Burn the Fedora!"

"Fedora?" Thomas asked.

"Metaphorical," Beautiful replied.

"What's metaphorical about a fedora?" Thomas asked.

"Everything," Beautiful said, "including the rim," as Ida went on. "Because this has to do with your self-esteem, ladies! How many nights do you lay food on the table to have some incon-fucking-siderate louse look at it like he'd leave it for the dogs? How many loads of laundry must you do before your side aches and you groan, 'Can't I get some help?' Now, I know I've suggested radical solutions before. These fall in line with the Radical Solutions open-call advice hour, but some situations are more nuanced, as they say."

"I don't even require his done laundry or dinner appreciation!" Beautiful said, vigorously incensed. "I never, not once, did his laundry or made him dinner, Ida! What I require is time, attention, adulation, and that he stops leaving!" Ida, of course, was deaf to Beautiful's remarks, a fact that never failed to irritate Beautiful but was somewhat ameliorated by the intermittently working call line that could be used, should Beautiful truly wish to communicate, though Beautiful had never used it due to extensive awe and fear of misrepresentations.

Still, Ida continued, "Radical solutions include leaving cold, bad food in the refrigerator and pretending you're too sick to cook more. Throwing the laundry away until your point is made…"

Beautiful looked down at her journal and doodled on the cover, drawing a wending line that spun side to side and resembled a series of cords wound around the neck of a rabbit, if one saw the ink blot where her pen paused as a possible rabbit and viewed journal cover art as mystically as one might view a moving cloud. Beautiful tightened the ink noose, made the rabbit larger, and subsequently said to Thomas, "Isn't it wonderful that neither of us have spouses, but we both know exactly what she's talking about? General disrespect. Heartbreaking, unresolved disrespect."

"Ida's right," Thomas said. "I had an ex-girlfriend or two who qualified as lemons. I think the subject bridges the gap, whether or not marriage enters the equation."

"Your lip skin is so soft without those tufts of mustache hair," Beautiful observed. "Watching you talk, even in the rear-view, seems different today."

"Maybe it's like keeping a tiny bit of my experience as a girl, saved by depilated skin," he replied.

"Maybe," Beautiful said. "I still think you would have made a beautiful girl, Esmerelda. You could've been one of my favorite girls ever! But don't worry, Thomas. I still like you as a boy."

"Thank you, Mama," he said.

They listened quietly a while longer as Ida continued until Beautiful announced, "Satellite Radio is so splendid. I don't know what I'd have done without Ida's teachings all these years. When the friends made me feel poorly, I mean."

"Ida's great," Thomas said. "Truthful as a tumbler of bourbon makes a sailor."

"Right," Beautiful said. "And further, I respect Ida for her willingness to put her real feelings out into space. Even when she's angry. Angry as I, myself, am angry right now. Angry and confused...."

"...Ida says *RAGE* is your power." Ida went on. "Each time you encounter your own rage, don't *discourage* it! Don't *suppress*—"

"I don't suppress, Ida," Beautiful enthused, chiming in. "Ever!" They listened pleasantly until Beautiful's cell phone rang like an escalating police siren, which meant her father's main phone was working.

"It's Daddy," she said to Thomas, and then answered, "Hello, Daddy."

"Did your mother tell you about Cisco?" her father asked, without prelude.

"What?"

"What did your mother tell you when you last spoke? Was it about Cisco? I need to know."

"What? Mother didn't speak of Cisco at all."

"She lied then," her father said, with a pained voice.

"She lied, knowing that what she said would force me to divorce her!"

"Oh, no."

"Then she took off."

"Oh, dear."

"Now, I have to get her back. She didn't speak about Cisco at all?"

"No. Daddy, Cisco wasn't mentioned. She told me how you two fell in love. A beautiful story! Typo! And then when I asked about whether I had ever had a fetal twin that I might've accidentally eaten, she said that I might because I'm left-handed, but I've no idea what you're talking about regarding Cisco. Can you please be more specific?"

"I'm too busy for precision or painstaking explanations, Beautiful. Do you have your mother's location? She's not wearing traceable shoes."

"No."

"But is she talking to you?"

"When she feels like it."

"When she next calls, can you tell her I've hired a technician to put back every piece of disassembled household machinery? Tell her I want to know the reason for this confounded getaway. Tell her I can't track her, so she must call me."

"Yes, Daddy, I'm sure I—"

"And tell her I love her, Peanut. I love her so much; be sure to tell her that..."

A lump of fear, anxiety, and sadness sat in Beautiful's throat. Daddy never sounded so desperate or so helpless. "Okay, Daddy," she agreed.

The line clicked silent. "Thomas," Beautiful said, dropping the glass between the seats. "This is a fine pickle. It would seem that my father's eager to get my mother back. It would also seem that she lied to him about telling me anything about his brother—or that he misinterpreted what he thought she said to me, but now I've no idea what either of them said."

Her phone beeped. Another text arrived, from Fedora Man. "I'm not thinking about you or anything. Just to let you know I'm not mooning."

"Fuck you," she replied.

"Am I supposed read that erotically?" he asked, moments later.

"Read it any way you want," she replied.

"So you aren't missing me at all?"

"Not at all. Stop talking to me. Isn't this what you wanted? Except I wish you hadn't left, but leave me alone now. I'm busy, and it's over. Go take over some evil empire."

"It was supposed to be over," he said tersely, as terse as a text could get. "Except for the distant friendship..."

"Your point?"

"We agreed."

"On what?"

"We agreed on dissolution, and then you enticed me into sex with you."

"What kind of agreement is that? I think it's non-agreement."

"No, we verbally agreed while I ravished your body."

"Even were I to entertain your idea that we agreed, distant friendship, I'd think," Beautiful replied, "should not take place *the day after* a tryst. So why are you writing me now?"

After a ten minute delay, "Because I wanted to," he finally said.

"Well, then, perhaps we should reconsider the welcomeness of distant friendship?" she queried. "And you should simply choose to be my boyfriend! I wrote you a horrid poem this morning, in which I cut off your balls. And then I fed you to the sharks. I also maligned the name of your family."

"Can I read it?"

"No. I ripped it up. You'd think it bleak anyway. Bleak,

heathen, bleak, you'd say."

"I can't love anybody, you know? It's not personal to you."

"And then the shark fed on his balls / For lack of truth or wherewithal... It's imperfect rhyme."

"I really can't love you. I'm not that kind of loving guy."

"Ivor, you can love anybody you want," she shouted, then texted, regretting there were no italics in text messaging because she would have used them for the word *love*. Nonetheless, in her mind, she italicized the word *love*, but she also put a mental exclamation mark (!) after (!) every (!) word (!), and hoped he heard her message as she thought it, letting the ideas and sentiments live in his eyes as if she had spoken the words directly to him. "What you can't do," she went on, "is let yourself be loved. I could love you very well, for example. I, myself, am very expansive on my ideas of love. You could be loved. But you don't want to be loved. I don't care if you're evil or whatever you think you are. What I think you are is a scared little chicken who fears real love doesn't exist because he hasn't experienced it or hasn't let himself experience it—but you never give yourself a chance. Can't has no place in this discussion. What you struggle against, Ivor, is won't." Again she craved italics—something more fulfilling than stroke and tapping the tiny phone keyboard.

To satisfy her craving for emphasis, she then sent a full message of exclamation marks, followed with, "So what you seem to do, if you won't love, not can't, and you should consult your past history in this matter, particularly the episode in which you killed your mother, is to push the other person away or diminish their value such that they become invisible to you—to crush them into not loving you so that loving will no longer be possible on their to-do list, but you know what, Fedora Man? Bah! I choose to love you and I choose to believe you can do more than you think you can. Though there are many things we don't agree upon. And I never wanted us to be second-date U-haul lesbians or something like that, which, if you're unfamiliar with lesbian culture, is a thing my friend explained as the need to fully combine existing lifestyles with unusual rapidity, and so forth. So what do you think? Will you be my boyfriend or what? We can discuss the terms in a mediated, co-counseled discussion and even call lawyers in if that would help."

He sent three texts after that. "?," "?," and "?."

"Fucker," she texted back, "You know exactly what I mean!" He didn't respond again, so half an hour later she continued into the void of data transmission, "Ivor, my pet, I love you without games and without conditions! I am Beautiful Ape Girl Baby Chef, BAGBC, and I'll do what I damn want, little fm! I have more and stronger letters than you—and I may not have left the estate before this, I may not be as worldly as all the other fancy polyglot women you meet, I'm not a skinny little toothpick because I am strong and aggressively muscular, but I'm real and I care. Tune your dial to the frequency of authentic love. We can have it together. I, at least, know what it is. Only one of us has to know what it is to teach it to the other. Chew on that. And take off your fedora. Wear only your whitest suit the next time you see me. A white hat, too. Symbolically, that will help."

It felt good, she thought, to tell him off.

He ventured forth with nothing more.

~

After another few hours on the road, the lights of the Vegas strip appeared. Through the drive, due to the beautiful hills they passed that were colored in multiple shades of brown, Beautiful had reconsidered her view of the desert. It could be a beautiful place, she decided, provided you were not dune walking and could drive. Still, "I thought we'd never get here," Beautiful said as the rural swath of manmade buildings changed to a more urban display. "Do you have Sandra's address?" she asked Thomas. "Does she live near here, where the lights begin?"

"No. We'll be at Sandra's in twenty more minutes."

"All right," Beautiful said as they drove toward the city. "Please, step on it."

When they finally arrived at Sandra's address, her house was a mobile home adjacent to a larger dwelling in a patch of sand far off from the main house and the glitz and the glamour of casinos. A dusty wind blew through as a small, white dog barked out front. Sandra's mobile home was old and dingy and appeared light pink before its coating of dust beiged it. There was no carport and Sandra's old Pinto sat beside the entry. Beside that was her Honda. Though Beautiful hadn't yet walked to Sandra's door, the sight of the Pinto created a nostalgic wave of love for times already gone. "I'm here!" Beautiful shouted. "I'm here!"

Eager to see her friend, Beautiful held her breath without realizing she did this. Thomas walked behind her while the white dog, a nasty varmint, followed to nip at her heels, but she was not required to kick it since it did not bite her. She gave it one look, barked back, and it immediately sat, cowed, licking its genitals.

She rang the mobile home doorbell and knocked. "Sandra?" Beautiful asked, looking up as the door partially opened.

"This isn't Sandra," a gruff female voice replied. "Take your shoes off and chuck them toward the Lincoln. My new name is Thrasma." The door then yawned outward fully, and Beautiful gaped, for there stood her own mother, tricked out like a Vegas Showgirl, with an orange group of feathers as tall as a toddler atop her head, wearing a gold glitter costume and nipple pasties. Her mother also sported gold dancing shoes.

"No shoes in the house," Sandra called toward the

new arrivals from the recesses.

After Beautiful chucked her shoes toward the Lincoln, "Come in," her mother said. "You like my disguise?"

"Oh, Mother," Beautiful enthused. "You're quite glamorous! So much less staid than your steno-pool outfits. I love the makeover!" Beautiful turned to Thomas and advised, "Baby, if all things work out, this will be Grandma."

"Hello, Mrs. Chef," Thomas said.

"Hello, Driver," her mother replied.

"Thomas's name is Thomas, Mommy," Beautiful said. "He regresses to childhood, and I'm now his mother for this trip out to see Ida, like a matriarchal ambassador to the foreign realm of childhood."

"I like your orange feathers, Mrs. Grandma Chef," Thomas said, bashful but proud to have been claimed.

"Your father said I was never to call drivers by their given names," Mrs. Chef told Beautiful, avoiding Thomas's eyes. "It was part of his jealousy and insane desire that I never speak intimately with other men. For years, I've followed his dictates." She glanced at Thomas as if unsure what to say next.

"You left my father," Beautiful replied. "It's a brave new world."

"Thank you, Thomas," her mother said, again without regarding him. "Mr. Chef liked orange feathers too. But we aren't speaking."

Her mother then brushed Thomas to the side and embraced Beautiful. "Oh, Baby," she said. "My daughter, my lovely, my Beautiful precious, adorable, rebellious girl! How are you? I'm so glad to see you still alive."

"Hey, hey, is Beautiful here now?" Sandra called from the back of the dwelling, her mouth full of something. Then Sandra came up behind Ethel Chef, and embraced them both. "Oh, Beautiful," she said, hurriedly chewing, "I've missed you!"

"Sandra," Beautiful said. "You're eating peanut butter

and celery and wearing those dear pajamas! I'm so glad to see you, too!"

"Oh, wow, this is wild," Sandra said. "Let me look at you! I see you haven't been shaving. Did you give that up?"

"Yes. I must be myself," Beautiful said. "I feel more selfly while hairy."

"Have you been leaving the car?"

"Yes. I leave the car whenever I want! I won't be restrained by common fears. It's like Ida says, 'fear is the death of all ambitions for growth.'"

"Don't worry, Sandra. We go out together," Thomas interjected. "We've had some enjoyable times. On the dunes, otherwise..."

Beautiful rested her hand on Sandra's stomach. "You're pregnant?" She stared hard at her friend's round abdomen before saying with awe, "Is something really in there, Sandra? A baby thing! Something that'll make a little Sandra, a rascal Sandra, a babe Sandra incarnate? Oh, wow."

Sandra didn't respond with anything at first, just stared with a misty-eyed demeanor. A moment later, "I suppose yes," she said. "I'm going to have a child."

Beautiful replied, "But you had to do it out here, really? What the hell do you do in all this sand, Sandra? Please tell me I'm missing something. A big tic-tac-toe game with large sticks? Light fires without fears? Make enormous hour glasses? Why would anyone move out here?"

"It's cheap," Sandra replied. "And pretty. In a sparse way."

"Hmmm, yes," Beautiful said, glancing at the minimal furnishings Sandra had brought with her from the estate that now glimmered like fine objects in her dusty trailer.

"Fucking Eugene's here too," Sandra told Beautiful as she watched her survey the home. "He came back. I guess he didn't care much for his stripper."

"How long did she last?"

"Two days. Until he ran out of money."

"So you took him back?"

"I had to think about the long-term. And the baby. So, yes. Too, unfortunately, I love him. Don't you do that when you're in love, take the beloved back?"

"I don't know," Beautiful said. "I don't know much of anything about love, it seems! I take hardly anything back. Before I was in love, I felt I understood love much better. In fact, the longer I'm in love, the less I seem to know. Love's confusing. And besides, you can try to take the beloved back and then have them spit in your face! I know that. Not to mention what you get when you try at the wrong time! In case you don't know, that's radio silence, which leads to hate!" She lifted her cell and texted Fedora Man with four texts: "Give me." "Everything." "I want." "I have clout." then left things alone.

"Beautiful, put that damn thing down," her mother replied, caressing her and tugging at the hair that once curled on Beautiful's cheeks. "You're here now! We've missed you."

Since Sandra planned to cook dinner, they decided they'd wait till the next day to ride into the barrio. As Beautiful looked on, Sandra made green-bean casserole and baked chicken. Beautiful watched her cook with admiration. "You touch that cold nasty stuff and pull off the white fatty skin and then put it in the oven?" she asked.

"Yes," Sandra said. "That's how it's done."

"So this," Beautiful remarked, "is how it happens from the store. The regular person takes raw meat home, throws things on it, and then heats it, right?"

"Yes," Sandra said, hands coated with egg and breadcrumbs.

"And it takes a long time?"

"At least an hour when you bake chicken," Sandra said. "Sometimes longer at higher elevations."

"Being a regular person who cooks seems like a lot of work," Beautiful said. "Grocery shopping, too."

"It is," Sandra agreed.

"I'll be right back," Beautiful said. She stepped into the living room, which was a matter of a few steps, to discover her mother reading a magazine article to Thomas, Thomas's head on her mother's knee. "We wanted to read him a story like a grandmother might do," her mother said. "But there aren't any children's books here." Ethel Chef then kept reading, "The second step in a perfect manicure is buffing. Top coat quality makes a difference. As you apply the polish—" Listening, Thomas smiled so contentedly that Beautiful felt both he and her mother were comforted.

"Daddy said he loves you," Beautiful said when the article concluded. "And that he is having everything at home reassembled, as you'd like."

Her mother's brow furrowed deeply. "That's nice, honey."

"Daddy said he doesn't know where you are."

"He can't and he won't. I myself am having an outing from the estate, but let's talk privately."

"All right," Beautiful said. "Where?"

Beautiful's mother excused herself from Thomas, pulling at Beautiful's arm. "Outside. We need to take a walk," she whispered to Beautiful. "My darling, I think it's important that you know why we never let you leave the estate. As a result, I rarely left the estate myself. This is the extent of a mother's love." Her mother pulled on a sweater and replaced her gold shoes with ugly tennis shoes she also must have bought on the way.

"I don't even recognize the shoe brand," Beautiful said. "Those are beyond ugly."

Her mother smiled and laughed, handing Beautiful a new pair of ugly shoes all her own and then grabbed Beautiful's hand and dragged her outside, saying simply, "They're cheap and ugly. But they've no trackers. Let's go, Beautiful. Yes, let's go! Before he finds us."

~

Beautiful and her mother sat together on a dune, watching a lizard scurry up a hill. "Do you really think all my shoes have trackers?" Beautiful asked.

"That or wire taps. Can't hurt to be safe," her mother said. "Some shoes might be clean, but let's not take chances."

"My butt is cold," Beautiful admitted, shifting in her Juicy Couture sundress. She wanted a sweater.

"Just sit still on it a while," her mother replied. "It'll warm."

"Are those sidewinder tracks?"

"I think so," Ethel Chef said.

"Wish I saw the snake. Right now. That'd be exciting!"

"You could go looking for it."

"No," Beautiful said. "I'm here for you. Why'd you ask me outside?"

After a comfortable silence, her mother spoke again. "Remember when you were quite small and asked me why the friends looked so different?"

"Yes, and mother I understand I was never quite feminine enough for you, so you don't have to rub it in. I tried my very best! I developed a very feminine style of dr—"

"I loved you just the way you were, Beautiful," her mother said. "I just worried about you, never wanted you to be lost or endangered. Out here, in the real world, you can't just kill or injure people. People out here go to jail."

"Daddy doesn't."

"Your father doesn't kill or injure," Ethel Chef corrected, "He has others killed or injured... But back on the estate, we controlled the world you saw. Checked people's backgrounds. Evacuated them. Introduced new candidates we thought might befriend you and paid them decent salaries to make your life enjoyable. There were certain things we couldn't arrange, like romantic friends in the appropriate age groups—because you were a minor, because we worried about people of the hired stripe who were compensated for romance, and because we were worried you might come to care for them, but they would leave you and break your heart. You have such a big, open heart, Beautiful. We couldn't meet all your needs. But we did the best we could—you were an adorable and thoughtful child, if vehement... And when we found Ida's radio show, we thought it was a perfect match since you had an uncommon amount of rage that your peer-group couldn't understand. We tried so hard, but—" Ethel Chef's voice broke before she went on more calmly, "we couldn't stop time or control your life forever. Even your therapists were trained what to teach you what we wanted them to instruct. We always knew what we wanted for you. Early on, your father said, 'I want my daughter to love herself, above all, to adore herself, and find the acts of others only partially concerning. People who love themselves are the least like animals. Self-love will be her cure for this visual anomaly.' So it was most important that you came to be confident, no matter what happened in the outside world, which we kept under wraps for as long as you stayed on the estate, although that could not and would not last forever—because you are so bright and so brave, so would certainly want more exposure to life eventually—and you know why we did all this, Beautiful?"

"To confine me," Beautiful said. "Because you wanted me on lockdown?"

"Because we loved you, and because of Cisco."

"Mommy," Beautiful said, remembering the escalation in her father's voice at the mention of his brother's name. "Daddy said never to talk about Cisco."

"He was afraid of talking about Cisco," her mother replied.

"Why?"

"Because Cisco looked like you and he died."

Beautiful's heart fell into her feet. She desperately

wished she'd met Cisco before he died, even just once, but this desire was quickly quashed since she knew her uncle had been deceased since long before she was born. "Like me, really?" she said.

"Yes. But he was unhappy. He was wild. Violent. Institutionalized after a time. And your father feared that if we didn't make you happier than Cisco as we raised you," her mother said in slow measures, looking out at the dunes and the sparkling city on the horizon, "the same bad end would happen to you. He feared the effect of too much knowledge, the knowledge of how you and Cisco were alike in particular."

"But Daddy always said knowledge was power," Beautiful replied. "That makes no sense. Why didn't he tell me Cisco looked like me? Why didn't he show me pictures? I asked so many times if there were others like me. He always said, 'Only the pop stars, Beautiful. Only the beauty queens.' He never said, 'My brother' or 'My brother, who I loved and who died in misery.'"

Her mother shrugged. "Nothing makes sense all the time, if you only think of it one way or the other," her mother replied. "Some knowledge is damaging, whether you know more or not, and you must weigh the gain in growth with the risk in receipt. Because, Beautiful, some truth is hard to swallow, but all truth is relative. Do you want to know more about Cisco, or not? I'll respect your wishes."

"Mother, I want—" Beautiful replied, but felt unsure how to go on.

"What do you want, Beautiful?" her mother said, unshed tears gathering in her eyes. "I'm listening."

"I want to know everything about him," Beautiful finally replied. "I don't care how much it hurts. I'm my Daddy's daughter, and I am strong."

"So be it," Ethel Chef said. "It was a dark day in May when Cisco died. He wanted to leave the asylum. He'd been held in solitary confinement because he killed a guard, but he wanted to leave. Your great grandfather came and attempted to persuade him to stay in confinement. Your father accompanied your grandfather, to help persuade Cisco because Cisco loved your father. They were quite close as boys. But on that day, Cisco said to your grandfather, 'I'm leaving here now because I'm so unmanageable, such an embarrassment, that I'll go where no one can see me. Can't you see this asylum makes me more crazy, Papa—makes me more violent? I wasn't a violent child until I was harassed, but I feel unmoored here. So I'm leaving. I'm not an animal, though I may look like one. I have to get away…' And then Cisco started to walk free of the facility, knocking guards out of the way, knocking their weapons to the floor, and your grandfather was afraid Cisco would ruin them all or do far more damage. He went to his car and got his shotgun, thinking he could persuade his son by force. Your father watched as their father ordered, 'Cisco, get back to your room! Stay there. I'll help you into the straightjacket until you feel all right,' but Cisco declined. He'd never wear a straightjacket again, declaring it unnatural. And, 'Shoot me if you won't let me leave, Daddy,' he said. But he had to walk past your grandfather to get out of the asylum gate. Cisco tried. His eyes were sad and red, your father remembers, but he planned to push right past. Your father also distinctly remembers watching your grandfather lift his gun and hearing your grandfather say, 'You can't be out there with the normal people, Cisco. You aren't normal. Don't cross me.' But Cisco said, 'Fuck you,' and kept walking. And then your grandfather shot his son, shot him ten times before knocking Cisco down as your father watched, in tears. Sometimes, your father dreams this scene, when he cries his brother's name in his sleep, and he used to tell me, 'Ethel, we can't let Beautiful know how sad and unprepared Cisco was for the real world, how it treated him… She must never be our, or anyone else's, monstrosity. We won't let people abuse her. She must be shown only love in this family. And if that means we have to hide that love away on the estate, we'll keep her safe and happy there. We'll pay people to be kind to her. Always. We'll make her a different world in which she might be happy. To this end, I'll spare no expense. But you must never tell her about her uncle Cisco. Not a word. Promise me that right now…' And then I promised. But you've left the estate. He let you go. I let you go. You asked to know. So now, I've broken my promise to him, but I already left your father, so who's to blame? The times have changed. You wanted to know more."

~

After Sandra's chicken dinner, which Beautiful heartily praised, she sat behind the trailer, listening to Sandra's problems as distraction from the weight of the information her mother had divulged. "… And then, Eugene left me," Sandra said. "So I thought, well, this is the end."

"And then what?"

"Then it wasn't the end."

"Fedora Man did the same with endings," Beautiful replied. "Left. Wavered. Women don't waver. If we like someone, we just stick with them. It must be that whole argument about men creating as many pregnancies as possible, seed scattering. When you're female and you have an egg, you don't feel compelled to scatter seed. You want someone to help guard your egg. Men want to go their merry way."

"But Eugene kept leaving and returning," Sandra remarked, laughing. "What is it with these guys who leave because they're scared, yet keep coming back?"

"You're very loveable, Sandra," Beautiful said. "If you were my lover, I'd come back time and time again. But then, I'd never have left you."

"You're very loyal, Beautiful."

"Yes. That's my defining trait." The friends clutched each other's hands. "Do you really think Daddy put trackers in all my shoes?"

"I wouldn't put it past him. Bugs too," Sandra said. "But Beautiful, even though you won't ever have to worry about money, your father's not powerful enough to keep you from harm in the real world if you kill people. Don't kill people anywhere here. You need to not injure others so as to avoid going to jail if you want to stay in the free world."

"I do a countdown from twenty when I get mad. That helps."

"Good, but you'll need more impulse control. What if you're still furious after twenty? It might help you to practice this meditation practice I've been reading about called Falun Gong."

"That's very nice to suggest, Sandra, but I've tried to meditate," Beautiful said. "Many times! And I'm too high-strung. I start thinking 'meditate' and end up thinking, 'massive new plan for action' and sometimes 'such inaction nauseates me,'" But then she thought again of Ivor, the strange *oooms* and *umms* he made, and the fact that he meditated. "Well, I guess Ivor did that meditating thing," Beautiful went on. "My shrinks did it, but in light of what ridiculous rules they had to work around, those shrinks, it's a wonder they could respect themselves near me, even with meditation. How could they counsel me? I was completely selfish and other. I had no real concerns. I didn't know what a real concern was, apparently, Sandra, as you mentioned before. It's part of my flawed and sheltered upbringing. I'm sorry if that harmed you."

"Beautiful, I think there's nothing wrong with you," Sandra said. "Except that you get too excited."

"Sandra," Beautiful replied. "I should tell you about Cisco. There was someone like me." She then told Sandra what her mother had said about her uncle, but when she came to the part about Cisco being held in the asylum, about his lifelong depression, mania, and exile, about his being shot, she began to cry. "I never met him, but that's why, Sandra!" she exclaimed. "That's why Daddy paid friends and never let me make real friends. Because he thought that would be impossible! That's why he built the estate! Should I hate him for confusing me so much? It's probably why I don't know how to handle this thing with Fedora Man! I wasn't raised for it!"

Sandra crammed her hands in her pockets. "That's some deep love," she said. "He spent and gave up a lot for your protection."

"Not for my protection," Beautiful argued. "For his sanity. My father's restrained me because I'm a monster. He protected me to protect himself, because I'm too violent. Like Cisco. He feared if I came out here, I might be shut away. So, he had no real faith in me, really. That's why he sent Thomas so quickly when I messed up a little—to spy on me. He loved Cisco, but he didn't want what happened before to happen again… So, to keep everything simple, he wanted to shut off my world in his own gilded cage."

"Oh," Sandra said.

"Yes," Beautiful replied. "Closed off like his silly cockatoos! I should have killed them all."

"And did your mother tell you whether you ate your fetal twin?"

Beautiful momentarily stopped reflecting on Cisco and her father to reply, "Thank you for the change in topic, Sandra. That's not clear. Mother eventually said I had a twin she lost in the second trimester, so I probably beat my twin's emerging cell clump to pieces, with my emerging cell clump, probably eliminated any chance of mother ever having a normal girl child if I got aggressive in her womb. But my sister had a heartbeat once. Subsequently, she disappeared. 'Reabsorbed' is the word Mother used, which likely means I did eat my own twin before I ever made a choice knowingly. And now, I have a driver doubling as my child, and a boyfriend who leaves all the time, along with a mentor I've never met who lives in the barrio and likely won't want to meet me—and only one real friend in the world, who is you, Sandra, but I still feel so alone I can hardly breathe. I don't know who I am! I've been trained all my life to be a confident person, but that person lived in a world that doesn't exist. A fabrication. Nothing will ever be the same, not back home. Not here. Not anywhere. Daddy has ruined my life with his deception. Did you ever feel, Sandra, that life is just one increasingly horrifying nightmare you go through only to reach the next room of hardly understandable terror? What if Ida hates me? What if Ida backs away in fear because I'm frightening and she's not a paid friend? I couldn't bear it. I've dreamed of meeting her for so long and I love her so much that it would hurt me unbearably if she rejected me, so I don't know if I should even risk meeting her—because the best outcome is only mildly good, but the worst outcome is potentially wracked with devastation or despair and I'm so—"

"*Tck-tck*," Sandra said, her eyes filling with tears, her arms wrapping around her friend and muffling the rest of Beautiful's speech. "*Tck-tck. Tck-tck. Tck-tck.* Please don't say more."

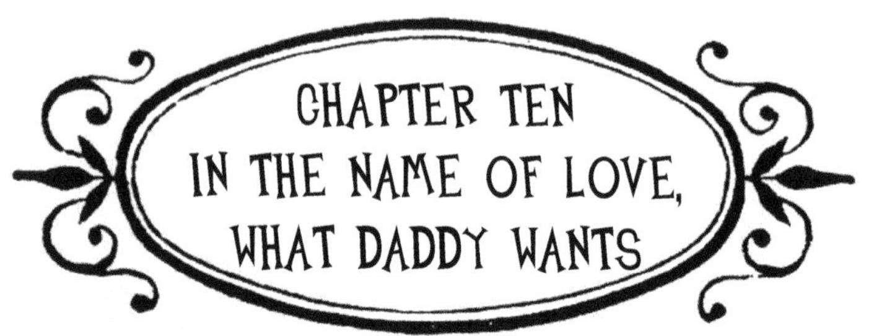

~IN WHICH, THE CHEFS VISIT THE BARRIO, IDA IS FOUND, AN EXTERMINATION TAKES PLACE, FEDORA MAN BETRAYS BEAUTIFUL, SHE JUMPS A CLIFF, AND BEAUTIFUL TAKES A LONG, EXHAUSTING SWIM...~

Ethel Chef decided to accompany them to Ida's the next morning. Everyone readied themselves, all parties except Beautiful wearing black sweatpants, cheap tennis shoes, and the K-Mart t-shirts Sandra had decided were barrio friendly, when Beautiful's father again called, saying, "I want you to come home now, Beautiful. I'm so lonely. I've no one here but maids, cooks, and drivers."

Beautiful wore an electric blue Prada dress. She said, "I'll come home as soon as I finish meeting Ida. Daddy, please, be patient."

But her father sounded ragged as he replied, "Are you okay? Have you heard from your mother?"

"Yes, I'm okay. No, I have not," Beautiful lied, watching her mother play with Thomas in black sweats and a lilac women's T. Ethel Chef looked quite nurturing as she then helped Thomas decide not to wear his chauffeur cap, though Thomas obviously resisted. The hat was tugged back and forth.

"No drivers except for drug dealers, in the barrio,

Thomas," Ethel Chef said quietly. "No drivers, so no chauffeur caps."

"Did you speak to her yet and tell her I love her?" Enrique Chef asked.

"I did and received no reply," Beautiful said. If she felt badly for fibbing to her father, which she mostly didn't since he was such a good and frequent liar, she let this pass. She looked affectionately at Sandra, at all of them.

"Did you tell her I re-assembled the house?" he asked. "Do you have any idea where she is?"

"I did tell her that," Beautiful said. "No, I don't have any idea." It was not fortuitous, however, that as soon as Beautiful said this, her mother shouted, in ebullient spirits, "Thomas, I think it's high time we get in the car and go!"

"Your mother's there!" her father boomed. "Right there! Beside you!"

"Fuck," Beautiful said. "Yes, Daddy."

"With another man!" he shouted. "She calls another man by his name! That whore! That cheat! Your mother's there, calling another man by his name!"

"Double fuck," Beautiful said, glad her father wasn't on speaker. "Calm down, Daddy. Please don't worry about that business. Thomas is Mommy's grandbaby. He's not her other man. He—" She tried to explain, but her Daddy had already hung up. Probably after "Double fuck," probably about to call a raid on Sandra's house just as soon as his helicopters could be assembled. He now knew exactly where they were, she surmised, because he could certainly track the Lincoln once he figured out the Thomas connection.

"Mommy," Beautiful said, as calmly as could be mustered. "Daddy was on the phone just now. He knows you're here. He thinks you have another lover named Thomas, whom he will likely soon piece together is our driver. And so, let's not hesitate. We have to go to the barrio."

In that moment, Beautiful was never gladder she'd

learned to make concise summaries in her Childhood Disaster Survival Training, yet a new pall fell over the room, each person considering the detrimental effects of Mr. Chef's awareness.

"But we're in the desert now," her mother howled. "This is where he buries people."

Sandra twiddled her fingers nervously, remembering Mr. Chef's many previous rages and the recent friend evacuations. Thomas paced. Only Fucking Eugene sat like a lump, too stupid to even register danger; however he rose to the occasion somewhat by saying, "That's bad, right?" as Thomas frantically searched couch cushions for his keys.

"We better go now," Beautiful said wearily, "before things get any worse. At least I can dress cute now."

When they all walked outside, she went right to the Lincoln and extracted a pair of electric blue Manolo Blahnik satin Sedaraby Open Toe d'Orsay Pumps to match her dress. "He's discovered where you are, Mommy," she said, chucking the no-brand shoes in the trunk. "So I guess my own shoes are fine, and these go so much better. But we don't have time to get a beater anything now, do we Thomas? Or the neck clocks?"

"I'd say not," Thomas said. "Let's go."

"That's okay," Beautiful said. "You're the best driver we've got and you know the Lincoln. Let's skip the beater. Still, what's the worst case? They steal the car? Someone tries to beat us up?"

"You do look pretty, Baby," Ethel Chef said.

"Thanks, Mommy," Beautiful replied. "I needed make-up today, too."

She was glad she'd refused barrio wear earlier, certain that she must impress Ida upon their first meeting. If she didn't impress Ida then, she feared, she might never see her again. "I need everything I can wear that makes me feel strong and confident today," she told those amassed. "Daddy might make me go back soon, and it's not every day you meet someone so important to you. I only have one chance to make a good first impression."

~

While they drove, Ethel Chef practiced hyperventilating in a paper bag while Beautiful received a text from Ivor that read, "Please don't visit Ida May Haze."

"You've got a lot of nerve," she replied, her fingers flying. "What makes you think the first time you try to order me to do something, it should come as a text? If you want to get assertive, you should call. Or show up! C U L8R. You going to call or not?" She still felt pissed.

He gave no response. It occurred to her, of a sudden, that this was exactly fm's way; he replied only selectively, and while she may have let this go before, whilst in the full bloom of hormone-induced delirium, now that she had spent due time considering him, his silence came as a shocking breach of authority. "ANSWER ME," she text-shouted.

"I don't use the phone except rarely," he reply-texted. "It makes me nervous."

"Well, I'm MAD. Use it now."

Her phone rang seconds later. "Just don't go," Ivor begged.

"Why not?"

Again, no reply.

"Ivor, why do you care if I go to Ida's?"

"It's just that—to see her might change everything, and I don't want you to lose the sacred cow of loving your mentor. What if you meet her and she's not what you think? Maybe she's just a boring, scared, old woman, afraid to live, no superwoman at all. A weak and cowardly—"

"Ivor, why are you worried about Ida? I'm not worried about Ida. I'll love Ida no matter what her current circumstances because I'm just that loving! Because Ida is strong and beautiful and profound and—"

"All right. Maybe I just wanted to talk to you today," he said.

"You did?" Neither spoke for a moment until Beautiful replied, "It sounds like you might be mooning over me after all. I'm hearing a big blue moon swell in the background."

He again failed to speak, and while he failed, she felt a swell of joy unequal to any she'd felt before, so asked, "You really like me, Ivor, don't you?"

"And if so?" he asked.

"I like it. Protective. Sweet. Definitely not evil."

"I'm not sweet, but I've researched Ida's house, and it's a dump. I don't want you to go there—"

"Ivor, how'd you get Ida's address?" Beautiful asked. "It's not available to just anyone. The only publicly available address is a P.O. Box. Were you checking up on me? Were you doing cute surveillance of where I'd go? You were spying! You're acting so much like Daddy! My Daddy Boyfriend!"

"Heathen," Ivor said, his laughter tinny and distant. "You know what I do. Did you really imagine I wouldn't hunt down any information I needed about what you've been doing?"

From his tone of voice, she imagined him wearing his supercilious look, which was one she was actually quite fond of, but she replied rather coldly so as not to expose her sudden vulnerability: "So what do you think of my earlier proposal?"

"Which one?"

"There was only one earlier proposal and you know it, you jerk!" she shouted, dropping her phone and staring furiously out the window. "Daddy, Daddy," Beautiful next texted, "Thomas is my driver. Mother is not involved with him or anybody else. Maybe you should say you're sorry. She'd likely take you back." In direct contrast with her Ivor interactions, she figured that at least her father should have the satisfaction of knowing the truth from someone, especially if she herself should be have been so robbed, so many times, regarding remaining in the loop, not by just them but now, also, by a man who spelled his initials in lowercase like a *setting* on the *radio dial*.

"Mama," Thomas said. "Sandra wants to know if you want her to sit in the backseat with you on the way to Ida's, for moral support."

"Of course I do, Thomas," Beautiful replied. "Sandra is always welcome here. Sandra and I have no secrets. And you know why? Because she is Sandra and she is not MALE."

~

They drove through a few dumpy cities in the boonies before they reached Ida's barrio. Businesses were few and far between, but they'd not yet entered serious traffic and Beautiful turned to Sandra and asked, "What is it about Fucking Eugene that you like?"

"He doesn't say much," Sandra said, knitting baby booties.

"That's it?"

"He does what I say," Sandra added.

"Sure, sure," Beautiful said. "But how does he make you feel? Does he make you feel like you have a migration of butterflies in your head? Does he make your heart beat so fast you can hardly move?"

"Beautiful, that stuff's for stories. Eugene makes me feel I can live my life with a warm body in my bed," Sandra said. "I don't have to give up anything. It's just comfortable; I'm not special like you, not rich, just an everyday person. I don't expect you to understand how low my expectations are, but Eugene, well, aside from the stripper episode, he makes me feel like I have no risk of losing him."

Beautiful listened and said, "Has he killed anyone? Does he say things that make you mad on purpose?"

"No and no."

"Oh," Beautiful said. "Well, I think you're far more special than Eugene and always will be, Sandra. I guess he's just lucky to have you."

~

Upon exiting the mountains, Beautiful's father finally called Beautiful's mother. The two spoke in code. "G P rr queos Nine," Ethel said, then, "10 sunset DRV," then "Quimere 70-64."

Another few exchanges of this nature took place. It was only when Ethel Chef gestured for Thomas to pull over and the others in the car watched Beautiful's mother walk off privately on her phone that a voluminous and animated conversation begin.

Parked for over an hour, they waited, despite that all were hungry. Beautiful wrote in her journal. She wrote about Cisco and her father and Eugene.

She closed the journal and thought about John Henry, and even about Jake, especially the expression on his ugly face as she'd banged his head against the dirt. She thought about Ivor, too, about the first night and the second, which were now to serve as her difficult and varied initiations into the shrapnel of love. "I think I just liked things better before," she said aloud. "When they seemed more simple."

In her mind, she heard her mother reminding her not to kill. She didn't want to kill and had never wanted to kill, with the exception of small and varied estate animals, but some people necessitated their own murder. She liked that Ivor appreciated this. If I have such power, she thought, it behooves me, where necessary for the safety of others, to use it. In this, Daddy had always complicitly agreed—while her gentle mother had often taken opposing sides.

Without her mother beside her father, Beautiful realized, their lives assumed an imbalance. There must be soft with the hard, weak with the strong, gentle with the sharp. Ivor, strangely, gentled her. It might have been his need to wear a hat—yet it was her mother, not her father, who wore hats. Watching her mother now, she realized she had never seen her parents separated.

For this reason, as they spoke with the invisible phone current as their remaining tenuous connection, she found herself issuing a silent prayer to the road that went something to the effect of: Mommy, take Daddy back. Make him kind. Love each other. It's been too hard for too long. Forgive him his way and start again.

But no one would know what happened during that distant conversation. The only clue was to be that when Ethel Chef re-entered the car, she fixed her eyes and lips using cosmetics and a purse compact, then said, "Driver, make good time. We must progress."

~

Ida May's home was adjacent to a poorer barrio, on a cliff of the Pacific shoreline. In most of her research, Beautiful had found that poorer enclaves often lacked ocean access, so this was a surprise. The fence in front was chain link. A cop car rested out front. Two mottled pit bulls sat on chains beside a dilapidated car on blocks, the front yard strewn with garbage. "Ida lives here?" Beautiful asked. "Thomas, re-check the address."

"I already checked it twice."

"It's not a Christmas list. Check it again."

"I checked it three times."

"Fedora Man already told me it was run down," she said, sighing. "He was right. How a fancy advice maven like Ida could live in—"

"I told your father you shouldn't come see Ida due to location," her mother said as a few men strolled by in stocking caps. "But I'm not worried. I'm packing heat." Ethel displayed a small pearl-handled gun yanked from her Guiseppe

Zanotti handbag, the handbag that Thomas said she should have to leave at home if he left his chauffeur hat home, but "Grandmamma knows best," she'd told Thomas in a voice that brooked no argument. "Besides, I need the handbag to hold my gun. If I have no purse, where will I put that? You already know where your head's supposed to go, with or without the hat."

"Mommy has such a beautiful, delicate gun," Beautiful murmured appreciatively.

As they sat in front of Ida's, Sandra stuck her hand into her recycled shopping bag and grabbed a snack of bagged pretzels while eying the pitbulls, but announced, her voice atremble, "Don't worry. I'll go up with you, Beautiful."

"Me too, Mama," said Thomas. "You won't go up there alone."

"Does anyone think, for one second, that I'm not going?" Ethel Chef asked.

"Of course you're welcome to come, Mommy," Beautiful said. "Did things go well with Daddy?"

"As well as can be expected."

"What does that mean, exactly?"

"What do you think?"

"I'm trying not to think about it."

~

As they walked toward the front door, both dogs ran at them, choked short and barely restrained from reaching the walkway by their choke chains. Beautiful rang the doorbell, thinking: Those *dogs should be able to access whomever they need to bite! Who arranged those chains?* But when one of the two snarled at her, she snarled back, and he took to immediate cowering. Then "Ida?" Beautiful called out in a much sweeter voice. "Ida May Haze, are you in there?"

"Who the hell is it?" came a quiet voice.

"It's Beautiful Ape Girl Baby Chef!" Beautiful shouted. She turned to the others to say, "Oooh! It's her! I hear her dear voice!" She could not prevent herself from grinning so widely it infected the whole party until everyone stupidly grinned.

Even so, Ida took a while to open the wood door behind the wrought iron gate, but when she did, she looked out at the strange group assembled on her doorstep and repeated, "Who in the good Lord's name are you?"

In that moment, it took all of Beautiful's patience, never been in abundance, to keep from ripping the screen off and swooping her mentor up in an enormous hug. "I'm your biggest fan, Ida," she said meekly but with much enthusiasm. "My name is Beautiful Ape Girl Baby Chef. And, oh, Ida! I love you so much!"

"I don't have any fans," the woman said, irritable, "I don't even have any children, well none that will talk to me," and she slammed the door shut.

"Yes, you do!" Beautiful yelled as she rang the doorbell again. "You have Liza."

"Go away," Ida bellowed from behind both doors.

"Ida, I know it's you," Beautiful said. "You don't have to be afraid due to your celebrity. We're not what they call paparazzi, those strange people who want to camp on your lawn and take your picture. I just came to thank you. I'm simply a longtime fan who wants to tell you how much your show has meant to me. I've traveled across the country to meet you. In that way you might call me a zealot, but never in an offensive way. Anyway, I'm really hoping you'll like me."

Ida opened the locking screen gate at this, squinting at them with a baffled face, and Beautiful said, "This here is my son and protégé, Thomas. This is my best friend Sandra. This is my mother Ethel. They didn't want me to leave the estate but decided to come with me and visit you after all."

"I don't believe you're my fan," Ida said, regarding them all closely now. "Like I said, I don't have any fans."

"Thomas, let's show her we are true fans," Beautiful replied. "Let's recite the *Strong as Animal Woman* show theme. Or let's do the rage dampening chant we learned last week. Oh, Ida, I've had so much rage I've productively channeled because of you! So much! And you showed me how to use my rage constructively. I've made things with it! Thomas and I had orange juice on this trip. Thomas also satisfactorily performed the glass-tossing maneuver. He didn't graduate to the full panes of glass I'm capable of, an expansion on your thoughts, but he's young yet, just a child by expression."

"I swept the glass, too," Thomas said. "The calming exercise after the storm. I did it very gently, Ida, just as you described on your show."

Ida stepped back. A small white slipper fell off her foot. "You been getting my show?"

"Oh, yes! Every episode!" Beautiful said. "I tape them. Since I was a little girl. I'm not trying to be forward, but do you think I might—that is, could I please see your broadcast room? I've imagined it so many times. Sometimes, when I turn on your podcast, where there is video, I try to brighten it so I can see it better, but you seem to like things dim. So, I could see that room. Or perhaps we could just chat a bit about creative visualization of our perfect worlds? That is one of my favorite themes from your shows, when you are in a hopeful mood, but your voice slurs just a bit as if you're half-awake."

"It's the whiskey," Ida said, but put her foot back in her white shoe and stepped aside to let them in. She wore a purple bathrobe with small green leaves. As they rapidly filled her hall, she announced, "There isn't much room here. We may need to go out back. Howard's just waking up." She also shouted, "Howard? We have guests. I'm showing them to the yard."

"Who the hell're they?" he replied from a back room.

"Nobody we know."

"So why you letting them in?"

"Because I want to," Ida replied, her small upper lip trembling. "You'll be going to work in a while; do you really mind?"

"Yes!"

"I'm actually certain he does not mind," Beautiful enthused at the same time. "Because any man married to you, Ida, must be the perfect example of a well-behaved spouse. You've offered so many great shows on training men. I have a man who needs training, but he's relatively difficult by standard measures. Surly. Deceptive. A bit secretive. Outwardly, emotionally unresponsive."

"Oh," Ida said. "Let's go to the back." She ushered them through the tiny dwelling and out to the yard where a patio table seated them. "I do the show from the shed," she told Beautiful.

"I want to see in the shed," Beautiful replied.

"It smells like grass seed... well, only if you really wanna."

"I really wanna," Beautiful said.

Ida let Beautiful follow her a few steps before she turned around, asking, "You aren't pulling my leg, are you? This isn't some group sent by my cousin Norma Rae to put me on some video show? Is that real hair on your face?"

"Of course it is. As to the other people, I have no idea what you're talking about," Beautiful replied. "But Ida, certainly I want to see your set up. I've been waiting for this moment since I was seven and you did the 'Rage Out with Tiny Bottles' show. How often can one meet one's idols in person? Oh, you can, but I've heard they let you down. Don't let me down. Can I embrace you? Oh, please? You have been such a great help to me!"

"I suppose you might," Ida replied, surprised, embarrassed.

Beautiful held Ida so tenderly, hugging the woman very lightly as Sandra had advised in the car. She pressed three tender kisses to Ida's cheek and said, "It is so good to see you, so very, very good. Mommy, wasn't that nice and ladylike how I embraced Ida? I was so gentle."

Ethel Chef nodded. Tears filled Beautiful's big blue eyes, tears of delight. Then Ida ushered them further into the yard and they heard the doorbell again.

"Who the hell is it now?" Howard shouted.

Ida shouted in reply that she didn't know, but left and soon returned, escorting Fedora Man out to join the others, muttering, "He said he was with you."

"What are you doing here, Ivor?" Beautiful asked, but to Ida, she replied, "He's certainly *not* with me," standing at the edge of a fence in front of the cliff, with Sandra elbowing her and hissing, "Be polite!" through clenched teeth.

"I *am* with you," Ivor argued.

"You are *not*. Since *when?* For *how long?* All of *five minutes?!* I'm on a serious mission to meet my idol Ida May Haze right now, Ivor. As we speak, I'm meeting her and things are going well, and I won't have you ruining it, so go *don't moon over me* somewhere else."

"So is he with her, or not?" Ida asked, scratching her head.

"Not," Beautiful raged. "He might have been, once—but he has ruined all chances for being involved with my future happiness."

"Yet, he's here with you now," Fedora Man replied, "Can't you see him before you?" to which "Saying something doesn't make it so," Beautiful instantly replied. "You may be here, Ivor, but you are not here *with me*."

"All right. Perhaps, I'm here to protect you then," Fedora Man said. "If not as your escort."

"Oh, really?" Beautiful laughed. Her mother laughed. Even Sandra and Thomas chortled. "Protect me from what,

Fedora Man?" Beautiful asked. "A sweet old woman named Ida? My mother? My child? My best friend? Go home, Ivor. I don't need you."

"I've now decided I'm now willing to be your boyfriend," he announced. "Just like I once decided I was willing to be your distant friend."

"Neither role of which you perform with any reliability," Beautiful returned.

He lifted his hand like a stop sign, interrupting, "Only now, I make more romance available. Not all the time. There must be breaks. But I'll spend whatever romantic energies I have on you. Keep in mind, these may be limited."

Because he spoke earnestly, "I'll think about it," Beautiful replied, but five seconds later she said, "Hmmm, no. I prefer a sex-fiend."

"What's the dilemma?" Fedora Man asked. "This is exactly the situation you proposed."

"Yes. Hours ago I proposed that," Beautiful said. "But I may not feel the same now. My feet are feeling—how should I put this? Rather chilly!"

"He seems a nice enough boy," Ida said.

"Well, he's not," Beautiful replied. "He's a liar and a lover and a leaver."

"Whether you want me here or not, I came to protect you, Beautiful," Ivor replied, "if not from being killed, then from killing."

"Ivor, you're the only person around here I'm likely to kill."

"You sure about that?" he asked. "I don't think you want to kill me." He put one soft hand on her shoulder.

She shrugged it away and replied, "Get your hand off my shoulder. Don't bet on your safety."

Then her mother's phone rang with her father's siren tone, but her mother omitted to answer. "Go ahead and get it, Mommy," Beautiful said.

"I think not today," her mother replied. "I know what

he'll say, and I've already had an earful." Ethel fondled the gold chain handle of her purse. "I tell you, I just don't want to hear it."

"Fuck's going on back there," a deep voice shouted from the house.

"Now Howard's up from all the chattering," Ida said, jittery, interrupting the intense looks that flew between Fedora Man, Beautiful, and Ethel Chef. "Oh, dear. He's up. We should all be quiet."

Beautiful noticed that Ida suddenly shook; a small bruise decorated her forehead, with several more on her arm. "Is there something wrong with Howard, Ida?" Beautiful asked.

"No, Howard's fine," Ida replied. "Howard is always fine."

Howard then loomed at the exterior house door. As he appeared, Ida shrank toward the shed. "Do you want to go into your shed now?" Beautiful asked her.

"Yes," Ida said. "Right away."

Howard was a tall man, broad across the shoulders and thick through the belly. His voice rang out as he asked, "You make my fucking dinner yet, Ida?"

"It's in the oven," Ida replied.

"Good. I gotta go in ten minutes. I'll get dressed. Get rid of these people."

~

Ida showed Beautiful the shed, but when Beautiful attempted to invite herself for dinner, moments later, Ida declined, pointing out that there was just one TV dinner in the oven. The rest were frozen. "I don't care for cooking for guests," Ida said. "I haven't got much in the freezer anyhow."

"We can eat TV dinners," Beautiful replied. "Whatever you have, we can eat." While she knew her mother would only pick at the fare, she didn't want to be impolite.

"There're only five dinners left in the freezer," Ida replied. "They'll take another twenty minutes to cook. But I can't afford to feed the nation. Maybe you could leave now and come back in a few hours for a cup of coffee, when Howard's gone? He told me to get rid of you."

"Oh, but, Ida, there's no need for us to go. We can go buy more dinners while those cook," Beautiful replied, "and eat with you here. Or we can use your last few and pay for more. Don't worry, Ida. I have plenty of money. I'll get you some money from the car."

"Good idea," Fedora Man said, "I'll follow you."

Believing them to be in the middle of a lover's quarrel, Sandra and Thomas did not speak, but Beautiful's mother said only, a propos of nothing, "I knew he'd be a good one."

When they reached the front of the house, however, Beautiful approached the trunk, angrily swinging her keys, and Fedora Man said, "Beautiful, we need to leave. Right away. Right now."

"Why?" she asked. "To where?"

"Anywhere. Away. Because danger's coming."

"There's no danger coming. How do you know there'll be danger?" she inquired. "Is there a danger sensor in your evil nose?"

"I just know," Ivor said firmly. "Like when your father hired that small cocky girl Elstad to play tetherball when you were seven. You broke her wrist—he could've predicted from the start…"

"How do you know about Elstad?" Beautiful demanded, thinking: Elstad, pudgy girl, copper curls. She'd forgotten about her entirely. There was no way she'd brought her up anytime recently.

"You told me," he lied. "Right before you went to sleep."

"I most certainly did not," Beautiful replied. "I haven't thought about Elstad in years, and I never talk about who I don't think about."

"You were very tired when you spoke of her," he replied. "That night we touched feet. Perhaps you forgot the mention?"

"I find that forgetting excuse hard to believe, Fedora Man. I remember everything that happens when I'm asleep and awake," Beautiful argued. "I never told you a thing about Elstad because it wasn't important enough for me to recall until you mentioned it just now—"

"Regardless, we need to get out of here," Fedora Man said, adjusting his fedora. "The law's inside. A sergeant wouldn't be easy to remove from the record, even for your father."

"What Sergeant?" Beautiful asked, noting Ivor again wore his white suit but had on his black hat.

"Ida's husband," he said.

Beautiful peered into his ever-watering eyes. It was like he could cry at any moment or had his sorrow put on tap. "I have no idea what you're talking about, Ivor," she stated, putting her key in the trunk lock. "I don't care about Ida's husband. I'm getting some money, and I'm giving it to Ida. Then I'm eating dinner with her."

"And then you're going to kill someone, so let's get out of here. I've seen all your past reels. I don't need more research..."

"What past reels?"

"The metaphorical ones, of your life, of your decisions, of your way of being, Beautiful. I know you."

"And so what if I kill someone?" she replied.

"We can't erase it this time."

"Like you did or someone else did last time? Who's we, Ivor? And, not that it matters, but why are you suddenly against killing people? Is it Ida? Am I going to kill Ida today? Oh my god! Oh, no! Can you read my aura? The future? Will I annihilate my favorite person in the world, Ms. Ida May Haze? Will I harm her?"

"No," Ivor said, putting his hand in his suit pocket. "I just know you well enough to guess what'll happen next, what you'll do..."

Beautiful pulled out two banded wads of cash from the open trunk. "Oh really, Fedora Man," she said. "Because I have no idea what you'd do. I don't judge people like you do. I don't leave them. And I don't lie. Besides, I'm not as violent as before."

"Really," he said. "I think you're just as violent."

"Well, you're wrong."

He scoffed. "Should we test this self-control you have and walk inside?" he asked, raising an eyebrow. "I can bet money it won't last long in there. I tell you it won't, not with what you'll see."

"What do you know that I don't, fm?" she asked him, worried about the strength of his sentiment.

"Nothing, Beautiful," he replied. "Nothing."

But re-entering the house, they walked into a hush. A policeman with his back to them leaned against the dish-sink counter. Ida curled on the floor, holding her abdomen, and Thomas had been flung against the dinette to rest crumpled against a chair. Beautiful's mother sat on the kitchen counter, ankles crossed, pointing her small pearly gun at the officer who stood, fork in hand, meditatively eating mashed potatoes from a cardboard cubicle of a TV dinner.

Sandra, horrified, stood crying, with her back against the wall. "He hit Ida," she said, hands on her belly. "And Thomas."

Though the policeman seemed interested only in lifting a greasy piece of fried chicken to his lips, into the hush, Ethel Chef pre-emptively announced, "Do not approach any more of my party or I'll have to shoot. If I do, I'll shoot your eyes out. I always shoot for the eyes."

Beautiful looked from Thomas to Sandra to Ivor to her mother to Ida to Howard and then back to Thomas. "Thomas," Beautiful said, whispering, leaning over him.

"What happened here?"

"I tried to stop him, Mama," he whispered. "When he hurt Ida, I tried to fight, but I wasn't strong enough. He hit her and shoved me down."

"It's about time you people got the hell out of my house," the man in uniform said. "I've got to go to work."

Beautiful dropped the money on the counter, asking, "Howard, did you hurt my friends?"

"Reckon so," Howard said.

"Why?" she asked.

"Because I felt like it," Howard said, unrepentant.

Beautiful's body adrenalized. In a flash, she approached Ida and knelt beside her, saying, "What's going on here, Ms. Haze?"

"Beautiful, you aren't allowed to kill this man," Fedora Man stressed. "Don't address him by name. As a police sergeant, he'd be difficult to erase. I told you."

"I'm not planning on killing the man, Ivor," Beautiful replied, touching Ida's gray disheveled hair, asking in her softest voice, "Where are you injured, Ida? You okay?"

Ida clearly was not. Blood trickled from the corner of her mouth. She said nothing, staring ahead with eyes as impenetrable and wise as an owl's.

Beautiful put her face directly in front of Ida's gaze, saying, "Are you still there, Ida? Is anybody home?"

"Precious peacock," Ida whispered, closing her eyes. "I'm glad you came, but you've got to get going now. Hurry! No good will come from staying. Don't worry. Ms. Ida May Haze will take care of this. Ms. Ida May Haze takes care of herself..." But her words came sharply between breaths.

"Ida, you might guess what needs to be done now," Beautiful disagreed, patting Ida's small, fragile head. "You've spoken of this path of action before, so don't let it surprise you if I must do what I must, according to your provided guidelines. Do you know what I plan to do?"

Ida nodded, then said, "But you can't win, my new friend. Don't even try. You're a woman. He's an animal."

Still, Ida May Haze really did not know Beautiful Ape Girl Baby Chef at all.

Already, Beautiful regarded Howard, assessing his weaknesses. She turned to Sandra and said, "Please get in the car, Sandra; you shouldn't see this," then bent over Thomas to return the Lincoln's keys to his hands. "Thomas, Baby," she said very gently. "You're now an adult. You've graduated! You're no longer my child! You stuck up for yourself. You acted like a man, a whole man, courageous and good; I'm so very proud of you, my son, for defending the weak. But go wait in the car."

"Get out of my damn house, all of you!" Howard yelled.

"Shut up, Howard," Beautiful replied. "Can't you see I'm busy?"

"You're not allowed to kill this man, Beautiful," Fedora Man repeated.

"What do I care if you're busy?" Howard said.

"You should care," Beautiful told Howard, and then asked Ivor, "And what are you going to do about it now, Ivor? You could try to stop me, but you won't kill me to protect Howard, will you? You love me more than you love this man, don't you? At least a little?" She regarded Ivor with a glare to make her mother proud before she said, "No, that's right. You don't love me a little. You don't love anyone, not even yourself. For you, everything has to be triangles, deceptions. All love requires loss. Well, that's not love. That's not even remotely love." Tears filled her eyes, which softened only when they lit upon her mentor, who still seemed disoriented. "Ida, I didn't know what I was doing here before," Beautiful said. "But I do now. You called me here, Mrs. Haze! Your shows called me here. I didn't understand what you were asking before, but I'm sorry now I took so very long to arrive."

"Fucking get out, all of you!" Howard shouted. "Now. I'll arrest you for trespassing!"

"Of course I wouldn't kill you," Ivor said. "Killing you is not part of the directive. I wouldn't even hurt you to protect him."

Beautiful ignored Howard, focusing on Ivor. "So I can now kill this tub of lard before me, and you'll give no direct resistance?"

"You can't kill *him*," Howard said, approaching. "*Him* is bigger. *Him* will kill you."

"Not bloody likely," Beautiful replied. "You're a blight on humanity, you stupid pig."

"How about you don't kill him today?" Ivor inserted, pulling her arm. "We could walk away from here and—"

"How about I do what I want instead?" Beautiful interrupted, turning to Howard. "Because he's a menace. Because he hurts my friends."

"Are you gentler or not?" Fedora Man asked.

"I'm gentler when I need to be, Ivor," Beautiful said. "Not when I don't."

At this, however, Fedora Man looked down at his phone, read a few more texts, panicked, and shouted in an agitated voice. "Beautiful, your father says not to kill this man, so stop. Stop everything right now! Everyone get out of here."

"Since when does my father tell you what to do, Ivor?" Beautiful asked. "Why are you communicating with my father?!"

"Oh, fuck," Ethel Chef said. "He told her."

Beautiful gave one glare to Fedora Man and grabbed Howard, stripping Howard's weapons. She held him by his neck and pinned him against the wall with one hand. Regarding Howard, she asked Ivor, "So, you're Daddy's employee, too? Well, I don't need you. I hope Daddy paid a lot of money for my virginity blood you spilled. Hey, Mommy, guess that means Daddy bought me a sex services worker after all, hand-selected for my first lover—isn't that fresh? We have even less control than we formerly thought." She wheeled to face Ivor without releasing Howard, saying, "That explains, I suppose, the reels you watched, right, Ivor—various home movie research from Daddy's vaults? You must be a high level flunky to be let in that far, paid or otherwise. And you seem to know his business. You must be on the inside of the inside. So there are no metaphors here, are there?! Well, watch this. Here's a metaphor of the active sort, embodying how I feel about ever having met you, you paid employee." She turned back to Howard and banged his head twice into the wall for emphasis, staring at his flailing limbs and enjoying their spastic quivers.

"Beautiful, gently now," her mother said. "Careful."

"No," Beautiful said.

Slowly, all color left Ethel Chef's face. "Please remember you won't solve anything by hurting Ida's husband. Please, stop."

"No, Mother," Beautiful repeated. "I'm sorry, but I can't stop this time. If you don't want to watch me kill this man, you should leave now. Ivor, I'd say the same." There was no warmth or emotion in Beautiful's voice; a feeling like death had gripped her heart, wearing Ivor's face. His betrayal rippled deep. "You're such a bastard!" she shouted.

"It wasn't like that," Ivor replied. "What we shared—"

"He paid you to like me!" Beautiful replied. "Like he's done with everyone else! Well, I'm sorry to disappoint you Ivor, but after I kill Howard, I may only have another few such murders in me. And what's my life to you, anyway? You never really cared. So go back to my father. I don't care."

Fedora Man stood still as Ethel Chef tried to rush the others out. "You're an ugly freak," Howard then said to Beautiful, spitting in her face. "You're an animal."

"That may be," Beautiful replied, wiping his spit back onto his own uniform. "But I have my hand around your neck, you lowly scum, and I'm very good at choking things, so answer me this, you stupid mammal, what power dynamic, as you stand pinned to a wall, is winning now—humanity with its technological superiority, secrecy, and weaponry—or brute animal force? Daddy, as you love naturalism so much, feel free to weigh in on this. I now know you're listening."

"Fuck you," Howard said.

"Hmmmm," Beautiful replied. "No. Wrong answer. Fact is, that's not even *one* of the *right answers*. Really, though, sex with a wife beater sounds flattering." She punched him in the gut and then regarded him again.

"You sure you're going through with this?" Fedora Man asked.

"He is so boring," Beautiful replied, glancing at Howard, "so there's no pleasure in this killing, don't you find? No pleasure in getting rid of big stupid men who think to destroy by vapid insult and attempts at domination? He's carbon. They're carbon. You're gaslighting carbon, too, Ivor. Get out of my way." She returned her attention to Howard, saying, "You're not dominant, Howard, by the way, so I plan to kill you today, but don't take this personally. This isn't murder, really. It's *an extermination*. You're like a fly. Or a spider, maybe. An *arachnid*."

"You. Won't. Kill. Me. Now. You. Fucking. Bitch. You. Can't," Howard replied, less and less sure as she banged his head four additional times.

"Ivor," Beautiful said. "Tell him that *I can* and *I will* kill him, as I've killed before, because he is terribly low. Because, for me, there are no repercussions, right, Daddy?"

"You don't have to harm him, you know?" Fedora Man asked. "There are other options."

"Oh, yes, I do have to harm him," Beautiful replied. "He's why I'm here, why Ida brought me..." She carried Howard closer to Ivor, planting him on the nearer wall, telling Fedora Man, "I thought maybe my journey was to find love, to find you, but you were paid, so you would've followed me anywhere. Ida was not paid. Ida's shows taught me lessons so I could save her. Because I can—because they seemed so angry and strong, and I learned from them, but Ida's guise of strength was *a cry for help*. So I have to kill Howard today, Ivor—because he does not deserve Ida, because he hurt my friends, because he's too stupid to stop doing his own violence, and because now he begins to piss me off, though that alone wouldn't normally have been enough to inspire murder. Say, Ivor, can Daddy hear me now? How's the reception?"

Ivor checked his phone. "Your Daddy can hear."

"Oh, good. Because now I want to ask you something, Daddy! How could you do this to me," Beautiful asked, "forcing me to examine the dirty nature of your clout when all I wanted was one trip off the estate to find a man who could want me for who I am—to make love and to meet my beloved mentor, whom you knew I cherished so dearly?" Each time her feelings surged dangerously high, Beautiful again clanged Howard's head against the wall, Howard dangling from her swinging fist, his body like a rag doll's in her hand, legs kicking futilely as his eyes rolled back. "But then I find out you paid my suitor? You couldn't even let me pick my own? Explain that, Daddy! Did you tell him what he could or could not do to your only daughter? Did you listen when we coupled, listen as we spoke? It's nice of you to play God, Daddy, but now you're just a voyeur of the most horrible kind, a sneaking, parental voyeur!" Just then, a cloacal scent arose from Howard, reminding her of the episode with Vick. *What stinking cops!* "Yet, it was nice of you to present me with a trained whore so knowledgeable about what I'd like," she continued. "Even one arrogant and confident enough to entice me, toying with the occasional feigned humility. But you had to both roll the dice and manipulate the felt? Well, guess what, Daddy? You can't control me! Like Cisco, I'll do what I want. Even if it's not acceptable." Beautiful then punched Howard in the gut once more before glaring at Fedora Man and saying, "I should have known better than to think there'd be a man who'd interest me at a motel. One so perfectly suited! You're a fake and a jacked up liar, fm." Under her continuous barrage, Howard's head fractured, making a bloody smudge on the wall.

"Stop, Beautiful!" Ivor said. "You agreed you weren't going to kill him while we were outside. That you'd changed! But you haven't. And it wasn't just money I wanted. I *wanted* you. I—"

Beautiful dropped Howard to the ground. "You didn't *want* me," she said.

"Yes, I did—"

"Fine! For a moment you forgot your employ, perhaps... Suffered through the culmination... And then you just wanted me to do what *he* wanted. Except, do you know what real freedom is, Ivor?" Beautiful asked. "It's the undeniable ability to change one's mind, at any time, after honest discourse. You can't be honest. So, everything's a trap. And maybe now, about you, I've changed my mind."

"Ch-change it back," Ivor stuttered. "Please."

"I might. Except who do you care most about pleasing today?" Beautiful asked. "I can tell you. If you and I were just a money sport, the answer would continue to be my father. But what does my father want? He wants this man to live, doesn't he? He said as much. So do what my father wants and pick Howard up. Call an ambulance. Let him live. He might survive." Beautiful walked around Howard's twitching body, saying, "If, however, the answer were truly that you cared about me above all, and you knew this man had harmed a person very dear to me, you wouldn't promote my father's agenda, but instead attempt to persuade me with a promised future between us, for love's sake, for sex's sake. 'Oh, Beautiful, don't kill this man because we could have a glorious life together.' Etcetera. OR, in the vein of the new distant friendship, if the friendship were worth more than clout or cash, you'd say, 'Kill the bastard, Baby. You know he deserves it!' in moral support, because you'd agree that he should die. Yes, if you had one ounce of feeling for me, you might approach this from a more humanistic angle or one more sympathetic to my interests, but Ivor, the truth is, you're again telling me instead about what my Daddy wants! Don't you think I have ALWAYS been TOTALLY clear about THAT?"

Ivor's response was silence. No surprise.

"I know what you want, Daddy!" she shouted up, nudging Howard's still body with her toe. "You want to put the ballerina in her box and wind her up. You want to keep her spinning in place, except you know that if she doesn't look like the other ballerinas, you must shut the box. Don't let anyone see her! If she cries, you'll build her a bigger, more elaborate box and populate her box with strangers who'll learn her history, seem familiar. You'll tell her she's dangerous if she gets outside the box, and so you'll do everything you can to prevent this until, one day, she ex-

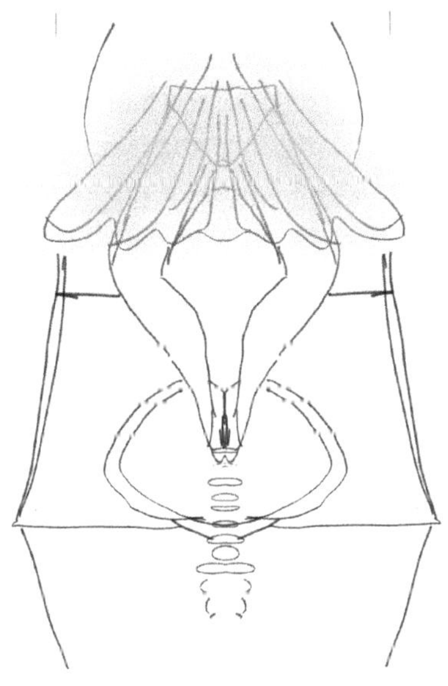

hibits the one thing she has that you, inevitably, cannot control. The broken spring. The sharpest departure. Her own free will."

Upon saying this, Beautiful kicked Howard in the face, removed her heels, and knelt beside him, saying, "In which shoe did your guy place the sensor, Daddy?" She lifted her stilettos, one at a time, talking into each, saying, "Can you hear me from this shoe, Daddy? How about this one? I don't want to kill him with the only shoe you can hear me through."

Howard, from the floor, raised one hand three inches off the ground.

"If I didn't care for you," Ivor said. "I wouldn't have come back to your hotel room in the desert."

"Oh, you're a liar!" Beautiful replied, staring at Howard's raised hand, her eyes burning and spilling over. "You'd have returned, just as you showed up today. There might be a bonus check in it for you. Seems you'd use anyone for your own *financial gain*. But what makes me so angry, Ivor, is that I loved you deeply. I loved you purely, loved you in the way of lovers who paint each other's portraits in the sky, those lovers who love with the beauty of real infatuation and desire, with nothing more to gain from continuing their exchange than their love's own fulfillment. I know you can't say the same because you never loved me that way at all." She closed her eyes briefly before saying, with finality, "Well, you can have my father's filthy stinking money. Take all of that you want."

"But I don't want your father's money," Ivor argued.

"All right. You must have pursued me for power then, for ambition?" she replied. "Researched me to discover the key to aligning with to the head of the empire because I was Daddy's most absorbing project? I don't care why now. You say Daddy doesn't want me to kill this man? I say, I think I should—because he deserves to be killed, and I'm that kind of animal, the ballerina who kills to save, so here, Ivor, fm., Fedora Man, for you and Daddy—the gift of my unrelentingly, honest, animal brutality." Beautiful lifted the stiletto, glanced at the heel, and slammed it into Howard Haze's skull.

"Oh my God," Sandra said from the hallway, unfortunately still watching.

Ida, on the floor, hyperventilated.

"No!" Thomas said, afterward, too late, agog.

"I had to kill that man, Thomas," Beautiful replied, explaining in her young girl's voice, "because I practice self-defense, but that also pertains to the ones I love. Ida, I love you! I've always loved you."

"I know you do, baby," Ida said, in shock.

Ivor stood coldly and silently as a sentry.

"Be sure my Daddy can still hear me," Beautiful told him. "Now, Daddy, I think I'll stand out in front of this house and let the police come shoot me like your father shot Cisco—and I'll do it proudly because you made me this way, strong, willing, biologically superior, self-confident, needing containment. Your genes made me this way, and I don't fit in this world. But there is something about average, everyday humanity that bothers me. Take you, for example, Fedora Man. You plot, deceive, cheat. You love with a surface kind of love that goes into hiding the instant you need to save your own hide. So I may be an animal, but I'd rather be an animal shot to death by men with better technology if that means I still stand for an inability to lie and for protecting those people for whom I actually would throw myself in front of a truck."

"Your father sends his helicopter to get you now," Ivor replied. "Ready yourself."

"No, Ivor," Beautiful replied. "Not today!"

She left her shoes in the house and walked barefoot to the yard before climbing the short fence in front of the cliff. "Daddy," she shouted upward, inhaling the ocean breeze. "You may control the people and things around me, but you don't control me." She stared at the several hundred foot drop where a slim strip of beach abutted the water, saying, "I always wanted to touch the ocean. And to fly."

Then she jumped from the ledge to fall with a sickening thud. All watched, shocked and quiet, as the small shape below them didn't move. From a distance, her father's helicopter approached, circled, and flew off to land on a distant hill. Sandra and Ethel Chef ran to Ida's kitchen and pressed a disoriented Ida to detail the best and fastest way to the shore: "What's quickest?" Sandra asked. "Tell us now. We have to reach her…"

"Way you get down in is the same way you got up!" said Ida, deluded, staring at the inert lump of Howard, who now had an electric blue pump sticking jauntily from his forehead. "Leaving and arriving come by the same roads, children," she went on, picking up the dropped empty shoe beside Howard's head, caressing the satin.

Thomas grabbed Ethel and Sandra to escort them out, saying, "She can't be asked. We'll drive the coast highway and double back. Or we can go residential and find a staircase down."

Ivor looked down from the cliff as the ocean air blew over and into his white jacket, inflating and deflating it. "Blue. So blue," he said, considering Beautiful's dress. He pulled his fedora down tighter over his head and eyed her body. A strong breeze passed over him, stealing his hat from his head and carrying it back toward Ida's.

He continued staring down at Beautiful's distant shape, but muttered, as the chill wind teased through his hair, "I touched you, like you asked. I came back for you. I even gave you permission to touch my feet."

But moments later, below, Beautiful twitched and shifted. She heard the sea's roar and stood up tall, saying, "Fuck, that hurt," but there were no sirens coming, no friends, and no concussions. She felt strong, indelicate, somewhat monstrous, recognizing the bounce back ability she always suspected she'd possessed. Stretching her firm, young limbs, she stripped her dress and undergarments, just in case her father had wire-tapped them.

She walked nude into the ocean, murmuring lightly, "They won't find me here, unless Daddy got under my skin. He may have done so. I've got no clue."

A block away, Sandra, Thomas, and Ethel got out of the Lincoln, searching for a path toward the beach.

Fedora Man still stood atop the cliff. "I did adore you," he then said, watching her from above, though the wind seemed to whisper *not enough*.

Inside the house, Ida crawled the floor, grabbed the trapped stiletto heel, and pushed it harder into Howard's skull. Round and round, her fingers wound over the expensive shock blue shoes.

She touched the satin of both the left and right heels, but also their leather interiors, touching them as if to feel the stranger's body that had once inhabited them, to capture the energy still residual or trapped in the remaining leather still warm from her visitor's skin. "I did it," she announced after a series of movements with her smooth old fingers, feeling she'd obliterated all other fingerprints on the shoes. "No one's to blame for this. Ida May Haze can take care of herself!"

Swimming below in the sea, Beautiful's body ached. The water was cold, but, "Daddy?" she said experimentally, almost sure he could no longer hear her. "What kind of clout do you have out here?"

For a while, she breast-stroked without pause. A mile or so out, she watched as pale fins appeared nearby in the blue-gray water. Abruptly, something bumped her left hip—a smooth body, then more. Soon, six dolphins flanked her, at play in the rolling tides, and Beautiful smiled. "You're sure speedy creatures," she said, retreating in her mind to the Darwinian primers she'd read as a child and the nature shows stolen in the wee hours of the morning at the estate while the false friends mated at the pool.

She marveled at the magnificence of the dolphins beside her now, those who swam five times faster than human Olympic swimmers, enjoying their low cost of transport. She imagined them as fleet birds or gliding insects of the sea. "Daddy, I love naturalism!" she said and again imagined dancing with the butterflies as she had in the early part of her trip, envisioning once more the butterfly that landed on her shoulder as if to guide her somewhere. *Butterflies tasted through their feet. Hers had touched her with his soul.* He was better than a man. He had come to her freely, without her asking. All of nature could nudge or touch her. *Only the natural*, she thought, *was real and true—could be no other way.*

With Darwin, she'd enjoyed imagining many such conversations about the animal kingdom, the flora and the fauna. Too, she recalled the joy she'd taken sitting under a tree at the estate and reading other dead people, when the shallow friends were elsewhere—how she'd talk to other authors from her books whilst seated under those trees, those authors whose thoughts were so unlike those of the everyday people who surrounded her, heavy thinkers, deep thinkers, those she could pretend to have reciprocal conversations with, despite the airy climate in which she lived: "There are so many things in your books I've wanted to try," she'd say. "But I'm closed off here, and they won't let me leave."

Now, she'd left, but nearly her whole life had been lived in a microcosm inside a microcosm, a sheltered construction of family embargo carried along as the ludicrous illusion of recognizable civilization. Attempting to forget this, with each stroke in the water she rejoined the larger animalistic magnificence of the great outdoors in a purely physical act, swimming, while considering her opposable thumbs.

What good were they? Even Howard possessed these. Jake, too. The fetus that may or may not have been. So it was *no good* to be human in particular, she decided, the egos of the thinkers be damned.

Her *toska* intensified until it was nothingness, a bland wall of the will to forget both what she'd done and what she hadn't done. It was bliss. Soon, she no longer felt her fingers or her toes. *I read about drowning once,* she thought. *I wonder what it will feel like... I wonder...*

In the distance, at last, the sound of helicopter blades and sirens came. *Tck-tck. Tck-tck Tck-tck,* she thought. *Someone is coming. Someone is coming for someone, for someone, for someone—but not for me. I'm alone now, as I've always been. Ivor, in the end, you failed me.*

The helicopters dropped nets into the water, but she disregarded these and, as always lately, as she swam, she saw flashes and lingering residue from her new and former nightmares, the weak female face of the twin she'd consumed in the womb, the broken necks of small cold estate birds, Jake's head in the dirt on a puddle of blood, the push of a faceless girl off a cliff of memory, and now the sight and sound of her spiked heel planting firmly in Howard Haze's forehead with what resembled the resonance of hitting the sweet spot, something her tennis coach had schooled her to understand years ago, which was the moment when the racquet made perfect hard contact with the ball.

She felt no pain or emotion as she went forward and told the sea, "I want to be reabsorbed in your womb. Take me down now," nakedly, and with purpose, stroking herself into exhaustion. But she played with no people or animals, so the dolphin pod soon passed. She ran a hand over the last animal's retreating back, saying, "I am being, just being," watching what seemed to be war games from a very foreign country above, her Daddy's clout and retrieval suspended in vehicles like primitive black wasps in the daytime sky as more helicopters arrived, circling fore and back, dragging their nets, looking for her, she supposed, but they could keep right on looking. They were not the someones for whom she'd stop.

There were no such someones.

Ignoring the commotion except to avoid it, she kept moving. She thought of how her therapist would be proud she'd reached such a perfect state of meditation in these last few moments, swimming with wide sweeps of her arms like a frog now, mostly below surface, obliterating the presence of nets and blades and motors in the sky as if they might be only the most radical static of a dream within a dream.

She wished, for an instant, that the dolphins had not departed, that money and clout had never existed, that Ida had been stronger or more able, or that Ivor had done what he'd needed to do to love her, to claim her. But she lacked a shrewdness, and she wished that her family had been able to fill in the needs of that absence. She wished that she could see more below the murky ocean's surface than a shifting mass of grays and greens and blues, but, like an invisible resting place lingered below her somewhere, rejoining the great pool of the amorphously unknown, she allowed her arms and legs to fall motionless to the sea.

She took one last, long breath. She set it free. And then, naked and unprotected as her body below her, her head slipped under the waves.

ABOUT THE AUTHOR

Heather Fowler is a fiction writer, a poet, a librettist, and a playwright. She is the author of the story collections *Suspended Heart* (2010), *People with Holes* (2012), *This Time, While We're Awake* (2013), and *Elegantly Naked In My Sexy Mental Illness* (2014). Fowler's *People with Holes* was named a 2012 finalist for *Foreword Reviews* Book of the Year Award in Short Fiction. Her fictive work has been made into fine art in several instances, and her collaborative poetry collection, *Bare Bulbs Swinging*, written with Meg Tuite and Michelle Reale, was the winner of the 2013 Twin Antlers Prize for Collaborative Poetry and released in December of 2014. Fowler has published stories and poems online and in print in the U.S., England, Australia, and India, her work appearing in such venues as *PANK, Night Train, Portland Review, Surreal South, Feminist Studies*, and more, as well as having been nominated for the storySouth Million Writers Award, Sundress Publications Best of the Net, and multiple Pushcart Prizes. She is Poetry Editor at *Corium Magazine*. Please visit her website at heatherfowler.com.

Other titles featuring Heather Fowler from

PINK NARCISSUS PRESS

PEOPLE WITH HOLES

Stories by Heather Fowler

Hailed as "magic realism at its finest," Fowler's stories reveal the small but essential truths that motivate sex, love, and tragedy in relationships. Whether in museums of solitude, airports of dreams, archers' fields, freak shows, urban cafes, or the cottages of dwarves, her stories explore love's inevitable consequences. Fowler's unique visions are thought-provoking, with a touch of feminist sensibility, and shot through with quirky and laugh-out-loud humor.

ISBN: 978-0-9829913-9-8

DAUGHTERS OF ICARUS

New Feminist Sci-Fi and Fantasy

"Throughout, the authors explore themes of gender, identity, and autonomy, with characters as diverse as miniature clones, stripper vampires, aggressive mermaids, and mystical crones. Many of the stories focus on gender roles and the pull of relationships, whether parental, familial, or romantic, among all kinds of people." —*Library Journal*

ISBN: 978-1-939056-00-9

RAPUNZEL'S DAUGHTERS

What happens after "Happily Ever After"...?

"Readers who enjoy discovering new writers or fans of imaginative approaches to familiar themes should relish this small press offering." —*Library Journal*

ISBN: 978-0-9829913-1-2

www.ingramcontent.com/pod-product-compliance
Ingram Content Group UK Ltd.
Pitfield, Milton Keynes, MK11 3LW, UK
UKHW020419250726
13967UKWH00007B/2720